Marcus was smiling at her; she was smiling too. There was a look on his face she had never seen before that Tia recognised as happiness and also relief.

The silence closed in on her, the sea sounds faded and so did the wind. Just as it began to threaten her, she opened her mouth to say something but Marcus stopped her by putting his finger to her lips.

'Will you do something else for me Tia, *annsacdh*?' he asked.

'What is that?' she asked, her voice so throaty it was almost a croak.

'Will you marry me, my love?'

For a moment, she did not reply, then her eyes gave him her answer and he grabbed her hand and they ran onto the shore; taking both of her hands, he began to spin her around and her world turned, faster and faster, until all she could see was him against the blurring backdrop of the sky and the ocean and the pearl white sand. Tia's laughter rang out over the land, mingling with the early morning cries of birds, the rush of wind through the grass and the music of the sea . . .

In a moment, her dream had become true, years before she had dared to think it would.

Kirsty White was born in London of Scottish parents. She worked as a newspaper reporter and in broadcasting and programme-making before turning to full time writing. Kirsty White lives in Dumfriesshire.

*By the same author*

My Little Oyster Girl

# Tia's Story

## KIRSTY WHITE

ORION

An Orion paperback
First published in Great Britain by Orion in 1995
This paperback edition published in 1995 by Orion Books Ltd
Orion House, 5 Upper St Martin's Lane, London WC2H 9EA

A CIP catalogue record for this book is available
from the British Library.

ISBN: 1 85797 491 3

Printed in England by Clays Ltd, St Ives plc

*W*inter was a wicked time.

The land was wild, a jagged rock cast up from the sea in the rage of Creation, battered ever after by the furies of the ocean until the edges were smoothed, honed like pumice stone. The anger rose far to the west, gales that struck like thunderbolts blowing everything in their wake; the crust at the ocean's edge was obstinate, but inland, the grass was vanquished and torn out by its roots, the soft underbelly of soil exposed and driven away, leaving the land tattered, frayed like a cast-off tweed, the weft unravelled, the warp thin strips of scrub drifting on the surface of inlets like jellyfish tails.

There are no mountains in North Uist; only Eaval rises in the south of the island, a nasal incline that sneers at the sky. On its slopes, even in summer, the grass grows thinly, like the fur of a mangy dog, in clumps and strands between the stones.

Between November and February, the tantrums of nature held the island in their thrall.

Day, when it came, was brief and anaemic.

Night could come again at any time. Long after they were grown, schoolchildren remembered the sudden onset of an ocean storm, the sky that darkened without warning, the wind that howled like a chorus of wolves. They would huddle in the schoolhouse and then walk home together, hands clasped, their bodies fragile against the might of the gale. Gaining the safety of home brought feeling back to their numbed faces, tingling to the skin and stinging to the eyes, the smell of peats burning and bread baking and comfort and kindness.

The cottages clung to the land like barnacles.

Indoors was warmth, tainted with the sharp smell of peat smoke, the light of the fire and sometimes a candle. Candlelight was a luxury, a luxury they often did without. In the gloom, reading strained the eyes; often it was better to pass the time in talk or silence, thinking or listening to the music of the wind.

Tia's father, Sorley MacIain MacLeod, was an elder, a churchman who preached the Lord's word. A long time ago, when Tia was very *young*, Tormod the bard would come to recite his poems, his stories of the glory of her people, as the whole family sat around the fire listening to him. There was her mother and father, her brothers and sisters; Tia, the youngest, in the lap of Mairead, the eldest, maybe friends and neighbours as well.

Tia loved these evenings. Listening to Tormod, she would look around at the faces; there was no age or youth any more, just her people and their stories, the melding of souls in the mask of the fire.

When, sixty years before, they had cleared the people they could not clear their houses; the backbones of their existence remained, charred at the edges, gathering moss and lichen, the shape intact despite the years that had passed and the things that had been done. The roofs were gone, but the walls stood firm. There was one like that just outside her village, naked boulders, the old mortar crumbling at the edges, topped by straggled weed like an old man's whiskers. It looked like a face made of stone with the hair of a dervish and empty eyes.

The people of the village wanted to knock the walls down, but Tia's father would not let them. He said the structure must remain as a memorial to the past.

Tormod would tell stories of the house and the people who lived there; it was not frightening then, it was only sad.

When Mairead ran away, when Tia was just toddling, Sorley banned Tormod from telling his stories, he said the nonsense had turned Mairead's head.

When Tia cried, her mother, Janet, comforted her; her brothers and sisters told her to hush, lest they got into trouble as well. Sorley would not let Mairead's name be mentioned at home after that, but he remembered her each week in the prayers he said in church.

Sorley said this place was God's land. Tia wondered if it was the Devil's as well; there were enough hiding places for him, after all, in the cracks of the rocks.

She began to dream for the first time in the year 1911, when she had just turned fifteen, after she had been to a dance at Creagorry on the island of Benbecula where her grandmother lived. Tia was pretty, the soft features of her face rimmed with honey-coloured hair; many of the men wanted to dance with her, but she only agreed to dance with one of them.

She had danced with one she had known for years, realising afterwards that in his years away from the islands he had become man.

Marcus was older than her, much older, twice her age, but that was all right in the islands, it took time to grow into the responsibilities of adulthood. Tia liked him, more than that; she hoped, dreamed and prayed that he liked her too. More than liked, if she was honest with herself, which she hardly dared to be.

She did not want to dream, particularly, because afterwards the rain felt colder and the wind more keen but the dream came unbidden when she slept. Yet the man was different, silver haired whereas Marcus's was brown. The dream crept into her consciousness, the knowledge that she would marry this man, but she thought it would be years yet, if ever. Her father believed that girls should marry when they turned sixteen; that worried her, because her sixteenth birthday was due the next year. She wondered if the dream was an illusion, a trick; the man not Marcus but an imposter, the Devil playing games with her. But the dream came back, again and again, the man holding out a hand to her and she taking it, the feeling that this was right and true and just.

The only book she had ever read was Pilgrim's Progress. Sorley MacIain believed that only it and the Bible were fit. Tia knew that in her father's eyes she sinned by dreaming, but she could not help herself.

She could not bear the thought of what would happen to her if she had to abandon her dream.

# Chapter One

North Uist, Spring 1912

*O*n a day when the sun shone thinly through the clouds, Tia and her mother went to the lazy beds to make the soil ready for the seed. The potatoes were grown in beds on the rocks close to the shore; the soil was stripped every winter by the rage of the elements and early in the spring they had to make good the loss. They dragged sods of peat into place over the dross that was left, spread seaweed over the peats, then another layer of peat to hold the goodness in. Later, when the weather was kinder, they would turn the fresh earth with a *cas chrom*; it would then be ready for planting.

It had not always been like this; within living memory crops had been planted on sheltered land away from the shore, in the time before people had been driven from the good land and left to cling to its edges. The sense of loss endured simmering but never quite boiling over; fuelling the determination of the remainder to stay. The irony of it struck Tia, as she carried creel after creel of weed from the shore, as her arms were numbed and her feet torn by the shard of shells. She laughed in defiance as she hefted the last creel from her back and set it down with a thud, exultant that again they had won the battle with the land. Every year the winter stripped the soil and then she and her mother made it again and the potatoes grew as if nothing had happened, the wiles of the landlord defeated again.

Janet looked up. Her face was as open as the sky on a clear day, her skin unlined despite the passage of time. You would never know that she was ageing unless you noticed the white that sprinkled her fair hair, heard the crick that sometimes came from her limbs after a day's work. Sorley MacIain MacLeod hadn't worked the croft for years, since his hand had become clawed with arthritis, but even before that he had devoted himself to God's work. To him, bodily survival was secondary to the succour of the soul; he ignored such mundanities as hunger, thirst and fatigue. Such feelings were tainted by sin, an implicit admission of the imperfection of man. He ate furtively, as if ashamed of the demands that his body made, impatient that despite the years of prayer and devotion his needs still ran the gamut of any man's. When he preached, he spoke of the sins of earthly riches, of humble poverty as a state to be desired, forgetting or maybe ignoring that the islanders had no choice in the matter.

Early in her life Tia realised that she could never live up to his ideals, so she gave up the effort though she maintained the appearance. She was quiet and obedient, as studious as anyone could be without an innate ability to follow the arid path marked out by her teacher. To her education was a penance, a dull preamble to the joy of life that she hoped to find later when she was old enough to strike out for herself. Joy was an emotion she had glimpsed in others; in her home such a feeling was a sin.

Janet stood up, scowling when she saw the ominous grey gathering in the sky above Eaval. The wind quickened. 'We'll be finished before,' she said, 'if we hurry.'

Tia knelt down to work the weed into the peat. Her hands were stained brown; the soil felt moist and hungry.

Janet joined her. 'You were laughing.'

'Only at us, Mama.'

Janet rocked on her haunches. 'You're lucky, if you find this funny.'

Tia remembered her father complaining about the potatoes, saying that they tasted bitter; her mother said nothing at the time, but later, when Sorley had gone to the elders' meeting, she glared at the tall, thin man striding towards the sunset and said, 'Bitter? I've a mind to put raw peat on the table instead, and then we'll see about that.'

Tia laughed again.

'You're not thinking about the road dance, are you?' Janet asked.

Tia's face straightened. 'No.'

Janet shook her head and turned back to her work.

The dance had been on Saturday night, when some girls walking home from Clachan had met some others on their way to Bayhead and then the fiddler from Baleshare happened upon them; he was on his way to Paible to play at a wedding but a high spring tide had blocked the causeway and by the time he started out the wedding was over but he wanted to go anyway, to make his apologies.

They asked him to play a tune and he did, just one, but one became another and the sound of music brought more people and the dance began, in the Field of Blood, no less, or the strip of track that ran alongside it. That made it worse, Sorley MacIain said, on Sunday morning when he heard about it; the dance had not only desecrated the Sabbath Day but the young people had danced on the bones of their ancestors, on the ground where the clans of North Uist and Harris had fought three hundred years before.

'You know,' Janet said, in the soft voice she used when he was angry, 'it was only a little road dance. It happened by accident, Sorley.'

'So lies the way to damnation, Janet.'

'They're young, that's all. They were having fun. To have fun is not to yield to temptation, Sorley.'

'Aye, it is, Janet. That is the way of Satan, is it not? To appear to tempt us when we least expect it? The Sabbath was desecrated. Seonag Morrison tells me that she was woken by the racket of them coming home just as dawn was breaking.'

Janet fell silent as he turned to Tia. 'You were not there, were you?' Sorley always spoke like that, enunciating each word carefully, never abbreviating, emphasising each syllable of the pearls of wisdom that scattered from his mouth as he spoke.

Tia turned away, so he would not see the look on her face that said she would have liked to have been there, but had not.

'You know yourself she wasn't,' Janet said quickly.

'That is just as well,' he said.

'You father wants the best for you,' Janet said to Tia, breaking into her thoughts.

They worked in silence for a while, racing against the weather. By the time the clouds broke, the peat was in place, the soil as good as they could make it. The air became water; to inhale carelessly was to choke and the women took their breath in short gasps, heads bent down as they struggled along the path that led back to the township, sliding over the treacherous gound. The rain abated just as they came into sight of Sorley's house.

'I know you want to go to the lowlands,' Janet said.

Tia did not reply at first, because she did not want to cause hurt. To want to leave was to reject her mother in a way, to spurn the work she did to make life bearable for her daughter and the confidences they shared.

'There's nothing wrong with that,' Janet said. 'You want to see a different way of life, to try things for yourself. We all want that, when we are young.'

'I don't want to stay there, not for ever,' Tia said quickly. 'I'd like to see it, that's all.'

Janet smiled. 'Like Mary.'

'Like Mary,' Tia echoed. Her grandmother, Sorley's mother, had been trained as a seamstress in a big house in the lowlands; she had worked there for five years until she came back to marry and she still told stories of her time in the south. Although decades had passed since then, Mary's stories were parables that proved to Tia there were other ways beyond that ordained by her father. Of the two of them, mother and son, it was Mary who seemed the younger.

'Your father'd not like it,' Janet said.

A look of exasperation spread over Tia's face.

'Not after Mairead,' her mother said.

'Why is it,' Tia asked bitterly, 'that I have to pay for something she did?'

Janet's face flashed pain. 'Peigi and Flo are happy enough.'

Tia thought of her sisters, a few years older than her, who had meekly obeyed the will of her father. Peigi had married a widower years older than her, a man respected because, like Sorley, he was a church elder; and Flo had married a man who worked on the estate as a ghillie during the season, a man whose face was a gaunt backdrop to a nose that rose from it like Eaval rose from the fields. They took their seats in the church on Sundays, to worship as earnestly as her father did. To the village they were dutiful daughters; if anyone thought they were too dutiful they did not say so. Only Tia wondered if they ever had any joy in their lives.

She smiled to herself. Her father's will had worked its way

out on Peigi and Flo; she knew as well as he did that there was no suitable husband for her within miles, no one who had not fallen prey to the temptation of a road dance or, worse, the inn at Carinish. Sorley's attitude to women was rigid; they were children or they were wives, because in spinsterdom lay the way to temptation. Peigi and then Flo had been married within weeks of reaching her sixteenth birthday; the mere thought of it terrified Tia until she realised that Sorley had already tried and failed to find a suitable match for her.

'It was hard enough getting him to let the boys go to the whaling,' Janet said.

Her brothers Donald and Iain worked on the whaling station on Harris; even in the off season they did not come home though it was money from them that paid the rent on the croft.

'There was an awful row when Mairead left.'

Tia hardly remembered her eldest sister, only the sound of her laughter and the feel of her body when she gathered her into her arms and ran along the sands, chasing the tide out, or so she said. It was Mairead who had shown her the causeway, who had first taken her to see Mary on Benbecula.

'What happened to her?' she asked in a small voice. She had always been afraid to until then.

Janet stopped. 'As God's my judge, I don't know, Tia. I hoped and prayed, but I never heard a thing from her all these years.'

The pain deepened on her mother's face. 'I'm sorry,' Tia said quickly. 'I didn't mean to hurt you.'

Janet shook her head. 'I was going to say, pet, there's always jobs in the hotel of a summer. You could go there and try for one. Your father'd not mind so much, not if you stayed on the island.'

'I'd rather be a herring girl. I could earn good money as a herring girl.'

'You know what your father says about herring girls, Tia.'

As they reached the cottage they stopped to wring the water out of their skirts, which had been soaked by the rain.

'There is a lad coming from the lowlands,' her father said after dinner, before he began the evening's reading of the bible. 'A minister. We will have to feed him. We will bleed the cow.'

9

Once they were seated by the fire Janet's eyes closed and she slept, and although Sorley noticed he said nothing, just carried on reading from the Epistles of St Paul. When Tia began to doze, though, he chided her sharply, saying there was plenty of time for her to sleep after she had listened to the word of God.

Janet dragged the old milk cow from the byre early in the morning, put a rope halter around its neck and cut the vein that rose upon its chest as Tia held the bucket to catch the blood. When the bucket was half full she loosened the halter and held a rag to the cow's neck until the bleeding had stopped, then she took the bucket from Tia and went indoors.

The cow stumbled as she ambled off towards the grazings; the grass was sparse so early in the year and her legs were weak after the long dark winter.

As Janet cooked the pudding with meal and wild onions, the smell of blood changed to one of food, though Tia felt nausea, not hunger.

Sorley was sitting at the table, trying to write a letter. He could hardly manage to hold the pen straight.

'Shall I do it for you?' Tia asked cautiously.

'No!' he barked, enraged that she had dared to ask.

She exchanged a look with her mother. 'I'll get away to Lochmaddy, then.'

'What are you doing in Lochmaddy?' Sorley asked.

'She's going to try for a job in the hotel,' Janet said quietly.

Sorley's face darkened. 'There is plenty work for her to do here.'

'I can manage fine,' Janet said. 'And we need the money. You know that.'

'The Temperance Hotel, I hope,' Sorley growled, before turning back to the letter and pursing his lips tightly, though another man would have cursed because a blob of ink had dripped from the pen and ruined the paper he was working on.

On the road to Lochmaddy, Tia met Ealasaid-of-the-sad-eyes just before she reached MacLean's store. Ealasaid fell in with her and they walked along together for a while. As the road turned inland, the wind dropped, but the tears in Ealasaid's eyes did not dry.

Her husband had sailed for Canada five years ago, telling Ealsaid that he would send the fare for her and the two young children when he had earned it. At first, his letters arrived every month but after two years the letters stopped and nobody knew why. As a girl, Ealasaid had the most wonderful eyes, so stunning that strangers would stop to stare at her. They were turquoise in the sunlight, changing to a deep blue as clear as a jewel when night fell. Once they had been only beautiful, but now they showed her grief as well and people remarked upon that.

'Are you going to Lochmaddy?' Tia asked her.

Ealasaid shivered. 'Only to Langass.'

The track ran past the sea loch now, the vast expanse of water that held the reflection of the sky and the land. The inland moors were like flotsam, the shiver of the wind through the grass kept time with the beat of the tide.

'Seumas MacAndrew is going to Canada.'

'Oh,' Tia said.

'He's promised to try to find Duncan.'

After a year without letters, Sorley MacIain had taken Ealasaid into the house one day, and tried to persuade her gently that Duncan must be dead because she would have heard from him otherwise and it was not unknown for someone to die in the wilderness of the Canadian winter. Tia remembered Sorley telling her mother that it was the kindest thing to do but Ealasaid had stubbornly resisted him, placing her hand on her breast and saying that he was wrong: her heart would tell her if Duncan was dead.

Tia did not often agree with her father, but this time she thought he was right. Before he talked to Ealasaid, he had written to a minister of the church of Canada, who had replied that Duncan MacDonald from Carinish had disappeared from his lodgings six months before.

'Seumus will look for him,' Ealasaid said. 'Seumas will look properly.'

His letters had been tender and full of love; Ealasaid had shown them to her mother and then the whole township had read them and waited eagerly for the next one.

'I'm going to try for a job in the hotel,' Tia said.

Ealasaid smiled softly. 'You'd have a better chance in the lowlands.'

'My father. . .' Tia said, her voice tailing off.

'You'd like to go to the lowlands, wouldn't you?'

'I'd like to see what it's like. Wouldn't you?'

Ealasaid shook her head. 'That's the strange thing about it. I never wanted to go to the lowlands. I didn't want to go to Canada. It was Duncan who wanted to go, not me.'

Tia watched her for a long time after she had turned on to the path to Langass, her figure forlorn against the might of the land.

She reached Lochmaddy in the middle of the morning. The town was silent but for the cries of the gulls that wheeled overhead. The Temperance Hotel was locked and shuttered; she hesitated for a moment before she walked on past the Court House to the Lochmaddy Hotel. It was a bleak stone building that was strewn along the line of the shore, facing the bay. The tide was out and the rocks rose starkly from the sea, stained black with iodine up to the high-water mark, pale grey speckled with yellow lichen beyond that. The low hills above, denuded by winter, surrounded the town like giant limpet shells beneath an opaque grey sky. Avoiding the front door, Tia walked around to the back and knocked at the kitchen door, not certain whether to open it or wait.

After a moment the cook opened the door; she was a tall, buxom woman Tia vaguely recognised from the September market where she had run a stall selling pies and ale.

'I've come about a job,' Tia said.

'Well, come away in,' the cook said. 'I'll ask Mrs MacFadyen, though I think they're all gone.'

There was a meal cooking of some sort, she could smell the richness of stewing meat.

'Sit yourself down, lass,' the cook said, ladling soup into a bowl which she handed to Tia. There was a motherly air about her, a cruel emphasis of her spinsterly state. 'You're from Carinish way, aren't you? It's some way to walk. You're Sorley MacIain's daughter, aren't you? I doubt he's happy about you working here.'

'We need the money,' Tia said.

'Don't we all?'

The cook went out of the door, coming back a moment later just as the soup was cooling enough to drink. 'It's like I thought, dear. Mrs MacFadyen's got all the girls she needs for the season, but there's maybe a chance of something at the Lodge down the road.'

Tia stood up to leave.

'Ach, lass, finish your soup first. The Missus says to leave your name and address and she'll ask the Post to tell you if you've to come in. The Lodge'll be busy in September, for the shooting. There's a good chance she'll be able to give you something then.'

Tia felt suddenly ashamed of her need. 'It doesn't matter,' she said, in a small voice.

As she left, the cook handed her a bag of scones.

Halfway back to her village, she heard the clatter of wheels beside her, then Archie MacCallum pulled his cart to a halt. She got in gratefully, aware that her legs were beginning to tire.

'Have you met the new minister, then?' he asked, shouting to make himself heard over the noise.

'He's coming today,' she said.

'I think Sorley MacIain's preacher enough for us, myself.'

Tia said nothing. Her father had led the worship since the old minister died.

'I don't know what they're thinking about, down in the lowlands,' Archie said.

'You have to study to be a minister,' she yelled.

'Your father knows the Lord's Book as well as any man.'

They rolled past the end of the tattered lochs, where the water lapped gently at the cleft of the land, and the horse strained slightly against the mild incline beyond.

'I doubt he'll even speak our language, this new man,' Archie said a while later.

'He does,' Tia said. 'My father made sure of that.'

Archie shook his head. 'And what of you, lass? You've grown up since I saw you last.'

Tia nodded.

'You don't have much to say for yourself, do you, lass?'

'Yes,' Tia said.

Archie waited for a while, then prompted her.

'I was agreeing with you, Archie. That's what I meant by saying "yes".'

13

She laughed, and he laughed with her, shaking his head. 'That's a wise head you've got on these shoulders,' he said, when he stopped the cart outside her cottage.

'You did not get a job,' her father said as soon as she was back indoors.

'I'll maybe get one later in the lodge,' she said.

'You will not,' he said gruffly. 'You will not work for MacFadyen.'

'Father, the Temperance Hotel is closed.'

'The Lord has spoken,' he said. 'So be it.'

For a moment she felt the walls of the little house close in around her; the air was hot and stale. Her mother was at the fire, turning the supper bannocks. 'Will the young Reverend be eating with us tonight, Sorley?' she asked.

'Yes,' he said, standing up. 'He is staying with Seonag Morrison. The manse is not fit for man or beast, the state of it. There is a job for you, girl. Tomorrow morning you can clean the place out and make it fit to live in.'

Tia pretended that she had not heard him.

'Tia, I am speaking to you,' he said sharply.

'I'll see to it, Father,' she said.

The new minister came in shortly afterwards, knocking at the door and waiting until Janet pulled it open. Sorley told him they did not keep these lowland habits in the islands, the house was always open to a minister; he did not have to wait to be told to come in.

He was tall and thin, his body encased in a black serge suit with wide lapels and baggy trousers that flapped around his ankles. His face was pale and angular, his eyes shaded and dark above a hawked nose.

There was something about him that Tia disliked instantly, a stagnant top-note in the smell of camphor that oozed from the fabric of his clothes and drifted around the cottage over the aroma of cooking, an arrogance in the easy way he sat down in the chair Sorley offered him, ignoring the women.

'This is my wife Janet,' Sorley said, as Janet turned from the fire and smiled shyly, 'and our daughter Tia. This is the Reverend Doctor Kenneth MacQuarrie.'

Tia felt his eyes upon her, and kept her own averted to avoid acknowledging him.

The Reverend said grace and for once Tia was grateful that he took an age, because she had lost all taste for food.

As she studied the small slice of pudding on her plate, and thought of the tired and anaemic cow asleep in the byre, she knew that she could not bring herself to eat and so she just pretended to, hoping that her father would not notice because he was so engrossed in his conversation with the lowlander. She felt bile rise in her throat, swallowed quickly and drank some water to take away the bitter taste, but he did not see her. He was busy telling the lowlander that it was a hard land, an unforgiving land, but they managed to survive, by the grace of God. They were poor and meek, but content, because that state was blessed, according to the Holy Book. The lowlander nodded knowingly and said that life in the south was too easy; a man risked damnation by ignoring the laws of God in the pursuit of worldly riches.

Her father talked with the lowlander deep into the night, as Tia and Janet cleared the dishes from the table and then climbed the ladder to the loft where Tia slept.

'I'll just bed down here,' Janet said, 'there's no stopping your father once he's started.'

Tia yawned. She was thinking of the longing in Ealasaid's eyes.

'I saw Ealasaid today,' she said.

'Looking for a job too, was she?'

'No. One of the men from the kelp works's going to Canada, and she says he's going to look for her Duncan.'

She heard the sound of her mother's lips meeting in the dark.

'I'm vexed for her,' Janet said.

'She's young to be a widow.'

'She's not a widow, pet, leastwise I don't think so. If someone you love dies, you know it in your soul.'

It was strange to hear Mother talking about love; Tia wondered what she knew about it, because she had wed Sorley. In the still of the night, Janet smiled, as if she knew what Tia was thinking. 'Time changes everyone,' she said. 'It'll be a weight off your father if this minister's come to stay.'

'What about his wife?' Tia asked sleepily.

'He doesn't have one,' Janet said. 'He's young, you see, straight out of college.'

'Father didn't want a stranger.' The church elders had the right to turn down an applicant for the vacant parish; under Sorley's guidance they had already rejected several.

'He's not a stranger, at least not completely. His grandfather's from Sollas. That's why he speaks Gaelic like he's one of us.'

A fleeting thought struck Tia then, that her father could be planning to marry her off to the new minister; but when she asked, Janet said it was ridiculous, she needed Tia's help on the croft, and the minister would have a mind of his own on the matter. For a moment the idea tormented Tia, though; at the back of her mind there had always been the knowledge that she would escape her father one day, when she got wed. The possibility that she might be tied for ever to a man like MacQuarrie was too awful to comtemplate.

They finished planting the seed in April, and Janet began to work on the fleece, as she always did. She did not have a loom of her own, or even a spinning wheel; she prepared the fibre for the spinners, washing each fleece by hand, carefully, and then carding the wool to make it ready for the wheel.

Tia helped her and when there was no more to do, she went to Lochmaddy again, to ask if there was a job, but the cook told her she was still too early, the season did not start until midway through August.

When the sun shone she walked to the high land to gather *crotal*, the lichen that clung to rock, to make dye for the wool, and when she had enough of that she went to the shore to get some *fiasag nan creag*, which was similar but gentler in hue. Sorley liked everything to be dyed in the darkest shade of *crotal*, or even water lily root, which dyed black; but she loved the lighter dye of *sealasdair*, wild iris, which gave a pale blue grey on its own, soft tawny pink with iron salts, ivory if you added alum.

The water lilies had not flowered yet, so Janet boiled some wool with lichen until it was the colour of oxblood, then she wrung it out and left it to dry. The Reverend Doctor MacQuarrie arrived just as she was starting on some *fiasag nan creag* for the spinner; he had taken to appearing unannounced and though it inconvenienced Janet because it interrupted her work and stretched her hospitality to the limits she would not even hint that he was unwelcome. These random visits disturbed Tia. It was as if he thought he had a right to put her under his scrutiny; his arrogance repelled her, made her squirm inwardly. Again, the thought came that, to her father, the Reverend would make an ideal husband for her, and this time it did not go away.

She looked at him, at the dark, haggard face on top of his scarecrow-like frame. The smile he tried looked like a mixture between a scowl and a rebuke. She knew then that her father had been plotting and was struck by a feeling of panic. succeeded by a wave of hatred. For a moment the feeling was so strong that she shook; a fleeting image of the Reverend touching her made bile rise in her throat.

'My father's not here,' she said rudely.

He hovered there for a moment as Janet dried her hands and then ushered him in, apologising on Tia's behalf.

'I wasn't being rude,' Tia said distantly, 'I just thought it was him you wanted to see, that's all.'

He sat down by the fire, took the tea and scone that her mother offered. The cottage was ripe with the smell of dyes and drying wool.

'I see you've been working hard.'

Janet blushed and muttered that it wasn't work, not real work; it was nowhere near as hard as working the land.

Tia felt anger rising, because the spinner wanted the wool the next day and they were not finished, nothing like it; they would have to work half the night to get it ready in time.

'That's a fine colour,' the Reverend said.

'Ach, its just *crotal*, Reverend,' Janet said, 'nothing special.'

'It's fine work, Janet, done by honest hands.'

Tia cringed inside.

'It's just for some socks for Sorley, a sweater for the winter as well.'

'Sorley's a lucky man.'

'Ach, Reverend, I could knit some for you easily, if you like.'

'I wouldn't want to trouble you, Janet.'

'It's no trouble, none at all.'

Tia was seething when he left. 'The cheek of him,' she raged, 'he could afford to buy his own.'

Janet said nothing.

'He watches me all the time.'

Janet turned away from the wool. 'It's nothing, Tia.'

'You know it's not. You know Father wants to marry me off to him.'

Janet shivered. 'Tia . . .'

'You know. But I won't, and he can't make me.'

'Tia, nothing's been said yet. Like I said, I need you to help me, and the Reverend must have a mind of his own.'

'He's got a mind like Father's.'

The Reverend Doctor Kenneth MacQuarrie came to eat dinner with Sorley in July, a few days before Tia's sixteenth birthday. Before they started the meal, her father said prayers and then Kenneth said more; by the time they got around to eating, the food on their plates was cold.

Kenneth MacQuarrie's face was as gaunt as his body, his countenance as dark as the sky before a storm. His expression rarely changed and when he smiled or, more commonly, frowned, the fold of his skin formed rocky fissures. He was the kind of man that a photograph caught perfectly, as if even a hint of colour was tantamount to the admission of sin. Tia glanced at him and shivered. When they finished eating he gazed at Tia openly, and his stare did not falter when she looked away. When she blushed with embarrassment he nodded and smiled to himself.

'Kenneth is a fine young man,' her father said, catching her eyes with his, clinging to them, his brows joined into a thick black line that promised hellfire if she defied him. Tia felt a tremor ripple at the edge of her stomach; the food, undigested, threatened to expel itself. She swallowed to quell the unpleasantness.

'You should be honoured that he has asked to take you as his bride.'

Underneath the table, Tia's hands bunched into fists.

'Well girl,' her father said, after a moment that felt like an hour, 'what do you say?'

Tia looked from him to her mother; Janet avoided her eyes. Tia smiled, not through pleasure but the realisation that her father had outwitted her. Deep within her soul, the image of her dream quavered, faded, threatened to drift away like smoke on the wind.

'Come on, girl,' her father said sharply.

The Reverend Doctor Kenneth MacQuarrie cleared his throat. 'Maybe she feels shy, Sorley. After all, we hardly know each other.'

*Hardly know each other?* Tia thought. *You've hardly ever spoken to me.*

'Maybe,' he said carefully, 'we might take a walk together. Just a short one, mind, Sorley. I'll take care that we stay within sight of you.'

'Aye,' Sorley MacIain said, 'that would be a good thing to do.'

Tia got up abruptly, brushing the crumbs from her skirt. 'I've things to do, Father, tonight. I've to sew my blouse, and your shirt needs mending.'

'All that can wait,' her father said.

She wasn't listening to him. 'And I've to mend Callum's breeks for him. Peigi asked me to; she's enough to do with the orphan lambs.'

'I said, that can wait,' her father repeated.

In summer, the land changed from serge to velvet, the new grass glass-sharp in the light of the sun. The inlet just beyond their cottage was covered with sea thrift, a pink carpet over the carapace of sand. She walked away quickly, not waiting for the Reverend Doctor to join her, listening to the sounds of his footsteps as he ran to catch up. The men of the village were standing talking by the lazy beds; they nodded to Tia, took off their caps to the minister.

'A fine evening . . .'

'It is that.'

She sensed his hesitation as he stopped to talk with them, used it to stride away until she reached the rise before the shore. Looking over the sea, she could see Benbecula, the streaks of peat smoke from the cottages hovering above the strip of land. The new wool would be spun now, ready in hanks to be woven into tweed. Last year she had dyed some wool with *sealasdair* to make a tweed for herself; Mary had promised to show her how to use the loom when she visited her next. She smiled bleakly in anticipation of her father's anger; the lecture on vanity and the lilies of the fields. The water lilies had flowered; the lochs were speckled white with blossoms and the *machair* scattered with wild irises, like a carpet of fallen stars. That afternoon she had walked out over the sands and collected seagrass, which she had left to dry to make a new bed for herself and one for her mother and father. The shore was strewn with wrack and bubble weed, plantain and ribwort, mermaid's hair in a tangle, softer than moss.

The bleakness of winter over, the island became a place to be loved again.

The Reverend Doctor had finished talking to the men now, she watched his figure break away from theirs and walk towards her. He seemed to labour as he moved; the black suit he wore was tattered, like the cast-off feathers of a crow. On his way he threshed a bed of irises, a clump of bog cotton cowered and then danced in his wake; an orchid growing just beyond was crushed carelessly, vanishing in an amethyst flash that made her blink and then wince with regret.

'Best not go any further,' he said, breathlessly, when he reached her. 'I told your father we'd stay within sight.'

Tia turned away.

'They say you're a good girl,' he said, 'that you'll make a good wife.'

Tia shook her head slowly.

'Your father is a fine man, a Christian man. I've not met his better.' He was so close that she felt his breath on her neck.

'Reverend Doctor MacQuarrie,' she began, turning to face him.

'You must call me Kenneth if we're to be wed.'

'Reverend Doctor,' she said, again.

'There's no need to use that tone of voice.'

'I would've like to be asked, Reverend Doctor.'

'I asked your father. He knows what's best.'

She turned to walk back, watching his shadow follow her as she did so. The evening was tender, the sky luminescent. The sun was a globe melting into the ocean. The light then was brilliant; it caught all the blemishes of the Reverend's skin, the pluke tipped with yellow and the little red razor nicks around his chin, the brittle growth despite the blade. She hated him then, for being ugly, for daring to challenge the transitory beauty all around him, for, worst of all, not even being aware of it.

'Whatever gave you the idea to marry me?' she asked him.

'I have my doctorate,' he said, 'and my parish, through the grace of your father. It is of the time that I should take a wife, and the Lord has found one for me. It is right, is it not?'

'It would have been better if you had found one yourself.'

For a moment, Benbecula hovered on the edge of her vision, then the island faded into the mist. She thought of the dances that went on there until all hours, of the fun and the laughter and the music. Her father had banished all music, except for unaccompanied singing in church; if he had his way, he would banish dancing too. Only the road dances thwarted him, the random nature of these celebrations that made them impossible to prevent.

The minister's face creased into a frown. 'But that is what I am saying. I am following the will of Our Lord. That is right, is it not?'

'No, Reverend MacQuarrie,' Tia said, 'it is not right. The Lord has not put me on this earth for the purpose of marrying you.'

For a moment he stared at her, then reached out for her hand.

Quickly she pulled away, folded her arms and hugged her hands tight to her chest.

'You will think again,' he said.

'Never,' she replied.

She started to run away and then slowed, knowing that her father would sense something wrong if he saw her doing that.

Janet was waiting for her. 'I'll talk to him,' she said, pushing a bundle into Tia's hands. 'Away you and stay with Mary.'

Tia hesitated.

'I'll not see you forced into a marriage you don't want.'

Tia looked at the shore. 'It'll be a while before the tide is out.'

'Wait for it, then. I'll walk with you as far as Carinish.'

'You don't have to, Mama.'

'But I want to, Tia. I want to make sure you're safe. Besides, Mary asked me for some wool. *Bun na rainich.*' She shrugged, picking a stray strand from the sack. The colour was soft gold, a shade lighter than the nascent sun. 'Daft colours they want for the tweeds, these days.'

Tia smiled. 'I think it's wonderful, Mama.'

'Don't worry, pet, I'll talk to your father,' she said again.

'Will he listen?'

Janet's eyes turned rheumy. 'He thinks he knows best. Married to the Reverend, you'd want for nothing.'

'Or everything.'

Janet sighed. 'Time was we went hungry so that the children could eat. In Campbell Orde's day, there was no work to be had for love or money; we only had what we could grow and what we reared. It wasn't always enough.' Janet stopped and smiled, her face gilded by the glory of the sunset. 'Talk about hard times; these times were the hardest. It hurts your father most of all. He's bitter, though he'd not admit it. He doesn't want his children to go through that.'

'It's not like that now,' Tia said evenly.

'I doubt it will be ever again.'

They passed the inn as the tide was fading, the sea a silken cloth that melted into the sands. Walking on to the shore, they passed a rock pool where a lobster threshed in impotent agony, stranded by the ocean's betrayal.

Janet knelt, laughing softly. With one deft movement she caught the lobster by the scruff of the neck and then wrapped weed around it to render the flailing claws harmless. 'You see,' she said, 'we might go hungry for a while, but we'd never starve.'

'Will you be all right, Mama?' Tia asked when Janet turned to go back.

'All right? I'll be fine.'

Tia stood watching her for a while, thinking of her relationship with Sorley, the way she seemed to acquiesce to him yet kept her own mind. Sorley had banned mention of Mairead, but Janet still spoke of her and Tia supposed that Sorley knew she did. She thought back to her other sisters' weddings, but they were different to her, they did not dream. Sorley would ban dreaming, if he could, she knew. He would ban eveything except mute obeisance to the Holy Word.

Janet would try, but deep down Tia knew that her mother

was not as strong as Sorley, she could not sway him. Her mother was naive; she wondered what Janet had ever seen in him, knowing somehow that Sorley *had* been different once – which made the notion of marrying the Reverend all the more terrible because he had no redeeming features, none at all. The one thing that humanised Sorley was his love for Janet, but Tia could hear her trying to reason with him and being deflected by his arguments. His love for his wife did not extend to his daughter.

The night sky was pale, yellowing at the edges, like a page from a book left too long in the sun.

The ford between North Uist and Benbecula stretched out, glassy grey in the low light, pockmarked by mounds left by burrowing worms. The way across was marked by boulders, dragged there by horses to make the journey safe. The remnants of the tide rested in the indentations made by waves on the sand, capturing the sky in fragments like scattered glass. In the trembling rye that lined the shore a corncake began its raking lament.

When the inn had faded into the distance, Tia stopped at an outcrop of rock. The stillness of the night closed in upon her, the soft, Hebridean blue as gentle as a newborn's eyes. The water was at an ebb, far away; the causeway clear past Grimsay, all the way to Benbecula. She had always gone in daylight before, this was the first time she had crossed at night and there was something mysterious about it, a spectral difference that made her feel like an explorer might, seeing it all for the first time.

She walked on, quickly now, not wanting to risk being trapped somewhere. The sack of wool began to weigh on her shoulder, and halfway over she shifted it to the other. The Reverend Doctor's face swam before her and then her father's; she imagined the pair of them calling upon God to bring her to her senses, to punish her for disobedience to them.

Like a mirage, a vision fluttered before her, the face of the man whom she had seen in her dreams.

She shivered, but not with cold.

As her thoughts drifted, she slipped, nearly stumbled on a stray strand of weed. She cursed herself for foolishness, wondering if God was chiding her, then looked up and saw the slight rise of Benbecula ahead, ghost-like in the predawn.

The outline of the cottages was vague, wavering, drifting in and out of the early mist, until the image steadied and she saw the glow of a candle being lit at a window, as if to light her way safely towards the shore.

# Chapter Two

*T*ia reached Mary's cottage as the dawn came to brush colour over the canvas of the night. Her grandmother was already up when she opened the door, fussing over the fire that glowed but had not yet given up its flame.

'Ach,' Mary huffed, 'I'm that blind these days, I can't see without my glasses, and because I can't see I can't find the blessed things. I was thinking I would be better to wear them in my sleep, but they dropped off into the bedding and I didn't see them for days.'

Tia put down the sack and began to hunt methodically, by the bed first and then by the loom, then on the table, where the washing bowl was full. She found them there. 'You must have taken them off to wash,' she said, handing them to her grandmother.

Mary balanced the glasses on the edge of her nose, then laughed. 'I'm daft as well. I forgot I had.' She attacked the peats with bellows, sitting back when they flared. 'I'll have tea ready in a moment, pet.'

'I brought your wool.'

Mary swore. 'I'll have to put you on the wheel, Tia, we're going through so much.'

'I don't mind. I'd like to, in fact.' She looked wistfully at the loom, with a half-woven tweed stretched over the frame and hanks for the next stacked beside it.

'Ach, lass, we've been that busy with the Home Industries Association. Some daft woman came round in the spring wanting to buy our tweeds before we'd even begun them, and the next thing is, she doesn't want them in normal colours, she wants *biolaire* and *freumh na craoich*, *lus Chaluim Chille* and *lus-an-fhilcadair*, only the Lord knows what else. It wasn't me, you see. She came around when old Anna from up the road was in, and she says, what a lovely jumper that is, and Anna starts telling her all about the dyes she makes and when that isn't enough she takes her off to her place to show her them and the woman comes back and nothing will do but she wants tweeds made up.'

She lit the oil lamp then, shaking her head at the tweed on the loom. It was pale yellow, with a check of *lus na fearnaich le sugh chabair*, sundew and ammonia, the colour of the sunrise.

'It's wonderful,' Tia said slowly, thinking about the dress she could make with cloth like that.

Mary shook her head again, caught the kettle as it boiled and made tea. 'You know where everything is, pet, just make yourself at home.'

Ceit the weaver came in then, telling Mary that she hoped she wasn't too early but she wanted to get that tweed finished and another one set up. The loom was Mary's now; it had belonged to Iain, her husband, and had become hers on his death. Mary was a seamstress by trade, and she had plenty to do with that so she let others use the loom. That way, all through the year, her home was always full of people; she did not mind the bustle at all, it meant that she was never lonely.

Tia watched as Ceit sat down and straightened the shuttle, then began to pedal, slowly at first until she had the rhythm and then quickly, humming a tune in time with the clacking of the loom, as the cloth wound slowly round the rod at the end. 'How much of this does she want?' she shouted to Mary, who fumbled for a bit of paper and then told her two lengths at least.

'I'll run out of thread before that,' Ceit yelled.

Mary began to search through the sacks piled against the wall; finding two the right colour she beckoned Tia out to the shed against the back of her cottage, where she kept her spinning wheel. Taking a hank of carded wool in her hand, she twisted it slightly and fixed it to the wheel, feeding more on as it began to turn.

'I can manage,' Tia said, moving to take over.

'Steady and even,' Mary said, 'that's the way.'

Tia sat on the low stool, bent over the wheel, biting her lips in concentration as she kept the wheel turning smoothly.

'That's right,' Mary said, 'not too fast, else it might snap.'

Tia smiled to herself.

'I'm that glad you're here,' Mary said. 'I said to Peter to ask your father when you would come. I told her, you know.'

'You told who what?'

'I told the woman from the Home Industries, it takes five spinners to keep a weaver in wool, there's not enough of us on the island if she wants the tweeds in these funny colours.' Mary shook her head, and went back to her work.

They had a break in the early afternoon, for a bowl of soup and some of the bannocks Mary had just made. By then, Tia had finished the *lus na fearnaich le sugh chabair* and had started on her mother's *bun na rainich*, a yellow of a slightly different shade. Her back was stiff from being bent over the wheel; her vision blurred because she had to peer so hard in the dim light.

The tweed of the morning was off the loom, *biolaire* and *sealasdair* in its place.

Ceit ate quickly, nervously. 'When do we get paid, Mary.'

'When the woman comes. Monday of next week.'

'Thirteen and six a tweed?'

'I asked her for fifteen with all these peculiar dyes. She wanted me to take it to Lochmaddy, but I said it would be eighteen shillings each once I paid to get it there.'

Ceit turned to Tia. 'I can't pay you yet, but I will soon's I get my money.'

'It doesn't matter,' Tia said quickly. 'I'm glad to help. I wasn't expecting anything.'

'Don't talk nonsense, you've done the work. I'd've been stuck if you hadn't turned up.'

'You'd only've had me, you mean,' Mary cackled, rubbing her glasses with her apron to rid them of steam from the kettle.

Ceit got up and studied the tweed, touching the cloth as gently as she would sooth a child's fevered brow. 'You did well, Tia.' She held it up. 'D'you think she'll be pleased with it, Mary?'

Mary shrugged. 'It's cloth, but it's not *clo mor*. It's fashion, they say. It's for Lucille, some great designer down in London. She's ordered a dozen tweeds; she'll want more, so they say. If they sell.'

Ceit looked wistful.

'I told her, forget fashion, fashion's too fickle. *Clo mor* isn't fashion, it's the fabric of the land. *Clo mor* will still be strong when Lucille and her ilk are all pushing up the daisies. It was the Duchess of Sutherland started it for hunting coats.' Mary's lips twisted as she recited the title. 'Bloody stupid foreigners, they want them in all colours of the rainbow now. What are they hunting, peacocks? The woman said, she said, "I'd like it made a little finer, a tighter weave; it's a little rough, you see. It makes it difficult to work with." "I always managed," I told her. The cheek of it. As if we should all undo the looms and set them up again because Lucille in London wants a tighter weave.'

'It's been a good year, though,' Ceit said.

'It'll not be so good next year, or the next again,' Mary retorted, 'just you wait. The fashion'll change and that'll be that. The orders'll dry up like a drought and we'll be left with piles of *biolaire* and *bun na rainich* that even a magpie wouldn't use for a nest. *Clo mor* is *clo mor*. Best to be honest and sell it for what it is than to try to make it what it's not.'

Ceit put the cloth back on the pile and returned to the loom. 'Have you enough pee for the waulking, Mary?'

Mary laughed. 'I've gallons more than I need. They were queueing up once I told them it was for the Duchess of Sutherland.'

Tia laughed. The finished tweed was soaked in urine for days before it was worked and dried into shape; the men were usually coy about providing it. Mary picked up the finished tweeds and kicked the door open. 'I've got them soaking in the byre. It makes for less of a stink in the house.'

Tia stood up. 'Can I help you, Gramma?'

'No, pet. I can manage myself. You'd best get back to the wheel.'

It was late in the evening when they finished work for the day, and Ceit left to go back to her own house. Mary pulled two chairs up to the fire, handing Tia a bowl of broth and a chunk of bread, then taking another for herself. 'You can stay a while, pet?'

'A month or two, I'm not sure.'

'There's plenty work for you to do, sure enough. I wasn't sure you'd be this year.'

'Why?'

'I thought Sorley would be wedding you off to someone.'

Tia paled but said nothing; Mary caught her expression.

Tia's fingers were stiff with the repetitive effort; she ate slowly, careful not to spill a drop. She was tired, but pleasantly so; in Mary's house there would be no long Bible reading to occupy the evening, just talk and then rest. Mary made the tea as Tia cleared the dishes away and rinsed them in water from the old bucket Mary kept just outside the door. Seeing it was near empty, Tia went to the spring and filled it, then carried it back and put the lid on to keep it fresh.

'Ach, lass, you didn't have to do that,' Mary said. 'You must be dead on your feet. You didn't have a wink last night, did you?'

Tia smiled. 'I'm fine, Gramma, honestly.'

'The joys of youth,' Mary sighed, then grinned. 'Time was in the lowlands when we sneaked out to a dance one night and stayed so late, by the time we got back it was time to get up again. The cook was such an old curmudgeon that we didn't even have time to change out of our clothes, we just put our maids' dresses on over our gladrags and went about our work as if nothing had happened.'

'I thought you were a seamstress.'

'That was later, pet. I was a maid first of all. I worked to pay for my lessons. Not that I learned anything worth knowing. We've always been good at the sewing, our women. My mother – your great-grandmother – and her mother before her. I was the first to go off the island. It was a woman my mother worked for, said I'd get a better training in the south, and my mother wanted me to have the chance. So I went, but I was a maid first of all. I didn't learn much about sewing; all I learned was fashion.' She smiled. 'It was the bustle then, a great bunch of cloth that was supposed to dangle from a woman's arse. Before that it was the crinoline. That was a skirt with enough cloth for three or four draped over a petticoat with hoops sewn in to make it stand out. Only thing was, you couldn't sit down right, because the hoops would catch the back of the seat and push the skirt up and any passing gentleman might get sight of your stockings, or even more.' She laughed, shaking her head. 'Daft, so it was. You had to howk the hoops up at the back and push them down on the front and sit on the edge of the seat. It must've been like sitting on a barrel. But the blouses were beautiful, pet. They were embroidered and edged with lace, there were pin tucks on the bodice and little buttons made of pearl.' She got up and went to the chest by her bed, opened it and after delving for a while pulled out a bundle, which she held up to show. 'This was for everyday wear.'

The blouse was made from thick ivory silk satin that glowed softly in the light of the candle. The neck was very high, several folds that met at the throat in a line of tiny buttons. On either side of the buttons was a strip of *guipeure* lace, the same lace that edged the cuffs, which ended in a frothy tumble.

Tia got up to look more closely; when Mary handed it to her she exclaimed in surprise, because the fabric felt smooth as a waterfall, the pattern of the lace perfect in every little detail.

'That lace is made by nuns,' Mary said. 'Nobody else has the patience.'

Tia folded the blouse carefully and gave it back to her.

'Like I said, that was for everyday wear,' she said as she put it back in the chest.

'What on earth did they wear for best?'

Mary laughed again. 'Best didn't come into it, pet. They would wear something like that in the morning, with a skirt, then they'd change for lunch into an *ensemble* perhaps and then into an afternoon dress, which was similar but a little more elaborate. In the evening they'd wear a dinner gown if they were staying in, that'd be velvet or satin. If they were going dancing, they'd really dress up. Brocade, furs, jewels, it'd blind you just to look at it and even then they complained because Victoria wasn't one for dolling herself up and so everyone else had to keep their taste in check. Daft it was, I tell you.'

Tia's face had taken on a far away look.

'It fascinates you, doesn't it?'

'What's wrong with that?' she asked, a shade too sharply.

'Nothing, pet, so long as you keep your head on your shoulders. With looks like yours, you could easily become vain.'

Tia shook her head. 'Never.'

'I don't know, lass. Stranger things have happened.'

'I've never thought of myself as being pretty.'

'But you are, Tia. Like you mother was, when she was young. She was the best-looking lass on the islands, and one of the nicest, too. Your father was lucky to get her because he wasn't the only one after her, not by a long shot. He trained to be a teacher, but you know that.'

'I did not.'

Mary's eyebrows lifted. 'Aye, pet, he did so and that was the shame of it. Sorley went to the college and passed the exam, then the school board said the faith he should teach must be the faith of the established Kirk, and your father was a Free Kirker even back then. He would've done it if it wasn't for Janet. She said he mustn't, because it would hurt his soul to teach a lie.'

Tia was thinking of her father, of his clawed arthritic hand and the clumsy, resentful way he had worked the land before that.

'He was vexed, Sorley was. Mind you, he'd a right to be. The rheumatics took him early. That's the other thing that runs in the family, pet. I've been lucky, but it struck your father when he was a young man. It wouldn't've mattered so much if he'd been a teacher, as he was meant to be.'

Tia yawned, through confusion not fatigue. It was always the same, when she talked to Mary. She saw her father in a different way. 'He wants me to marry the Reverend Doctor,' she blurted quickly, bringing back the anger that had flickered briefly.

Mary gave her a knowing look. 'Sorley's aye one for making other people's choices for them.'

'That's why I came last night. Ma said she would talk to him.'

'I'd not bother yourself about it then, pet.'

'She didn't with Peigi and Flo.'

'You're different, pet.'

Tia listened to the silence of the night, which had fallen outside the cottage; everything was still, all of a sudden, and the emptiness dwarfed her resentment and her shame.

'Sorley'd think that you'd want for nothing, being wed to a steady wage.'

She smiled wistfully. 'That's what Ma said. But, you see, if I wedded that man, I'd feel I'd wasted my life, even before it began.'

'Why would that be, Tia?'

'I've never loved, you see. If I wed him, I never would.'

Mary knelt by the fire to smoor the peats, whispering the old prayer, the Catholic prayer, as she did so. Though North Uist was Presbyterian, South Uist was Catholic; Benbecula, between the two, a mixture of each. It was difficult to think of her father growing up here, so close to the popery that he thought of as worse than Satanism, reckoning that, if there were those who worshipped the Devil, at least they were honest about it. To him, the Church of Rome was Auld Nick in disguise, gilded and scented with incense to mask the stench of sin.

Mary finished, straightening her back before she got up to wash her hands. Her legs creaked as she moved; her face tensed before she threw the pain away with a grin. 'You can bed down with me, lass, or I'll make a pallet by the fire. What'll it be?'

The bed Tia usually slept in was piled with tweeds.

'With you,' she said, smiling.

Once she had washed and changed into a nightshirt of Mary's, she put out the lamp and lay down beside the old woman in the big double bed she had once shared with Tia's grandfather. Mary had become scrawny with age, her skin loose folds over limbs as thin as sticks, her body slight beside Tia's.

'Thank you,' she murmured.

'Ach, lass, there's nothing to thank me for. Just be yourself, you don't have to worry about vanity, or owt else.'

'Why's that?'

'Because you're honest first of all. Honesty is the opposite of vanity, don't you know? If you're honest, you can't be vain.' Mary stopped to think, then cackled at herself. 'Lest you become vain about being honest, that'd never do, would it pet? Ach, I'm that old my brain's getting addled. You would be as well listen to the cows in the fields as me, pet. They'd probably make a sight more sense.'

Tia whispered a prayer, then immediately tried to take the words back because the thought was so wrong that God would surely punish her, then she fell asleep, with a smile on her face.

The Reverend Kenneth MacQuarrie came to Benbecula two weeks later, when all the Home Industry Association tweeds were finished and Ceit was making the darker ones that were sold to the tailors in Oban and sometimes to the store at Balivanich, where tourists to the islands occasionally stopped off.

The minister arrived by boat, having inveigled someone into rowing him over the Oitir Mhor as the tide was turning; if he had started earlier he could have walked over the ford, like everyone else. Some children playing in the dunes saw him walking up the sand, his trousers rolled up to his knees and his boots in his hand. The boat couldn't bring him right to the shore and he had to get his feet wet anyway. When he reached the scrub at the top he stopped to put his socks and boots on again, and asked the children where he could find Mary MacLeod.

So it was that Mary knew he was coming long before he arrived, and so did Tia, because the children directed him towards the Committee Road, that almost completed a circle before it reached the croft houses, just a few hundred yards away over the scrub. The Reverend Doctor had been nearly to Creagorry and back before he reached Mary's; a walk of several miles that was nothing to a native islander but a major undertaking for a man, even a young one, dressed in the unwieldy garb of a lowlander.

Mary welcomed him in and gave him *stapag*, a cooling drink of spring water and oatmeal, which he put aside after politely taking the smallest sip.

'Ach,' she said pleasantly, 'I was forgetting myself. I guess you'd rather have tea.'

The answer he gave was not words but a croak.

'The children would be thinking you'd be better on the road,' Mary said. 'What with your boots and all. The salt ruins the leather, you see.'

He drank the tea, then rose as Mary poured another cup, looking out of the door, listening with his head cocked to one side to the laughter of the children playing. His eyes narrowed as a mask of anger spread over his face. 'I suppose they think it's funny to make a fool of a stranger.'

Mary shrugged. 'It depends what you asked them'

'I asked them to show me to road to Mrs MacLeod's cottage, Mrs Mary MacLeod, that is.'

'Well, Reverend Doctor, I don't see that you can blame them. You asked them to show you the road and that is what they did.'

'They knew fine well what I meant.'

'Ach, have a bannock. I've just made some fresh.'

Tia was wearing a cotton dress that Mary had made for her from scraps she had saved over the year. It had a bodice of shirting and a skirt panelled with a Paisley print that Mary used to make backs for waistcoats. Though Mary said she was almost ashamed to give it to her, Tia loved it. 'See, pet,' Mary had said, 'I ordered some special, a lovely shade it was, a wine colour that only someone as fair as you could wear, though it was dark enough that maybe Sorley would let you keep it back home, and blow me, but didn't Ceit's niece Elsbeth decide to get wed and that was the only bit I had that was enough for a dress?'

From the corner of her eye she saw the minister study her for a moment before he shook his head. He rose then, abruptly, rudely brushing the crumbs of the bannock from his suit on to the floor. Mary's eyes met hers; that look told her everything.

'I'll not keep you, Mrs MacLeod,' he said. 'It's Tia I've come to see.'

Mary folded her arms and faced him; he clenched his jaw because he could ask for no more privacy than she was prepared to give.

'We're to be wed, you see,' he ventured.

'Is it just you who's decided that, or does Tia have anything to do with it?'

He ignored her and turned to Tia. 'Perhaps you would take a walk with me?'

'I thought you'd walked far enough today already.'

Mary mouthed Sorley's name; Tia frowned then thought better of it.

She strode out of the cottage before him, shrugging off his effort to link arms with hers, walking briskly until she reached the rise that overlooked the ford, laughing inwardly at his breathless efforts to keep up with her.

The minister's manner softened suddenly. 'I just wanted to say,' he said cautiously, 'that I still want to marry you, and I would be proud if you would agree to be my wife.'

She saw doubt now, not much but a little; as he waited for her answer she caught a brief glimpse of the man beneath the guise of a minister of the church. Though the arrogance remained, there was also a studious air about him, as if he would excuse his lack of understanding as merely lack of knowledge, and rely upon study as a remedy for that. Somewhere far beneath the surface, she sensed that he had feelings, but they were buried so deep down that she doubted if he recognised them as that. He had given up his personality to the strictures of his creed, to him religion was not belief or faith but simply obeisance to a set of rules that rubbed the hard edges off the path of life, removed the need for choice or decision, anything more difficult than acquiescence to a code that, most often, answered a question with one of its own.

The Bible held the answer, so many different answers that by the time you found the one you sought you might well have forgotten the original question.

Tia knew that. She had asked questions of the Bible more than once in her time.

'I would make a good life for you.'

*Ha, but do you love me?* As she looked at him, she knew that he did not even know the meaning of the word; she did, or so she thought. She knew enough about it to know that she did not feel love or anything but revulsion for him.

For a moment she thought she felt something more until she realised that it was pity.

She threw her head back, shaking it like a filly facing the halter for the first time. 'I'm sorry,' she said, 'but as I've said, I cannot.'

His face crumpled into confusion. 'Why not? Whyever not?'

She smiled slowly, wickedly. 'You see, Reverend Doctor, it would be the most terrible sin.'

'A sin? I don't understand. How could it ever be sinful?'

The thought had bubbled out of a spring in her mind, in jest at first before she realised that it was her answer. She leaned close to him, so that no eavesdropper could possibly overhear what she was about to say. 'I'm not a maiden, you see.'

His eyes widened in astonishment.

'I took a lover, you see. I am, what do you call it in the lowlands? Deflowered?' She had heard the word from a herring girl, home from Lowestoft, who said that fate had befallen her sister, who was now stranded in a home for unwed mothers. Her family had to raise £10 to get her back, and she was not allowed to keep the baby.

The Reverend Doctor Kenneth MacQuarrie recoiled as if struck.

'But Tia . . . Miss MacLeod, I had no idea. Your father doesn't know, does he?'

Tia fixed her eyes on the ground, so that he would not see the laughter welling up inside her. 'Please don't tell him,' she whimpered.

'Oh, dear me. I really don't . . . Gracious, what a quandary you've put me in.'

'I had to tell you.'

'Of course you did.' He stood up straight, gazing out over the bay. Already he had forsaken her, replaced her in the herd of the parish rather than at its head with the shepherd. 'I will pray for you, my dear.'

'I would be obliged, Reverend Doctor, if you wouldn't tell my father?'

He shook his head; then shuddered, as if to rouse himself. 'I'd best get back now. D'you know someone who can row me over?'

Tia looked at the waters churning in the pools around the causeway. 'You could walk it easily, Reverend. See these stones? That marks the way.'

He looked at his feet. 'I don't want my boots to get ruined.'

'They won't, not if you hurry. I'll walk you to the shore.'

'No,' he said quickly, 'there's no need. I can manage myself.'

She watched from the dunes until his figure had become tiny, the size of a crow, his reflection beginning to break up as the waters of the incoming tide surged around him.

Mary had to wait for ages before Tia stopped laughing.

When she heard what Tia had done, she ran to the headland and sent a boat after him; the men searched the route twice until they found out that he had been stranded in Grimsay, the smaller island between Benbecula and North Uist, where they thought it was better to leave him. They said he was yelling so loud he could be heard on Berneray.

'I knew he wouldn't drown,' Tia said, when Mary tried to chide her for it. 'D'you think he'll tell my father?'

'It'd serve you right if he did,' Mary said, but there was a smile on her face as she said it.

'There's a dance at Creagorry tonight,' Mary said, a few days later, 'though I doubt you want to go, the state of you, what with being deflowered and all.'

Tia smiled to herself. The laughter in Mary's eyes told her that she was not serious. The minister was back in his parish, no worse for his adventures.

She wore a new skirt of tweed Ceit had give her, from a length that she couldn't finish because there wasn't enough wool of the shade she needed. Mary had found some cotton lawn in her press, dyed it to tone with the skirt and then made her a blouse with a pin-tucked bodice and an embroidered collar. Tia had never felt happier in her life, though the thought of her father still hovered on her mind's horizon, and like the chill wind which started that day spoke bleakly of the end of summer. Within the week she would have to go home; her mother had sent a note to say that Mrs MacFadyen had offered her a job as a kitchen maid at the hunting lodge from the end of August until mid October. Janet had told the Post that Tia would be there.

'Mightn't happen,' Mary said, seeing her glum face as they set out for the south side of the island.

Tia tried to smile, but she smiled properly only when, with Mary and the others, she crested the rise before Creagorry and heard the music that had already begun.

The hall was packed with people, from South Uist as well as Benbecula. As Tia walked in, one of the men from her grandmother's village pulled her into the swirl of dancers and she danced with him until she was dizzy. When the music paused she waited for the crowd to settle and then looked around anxiously, then again when she did not see what she was looking for. She walked right round the hall, on the pretext of going to get a glass of water, before she came to accept that her hope was forlorn. God had not answered her prayer; maybe He had not even heard it. She walked outside and breathed slowly for a moment, listening to the sound of her heart as it returned to its normal rhythm.

Far to the west, the day was ending; on the edge of the ocean the sun melted like butter. She watched the light flare and then fade as a chill wind began to mat the *machair* grass. As the island to the north took on the colour of night, she thought of her father at home taking his seat by the fire to begin the evening Bible reading. Perhaps the Reverend Doctor would be with them; he often joined Sorley MacIain for the evening reading and then prayers.

Even Mary didn't understand. When Tia was very young, she had thought that every house was like her own. Then, when she was at school, with the other village girls, she had gone into homes where there was laughter and joy, where the pursuit of happiness was not, by definition, a sin. She was shy at first, nervous that her hosts might know what her father said of them, that so-and-so was foolish, simple, a sinner whose natural tendencies must be strictly controlled. They would tease her about him sometimes, tell her that with Sorley MacIain for her da she'd not be worried about going to heaven, as Tia bit back the remark that she had her life on earth to live first. Her father was respected in the village, but apart from the elders he had no friends. Sorley MacIain would not care about that, even if he realised it. He often said that the only friend a man needed was Jesus, or a woman, come to that.

Tia wanted more than that.

Years ago she had thought that escape from her father would come when she left school with the other girls and went away to work; it was only now that she realised there was no escape, there never would be unless like her sister Mairead she broke the ties for ever and ran away.

She had saved the money Ceit had given her; it wasn't enough yet, but it would be after she had worked at the hunting lodge.

In all of her life her only act of open defiance had been that one dance with Marcus Cameron last year. She had met him the first time she had ever visited Mary's; as a child, Mairead had played with him; as a young man he would ferry people across the south ford to Iochdar when the tide was in for a fare of a farthing or just a smile. Tia saw him every year after that, and made a point of searching him out. At first they just talked shyly, reminding each other of the passage of time, but last year he had asked her to dance with her and when they parted he told her that he would look forward to dancing with her again, the next year. Tia had been afraid at first, when she learned that Marcus was a Catholic, scared that her father would get to hear what she had done, but on Benbecula nobody cared or even noticed. She had wanted to see Marcus again, had been looking forward to it, but he had not appeared this summer; he was away on his ship and she did not want to excite Mary's interest by asking if she knew when he would come.

He's just a friend, she thought. It was silly to feel anything more about someone she only met once or twice each summer. Though she had known him all of her life, she hardly knew him at all.

'Hello,' he said suddenly.

She spun around, astonished. It was as if magic had brought him to her; that he had some power she did not understand.

'I didn't mean to startle you,' he said.

She tried to tell him that he had not, but no sound came from her lips.

He smiled. 'There was a queue waiting to dance with you. I stood at the end for a while, and then I thought I'd wait out here, hope that you got tired.'

'Oh, Marcus, I didn't even see you.' She wondered then if the power that had brought him to her also enabled him to read her mind.

'Like I said, I was standing at the end of queue.'

The music started and he took her hand. 'Will you dance with me now?'

'Yes, Marcus, I'd love to.' Tia felt joy then, the emotion so strange that she wondered, at first, if it was giddiness, knew only for certain when he took her in his arms as the music began.

He was a sailor on the North Atlantic route; he had travelled the world on the ocean steamers before he settled down on a ship that sailed between Glasgow and America. He had done well, for a boy from South Uist who had started with nothing. He was a first officer now; he had a navy uniform with shiny brass buttons and braid around the collar and cuffs, which she had seen last year when he left on the Oban ferry to return to his boat.

'So you did wait for me,' he said, just before the reel parted them.

'I did not wait for you, Marcus Cameron,' she spluttered, as he spun away, laughing.

As the dance ended, Mary tapped her shoulder and said she was going home. Tia gasped. To her, the dance had only just begun.

'I might be old and stiff, but I'm not a killjoy. You stay, pet. Enjoy youself,' Mary said.

'I'll bring her home,' Marcus said quickly.

Mary nodded at him. 'Aye, you do that, Marcus Cameron. That's straight home to me, not home by way of Glasgow or New York or Shanghai or wherever it is you're headed next.'

Tia felt a surge of pleasure to know that for the rest of the night she would be with him.

He smiled at her as the music started again. 'Do you want to dance some more?'

She shook her head.

Outside, the sky was the ivory gauze of the summer, dark streaked in the east with the veil of night. Marcus stopped to light his pipe; as he did so she caught the strong line of his jaw. He had changed since she'd last seen him, she saw now as if for the first time the lines of experience on his forehead and ones of laughter at the edges of his eyes. The pale light made a veneer of his tan, made him look polished, like a gypsy, but his eyes were still the cold, clear, crystal blue of a winter dawn that lit like sapphires when he smiled at her. His hair, once dark auburn, had turned pewter grey. She counted up and realised that he was thirty-three years old now.

The tobacco lit and he inhaled deeply, then cursed and knocked the burning leaves out on a stone where, one by one, he extinguished them.

'Ach,' he said, 'it's the Devil's habit. I'm not going to bother with tobacco again.'

They began to walk along the shore path towards Lioniclett.

'D'you know,' he said, 'my uncle used to go to sea like me and when he made Captain on the old Boisdale ferry, he bought himself a plug of tobacco every month and he would come home and sit there, smoking his pipe like a king. I thought, when I grew up, came like him, I'd get a pipe and smoke it too, but when I did, I discovered I don't enjoy it. Not even when I get it free.'

He threw the pipe into the grass, disturbing a duck that squawked and honked, then changed his mind and went and got it back. 'I'll give it to Hector, that's what I'll do. He's daft enough to enjoy it.'

She shivered in the chill. Without a word he took off this

sweater and wrapped it around her shoulder. The path dipped down towards the sea; there was a rock there, sheltered from the wind by the rise of the land. He stopped and folded his jacket to make a seat for her.

'So what has life been doing to you since last year?' he asked, when she was settled shyly by his side.

She smiled grimly; she did not want to tell him about the Reverend Doctor or the lie she had told to escape marriage to him.

'I'm going away to work,' she said suddenly.

He grinned. 'I heard your father wouldn't let a daughter of his off the island.'

'That's true, but I'm going anyway.'

Marcus said nothing, but the skin around his eyes crinkled as he looked towards the distance. 'My brothers have their boat now,' he said.

He had told her last year about the boat, that if he could buy his brothers a fishing boat his family would be secure. He had supported them all for years, since his father died. Ever since she had known him, he had been working away from the islands; he had been only twelve when he started on the ferry, fifteen when he had gone to sea proper. There had been a year in which she had not seen him, and the following year he told her that he had sailed right around the world.

When she asked him, he would tell her stories of these far-off places, of the other side of the world where winter was summer, of oceans so wide that you could sail for weeks and not see land. The strangeness of it all both frightened and intrigued her; she thought Marcus very brave to venture so far from home. She told him that once, and he said it was nonsense, that people were the same the world over; some good, some bad, most just foolish.

'My sisters are wed, 'cept Bridie, who won't, and Cal's off to the Scots College in Rome,' he told her.

'Will you be coming home, then?' she asked nervously.

He shook his head. 'I think I'll head west. In America, a man's judged for what he does, not what he is.'

The thought of him leaving made her shiver again.

'Are you cold?' he asked her.

'No,' she said quickly.

'When are you leaving, Tia?'

As he looked at her, she wondered what he meant.

'You said you were going away to work . . .'

'Yes. Soon. I don't know when.'

'Are you going to run away?'

'Yes.'

He sighed. 'If I can help, I will.'

'Help?'

'I can take you down to Glasgow when I go back to the ship. I can help you find somewhere to live, maybe a job as well.'

'That would be very good of you, Marcus.'

He shook his head. 'It's nothing.'

The wind changed from chill to cold, brought rain as soft as thistle-down that painted Tia's hair to her face.

Marcus looked at the sky and swore softly. 'I'd best get you home before you catch a cold.'

'Yes,' she replied, deflated, because she wanted to talk some more.

'Will you do something for me, Tia?'

She looked up at him and saw herself reflected in his eyes.

'Will you let me kiss you?'

She blushed and whispered that she would.

Very slowly, his face closed in one hers, until she could no longer see the sky but only his features. She closed her eyes and felt his lips brush hers so softly that she wondered how the sensation made her tremble and fall towards him; he wrapped her in his arms and held tight for a moment before he let her go.

She took a breath and felt the giddiness recede, found herself thinking of the other women he had touched, of the other women he had kissed; she was jealous of them. Through the cotton of his shirt, she had felt the muscles of his chest, hard as steel.

He was smiling at her; she was smiling too. There was a look on his face that she had never seen before, that she recognised as happiness and also relief.

The silence closed in on her, the sea sounds faded and so did the wind. Just as it began to threaten her she opened her mouth to say something but he stopped her by putting a finger to his lips.

'Will you do something else for me Tia, *annsachd*?' he asked.

'What is that?' she asked, her voice so throaty it was almost a croak.

'Will you marry me, my love?'

For a moment she did not reply, then her eyes gave him her answer and he grabbed her hand and they ran on to the shore; taking both of her hands then, he began to spin her around and her world turned, faster and faster until all she could see was him against the blurring backdrop of the sky and the ocean and the pearl white sand. Her laughter rang out over the land, mingling with the early morning cries of the birds, the rush of wind through the grass and the music of the sea.

Breathless, she collapsed towards him, and he caught her and let her sink into his lap, waiting for her dizziness to subside. For a long time they sat in silence, gazing at the frothy peaks of the waves, watching the tide as, inch by inch, it took the shore. Tia was thinking of the chance, of the risk that she might have missed him; her heart was fluttering like a baby bird as she looked at him and knew that he was now the man in her dream. His hair had gone grey in the year he had been away and she wondered how she could have known that, took it as a sign that her destiny was with him, as she had hoped it would be. In a moment her dream had become true, years before she had dared to think it would. She turned to look at him, felt a wave of love so strong that she shuddered, smiling shyly as his arms tightened around her.

'When did you know?' she asked him, in a small voice, when the first droplet of spray brushed her face.

He looked deep into her eyes. 'I've always known, *annsachd*. Right from the first time I saw you. I loved you then, as I love you now.'

She trembled slightly.

'And you?'

She smiled shyly. 'Last year, when we danced last year. I began to hope then but I hardly dared. I was scared, you see. I thought . . .'

'You thought what?'

'That you were my friend, as you've always been. I . . .I don't have many friends. After you left, I felt empty inside. I thought you'd forgotten, that you weren't going to come . .' The chance seemed so fragile that she shivered reflexively again.

43

He grinned. 'That was never in doubt.'

She looked at him questioningly.

'I'd home leave coming, a year's worth. You know Willie Beag just along the road from Mary?'

She did not.

'Well, Willie Beag's a cousin of my mother's. I told Willie last year. I made him promise to send me a gram the moment he saw you. It was waiting for me when I docked last week. I came then.'

Tia thought for a while, then remembered the small, thin man who had smiled very broadly when she passed him with an armful of dried tweeds after the waulking.

The air sparkled with the dawn, the changing colours had never been so clear, or so beautiful. The tide began to lap softly at her feet. Relishing its caress, she watched as the water broke between her toes, feeling the ocean's energy pulse against the sole of her foot. A bit away, a wave reared and then broke, tumbling towards them in a shower of froth. Marcus snatched her up just in time but his trousers got soaked and his laughter sounded like a heavenly chorus as it rang out over the beach. He carried her all the way to the top of the dunes, then put her down as he found his jacket and shrugged it on. The breeze had quickened; she could see goose pimples on his skin under the open collar of his shirt.

'D'you want your jumper?' she asked him.

''Course not,' he said.

It was an Eriskay seaman's sweater, the special pattern known only to the women there.

Marcus was scrambling around, peering at the ground, cursing softly under his breath.

'I never used to believe in miracles. I do now,' she said.

He stood up straight, flexed his shoulders then let his arms hang loose. 'A miracle, is it? Perhaps you could magic up another one, *annsachd*.'

'What's that?'

'Help me find my *galach* boots.'

She began to laugh.

'I had the blessed things when I walked over. I had them at the dancing. I had them walking along the path with you. I don't have them now.'

The confusion on his face made her love him more. For a moment she gazed at him, then she flung her arms around him, breathing in the scent of him, the salty muskiness, the bleach of his shirt, the rough sharp tang of the damp tweed of his jacket.

'I can try.'

They linked hands and ambled slowly over the dunes, searching for the boots occasionally, more often gazing at each other.

'I've lost the *galach* things,' Marcus said when they had walked the line of the shore twice and arrived back where they started. 'I don't know what I'm doing anyway, looking for a bloody pair of boots when we've a wedding to organise. Who do we tell first?'

Tia frowned a little. The sun was full now, its harsh rays stung her eyes. 'What do you mean, Marcus?'

'I mean, do we tell your family or mine?'

His hand tightened on hers. 'Iochdar's nearer, we should go there first, to my mother. We could just make the south ford if we rush.'

'What about my grandmother?'

'She'll understand when we tell her we're getting married.'

Smiling, she began to run but her legs were shorter than his, her pace slower. Marcus jogged alongside her for a while; then, when the ford came into view, the waters just glazing the sandy channel, he stopped and rolled up his trousers, then swung her into his arms and began to run full tilt towards the rise of South Uist. The water was midway up his calves but he raced on, gulping air, his breath hot and fast with the exertion. Halfway along the narrow passage, they passed a lobster boat, the fisherman gazing at them in amazement.

'I love her,' Marcus roared. 'I love her and she loves me.'

The spray slapped Tia's face and she began to laugh.

'She loves me and she's going to be my bride,' Marcus roared, as the gulls cried and the oyster-catchers squawked and the puffins dived and the kittiwakes stopped jousting for a moment to stare at them.

'We're getting married,' Marcus yelled, as the fisherman's face broke into a smile and he waved so hard that the little boat rocked and nearly capsized.

Long before they reached the shore, the whole of the north

end of the island knew what had happened and was waiting for them.

# Chapter Three

$A$s they walked over the *machair* to Marcus's cottage his mother Eunice ran to meet them. She folded Tia into her arms, rocking her as she whispered a prayer. She was a tiny woman, as broad as her own son was tall, the only similarity between them the colour of their eyes and the easy way they smiled, as if happiness was not a blessing but a right.

'I doubt the Father'll wed us,' Marcus said once they were indoors, huddled around the fire as Eunice dried Tia's shawl and then began to hunt for his old boots.

She winced. 'I know he won't. 'Lest you convert, Tia, come over to us.'

'I'd not ask her to do that,' Marcus said quickly, 'not unless she wants to. We'll marry at the town hall at Oban. We'll be wed just the same.'

Eunice's face became wistful for a moment, then she smiled determinedly. 'God's not blind to love, you know that. Not blind like the Church can be blind. Are you staying long?'

Marcus looked out of the window, at the clouds rising over the ocean. 'We'd best away, Ma. We've to cross to Benbecula, then the North, to see her folks.'

Eunice looked away briefly, then knelt beside Tia and clasped her hand. 'You're not gone for ever. You'll come back to see us.'

Tia smiled. 'I promise. Of course we will.'

Bridie, Marcus's older sister, came in then, her expression bland.

'This is Tia,' Marcus said, rising. 'She's going to be my bride.'

Bridie ignored her. Marcus's eyes followed her for a moment, then he shrugged.

Eunice had taken a jacket from a hanger dangling from a hook on the wall. 'It's steamed and pressed, son, good as new.'

He put it on easily. Tia noticed there was another gold ring around the sleeve.

'He's captain now,' Eunice said, 'made up since last December.'

Marcus turned away, embarrassed.

'I'm so proud of him,' Eunice said.

'So am I,' Tia murmured.

Bridie spun round then. 'I know your type,' she hissed. 'Just don't play any of your tricks on him.'

'That's enough!' Marcus said, so sharply that Tia flinched.

Outside, as they walked over the *machair*, he told her that Bridie was bitter because the man she had been about to marry was killed in an accident at sea.

Tia shrugged her shoulder, trying to shake off the hurt as well, but Bridie had cut deep, well below her skin. It hurt to know that Bridie even thought like that.

'It's not true,' she said.

'I know it isn't, and so does she. Give her time, and she'll love you as I do. She hurts so bad, she's blind to other people.'

The plain perched on the ocean's edge was glorious in late summer, a carpet of wildflowers and cotton tufts, with wild orchids scattered like windfall over the iridescent grass.

Marcus tugged at her hand, pulling her to a halt as he pointed to the ground. A single orchid grew there, the flowers pulled tightly together, pink petals that deepened to a crimson over a golden labellum. It seemed to sense the human presence, because it quivered slightly in the breeze.

'You would have stood on it,' Marcus said, 'if I hadn't pulled you away.'

'I'm glad you did.'

She noticed then the strange quality of the time she spent with him, the way a moment could stretch into an hour and then how, when looking back upon it, it was not as if the time had passed, but that it had been snatched away. It was late afternoon, going on evening, nearly a whole day had gone, without her noticing even the movement of the sun across the sky. At the place where the *machair* met the sands, white and lonely, she stopped and looked back at the wind sweeping a wave through the grass, rippling olive on emerald, as the wild cotton surfed and jigged on the current.

'We will come back, won't we?'

'Yes,' he said, roughly. 'You could go the world over, *annsachd*; there isn't a place that comes anywhere near to this.'

When they reached the south ford, he carried her over his arms.

Mary was waiting on the other side. 'There you are, pet,' she said, pressing a bundle into Tia's hand, 'God bless and good luck.'

'How did you know?' Tia asked her.

'I guessed, when you didn't come back, then I heard you'd gone to Iochdar.'

'Marcus took me home.'

Mary patted her cheek. 'Everybody knew he loved you before you did, pet. Have you time for a *strupag*?'

'I'll always have time for a cup of tea with you,' Marcus said as he took her arm.

As she saw her grandmother in the hard light of day, Tia suddenly realised how much she had changed over the year, how old she looked now. She felt cold suddenly, wistful somehow, as she tried to shake off the feeling that she would never see her again.

Watching Marcus and Mary, she was glad that her marriage had her grandmother's blessing.

When the Reverend Kenneth MacQuarrie had got back from Grimsay, he closeted himself with Sorley – unthinking, perhaps that Janet listened from the loft.

'I cannot marry her,' he said, 'she is fallen, she tells me.'

'What nonsense is that?' Sorley roared. 'There had been nobody for her to fall with!'

'That is what she says.'

'It is not true.'

'Even so, that she even thinks of it is enough.'

Janet shivered.

'She is pure, I would pledge my life on it.'

'Her thoughts are impure.'

Sorley's face was like thunder when the Reverend left.

'She has a mind of her own,' Janet tried.

'She has a mind to hold her father up to ridicule,' Sorley raged. 'She will come back and apologise for misleading him.'

'It will never work,' Janet said.

'He will see the sense of it too,' Sorley said gruffly.

With a mother's instinct, Janet knew as soon as she heard of Tia's journey with Marcus to meet his mother, that Tia would never come back. She crept up to the loft and packed her daughter's nightgown and spare set of underclothes, then wiped a tear from her eye as she took her shawl from the hook.

'Where are you going?' Sorley asked her.

She started because he had been engrossed in the Bible and she'd hoped he would not notice her.

He saw the bundle of clothes in her hand.

'Tia is leaving.'

'Over my dead body.'

'Sorley, the girl has a right to her own life.'

'Is not the life she has good enough for her? What is wrong with her?'

'There is nothing wrong with her.'

'She is like the other one.' He was referring to Mairead. 'And you are standing up for her.'

'I am not going to stand in the face of the inevitable,' Janet said. 'She has a mind of her own and she has chosen her own man.'

'And who is that, pray?'

'A good man, I hear. A man from South Uist.'

'A papist.' His face twisted into a look of disgust. 'Why does she have to shame me so, and you too?'

Janet breathed in deeply and then stood firm. 'I am not shaming you, Sorley. You are shaming yourself. Do you remember nothing?'

'What do you mean by that?'

'My mother was a Catholic, a papist as you would say. That didn't stop you.'

'That was different. She had come over to us.'

'You say yourself the sin is the Catholic Church and not the people.'

'I will not have my daughter marrying one of them. I forbid you to go to her.'

'You will not keep me away from my own daughter, Sorley MacIain. Not even you can do that.'

\*

Tia fell into Janet's arms when she met her below the inn. 'Oh, Mama, Mama, this is Marcus.'

'I know, pet,' Janet said, turning to the tall man who stood beside her daughter. 'Ceit's sister, Anna, came by with the news. I've brought your things for you.'

Marcus shifted. 'We'll not sneak away like thieves in the night. I'll go to Sorley and ask his blessing.'

'Best not to. He's not in a mood for giving it.'

Marcus folded his arms. 'I'll ask him, nevertheless.'

Tia turned to him. 'You don't know what he's like.'

'I've heard. But there's no man who would keep me from you, *annsachd*.'

Janet nodded slowly to herself. The wind had turned chill; Marcus saw her shivering then with one swift movement he took her into his arms and carried her over the dunes as he had carried Tia over the ford.

Janet began to laugh, she was shrieking with joy as he swung her in time with a sailor's song he sang. When they reached the first rise of scrub, he let her down gently and then took her by the hands and spun her around in a reel.

'Stop, *stop*!' Janet wailed. 'My old bones, can't stand it!' She was laughing as she said it, and Marcus did not stop; his voice just changed rhythm slightly, from the sailor's song to a bawdy waulking tune. Janet was as happy as the sunrise in the wake of the storm, as radiant and triumphant. Tia felt pure joy then; she watched Marcus's lips as he launched into mouth music, mimed for a moment until she caught the beat, joined in tremulously at first, gaining confidence from the sound that she made. Under the big sky, against the emptiness of the ocean, the music gained a life of its own. The beat rang out over the sands, reverberating against the rocks and rise of the land, coming back on itself in counterpoint and then in perfect time.

*Rarra-rho, rarra-rho, rarro-rho-rho-rho, cracka-co, cracko-co, cracko-co-co-co; bhabha-bho, bhabha-bho, bhabha-bho-bho-bho.*

Marcus's strong baritone rose in words that he made up as he went along:

*I left my love when I went to sea-ee,'*

*Rarra-rho, rarra-rho, rarra-rho-rho-rho, cracka-co, cracko-co, cracko-co-co-co; bhabha-bho, bhabha-bho, bhabha-bho-bho-bho.*

'*I left my love but she followed me-ee,'*

51

*Rarra-rho, rarra-rho, rarro-rho-rho-rho, cracko-co, cracka-co, cracko-co-co-co, bhabha-bho, bhabha-bho, bhabha-bho-bho-bho.*

The door of the inn opened and two people came out, strangers, to see what the noise was about. As they watched, others came from the fields and the sands, waiting for the pause between phrases, joining in when they caught the beat. For a while, Marcus and Janet danced alone, then Marcus pulled Tia into their circle and Archie joined in too, then Iain MacDonald and Tam McPhail, Jessie MacKenzie and Jean MacCallum, Seumus MacAndrew and John *beag Mic Ailean Mor*, Effie MacInnes and Morag Maclellan, even Samuel, home from the shooting, with Flo, and Ealasaid-of-the-sad-eyes, drawn into the knot of dancers by Seumas, who cajoled her and coaxed her as gently as he would an orphan lamb.

The dance went on and on, fuelled by the music and great jugs of ale that the innkeeper brought on to the sands when he realised that he would get no custom at the inn that day. Marcus put his hand into his pocket for some coins; the innkeeper shook his head, refusing absolutely to take money from him or anyone else.

The whole village was there, apart from Sorley MacIain and the Reverend Doctor.

For a while nobody thought beyond the moment; the dance just happened, as such things do. It was deep into the evening, long after night had fallen and the way was lit first by the moon and then by some torches that the innkeeper kept to light the way for travellers, that they remembered themselves as the wind quickened and became tainted with rain. The music faded then died, though its echo continued long after, like a stream that seeps into the earth to escape the assault of drought will return to life again at summer's end.

They walked home in silence, hands linked, all three of them, Marcus and Janet and Tia. Just as they reached the door, Marcus stopped and held Janet tight.

'Thank you,' he said quietly.

Janet looked at him.

'For accepting me.'

Janet shook her head, embarrassed by his attention. 'You'd best let me go, Marcus, else you'll make her jealous.'

'No.' Tia smiled.

'If I didn't have Tia, I'd be after you.'

Janet laughed. 'Away, Marcus. I'm old and I'm done.'

'You'll never be done.'

The door opened so fast that in the rush of air Janet stumbled and Marcus reached for her arm to steady her.

Sorley's face was the shade of damnation. 'I heard the dance,' he said. 'So it is not enough to turn down a good man for a papist, you have to breach the peace of God as well?' He reached for Janet. 'Get away in, woman.'

She stood there. 'This is a good man too. He has a right to a hearing.'

'He has a right to nothing after what he has done!'

Marcus folded his arms. 'I've heard that you're strict, Sorley MacIain, but it was only a little dance . . .'

'Only a little dance! The noise of it! Decent god-fearing people disturbed in their homes and all the lewdness of Gomorrah right on their doorsteps! Only a little dance, you say. You are not content with corrupting my daughter, you will corrupt the whole place as well.'

Marcus flinched then stood his ground. 'I have come to ask for your daughter's hand in marriage.'

'Over my dead body!' He reached for Tia's arm, but she slipped out of his grasp. 'Get in here this instant, girl!'

'No, Father. I am going to marry Marcus, whether you like it or not.'

He reached for her again, this time grabbing her arm and shaking her. In an instant, Marcus stopped him. 'Leave her be, Sorley MacIain.'

Sorley gazed at his daughter with hatred. 'Very well, but if you leave now you are no longer my daughter.'

'Sorley, no,' Janet said, 'not again . . .' She flung her arms around Tia, crying, as Tia began to sob too. For a long time the women held each other, as Sorley turned away and slammed the door in their faces.

'He doesn't mean it,' Janet said, 'he will come round in time.'

'You know he won't,' Tia murmured.

Suddenly the door opened and Sorley flung himself at Marcus, pummelling his chest with his clawed fists. Janet screamed and flung herself at him, dragging him off as he yelped with impotent rage. The door closed and Marcus was

53

left standing with Tia; very gently he wiped the tears from her eyes.

'He didn't hurt you,' she said, 'I hope he didn't hurt you.'

Marcus shook his head. 'He couldn't hurt me, *ban-righ*. No man could. Only you.'

She shivered with the strength of her feelings; she wanted to hold him, keep him close always, to cherish him as he cherished her. Belatedly, she realised that he had called her Queen.

He slung her bundle over his back then picked her up and began to stride away.

'Where're we going?' she asked him sleepily.

'Lochmaddy, of course, for the boat to Oban and our wedding.'

Her heart flipped. 'Aren't you tired, Marcus?'

'No, *ban-righ*. I'm not tired, I've waited for you so long.'

She slept guiltily in his arms, waking only briefly as they boarded the steamer and he settled her once again in his lap as he took the only chair left in the passage just down from the bridge.

'Bloody, tub,' he said, as the *Hebrides'* engine began to turn slowly.

'What's that?' Tia murmured.

He looked down at her, his face filled her eyes. 'This ship, beloved, a bathtub if there ever was one.'

'Awa' to hell, Cameron,' the captain spat.

'If you pulled the plug on her, she'd sink like a stone,' Marcus said loudly.

'That's not the only thing the plug'll be pulled on, soon's we get moving. You'll be over the side in a barrel, Cameron, if there's any more of your cheek.'

'The engine sounds sweet,' Marcus said wryly.

'It does too,' the captain retorted.

'Is it treacle you feed her to keep her moving? The racket of the piston, what holds this thing together, string? Or glue, maybe?'

The door of the bridge swung open and the captain hovered threateningly.

Marcus held up his hand in a gesture of peace.

The captain smiled at her. 'Who's the lady?'

'My bride to be.'

Tia fell asleep to the background of their banter, with a smile on her face.

In Oban the registrar's clerk looked at her and then at Marcus. 'The lady looks a mite young to me.'

'I'm sixteen,' Tia said defiantly.

'Well, you'll have to wait fourteen days for the banns.'

'No,' Marcus said. 'We'll apply for a special licence.' He asked directions to the sheriff court and they were out in the sunshine again.

'How did you know?' she asked him.

'I told you, *ban-righ*, I've waited for so long. I've planned this for a year.'

'The sheriff might not give us a licence.'

'He will. You'll see.'

At the court, the sheriff clerk directed them to the sheriff's house. The town was busy; Tia saw a car for the first time but hardly noticed the bustle, because her attention was on Marcus. When they reached the door of the house he squeezed her hand to reassure her.

The sheriff of Oban was a doughty old man called Jeremiah Muir, of a gruff, open manner and twinkling eyes who first of all asked Marcus who he thought he was to come banging at his door at that time when everyone for miles around knew that he took a nap after lunch and did not surface again until the sun had fallen beyond Kerrera. 'I need my rest,' he said, 'the law's such a stramash these days, it'd test the patience of a saint, never mind a mere mortal like me.' Marcus coughed and said that they would come back later, but the sheriff asked them in, saying that since they had woken him they might as well explain what all the fuss was about.

Tia's nerves jangled. In her dreams it had never been like this. She had never thought that her marriage would depend on the whim of a sheriff, that she needed permission to marry the man she loved. She felt anger rise suddenly, at the process that put her future in the hands of a grumpy old man.

Marcus's hand on hers was firm, his grip certain. As the sheriff shuffled amongst his papers for his glasses, she leaned close and in a whisper asked him what to say. 'The truth, of course,' Marcus murmured under his breath, as the sheriff suspended his hunt for a moment, to glare at them and say that though he was old and half blind, he was not yet deaf. He went back to his search for a while and then abandoned it for the time being, sat down on the other side of his desk and folded his hands prosaically. 'Well, get on with it, man.'

Tia opened her mouth to speak, but Marcus began first. 'We want a special licence to marry. What do you want to know?'

'The truth, of course, like you told the young lady. I've heard that many fibs in my time, I've aye got ears for the truth.'

Tia shivered inwardly, she did not share Marcus's confidence. As Marcus began to explain that he was a captain with Rankine's, she gazed at the sheriff's impassive features, wondering what thoughts were running through his mind.

'What's to stop you just carrying her off and marrying her yourself?' The sheriff said. 'You have the right, you know. A ship's captain can do what he likes at sea.'

'It wouldn't be right,' Marcus said.

'It would be legal.'

Marcus smiled wryly. 'I'd not know how to go about marrying myself. I want to be wed by the laws of my country. Like you say, the ocean's a law to itself.'

The sheriff nodded slowly.

'You see, I'm a member of the Roman Church, and Tia, she is a Presbyterian. They each of them won't recognise the other. If we wed in church, in either church, we'd aye be fornicators in the eyes of the other.'

'You could choose, one of you converts to the other.'

'Why should we? I love her as she is and she loves me. God never told Adam and Eve that they must choose one church over the other.'

The sheriff's eyes had turned rheumy. 'As yet, I've heard nothing that merits a special licence.'

'It doesn't matter,' Tia said suddenly. 'We'll wait the fourteen days. It makes no difference.' She did not want this man to decide for her, she was sure without him and the time did not matter.

Marcus swallowed; underneath the desk she gripped his hand tightly and his squeezed hers in reply. 'Tia has no means of support. We went to ask her father's permission. He withheld it. He said he would always withhold it. He said that if she did not forsake me, she would never be allowed to cross his doorstep again. As you can see, she's still with me.'

Tia closed her eyes against the pain of the memory. The sheriff shook his head, then rang a bell which brought a moment later a maid with a tray laid for tea.

His study faced the bay; the light of the afternoon bisected the window, made shadows that crossed the floor and then climbed the walls, ending only when they met the ceiling. The sun had fallen beyond Kerrera, the jagged edge of the hill biting a chunk out of the flame that flared over the island like molten ore into a forge, hissing and sizzling as its energy gave way to the hardness of rock. Tia gazed at if for a moment, then realised that now was the time when the sheriff began his work.

The sheriff poured the tea himself, ignoring Tia's offer of help, and then swore softly as he reached for a bottle of whisky and two glasses, leaving Tia with a little porcelain cup and saucer and a full pot to herself.

'What of your people?' he asked Marcus.

Marcus sighed. 'I have my mother's blessing. My father is dead.'

The sheriff nodded in acknowledgement.

'My eldest sister's the only one left at home. Her man died before she had a chance to wed. She is bitter. She might not mean to, but she can hurt.'

Tia trembled reflexively, until his hand found hers.

'That I can understand,' the sheriff said, turning to Tia. 'My dear, all I can say is this. The law is not heartless but it can be strict. All rules have a reason, at least, good rules have reasons, and the reason for the rule that says you must give fourteen days' notice of a wedding is to save the fool from the worst effects of his folly. We can't have every scallawag in England thinking they can come to Scotland and get hitched overnight. And the same goes for our own. We're already generous in that we allow a girl of your age to wed without her father's permission. We temper that with a request for sobriety and reflection because the marriage vow is the most serious promise you will ever make in your life; it is a promise that I believe should never be broken. We want evidence of your maturity, that you have reached your decision freely, without duress, without undue influence by any person. You might be certain in your own mind, but I need to be certain, too.'

Tia began to say that she was, so certain, but he raised his hand to silence her. 'I might be old, girl, but I'm not blind. I know love when I see it. I am prepared to grant a licence not now but tomorrow morning on condition that you stay here with me and my wife and spend the evening in reflection. If you feel tomorrow as you do today, then you will have my permission and also my blessing.'

Marcus looked as if he was about to say something but the sheriff stopped him too. 'As for you, lad, I sense you've been planning this for years, but the way it's turned out has been rather sudden. The MV *Hebrides* is with us overnight, I hear. Something the matter with her boiler. I suggest you spend the evening with your friends and come back again in the morning.'

'But,' Marcus said.

'But what?'

'She needs some clothes. You see, she had only the clothes she stands up in, and the boots I bought from the chandler's when we got here.'

Tia looked down at the shiny leather and smiled at herself. When the boat had docked Marcus had carried her down the gangplank of the *Hebrides* and left her sitting on a bollard as he disappeared into the chandler's, returning a moment later with a thick pair of fisherman's socks and a brand new pair of boots. He handed her the socks to put on as he worked the boots with his hands, pulling and tugging the leather until it was soft and supple. 'I can't have you catching blisters,' he'd said, as he helped her put them on.

'That's not true,' she chirruped suddenly, remembering the bundle Mary had pushed into her hands and the bag that Janet had packed for her that Marcus had put in his own.

'I meant,' Marcus said, 'that she might want to buy herself some new things.'

'You should've thought of that before you decided to elope with her,' the sheriff growled, staring him down. 'I'll have you know I've three daughters of my own, wed now, thank goodness, but I'm sure my wife can manage something.'

As Marcus rose to leave, he bent down and kissed her on her forehead.

Tia was too excited to eat; after a dinner that she hardly touched, Mrs Muir showed her to a bedroom and explained how the bathroom worked. Tia was embarrassed at her lack of knowledge; she thanked Mrs Muir in a very soft voice. The cotton nightgown she was given was softer than anything she had ever worn before.

Alone, she changed and got into the strange bed, feeling the cool comfort of linen sheets. For a while she tried to sleep, but her mind was whirling; when she closed her eyes the image of Marcus appeared, smiling, as he had been when he said goodbye to her.

She got up and walked towards the heavy drapes, pulled them aside and stared at the night. The moon was risen, streaking the bay and Kerrera, making the sea silver and ephemeral. The dance at Creagorry had been two days ago; she had hardly slept since, yet did not feel tired. She closed her eyes and saw Marcus, wondered what he was doing, where he was. She shivered, and hugged herself. Tomorrow she would be his wife.

Her dream had become true, so soon and so suddenly that she could hardly believe it. She thought of her mother, felt a stab of remorse because Janet was left with the work of the croft; but her sisters would help, or somebody else. Her mother was happy for her, she knew that, but she wished Janet could have come to Oban with her, to share her joy. It seemed as if only a moment ago she had been on the island, struggling with creels of peat for the lazy beds, dreaming when she dared, disbelieving that anything she dreamed could ever become real. The Reverend Kenneth MacQuarrie flitted across her mind; she shuddered.

'I love you, Marcus Cameron,' she said, very softly. She had not told him that; she felt suddenly terribly remiss, she should have done. She felt free, with the whole of her life before her. The strictures of her father had vanished, she could dance and laugh and love without fear.

'Mrs Cameron, Mrs Marcus Cameron,' she whispered, wondering where they would live, whether he would leave the sea. If not, he would be away a lot and she would have to wait for him, but he had said something that made her think he might give up his captaincy. She did not know; she did not think she had a right to ask him to stay home with her. She would be lonely, yes, but she would have children or, maybe, a job of her own. There was no doubt in her mind; Marcus was the man she loved, the only man she could ever love. She closed the drapes and went to bed, hugging herself.

The morning came suddenly; she had not slept until the fingers of dawn seeped in beneath the heavy curtains and then she fell into a slumber so deep that the sheriff's wife had to shake her hard to rouse her.

'My husband's waiting downstairs to talk to you,' she said.

Tia dressed quickly and went down to the study.

'Well,' the sheriff said.

'I'm still sure.'

'You are very young, just a few weeks past your birthday.'

'I've known, I've known that I love Marcus for a year now.'

'Is it the thought that you can't go back home?'

'I wouldn't go back home anyway. You see, my father wants me wed to a man of his choice. . .'

'And Marcus is your way of running away.'

'No. He is *my* choice, freely made.'

The sheriff sat down and indicated that she should do the same. Taking a piece of paper and inking his pen, he scrawled a note. 'There you are, my dear. You have my permission. The registrar will marry you at twelve noon today.'

Tia got up and threw her arms around him.

Shaking, Tia heard the clock chime nine; she had three hours to wait. Mrs Muir asked her if she would like a bath, then showed her how the taps worked and left her alone. Tia filled the tub full and washed her hair first, then her body. The sensation was new to her; the tub at home was only big enough to sit in and then not for very long; she laid back and closed her eyes, letting the warm water caress her, feeling luxury for the first time in her life.

The towel was soft and warm and big enough to wrap twice around her; she dried herself carefully and tousled her hair, pulling at the tugs with her fingers. When the door knocked softly she opened it to see Mrs Muir and a maid standing holding two boxes.

'We came to help,' Mrs Muir said.

'Oh, I . . .' Tia had been about to put her old clothes on.

'Here's a set of underthings,' Mrs Muir said, 'and Jean'll help you get your hair dry.'

Embarrassed, Tia turned away as she put on the bloomers and chemise and then the soft lawn petticoat. The maid began to brush her hair. 'I have a blouse,' she said, thinking of the one Mary had given her.

Jean smiled. 'Your young man brought you something to wear in these boxes.'

'But I'd like to wear my blouse.'

'Well, then, you can,' Mrs Muir said.

When the maid had finished brushing her hair, the sheriff's wife handed her a pair of fine silk stockings and a blue garter. 'For luck,' she said.

Tia smiled politely.

'You know,' Mrs Muir said, 'what a bride should wear? Something old, something new, something borrowed, something blue.'

On the island, brides wore their best clothes, a new dress if they were lucky, a new blouse if not.

'What have I borrowed?'

'Let's say the garter, but I don't expect you to give it back.'

Mary's silk satin blouse felt like featherdown against her skin; she looked in the mirror for the first time, studying herself, staring at the reflection of the woman who gazed back at her.

'You are very lovely,' Jean said, in her soft Islay accent.

'I was thinking of the blouse,' she said, 'my grandmother made it when she was a seamstress in the lowlands.'

'Ach, the blouse is nothing. It is the woman who wears it.'

Tia's hair was dark gold in the low light of the gas lamps, the folds that the maid had piled on top of her head glowing a shade lighter, as if the curls had been gilded and then carved in place. Her lips broke into a smile, shyly she looked at herself again and then laughed. Her features were as fine as her mother's, her skin like the petal of a water lilly just come to flower; she straightened her face once more, and then nodded as if satisfied with what she saw.

'You see,' the maid said, 'you are pretty.'

'I've never seen myself like this.' There were no mirrors in Cnoc na Clachan; Tia had never seen her face before, except in the rippled reflection of water.

The clock in the hall chimed eleven times.

Tia jumped. 'I have to hurry.'

'Tush, you have no hurry. My husband will drive you to the registrar's office himself. You will be a few moments late. All good brides are a few moments late.'

Tia opened one of the boxes, picked up a long garment that just reached her knees, frowned when she realised that it would show not only her ankles but most of her legs as well, until she found in the tissue beneath a skirt, cut straight to the knees, a shower of knife-edged pleated beyond that. The jacket was cut softly from fine ivory wool, edged with coffee silk piping around the collar and cuffs. A note tumbled out: 'Dearest, I saw this and thought you would like it. I described you to the sales girl and she said that it should fit you.'

'He said he wasn't sure if you'd like it but he thought the colour would suit you,' Mrs Muir said.

Trembling, Tia stepped into the skirt, fumbling with the buttons until the maid knelt to help. It was made from the same cloth as the jacket but the coffee piping fell from the waist in lines that curved into little rosettes at the top of each pleat, trailing a tangle of stems and leaves that ended in a velvet band at the hem; as she moved, the pleats opened accordion fashion, the inner edge lined with coffee silk. The fit was perfect.

She stared at herself for a moment and then burst out laughing.

'What d'you think?' Mrs Muir asked.

'It's wonderful. It's the most wonderful thing I've ever seen.'

The maid opened the second box, taking out an extravaganza of coffee chiffon roses perched on a crown of the same colour, which she balanced on top of Tia's head, telling her to hold her breath until she had fixed it with two hat pins and tied the chiffon scarf attached to it around her throat. Then she helped her into a little pair of light beige suede pumps.

'Can you manage?' she asked, anxiously.

'I wouldn't worry,' Mrs Muir said, 'she'll manage to float.'

They walked downstairs in a procession, Mrs Muir first then Tia, with the maid at her back to make sure she didn't catch her heel on her skirt.

The sheriff was waiting for them. He bundled her into his car and drove her to the registrar's office, handing the licence to Marcus, gruffly waving away his thanks and handing the parcel Jean had made of her old clothes to the registrar's clerk.

Marcus was wearing his uniform jacket, with the four gilt rings of a captain.

Tia looked at him and felt faint, stumbling just a fraction before his hand gripped hers. She loved him so much that she longed for the ritual to be over so that she could be in his arms. 'I love you,' she whispered.

His face flushed. 'I love you too.'

The registrar checked the names on the licence. As she sat down, Tia noticed the Captain and mate of the *Hebrides*, who were witnesses, heard the sound of the clerk's pen as it etched their names in the ledger.

'In my capacity as Registrar for the Dirstrict of Oban in the County of Argyll I have been appointed by the Registrar General for Scotland as one authorised to solemnise civil marriages in accordance with the Marriage Act,' he began, speaking so quickly that the words were a blur. Tia wanted to ask him to slow down, so that she could savour every moment.

He turned to Marcus. 'Are you Marcus Cameron, bachelor, Captain of the Rankine line, and of 8 North Plain, Iochdar, Isle of South Uist?'

Marcus said that he was.

'And are you Cairistiona MacLeod, spinster, of 3 Cnoc na Clachan, of the parish of Carinish in the Isle of North Uist?'

'I am,' she said, her voice taut with nerves; then 'yes' in case he had not heard her.

The registrar was a man in late middle age of sombre expression and a slightly stooped back. As he spoke he gave nothing away of the joy of the moment, of the excitement Tia felt bubbling inside her. She wanted to sing and dance and shout out her love for everyone to hear.

'We are now assembled here in order that I may solemnise your marriage in the presence of these witnesses in accordance with the law of Scotland,' he said. She gazed at him, wondering how he could marry anyone without smiling. Beside her, Marcus's face was flushed; she sensed he was shaking slightly. Her stomach fluttered; she began to watch the second hand passing on the registrar's clock, counting the moments before she would be wed.

'Please stand,' he said.

They did.

He turned to Marcus first. 'Please repeat after me . . .

'I, Marcus Cameron, solemnly and sincerely declare that I know of no legal impediment to my marrying Cairistiona MacLeod and that I accept you, Cairistiona MacLeod, as my lawful wife to the exclusion of all others.'

Marcus's voice was strong; she was afraid that she might sound weak until she looked into his eyes and repeated the vow, her voice crystal clear and sharp as the morning. 'I, Cairistiona MacLeod, solemnly declare that I know of no legal impediment to my marrying Marcus Cameron and that I accept you as my lawful husband to the exclusion of all others.'

Her hand was trembling as he slipped the ring on to her finger.

'You owe me one,' the Captain of the *Hebrides* said, as Marcus waved the certificate in the breeze to make sure the ink was dry before he folded it and put it in his wallet.

'More than one,' Marcus said.

'The hell with anyone owing anything,' the mate said, 'he always was a mean bastard.'

They all laughed.

'I mean, I vouched for you. I could've said, "I've never seen the fellow before in my life. Marcus Cameron? Captain Cameron? That's a new one to me. Cameron, you say? Are you sure you don't mean Captain Cook?"' He stopped and looked Marcus up and down. 'I mean, he's a lad yet, too young to be a captain. No more than a boy, he is.' His laughter was throaty and rich, it sounded of the sea and of whisky, the aged malt distilled in the islands, not the cheap blend passed off elsewhere.

The ferry captain insisted on a celebration. Tia's legs felt weak with the realisation that she was married now, that her dream had become real.

In the restaurant of the Marine Hotel he peered at the bottle of Haig the waiter offered then told him to take it away and come back with something decent.

'*Uisge beatha*,' he told him, 'that means the water of life, not the pee of some lowland devil.'

The waiter smiled thinly, returned with a dusty Laphroaig.

'That's better,' the Captain said, as he poured for the men.

The waiter was standing staring at them. 'What the bloody hell is the matter with you, lad?' the Captain roared. 'Bring us some champagne for the lady.'

The wine stung her tongue, flooded her throat with its warmth, tingled and sparked in her empty stomach. Beneath the table, Marcus took her hand and squeezed it.

'Happy?' he whispered.

She blushed deeply, shyly. 'Yes.'

'D'you like your dress?'

'Hush Marcus.' The Captain and the Mate were staring at them. 'It's the most wonderful thing I've ever had in my life,' she said. 'I never dreamed anything to wear could be so beautiful.'

'It's not anywhere near as beautiful as you.'

She turned poppy red then.

The Captain coughed. 'As I was saying, Marcus, I'm thinking of going over to MacBrayne's.'

The waiter brought a trolley to the table and then whisked around them, laying plates first for Tia and then the men, adding slices of rare roast beef and pudding, peas and carrots, mashed and roast potatoes. Tia had never seed food like that before, had only heard of it from Mary. She began to eat, then realised she was hungry. For pudding they had slices of chocolate cake in a rich, dark sauce. Once she finished hers, Marcus took her plate and gave her his, then lifted her hand and kissed it gently, making her tremble inside.

'I couldn't,' she said. 'It would be greedy.'

'It would not, Tia. It's not possible to be greedy on your wedding day.'

The Captain of the *Hebrides* said something to the waiter, then handed him some money. Marcus frowned at him.

'We'd best get on, leave you two in peace.'

Marcus rose, helping Tia up before he turned to him.

'We're getting the West Highland Line.'

'Rat,' the Captain said. 'Mind you, like I was saying, I'm thinking of leaving MacCallums myself and going to MacBraynes.'

They walked on to the esplanade towards the pier and the railway station. One of the MacBrayne ferries was coming in, the stately old *Iona*, a graceful paddle steamer, the timbers of the pier creaking softly as her lines were made secure.

'What's that, then?' Marcus asked him, once he'd noticed it, 'the Ark?'

'To hell with you, Cameron. Yon bloody thing you drive, it's more a barge than anything else. Four hundred feet, you say?'

'Four hundred and five, actually.'

'I ken the type. You can't see the bloody stern from the bridge, nor forrard either, not that you'd need to, the way you sail her. You have to take a two-mile hike to find out what the weather's like and the only time you're on an even keel you know you've grounded the bloody thing.'

Marcus roared with laughter. 'You're a tramp, Peter, you're not fit to go beyond the Clyde. Mind you, MacBrayne'd be glad to have you.' He cupped his hands around his mouth and roared at the *Iona*, 'Ahoy, there, is there anyone on board called Methuselah? No? Did you leave him at Tiree or haven't you picked him up yet? What about Columba?' He held his hand behind his ear as he waited for an answer. 'I can't hear you,' he roared, when none came, 'have you let the animals off yet? They never got on in the first place? They swam, did they? That'd be safer.'

The MacCallum's Captain was looking away, shaking his head as the Mate convulsed with laughter.

'David MacBrayne was a thief,' Marcus said, 'the biggest thief that ever sullied the seas. A pirate incarnate, so he was.'

'The old boy's been dead for years.'

'Aye, though, I bet he haunts these bloody tubs of his. Bet he swims underneath them to keep them afloat.'

'MacBrayne's'll be the biggest line on the Clyde soon.'

'Just you wait till it's the only one. That's what MacBrayne's wants. Once they've got it their way, you'll have to mortgage your soul to get off the island, your mother's to get back again.'

Tia listened to the easy banter; gazing at Marcus, she felt a rush of pride. She longed to be alone with him, to be able to talk to him without an audience, to be able to touch him, and have him touch her. The time had passed so quickly, she had hardly a chance to catch her breath. It seemed only a moment ago she had been at the dance on Benbecula, wondering where he was. Now that he was her husband, she had to pinch herself to believe it.

A whistle sounded; Marcus picked up their bags, took her hand and ran for the station, just jumping on the train as it began to pull out.

They had a compartment to themselves, two seats facing each other over a table next to a window. As the train picked up speed, the conductor came and asked them what sitting they wanted for tea.

Marcus looked at Tia, who shook her head.

He told the conductor they wouldn't bother with tea.

The track curved inland toward Glen Etive; the loch a glassy echo of Buchaile Etive Mhor, fir-capped slopes that rose sharply from the water's edge. The trees were deep olive, tinged with lime.

'New growth,' Marcus explained to her.

The colours were soft as moss, blurring as the train picked up speed.

Through the compartment door, Tia saw the flatness of the shore, the ruin of a castle tumbled over the rocks.

'MacColla burned that down,' Marcus said.

She shivered.

Five minutes later the train stopped, then it started again.

They were doing nothing, just staring into each other's eyes.

Marcus looked out of the window.

'Taynuilt next,' he said ticking off the stops on his fingers.

Loch Awe. Dalmally. Tyndrum. Crianlarich. The edge of the highlands, rising hills and falling valleys, passing swiftly, dream-like. Scattered images that were made unreal by the speed.

'How d'you feel?' he asked her.

Tia closed her eyes. 'Like a dream.'

He grinned and reached for her hand, began to play with it, tickling her palm and running his fingers along the insides of hers, doing that for ages until he drew her hand to his lips and kissed it. Tia felt as if she was melting.

'You won't be alone, you know.'

'What?'

'Rankine is selling the line, his ships. Once he's sold it, I'm leaving. I have money saved.'

'Oh.'

He picked up her other hand and began to tickle it.

Beyond MacIains glen, the track passed Lomondside, the loch so calm it was as if the sky had fallen to the ground, the sight so beautiful that Tia gasped.

'I think I've loved you forever,' he said.

She blushed.

'You were special even then, when I used to take you and Mairead over the causeway.'

She flinched when he mentioned her sister's name.

'I'm sorry, *ban-righ*. I forgot.'

He leaned over and kissed her on the lips, sending shivers down her spine. She gazed at him.

After Garelochhead, past the inlet, the track swooped down to lower ground, following the path of the coast. After Helensburgh she saw a factory for the first time; passing Greenock on the other side of the firth, Marcus pointed out the deep docks and she strained to see cranes that rose almost to the height of the hills beyond the town.

He was still holding her hand.

The sprawl of Glasgow was grey, the colour of the smoke that seeped from the chimneys. The sky had faded in a wink.

The train came to a rest at Queen Street station. Tia did not want to move.

Marcus leaned over and kissed her softly. 'We have to get off the train, *ban-righ*.'

She stood up slowly, weak-kneed. He opened the door of the carriage and helped her out.

'Look up,' he said, and she did, to see curved glass panels that seemed to float on air, though heavy steel struts held them secure.

He told her to close her eyes as they walked down the stairs that led to daylight.

'Now open them,' he said, and she did, to see the wide open

space of George Square with the fountain in the middle and the arrogant assertion of the Town Hall.

'It is all like this?' she asked in wonder.

'Lord, no, *ban-righ*. Most of Glasgow is slums, this is just for show.'

She looked at him, wide eyed. 'Where now, Marcus?' She was like a child let loose in a fair, a child allowed to play for the very first time.

'If you can stand it, *ban-righ*, we'll take another train to Troon. There's a hotel there that we can stay at for a strange lowland custom called a honeymoon. Yes?'

'Yes,' she smiled. 'Yes, of course.'

# Chapter Four

*T*he hotel room was decorated in crimson, gilt and ivory; with the heavy plush drapes closed it was lit sparsely by little lamps with pearl glass shades that shed puddles of rosy luminosity to dapple the ruddy gloom. When the bell boy threw the door open with a flourish, and Tia stepped in from the hard electric glare of the corridor, she had a feeling that in this place she would be reborn as Marcus's wife. She was not sure what this process entailed, but she trembled in anticipation. Something deep inside made her want him and yet she hesitated and he caught her hesitation and smiled. He handed the bell boy a penny and he scampered away, leaving their baggage looking morose and slightly scruffy against the peony velvet pile of the carpet.

Marcus looked around, apparently nonchalant, but as he reached to pull back the curtain she noticed that his hand was shaking.

The sun was teetering on the western horizon, its legacy a silver-mirrored sea on which islands were settled like drying cow-pats. There were french windows which led to a balcony; she didn't know what they were called at first, she learned all that later, when she found the hotel's brochure in the drawer of her bedside chest, along with a menu and copy of the Gideon Bible. Marcus fiddled with a catch and the windows opened, letting in air that was tart and salt, stale somehow. There was no breeze; she noticed that when the lace curtains underneath the drapes stayed motionless.

The air in the room was sweet, heavily perfumed, hard to breathe.

'Come, my love,' Marcus said, reaching for her.

She walked to him and he put his arm around her.

There was an iron table on the balcony that had been painted white; the paint had chipped off, leaving rusty stains like ulcers. Beside it were two wickerwork chairs with canvas cushions that rustled when sat upon. Marcus sat opposite her cupping his chin in his hands.

She was alone with him now, the future, her future, like a blank page in a book yet to be written. The thought occurred to her, frightening in its intensity, that perhaps she should flee now before the magic vanished; that way she could keep for ever the perfection of the dream. It was so strange to be there, in a hotel in a seaside town in the lowlands, a tourist herself when she should have been at the hunting lodge, caring for the needs of visitors to her own island. She had no regrets about leaving her father, too many about her mother; for a moment she wondered about Janet, about how she would manage the croft, about whether Archie would help her cart the potatoes home, if she'd have to drag the *cas chrom* over the soil herself. Her eyes turned wistful and sad. Still Marcus watched her, saying nothing. She turned to the sea, watched a gull catch a draught in the air as a motor car passed along the shore road, its angry exhaust blurring the vista then rising in tendrils to sting her eyes. She blinked, looked over his shoulder at the oak tree in the hotel garden, its leaves singed and curled at the edges, already beginning to shed. There were no trees on her island, there had not been, according to legend, since the Vikings had burned them all down a millennium before. She knew about oak trees and autumn leaves because she had once started to read a novel by one of the Brontë sisters before her father had confiscated it and then banned all such works from her home on the ground of lasciviousness. Only one book, apart from the Bible, had Sorley's approval, that was an old, tired copy of *Pilgrim's Progress*, a saga she had read from end to end more than twice through sheer boredom in the inertia of the winter months. Anything else, he tossed on the fire; in his *auto-da-fé* Sorley had burned her Brontë and her brother Hugh's *A Christmas Carol*; also a copy of *Cassell's Magazine* that Mary had sent to Janet. It was the *Cassell's* that first incited his ire; when he caught sight of an article called 'The Confession of a Rebellious Woman' he snatched it out of her hands and threw it on the flames as Janet forlornly protested that she hadn't even started reading it yet, and she would skip that part if he did not want her to see it. He had cleared all their books off the shelf on the dresser, apart from the Bible, the Hymnal and Bunyan's tormented meanderings.

She could almost recite the story by heart; smiling, she wondered, if Marcus was Christian who was she? Discretion, Prudence, Piety or Charity, or one of the harlots or ne'er-do-wells of Vanity Fair?

A breeze began to whisper then, a soft cool puff that touched her face, sending the chiffon ribbon of her hat in a trembling frill in its wake. Her eyes met Marcus's; carefully, she reached for the ribbon and unravelled the bow, then lifted the hat off and put it on the table after wiping the flakes of rust away with her fingers. Something moved in the room beyond; she looked up and in the gloom perceived a maid unpacking their bags and putting things away.

Marcus reached out and tickled the soft skin beneath her chin. 'Are you hungry, *ban-righ*? Thirsty, maybe? Would you like some wine?'

She smiled shyly. The champagne at lunchtime had made her feel strange; she could not be rude to the Captain of the *Hebrides* by refusing to drink it, but it had dulled her senses, soothed the edge of her perception, made the day for a while feel mundane when she wanted to keep it magic, alive. She had only one glass, even that had gone flat before she had finished it, for she had carefully left a little in the bottom so that the waiter would not replenish it. The Captain and his mate had done the drinking; after raising his glass in a toast Marcus had drunk only water, held his hand up when the waiter offered more.

'Tea, perhaps?'

He smiled and turned to tell the maid.

'How do you feel, *ban-righ*?'

'It's difficult to believe it, Marcus. I keep thinking I'll wake up suddenly, find myself back at home.'

The breeze quickened to a wind, sharp, slightly chill. The air moved and the staleness vanished, a sprinkling of rain fell; sheltered by a canopy, they watched as it damped down the dust on the road and burnished the grass, made the world seem fresh again. She reached for her hat and held it until the wind died, then reached up to smooth her hair, the taut curls all a-tumble in the eddies of the draught.

The wind gusted then, catching her hat before she could trap it and lifting it away, the ribbons streaming just out of reach, sending it spinning like a top and then flopping to the garden below where it settled for a moment before the wind gusted again and it began to cartwheel madly over the lawn.

She gaped, horrified, stunned; watching her, Marcus shook his head then vaulted the balcony, dropping on to the grass with feline grace before he pounced, just missing the ribbon as the hat lifted again, clearing the garden wall. Marcus paused for a moment and then, catching a glimpse of chiffon, set off in pursuit, swearing roundly as he leapt the wall and landed with a thud on the other side, then taking off at a gallop after the hat that was spinning along the road like a wheel snapped from its axle, veering crazily from side to side. A car rounded the corner, a great solid mass of clanking, wheezing metal that made her shriek with terror and close her eyes before she opened them again to see it swerving out of the way, avoiding Marcus but just clipping the crown of the hat, sending it reeling like a drunkard and then tumbling over the pavement on to the rocky escarpment that led to the shore. Marcus following, skiting over the rocks then sprinting over the sand, sending up a trail of spray when he hit the damp sand before the water's edge. The hat was floating now, bobbing up and down on the soft swell of the neap tide. As the sun set in the west, the moon was risen in the east, the two squaring up to each other at opposite corners of the plane of the sky.

Tia was distracted by a soft knock at the door, then the maid came in, wheeling a covered trolly. 'Afternoon tea, Madam, Mrs Cameron. Would ye like it served on the balcony?'

Tia smiled. 'If you leave it, I can manage.'

'Och, no, Madam. That widna' be richt.'

The maid looked young, her face was plump though her eyes were tired. Her accent was guttural, the language not English, but a strange bowdlerised form of words that subverted the arrogance and the orderliness of the tongue. Tia could hardly understand her at first, had to listen carefully and think very hard.

The maid lifted the cover from the trolley and set out matching plates, cups and saucers, then a plate of buttered bread and a full cake stand, a plate of scones and a bowl of jam, another of cream. With a flourish, she lifted a lid from a platter that let of a cloud of steam. 'Will ye have halibut or the salmon mousse or chicken fricassée or the sirloin, Madam?'

The conflicting smells confused her. 'I only wanted a cup of tea,' she mumbled.

The maid's face fell. 'Oh, Madam, Mrs Cameron, Madam, I'm gey sorry. When the Captain esked fir tea, I thocht it wis high tea ye wantit. I thocht ye'd be hungry.'

Tia smiled slowly. 'It doesn't matter.'

The maid looked relieved. 'Whit d'ye want, then, Madam?'

Tia smiled again. 'My name's Tia. You can call me that.'

'Oh, Mrs Cameron, Madam, it'd be more than my job's wirth. I'd git the sack fir familiarity, be bootit oot wi'out ma wages, most like.'

'You see,' Tia began carefully, 'I only got married this morning. You're the first person who's called me Mrs Cameron. It sounded strange, at first.'

'Ye'll git used tae it, ye'll huff tae.' She beamed broadly. 'I'm that pleased fir ye. Gey chuffed, so I am, Madam, Mrs Cameron, Madam. Now, whit'll ye hae tae eat?'

'Just a little chicken.'

'An the Captain? It's a lovely bit o'beef, Ma'am, richt' rare an' aw'. They like that, so the men do.'

Tia watched her carve the meat and then add gravy and vegetables.

'They shoulda sent a waiter but there were aw' busy wi' the resta-wrong so I brung it ma'sel.' I'll leave the covers, tae keep it warm. I'll knock the door of the bath an' tell the Captain.'

Smiling to herself, Tia thanked her.

The soft kid pumps were pinching her instep, so she slipped them off and then unrolled her stockings, flexing her toes on the warm stone of the balcony floor. The coils of her hair were loose, so she took out the pins and shook it free, running her fingers through it gently until the knots were untangled. Distantly, she thought of combing it until she remembered her comb was at Mary's where she had left it, she had been too tired during the journey and the maid had combed her hair at the Muirs'. She wondered if her mother had packed one for her, but she did not go to see.

The gravel tinkled on the path below, there was a shuffle and a sigh, then Marcus's hand appeared on the balcony parapet as she got up and leaned over, letting her lips brush the top of his head as he reached up with his other hand and handed her the hat, the chiffon bedraggled now, the ribbon trailing a wisp of drying maiden's hair. He pulled himself up to waist level, then lifted one leg over, straddling the balcony for a moment before he dismounted and stood before her, salt water dripping from his sodden trousers. He shook his head.

She began to tremble, knowing that the time had come. All she knew of the act of love was of animals, of the bull covering a cow, the clumsiness of mating, yet suddenly she wanted him like that, she knew that it would be different. The food lay forgotten; she was no longer hungry, never had been if she was truthful. She wanted him but was nervous, shy, afraid to tell him so.

'Thank you,' she said, as he reached for her and folded her into his arms, hugging her so tight that she lost her breath before his hold loosened slightly and she felt him nuzzling her hair, his breath coming quickly as his lips and then his tongue glanced against her earlobe before he nibbled gently at her throat.

'*Ban-righ.*' He backed into the open door, drawing her with him then kicking it shut with his foot as her tremor became a quiver and then a quake that spread through her body from its epicentre where he kissed her to the tips of her toes.

She was shivering, shaking so much that she did not trust herself to be able to touch him as she wanted to, there was no longer the power in any of her limbs. Instead, she let herself melt into him; the ice formed by the echoes of Calvin, the rage of her father, and the hurt of her failures to live up to either softened to moisture that evaporated and drifted away in the wake of the wind. Marcus sighed softly, kissed her gently and then with insistence as she reached for him by instinct, the flicker in her fingers quieting when she felt the soft skin at the back of his neck, pulling him closer until she could feel the thud of his heart. His hands moved to her jacket; as he unbuttoned it, she felt his anxiety, shared his need to rid her of the irrelevance of things like clothes. He was methodical, careful and precise in his movements, when she wanted him to throw away caution, abandon the pretence of separateness. When he lifted her up and then let her down on the bed, his lips parted from hers briefly and she whispered that. She lay prone as he eased her breast from her bodice, touched its tip then bent to tease it; she murmured as his hands moved to her waist, loosing her skirt, easing under the ties that held her bloomers. He moved closer then, her toes touched his damp trousers, her knee lifted and her legs parted; she cried when she felt his fingers there. He lifted his head; she opened her eyes and saw him gazing at her, drinking her in. 'Please . . .'

'*Ban-righ.*'

'My love.'

'*Ban-righ.* I could not dare to hurt you, *ban-righ* . . .'

'You could not hurt me, my love.'

She heard the rustle of fabric, felt apprehension fleetingly like the moment of stillness between lightning and thunder; she called to him, cried out when she felt the touch of his skin.

She was not flesh any more, but water, fire and air.

She was salt to his ocean, soil to his earth.

She groaned when he edged into her, begged him to be gentle no more, to let loose the need he had of her as she had of him. Her body closed around him like a whirlpool; he felt her power, like a tidal wave, he cried out in reply and they were unique then, no longer earthbound but floating somewhere, far beyond.

He kissed her to wakefulness in the quiet hour just before dawn, complaining of a ravenous hunger groaning in his stomach that might have disturbed her if he had not done so himself.

She smiled sleepily, contentedly; he kissed her again, his stomach forgotten for a moment, as he played with a strand of her hair, brushed the sleep from her eyelashes.

'I love you, Marcus.'

'I adore you, *ban-righ.*'

Her eyes opened wide. 'Are you really hungry?'

He grinned. 'I was, I'm not any more.'

Their bodies met, softened like candle-wax, languorous until the heat became fire and their limbs fused and then their minds. As a bird called out to mark the morning, they tangled like weed caught on the waves, surfing the rollers, soaring and diving, tumbling over and over like a strange new sea creature bound by the fronds of her hair and the sinew of his limbs. Briefly, Tia opened her eyes, saw not colour but light and shade, the sheen of moisture like filigreed silver. When she cried out, he answered her, echoed her as if he was not only her lover but also her shadow, the mask of her soul, their melding so complete that she could not bear the thought of parting, of being only one again.

The ocean played out its rage, sending off showers of spume that fizzled and spat like droplets on a griddle, foaming rabidly as water became steam that in turn was cooled by the draught of its wake. Relinquished by the furies, like flotsam she lay in his arms, listening to the sound of his heart as it settled and then syncopated with the beat of her own.

Marcus sighed and opened his eyes. In the low light they were glassy, the bright blue like a beacon in the gloom of the room.

'Are you still hungry?' she asked him.

He smiled. 'I never want to leave you, *ban-righ*. Never. Not even for the briefest moment.' He stretched, brushed the hair from her face and then began to draw circles upon her stomach.

She smiled slowly, lifting his hand away.

His face twinged, as if she had struck him.

'Don't go,' he said.

She kissed his forehead fleetingly. 'Only for a moment.'

Wrapping herself in his discarded shirt, she parted the curtains and opened the french windows. Shivering in the chill, she started at the sound of wings, felt the shaking of the air as the birds lifted, chattering angrily. All that remained of the bread and cakes was a solitary crumb. Just as she saw it, an angry starling swooped down and grabbed it, as if to challenge her to a duel. She laughed. Quickly, she lifted the two dinner plates and carried them back into the room. The covers were icy, misted with condensation.

The food was cold, the gravy congealed; on the island it would have been a feast but Marcus frowned at her, mock anger overlaid on the curve of his smile. 'What's this, *ban-righ?* Cold potatoes for my breakfast? Do I get a cup of tea too, or just a couple of ice cubes?'

Her face fell; when he saw that he could have punched himself, struck the words that had hurt her out of his teasing, joking mouth.

'Marcus, I . . .'

'*Ban-righ*! Don't you dare!'

'There was cake too, and scones, but the birds ate them.'

'*Ban-righ*, this is wonderful. Just what I wanted.' He scooped potato into his mouth, then some peas, still wrapped in their halo of solidified butter. His eyes closed in mock ecstasy; he chewed voraciously and then reached for some more. 'I was just lying there thinking, thinking about what I wanted to eat. I was dreaming of cold potatoes and cool buttered peas. . .' He laughed as she swiped him with a pillow, held his hands up in surrender then grabbed hers when she let the pillow go.

'Seriously, my love, I didn't marry you to cook for me, or to clean for me. I don't want you to waste your life doing that.'

She looked down at herself, at her legs beneath his shirt, at how pale her skin was beside his ruddy tan. 'Why did you marry me, then?' she asked, in a small voice.

His expression became serious. 'Because I felt the empty space beside me that only you could fill. So that we could love each other and build our lives together. If I'd wanted just a cook, or a housekeeper, don't you think I'd've found one before I turned thirty-three?'

He got up and went to the bathroom; as he came back he opened the wardrobe and took something out. 'There you are, *ban-righ*,' he said, coming back to bed and easing his shirt from her shoulder, then wrapping a gown around her that was so light it felt like a feather.

She looked at it, at the satin piping around the collar, the broad satin belt that tied around her waist.

He reached for a bedside button and pushed it. 'The good thing about a hotel, *ban-righ*, is that you don't have to bother about food or any of that nonsense. You just ring a bell and they bring it for you.'

A moment later there was a knock at the door, which opened immediately on a steaming trolley pushed by a waiter. Suffused by embarrassment, Tia dived under the sheets.

'It's safe to come out now.' Marcus stage-whispered, after the clatter ceased and the door had clicked closed again. 'There's nothing to be ashamed of, no need to be embarrassed. We're husband and wife now.'

She blushed.

'You aren't, are you, Tia? You're not ashamed or embarrassed?'

'Marcus, I. . .' She smiled and her cheeks dimpled. 'It'll just take a while to get used to it.'

The table was laid with pots and plates, a steaming server with bacon, eggs, sausage, kidney, smoked and fresh herring, porridge in hillocks that were beginning to dry at the edges.

Marcus got out of bed, arrogantly naked, carelessly wrapping a towel around his waist before he sat down.

'You really don't care, do you?' she said, still cocooned between the sheets in the robe he had wrapped around her.

He winked.

The curtains were open, the room lit by sunlight that danced off the sea. The morning sounded of gulls and waves, people talking, the cranking of a car engine sparking to life.

'Should I care?'

'Well,' she shrugged, 'I mean. . .' In the light of the day she was aware of the frailty of her body, of the whiteness of her skin beyond the rosy areolae of her breasts, of the downy hair underneath her arms and at the cleft of her legs. The pallid ivory of her skin seemed to be afraid of the day, like a mussel that shrinks convulsively when its shell is breached. As a soft breeze ruffled the edge of the curtains she felt goose bumps form and hugged herself; then she put her arms into the sleeves of the gown and tied the belt tight.

Marcus was devouring an egg, he had already eaten half a dozen sausages and stack of toast.

He smiled at her again, wiping a spot of bright yellow from the edge of his mouth.

Her hat was balanced carefully on top of a coat stand; intrigued, she forgot her shyness for a moment and got up to study it. The roses were only slightly rumpled, the chiffon unscathed but for a white line where the salt had dried.

She touched the fabric wonderingly; she had never seen anything like it before in her life.

'Where in Oban did you get this, Marcus?'

He turned from buttering his toast and smiled at her. 'That's a secret, *ban-righ*.'

'Please tell me?'

He smiled again. 'Nowhere.'

'Nowhere?'

'Nowhere in Oban.' He picked up a forkful of bacon and began to chew.

'Marcus?' She was frowning slightly, gently puzzled.

He finished eating and grinned again. 'I got it in New York, *ban-righ*, That and the suit and the robe you're wearing. I picked them out there and brought them over and left them at MacCallum's in Oban because I didn't want Bridie or anyone to find them and start nagging me.'

'You were so sure of me?'

'I was.'

He reached for her, drew her towards him and settled her in his lap as he began to feed her scrambled eggs and buttered toast, and a cup of creamy coffee. 'Happy now?' he asked her, as he tugged at the bow of the belt she had tied. She murmured something but the words got lost in a sigh.

In the early hours of the next day they dressed quickly and crept out of the hotel through the back door, wedging it ajar with a broken umbrella.

The air was cold and crisp and invigorating; the tide, in retreat, had left the shore empty for miles.

Tia walked along in the crook of his arm; they hadn't bothered with shoes, and walked far beyond the tide line, until tiny wavelets lapped half-heartedly at their feet.

'I didn't know that you were a captain,' Tia said. There was another side of him that she was just beginning to understand, the veneer he had acquired because he had left the island and had to find a way to deal with the world beyond.

'I told you in my own way, *ban-righ*. When I tried to smoke that bloody pipe.'

She laughed.

He gazed deep into the distance, his eyes crinkled, radiating lines of latitude.

'Rankine's is changing,' he said, ''fact, soon it won't be Rankine's any more. The old man sold it, you see.'

'Why?'

His face tightened. 'His sons, his heirs, the pair of them are just bloody wastrels. If he left the line to them they'd wreck it. Allan Rankine, that's the old man, he only ever held half the shares. That pair have the others. He knew that if he left it to them, they'd wreck everything he worked for, so he sold his interest to an English line. At least, that way he has some money.'

'I don't understand.'

He grinned cynically. 'I don't either, but that's the way it is, *ban-righ*. It was the old man gave me my job, you see. He taught me everything I know about the sea. Last year, when he made me Captain, he asked me if I'd stay on. He knows I don't like the idea of working for a stranger. I said I'd stay on to the year end, but only for him. It's not a big line, Rankine's, just half a dozen ships, though we've got some good routes and a couple of New York berths. Thing is, it's too small now.'

She looked at him quizzically.

'It's all about speed now, *ban-righ*, about how quickly you can make the crossing and come back again. Time is money, they say. Like cargo's money and passengers are money. Rankine's never lost money, but he never made a fortune either. The sons, when they came in, they didn't want to sail his boats, they just wanted to make money from them. Y'see, he's an old salt, and they're landlubbers.'

'Are you an old salt, Marcus?'

He squeezed her. 'Only a fool loves the ocean, *ban-righ*. The ocean never loved anyone but herself. Her mood might change, but her nature? Never. The best she'll do is tolerate you, forgive you the odd mistake. I'd rather take my chance on land.'

'Won't you miss it?'

'Miss what?' He frowned at her. 'The gales, the storms, the fog so thick that you can't see beyond your own nose? Salt herring and biscuits for breakfast, dinner and tea? The empty, grey Atlantic for days and days on end? The rain, the sleet, the ice that cuts your face, the cuts that won't heal because the air's full of salt? I won't miss any of that, *ban-righ*.'

She shivered. 'You shouldn't've gone. You didn't have to go.'

'I did,' he said cynically. 'My father was a seaman and my grandfather before him. I was the oldest so I got the job on the ferry he had when he died. I had to put food on the table somehow.'

'But your brothers, the ones that have the fishing boat.'

He shook his head. 'Kenny and Donny were too young. I'm

the oldest, Bridie's next, then Seonaig and Morag, Silis and Peg. I've eight years on Kenny, ten on Donny. Cal's the youngest. He's off in Rome, going to be a priest.' He shook his head, smiling. 'That was Ma. Cal's the bright one, and she'd have nothing but Cal'd be a priest.'

She hugged him. 'You're bright too.'

'Not like Cal. Cal speaks Latin. He went to the Brothers at Maynooth, they sent him to Rome.' He shook his head again. 'We'll see.'

They turned to walk back when the sky lightened in the east.

'You know everything, Marcus,' Tia said dreamily.

'I do not.'

'You've been everywhere.'

'I have not.'

She stopped. 'You told me you'd sailed around the world.'

'I have. That's different.'

'How is it?'

'I've spent half my life on the blankness of the ocean. I haven't seen the world. I've seen its edges.'

The crept back into the hotel like naughty children, slipping along the corridor silently and then laughing, gleefully, when they were alone again, the door closed behind them.

After five days they left the hotel to go to Glasgow. As the train pulled into Central station, Marcus lifted her chin and stared into her eyes.

'We don't have to do it this way, *ban-righ*.'

She smiled. 'I don't mind.' She knew that he was a man of honour, what his promise to Allan Rankine meant to him.

'I don't want you to get lonely.'

'Don't worry. I won't be.'

The train came to a halt, he opened the carriage door and got out first, then helped her down. Linking hands, they walked around to St Enoch's to take the subway to the boarding house where he had rented rooms.

'I've known Mrs Anderson for years,' he said, 'she's a good woman.'

Tia was terrified of the roaring the train made before its demon's eyes pierced the black of the tunnel and it thundered towards them, crashing to a stop in a shower of sparks. The doors opened and they got on and sat down, as she mimicked his nonchalance, smiling to herself.

'We'll get the tram next time,' he said, 'but this way's quicker.'

'I could get a job, Marcus, while you're away at sea.'

The carriage began to shake, and they were thrown together, laughing.

'You could,' he said, as it came into a station and the other passengers got off. 'Maybe I should retire. Maybe I will, and you can keep me.'

The doors stayed open for a moment, as if waiting for someone, and then closed, leaving them alone in the carriage.

Marcus looked deep into her eyes. 'Maybe you shouldn't get a job just yet,' he whispered, as his fingers traced rings around her stomach. 'Maybe there's a job there for you already.'

She shivered and leaned close to him.

'Then again,' he said, taking her hand in his, 'maybe not just yet.'

'Why not?' she murmured.

'Because,' he said, moving closer, 'I love having you just to myself. I don't want to have to share you with anyone for a while.'

Giggling furiously, she turned bright scarlet, pushing him away frantically when the train slowed down before it reached the next station.

'Maybe your father was right about me,' he said, 'I might be a werewolf, really.'

He was teasing her so much that he missed their stop and they had to go round the whole of the subway before they reached it again. He told her that it didn't matter, because the tracks ran in circles anyway, you could sit on the train for ever and never go anywhere at all.

Mrs Anderson was a tiny little streak of a woman of constant, nervy energy, always doing two things at once and talking non-stop, pushing words together, squashing sentences between anxious little sighs; often she asked questions which she answered herself.

She was already holding the door open for Marcus and Tia,

polishing the brass door knob with one hand as she said 'hello' to them and grabbed Marcus's kit-bag with the other.

'You'll be fer wabbit,' she said, as she led them into the hallway and then up three flights of stairs to a door wedged open with a chair. 'I aired the room fir ye, acos I wisna sure when ye'd be. I didna licht the range, but, I didna want tae waste coal, ye ken? Ach, I'm babbling. I'll awa' an' put the kettle oan an mak' ye a pot ma'sel. Yous jis' get yersel' settled in, an I'll be back in a trice.'

Tia watched her go, shaking her head.

Marcus smiled.

'I didn't understand a word she said,' Tia laughed, shaking her head. 'I thought the maid in the hotel was bad.'

'She's a good soul, Tia. You'll understand her soon enough.'

She looked around the room, finding a bed in an alcove behind the door, a sink against the wall beneath the window and a big coal range opposite the door. The range was freshly scrubbed, she could see that; when she ran her finger along it, it came away clean.

Marcus was looking at her anxiously.

'Is it all right, *ban-righ*?'

She looked again. 'I doubt I'll ever get it working.'

He gathered her into his arms. 'You will.'

They parted as they heard Mrs Anderson's footsteps, swift as a mouse, running up the stairs. Breathing heavily, she put down a tray with a teapot, cups and saucers, then scuttled away again, coming back with a box which she put down on the floor. 'I got a few things in fir ye, lass, Missus Cameron. Marcus telt me ye wis jis' merrit, and ye'll no ken whit's whit yet, fir a while. I mind, it's gey strange at first.'

'Her name's Tia,' Marcus said quickly.

'Aye, but I didna want tae be forrard, like. Thaur's black-lead fir the range, hen, an' Lysol an' a wee bit carbolic if ye've a washing, a bit starch fir his shirts, a wee bit kindling fir tae git yees stairtit. Coal an' aw's in the box by the range. My, I've been up an' doon yon stairs that mony times the day, I'm fair wabbit.'

She plonked down on one of the twin wooden chairs, one with arms and one on rockers. Tia and Marcus were still standing. 'I'll pour, shall I, hen?'

Tia bent over to do it, apologising as she did so.

'It'll be gey strange fir ye lass. These first days're the hardest, so they say.'

Tia smiled.

Mrs Anderson gulped the steaming tea and rose again. 'Well. I'll leave ye to it.'

'Thank you,' Tia murmured.

'We're very grateful,' Marcus said.

'Well, ye ken whaur I am. Jis'gie me a yell if thaur's aucht ye need.'

As her footsteps faded, Marcus closed the door and locked it.

Tia shook her head again. 'I only caught about half of what she said.'

'You'll learn, *ban-righ*,' he said.


She woke, very early, to the stillness of an empty room. In the darkness she reached out for him and found only a cooling space beside her. The room felt cold, its contents sinister. Through the skylight she watched the sky until the night faded to a milky dawn. She was too panic-stricken to move; she waited, shivering, aching, wondering why on earth he had done this to her.

The morning brought clarity to the shapes of the room; she could see the range, the table and chairs, the cupboard in the corner where Marcus had hung his clothes, the hook on the door where his cap hung. She felt reassured when she saw that; without his uniform, he would not have gone far.

Somewhere, a church bell chimed six times, the sound empty and hollow; there was no echo but the bell continued to ring in her ears long after it had ceased. She heard his footsteps then, strong and regular, and she jumped out of bed and threw herself into his arms as soon as he opened the door.

'Never do that to me again,' she murmured.

He held her back and looked at her. 'You were sleeping. I didn't want to disturb you.'

'Marcus, never do that to me again.'

'All right. I won't, if that's what you want.'

His skin felt cold; his jacket was damp with the morning mist. She went to the sink and filled the kettle, then lifted the lid on the range and put it on to heat. Mrs Anderson had left some

85

oatmeal which she had soaked overnight; she put it on to heat gently and then began to slice a loaf of bread.

Marcus took his jacket off and sat down. 'I thought we's go into town later, *ban-righ*, buy you some clothes.'

'Why?' Hearing the water bubble, she made the tea quickly, then ladled his porridge into a bowl.

'You could do with some,' he said.

She smiled. 'I have my own. And the suit you bought me. That's enough.' She went to the cupboard and opened it as if to remind herself that her wedding outfit and hat were still there.

He began to eat ravenously. 'I went to the line. They want me to go to Liverpool to bring up a freighter. It's been in dock there.'

'When?'

'Tomorrow.'

Their eyes met.

'That's why I thought you might want to go shopping.'

'I'd rather stay here with you.' She picked up a slice of bread, buttered it and began to eat. 'Marcus?'

'Yes.'

'I'd like to get a job, Marcus. Until we leave. You see, if you're away, I'll be lonely if I don't.'

'If you want,' he said, 'but you don't have to.'

'I want to, Marcus.'

'Only if you want to, *ban-righ*. I can care for you. You don't ever have to work again, if you don't want to.' He stopped and looked at her, saw the earnestness of her expression, the strength of her Presbyterian upbringing that would not let her stay idle for long.

'Once we go to America, we'll find a place to live, and then we'll work together,' he said slowly, 'we'll find a town somewhere and run a store. I want to have some land, some good land. I want to have a house with apple trees in the garden and a place for the children to play and a field to grow my vegetables.'

'Three acres and cow,' she smiled.

'We might not even need three acres.' He smiled. 'There's gold and silver in America, *ban-righ*. Oil too. Paupers've made millions overnight. I don't want that, though. I wouldn't want to have people calling us carpetbaggers. I just don't want to spend the rest of my life at the whim of some *galach* landlord. You understand, don't you?'

'Yes,' she said, 'I do.'

# Chapter Five

*T*he room felt empty after he left.

Tia picked up the clothes lying on the chair, catching the scent of his body as she did so. For a moment she held his shirt to her face, then filled the sink with water and left it to soak. From the street the sound of children playing drifted up. She caught the odd word here and there but the language was foreign, the sounds harsh. Opening the skylight, she breathed in the tangy scent of city air, then made the bed and tidied everything away. Taking the cake of pink carbolic, she washed his shirt lovingly, easing away the ingrained dirt around the collar and cuffs and then rinsing it again and again to get rid of the strong smell of soap. When the rinse water ran clear, she wrung it out and hung it on the pulley that came down from the ceiling, watching it flutter in the breeze.

She heard the clock chime nine as she sat down and wondered what to do next. The day was empty, as was the next and the next again until he would come back at the end of the week. He had left her money on the dresser, along with a little leather purse.

'Just be a lady of leisure,' he had said, that morning, as she hugged him goodbye. 'Mrs Anderson'll show you where the tram is. Go into town and enjoy yourself.'

Her face had fallen.

'What is it, *ban-righ*?'

'It's not right. I don't want to waste your money.'

He had laughed. '*Annsachd*, you couldn't waste my money.'

There had not been time to ask him what he meant by that, because the clock had struck the hour and he had left at a run.

Resolutely she rose and began to sweep the floor. That done, she scrubbed it and then washed down the walls and dusted the dresser, the table and the chairs. She would have scoured the range as well, but it was so hot that the cloth sizzled and dried as soon as she touched it and she nearly burnt her hand. That would have to wait until the fire burned out and the metal cooled down; she wasn't sure about letting the fire burn out because she would have to start it again with paper and kindling and small lumps of coal. She had never even seen coal before, wasn't sure what it was until Marcus told her it was exactly like the peat they burned in the islands, except it took flame much more easily. The coal box next to the range was brim full with coal; he had filled it before he left and told her that would be enough to see her through the week, but that there was more in the bunker in the back yard if she needed it. Mrs Anderson would show her where it was.

She sighed deeply. She wasn't sure about Mrs Anderson either, though she felt her friendly manner and liked the easy way that she smiled. The landlady had told her that she had the Gaelic too; when Tia began to talk to her she grinned broadly and said she hadn't spoken it for years and then uttered something that sounded like gibberish. Tia spoke English instead, forming the words slowly and carefully like the teacher had taught her to do at school, listening to the sound she made and wondering if it was even the same language as the landlady used, because it sounded so strange and quaint. But the landlady understood her perfectly and said something about her lovely island accent, which Marcus translated afterwards when they were alone in the room. Alone, they had no need of English or even of language; they spoke by expression and touch and gesture; their bodies had a language of their own with syllables and words made up of feelings that ebbed and flowed like the tide that had swept them together, mingling as easily as the sand brushed by the waves. It was strange to know that love was like this, not the obligation her father preached of in church, but a living force that binds a man and woman together like a growing seed lays down roots that bind it to the earth. Love had made her whole, had made her feel truly alive for the first time as if her life before she loved Marcus had been like the game a child plays with rules that have no reason beyond being necessary for the game to work, or like the lines an actor would speak not for himself but for the sake of charade.

She blushed when she thought of it, of what it was like when they were together and at the same time felt a surge of need and longing so strong that she felt dizzy. She smiled to herself, even laughed when she thought of her father, of what he would say if he knew, of what he would try to do and the wondrous realisation that there was nothing that he could do to her, nothing that he could do to her ever again, because she was married to a man as strong, if not stronger, than he was. Through Marcus, she had gained the strength to be herself.

The door sounded, she had to think before she realised that it was a knock and that she had to open it. That was another thing about the city, the way that doors were closed and people knocked and then waited to be asked in; it was only if the door was open that you could go inside, calling out as you did so. Marcus had explained it all to her, the way that in the house there were other smaller houses, each home to a family and the doors that led off the stairway were like the front doors of the cottages in the village back home.

Mrs Anderson stood there, holding a plate full of scones. She smiled and Tia just smiled back for a moment before she realised that she was supposed to open the door wide and ask her in.

'Forgive me,' she said, as the landlady came in, flinching when as she sat down her face brushed against Marcus's wet shirt.

'Ach lass, it takes a while to get used to it,' she said.

Tia put the kettle on and spooned tea into the pot, sensing that the landlady expected her to do that.

'Must be very strange for you,' Mrs Anderson said, 'I mean, coming down from the islands, and you so young as well. Still, there's aucht wrong with that, being young, I mean. It's as well to marry young if you get the chance. Don't want to get left on the shelf. You could've put your wash in the yard, lass. It's a fine day for it, but it might turn later. You'd have to watch for the rain. 'T's not like the rain in the islands, lass. All the bloody smoke comes down with the rain as well. Makes a wash dirty and you have to start all over again.'

She laughed as she saw Tia looking at her, utterly bewildered.

'Ach, lass, don't mind me. Sit down and have your tea and we'll have a blether.'

Tia took the milk and sugar from the cupboard, feeling she

must be rich, to have milk and sugar with tea – a box of lumps of sugar and whole milk, not just the sour left after butter had been churned. At home, her old home, they never had even sour milk with tea, never mind sugar, it was only Mary who put sugar in tea with a little sour milk and then only for a treat on Sundays.

She put one lump in the landlady's cup, couldn't help looking at her askance when she took another from the box.

Mrs Anderson smiled again. 'It's a fine man ye've got in Marcus.'

Tia smiled. The landlady was speaking slowly and carefully, but even so she had to struggle to understand.

'Ye ken, he telt me about ye. I used tae esk him when he'd get hitched, I wis thinking he was still lookin', mind, and he said that he was bidin' fir ye tae come o'age. There was a lot o' the lasses efter him, mind. He wis here for a while when he wis at the college. That wis a few years back. He was staying at one of they places by the docks' – she made a face, a sort of frown that was also a knowing smile – 'an' came tae me to git some peace an' quiet sae he could study fir tae pass his exams. He's got his ticket, ye ken.'

Tie thought of what she knew about Marcus; she knew that he had his master mariner's certificate, but there was so much she didn't know of his life besides that, so many things that he hadn't told her because he hadn't had time or she hadn't asked. She did not know exactly how he knew Mrs Anderson; suddenly she wanted to know so much so that she thought of the words in English and then asked her, diffidently.

'Ach,' Mrs Anderson said, 'my man, Iain, that is, my husband; he wis a ganger at the docks afore he died. He brung him hame fir his tea. Marcus was so skinny those days; skin and bone he wis, when he wis a lad. Mind you, he's put on some brawn since then. An' grown intae a guid man. A guid provider, he'll be, lass.'

Tia smiled back at her, shaking her head, remembering Marcus from years ago; he had always seemed tall and strong to her.

'There isn't aucht wrong, is there?'

Tia shook her head quickly, looked around the room, shrugged. 'I don't know what I'm going to do all day, Mrs Anderson.'

'Ach, lass, enjoy being idle when ye can.'

'I was thinking, if I could get some cotton, I could make him a shirt.'

'Ye could do that, aye, but you'd be best to go up to the town, mind. There's only wee Jenny A'thing up the road, Mrs McCafferty, she's called, and she's gey dear for things like that. Ye're best to go up the town. Ye can aye pick up something cheap at the Barras. Mind ye, ye've to watch them, make sure you don't get sold a pup.'

Tia's face became confused again. 'I wouldn't let them, even if they tried to give me one.'

'Ach, lass, I wis firgittin'. It'll be strange fir ye yit. But ye kin git a tram at the top of the road, or e'en hoof it. It's no that far. The shops round here, there's a butcher's and a grocer up the road. But they're dear. That's why I gang intae the town. I'll take ye on Friday. Friday's my shoppin' day. I dae the shoppin', and then I clean the place efter. But I'll take ye up the road now, if ye like. I aye go tae pick up the paper.'

Tia smiled. 'I wasn't sure,' she said, 'I didn't want to go myself. I was scared of getting lost.'

Mrs Anderson walked with her to the newspaper stall, chattering all the way. 'See, lass,' she said when she had bought her paper, 'you just walk back down the street and take the second left and you're back home.'

Tia stared at the unfamiliar landscape.

'Ach,' Mrs Anderson said, turning for home, 'see if ye ask wee Jock, he'll put you right.'

The paper-seller grinned toothlessly; the road was long and wide and Tia thought that she could not get lost as long as she didn't turn any corners.

Tia walked along very slowly, her ears ringing with the noise of carts, trams and cars. The buildings reached four storeys into the sky, the stone a shade lighter than the clouds. She looked up at the sky, squinted against the muted sunlight, wondered briefly at life in the grey grime of the city. The crowds jostled her and she shrank back for a moment before pressing on; the people amazed her, the speed at which they moved, the way they passed by without a word, so very rudely by the standards of the islands. Yet they were not unfriendly; they smiled back when she smiled at them. A tram trundled past, throwing up a shower of sparks in its wake; she gasped in surprise but nobody else paid any attention to it. This street was different to the street where Mrs Anderson's was, in that street, children played, their faces and hands covered with dust, so filthy that she wondered how their mothers ever got them cleaned at night. There were no children at play here, just people, mostly women, going about their business. Some wore shawls, others jackets and capes; she sensed that to wear a shawl was to admit to poverty because the women wearing shawls often did not have shoes. There were many women in shawls, just a few in jackets.

Tia had never seen shops before, beyond the merchants' at Lochmaddy. There was a butcher's with great joints of meat on marble slabs, a shop with a white on black sign that read: Miss McCafferty's Haberdashery, then a grocer's that smelled of spice and coffee when the door opened and a woman came out, followed by a boy carrying her bags. Before the door swung closed Tia caught a glimpse of the interior, of boxes and bags piled high and a counter on which a dozen cheeses were laid out, as lush as buttercups in the gloomy gas light. Outside, apples were piled in a crimson tumble next to a box of oranges; Marcus had taken an orange from the bowl in their room at the hotel and showed her how to take the peel off and then eat the watery flesh. She hadn't liked it at first; the taste was tangy, almost sour, sweet only afterwards when the sting left her tongue. Marcus laughed when she said that; then he agreed when he tried one himself, tossing it away when he had eaten only half of it. 'Palestine's the place for oranges,' he told her, 'Palestine or Spain. They don't taste so good once they've come all the way here. I'll bring you some.'

'But you're not going to Palestine or Spain,' she said.

'No, but they have good oranges in America, too.'

'Is everything good in America, Marcus?'

'Everything's wonderful in America, Tia. You'll see.'

She smiled to herself as she walked along the parade of shops and then across the road, past the place where the shops ended and the houses began, large villas set back from the road with lawns in front and trees that were beginning to shed their leaves on to the pavement, where they cartwheeled along on the wind until they came to rest against the railings. She thought of the island storytellers, Tormod and the others, of their poems and songs, of the fable that explained the powers of the rowan trees; the storytellers had enraged her father, to him the bardic arts were debauched and sinful, a relic of pagan times best forgotten, along with the tales they told. There were enough tales in the Bible, he said, without all that mystic nonsense about the past.

Her sister Mairead fluttered through her mind; she must remember to ask Marcus if he knew what had become of her.

Tia came to the end of the road and turned back, slightly worried at first because she had been thinking and not concentrating on where she was going, but then she saw the shops in the distance and knew she could find her way back. When she reached the newspaper stall, she stopped and smiled at Jock, thanked him when he asked her if she had enjoyed herself. For a moment, she wondered if she should buy herself a paper before she remembered that she had not brought her purse. Jock saw the look on her face and gave her one anyway, telling her to give him the penny the next time she came.

By the time she reached Mrs Anderson's, it was only just after noon. She walked up the stairs, wondering what to do with the rest of the day.

Marcus's chest was by the wall, where he had left it when he brought it from the shipping company, the lid propped up. Very slowly, she read the label, and lifted out the books about seamanship and put them on the shelf on top of the dresser, and his spare boots under the bed.

Early in the afternoon, she felt hunger pangs, but did not eat until the evening, when she cooked some potatoes and a slice of ham. Sitting down by the open grate, she poured some tea and added milk and sugar, smiling at the taste and the sheer delight of it all. As darkness fell she lit the gas lights and the room closed in on her; it felt almost cosy although she was alone. Marcus had been gone for hours only, not even a day, but even so she missed him keenly, hated to think of the days that would pass before he came back, never mind the weeks on end he would be away once he went to sea again.

'It'll only be for another three months,' he had said. 'Once we go to America, I'll not leave you. I'll not leave you ever again.'

The time apart did not seem to matter then, it only mattered that they were together; she had not known how much his absence would hurt.

He needed the money; they needed the money for their new life together.

Idly turning the pages of the paper, she found lists of jobs, a whole column labelled Domestics. It was all so new to her, but she remembered one of the girls on Benbecula, who went to a job that the factor found for her, saying that she left it straight away and got a better one out of the paper. The advertisers wanted maids, butlers, chauffeurs, cooks, housekeepers, handymen, kitchen girls.

'Ach,' Mrs Anderson said, when Tia asked her how to apply for a job, 'Marcus makes plenty. Ye mustna gang upsetting him by makin' folks think he canna keep ye.'

'I won't upset him,' Tia said, 'he'd not mind. He said so.'

'E'en so, a man disna like his wumman tae wirk. My man wouldn'a stand fir it. Marcus'd be fashed, Tia. Best jis' tae bide at hame.'

Tia did not understand what she meant. 'Mrs Anderson, I only want to try. Please tell me how. Marcus won't be angry, I promise you.'

The landlady peered at her and then at the newspaper. 'Well, Tia, if ye're set oan it I wouldn' fret wi' the paper. Have a keek at wee Jock's board the morn, an' if thaur's nowt esk the grocer. He aye kens if someone's looking fir help.'

Tia thanked her and went back to her room, wondering again at the strange ways of the city. Finding a pen, ink and paper in Marcus's chest, she sat down and wrote Mary a long letter about it all, folding it and sealing it and then propping it on the dresser for him to take to the ferry office when he got back.

Next day Tia went along to Jock's newspaper stall to pay him the penny for yesterday's paper, and found the board where folk paid to advertise jobs. There were a few cards asking for domestic help, and she sought Jock's advice as to which one was the closest.

'That'll be the Baillie's,' said Jock, and pointed out the way.

The house was not far from Jock's stall, just along the road and round a corner, but not so far that she couldn't still see where she was. Tia thought that she would never get used to the street names; in the end Jock gave up trying to explain the address and told her just to turn right at the lamp post instead. The house was different to the others; it was set further back from the road and there was a tiny pond in the front garden.

Tia found it easily enough and walked up the driveway, horribly aware of the sound her boots made against the gravel. She didn't go to the front door, but walked around to the back and knocked at the kitchen door. Jock had been very particular about that; he told her it was an affront to the dignity of the household if she disturbed them by ringing the bell. Her timid knock was answered by a little girl who looked like a mouse, who told her to come in when Tia said that Jock had sent her about the job.

The door opened into a lobby outside a kitchen that was stifflingly hot, with a huge range taking up the whole of one wall and a fire burning on the one opposite.

'Miss Thompson'll see ye in a minute, if ye wait,' the mouse girl said, before she picked up a pan and brush and scurried away.

Tia waited, listening to the disappearing sounds of her footsteps. She wasn't sure what to do or to say and as the minutes ticked past on the kitchen clock she began to wonder if anyone was coming or if she would be left to wait for ever for someone who did not even know she was there. It was a cold day, so she had worn her thick island shawl that felt like a blanket now in the warmth of the room. The house was silent except for the bubbling of a pot on the burner and the gurgle of water in the pipes. The minute hand moved with a click; she watched it for a while, until a quarter of an hour had gone by. Then footsteps sounded in the hall and the door opened, riffling the pages of a cookery book on the table.

'You've come for the job,' the woman said. She was tall and broad, built like a man almost, with the sort of whiskers that grew on the upper lip of an adolescent boy. The sleeves of her dress were too short; her wrists were thick and her hands red and rough. 'Well, let's see your reference, girl. We haven't got all day.'

Tia wondered what she meant.

'It said in the notice that a reference is required. Come on, girl. This is a busy household.'

'I haven't got one,' Tia blundered.

'What are you doing here, then?'

Tia thought quickly. 'I haven't got it with me, I meant.'

The housekeeper's eyes narrowed. 'Well, I'll need to see it before I appoint you. *If* I decide to appoint you, that is. You know we're only looking for help with the laundry. It's a daily we need, for the time being.'

'I see.'

'You have worked before, haven't you?'

'Oh, yes,' Tina said, thinking of the croft, 'I have worked before.'

'You're a teuchter, I see. Oh well, I suppose a teuchter's better than a paddy. What sort of work have you done?'

Tia had to think before she remembered that 'teuchter' meant a highlander whereas 'paddy' meant Irish. She bridled for a moment before she mumbled that she had done all sorts of housework.

'It's not Mrs Beeton we need, mind, no cooking, it's not heavy work either, but I do need a girl who knows what's what. Just doing laundry on Monday, the Baillie's and the young master's shirts, their smalls, the linen and that. Most of the mistress's things go out. Then doing the ironing and that, and helping out in the kitchen as well, if you're needed. Could you manage that?'

'Oh, yes,' Tia said.

'Well, if you come back with your reference I'll give you a try.'

'I can't start until next week.'

The housekeeper glowered. 'Why ever not, girl? You work for us at our convenience, not yours, mind.'

'Oh, yes,' Tia said, 'But, you see, I've just come down here and I'm waiting for my things. My references and the like. It will not be here until the weekend and you said you have to see my reference, so I will have to wait until then.'

The woman snorted. 'You do not have to wait until then.

You can start work now and let me see the reference when it comes. If you want the job, that is.'

'Oh, I do want the job.'

'Well girl, I'll get you an apron and you can get started.'

'How much do I get paid?' Tina asked, as the house-keeper reached into one of the cupboards.

'Hah! You'll get, let me see, a ha'penny an hour, maybe a florin for the week, depends the hours you do. You start at six and finish when I let you go. That'll be mid afternoon most like, but you'll have to stay sometimes, if there's a dinner on. The family entertain, you see. This is an important household, girl. In normal circumstances you would not be even considered for a position here, so you've been lucky. I expect you to show your appreciation by working diligently and conducting yourself in a manner appropriate to your position here. Well, get on with it, girl. We haven't got all day.'

Tia put on the apron, managing to tie it behind her back perfectly through sheer luck.

The housekeeper led her to the scullery, where she told her to wash and dry the breakfast dishes and then to make a start on the vegetables for lunch.

Tia had finished the dishes and was peering at the mounds of vegetables on the scullery table when the mouse girl scurried in to fetch more beeswax.

'Ye took the job,' she said.

'Yes,' Tia said, still surprised at how easy it had been.

'Ye'll regret it,' the mouse girl said, 'the bluidy slave trade it is here. The Gold Coast's got naithin' oan this place.

Tia wasn't sure what she meant.

'Ye'll learn,' the girl said. 'I'm leavin' the end o' the week. Got a job jis' up the road. I'll be glad to see the back of this place, an' that auld bitch an' the madam. Ye'd think yon wis the bluidy King and Queen, fir the way they go oan. So ye would.'

'What do I do with the vegetables?' Tia asked her.

The girl's eyes lifted to the ceiling. 'Ye peel the tatties and top an' tail the beans, 'Cept ye better ask the missus if she wants the beans peelt an' aw.' Seeing Tia's confusion, she took a knife from the table drawer and showed her how to peel a potato, leaving Tia struggling and wondering why on earth anyone would go to the bother and waste, because so much of the goodness was left on the peel.

'I thought I was supposed to be doing the laundry,' she said, the next time the mouse girl scampered through.

'It's done fir the week. They sent it up tae the Magdalen. Ye'll dae it next week, but. Dinna hawd yer breath.'

Tia became used to waking before dawn and getting dressed in the darkness, then rushing along the road to work as the thin city sun lighted the sky. Her working day was long and onerous, more so because she had no experience and had to learn everything as she went along, but at least it made the time pass, quelled the yawning emptiness of the days when Marcus was away. At times her little deception worried her, but at others she was pleased that she had managed to get the job, despite her lack of a reference and experience. It was a victory of sorts; the job wasn't much but at least it was work.

Miss Thomson, the housekeeper, nearly found her out several times; Betty, the mouse-like housemaid, did because Tia had to ask her again and again how to do this or that and eventually confess that she had never had a job before. 'You won't tell, will you?' she asked anxiously.

'I don't bluidy care,' Betty said, 'it makes nae difference tae me. Jis' watch the missus disnae find oot. Ye'll be oot on yer ear if she does.'

The work drained her, but it also made her smile when she thought of what Marcus would say when she told him that she had found something to do while he was away. It meant a lot to her that her wage would go, like his, towards their future, and the meals she ate in the house meant she did not have to spend any of his money on food. Labour filled her day and made the time apart seem less onerous when she fell, dizzy with tiredness, into her bed, dropping into a deep sleep the moment her head hit the pillow.

Betty's wages were paid at the end of the month, though she said that Tia would get hers on Saturday, which was the end of the week. Miss Tompson had told her, pedantically, that because the household was faithful to the Lord, staff who lived out were given the whole of His day off. Only the boy who helped the chauffeur lived out, apart from Tia; both Betty and

Miss Thompson had rooms above the kitchen, and the chauffeur, Farquharson, stayed in the room above the garage. The man of the house had an Argyle, which made a sound like an army on the march and moved only slightly more quickly; the car company had gone bankrupt before the Great Exhibition, but the man Farquharson called 'the gaffer' insisted the car was kept as an act of civic pride. Tia learned all this from Betty and from overhearing Farquharson talking to Miss Thompson:

'See yon bluidy vee-hickel, Jessie, we'd be better wi' a cart and horse, we'd be better wi' a bluidy wheelbarrow, come tae that. Ye canna go twa mile in the beast wi'out the engine o'erheating, an' the Baillie's in the back an' I'm runnin' a' o'er the place tryin' tae find watter. It's possessed by auld Nick, so it is; naething earthly could tak' in sae much watter. Must be the fires o' hell burning inside.'

By the time Saturday came, Tia was so exhausted that she wondered if the money was worth it; her hands were ragged and scarred and her feet ached and so did her back; worse, she knew that her employers, for all their Christian faith and civic pride, paid the worst wages in Glasgow to staff expected to do twice the work for the privilege of working in the household of a man elected by his peers to serve the city as a member of its corporation.

'I'd walk oot if I wis ye,' Betty said. 'Jis cut yer losses. Ye'll get anither job nae trouble, e'en if ye tell them ye've no wirked afore.'

'I haven't even got a reference,' Tia hissed.

'Och, see, ye git yin fra' the minister, or the teacher at the school. It's jist tae mak' sure ye're no' jis' oot the Magdalen or the jail or aucht.'

Tia thought of the Reverend Doctor, and smiled to herself.

When the time came for her to leave work, she put on her shawl and waited in the kitchen as Miss Thompson fiddled with the food cooking on the stove. She couldn't leave until she had been told to; though her working day was supposed to end in the afternoon she had worked every night until ten o'clock or later, because the family did not begin their evening meal until eight and the housekeeper asked her to help Betty with the dishes and clean the kitchen afterwards. That night, they were entertaining; Miss Thompson told her that she could go because the domestics from the Civic Chambers had come to help serve the guests.

'What is it, Tia?' she asked after a while, when she deigned to notice that Tia was still waiting.

Tia cleared her throat. 'Miss Thompson, please, my wages,' she said, 'it's the end of the week.'

'Hah,' the housekeeper spat, 'that's all your type think about. You don't think about your duties at all, only how much you get paid. Well, I had a word with the Baillie and he said that it's quite all right about your reference, that is, he's quite happy for me to wait for it, but he said I've not to pay your wages until everything's regular. You'll get your money just as soon as I've seen it, but not before.'

'But . . .' Tia began.

'No buts, girl. You should be grateful for the Baillie's indulgence in this matter. Most employers wouldn't even have let you in the door.'

It was raining softly outside. Indoors all day, Tia hardly noticed the weather, but the cold wind whipped at her shawl and as she walked home passing cars and carriages threw up sheets of water that drenched her skirt. By the time she reached Mrs Anderson's, the drizzle had become a deluge and she was soaked to the skin.

Tiredly, she walked up the stairs. The stove was not lit, but Betty had shown her how to do it and she was an expert now, and had laid the kindling in the morning so that she only needed to put a match to it now. She took her wet clothes off, shivering in the cold.

As she waited for the fire to take hold, a feeling of despair settled over her. Marcus was due back that night; she wasn't sure when but he'd said it would be very late because the docks were busy and it took a long time to berth. She had wanted to go to meet him, but he refused – the docks at night was not a place for a woman alone. Instead, she had risen very early and cleaned the room until there wasn't a speck of dust anywhere.

At work, she had carefully watched Miss Thompson cooking, memorising the recipes so she could do it herself. She had seen her making a roast of beef with vegetables, then an apple dumpling so light that it seemed to float on the plate.

Knowing that Marcus loved beef, a rare delicacy in the islands, she had bought some from the butcher's then the other things she needed from the grocer, appalled at the cost but consoling herself that her wages would replace most of it.

She wanted Marcus to come home to a good meal that she had provided entirely by herself; to be as proud of her as she was of him, to know that as he was a good husband, she would be a good wife.

Taking the beef out of the pantry, she though how pathetic it looked, compared to the huge joint that Miss Thompson had roasted for the family's dinner. The vegetables, peeled and soaking in water, had the look of newly hatched ducklings, pale and sickly, too frail to face the world without the protection of the shell. The dumpling mixture made that morning, the blend of flour, butter and sugar, and a little cinnamon to add piquancy, appeared wan and tasteless.

Tiredly, she checked the oven then put the beef in; she had cooked it slowly overnight, since Miss Thompson cooked a roast all day to bring the flavour out. Once she had par-boiled the potatoes, she put them in the oven too, basting them with juices from the beef. Very carefully, she added an egg to the dumpling, then put it all in a bowl wrapped in muslin and set it to steam with apples over a simmering pot.

The smell of cooking comforted her. Looking at herself in the mirror, she unwound her plaits and brushed her hair until it gleamed. She heated water, took her clothes off and washed from tip to toe before she put on fresh underthings and her other skirt and blouse. She laid her nightgown on the bed, thinking it would be more comfortable to wear, but it would not be right.

She felt Marcus's proximity when he turned the corner into their street. Leaving the food, she opened the door of the room and went down to the front door, waited for a minute or two before she heard his footsteps and then opened it and threw herself into his arms.

The feel of his body drove away all her doubts, the remnants of her brief despair. Mrs Anderson's door opened, then quickly closed again.

'I missed you,' she murmured, into his neck.

'I missed you,' he replied, his voice thick.

When they were alone in their room, he kissed her and she

felt his hands touch her chin before they travelled down, undoing her blouse and casting it off as a ship casts off its moorings. She thought briefly of the meal cooking, wondering fleetingly how to turn the oven down. His hands were on her breasts now, his jacket rough as her nipples brushed against it. She whimpered softly as she felt herself melt into him.

She served the meal much later, in the early hours of Sunday morning as the night rolled towards the dawn. He ate ravenously, like a starved man, as she watched him, smiling to herself. She was worried that the beef was dry, but he said he liked it crisp.

'I got a job, you see,' she said, when he had finished the dumpling, 'after a day of waiting for you, I thought I'd go mad if I didn't, so I went and got myself a job.'

He grinned. 'I didn't marry you, *ban-righ*, for you to work to feed me.'

'Mrs Anderson said you'd be angry.'

'I'm not angry. The woman's daft. Why should I be angry?' He hugged her tight. 'I'm proud of you, *ban-righ*.'

Her face lit up, shone like a spring morning.

He smiled and tickled her chin. 'Tell me about this job of yours, *ban-righ*.'

'Oh, it's nothing much, just domestic work. I'm not even a maid, I just do this and that. In the kitchen. I'm supposed to do the laundry as well, but they sent it out. I'll do it next week though.' It seemed better now, when she thought of it, not nearly so hard as it seemed at the time. 'I get my meals on duty and they don't mind me living out.'

Marcus's face straightened. 'Who're the family? What are they like?'

She thought of the civic dignitary and his Argyle, of Betty the mouse-girl and Miss Thompson with her airs and graces, the raucous familiarity of the chauffeur.

'They're not too bad,' she smiled.

He took her hand and drew circles on it with his finger. 'Like I said, you don't have to work, *ban-righ*, but if you want to, then do.'

'Mrs Anderson . . .' she said again.

'Ach, stupid *ghalltachd* heathen customs. A married woman is not supposed to work. As if I care.'

'But, you see, Marcus, I didn't actually get my wages.'

His face hardened. 'What?'

'Well, the woman, she asked for a reference. I didn't know what it was. I just said I didn't have it but I'd have it soon. Then, when it came to the end of the week she said I'd get my wages when she got the reference.'

'*Galach* bloody nonsense. We'll go round there now and get your wages for you.'

'No, Marcus. I'll get them myself. I just need to get a reference.'

He looked at her askance for a moment, then he grinned. He opened the dresser, took out a pen and paper, sat down at the table and began to write. A moment or two later, he blotted the paper and handed it to her.

*To whom it may concern:*

*Mrs Tia Cameron has worked for this household in a highly satisfactory manner; she is honest, loyal, trustworthy and highly competent to perform all her duties. It is with great regret that we have learned that she has chosen to leave us, but we wish her well in the future and assure any employer that she is an excellent employee.*

Tia recognised neither the address nor the signature.

'Oh, Marcus . . .'

'Is that all right?'

'Yes, but . . .'

'What?'

'I'm not supposed to be married, Marcus. Least, I don't think I'm supposed to be married. The housekeeper, she said they wanted a girl. I think that means I'm not supposed to be married.'

'Ach, if you're ashamed of me . . . What'll it be next, *ban-righ*? A divorce???' Shaking his head, he took another piece of paper and wrote the reference again, this time using her maiden name and signing his own. The address he gave was Allan Rankine's old house in Kelvingrove. 'There you are, *ban-righ*.'

She folded it carefully. 'Thank you, Marcus.'

He reached for her and took her into his arms, ruffling her hair gently as he told her not to worry about the daft lowlanders and their silly references.

She grinned. 'You see, your meal, I wanted to buy the food myself, but I couldn't when she didn't give me the money. I had to use yours.'

'Tia, how often do I have to tell you, my money is your money?'

It was only in the morning, when they woke very late, and he said that he was hungry, that she realised she had forgotten to buy bread or anything for breakfast, she had been so busy thinking of the dinner she was going to cook. They had made love until after dawn; she was still drowsy, her limbs fluid. Sleepily, she told him that there was only the remnants of the beef and some cold potatoes; she had the makings of scones but it would take a while before they were cooked.

'Ach,' he said, 'to hell with food. Come here and I'll eat you instead.'

She shrieked as he began to mock-gnaw her shoulder, laughed convulsively when he pretended to cut a slice from her hips.

She tried not to think beyond the moment, of the next day when he would go to sea to sail to America and would not be back inside a month.

'Marcus,' she asked him, later, 'd'you know what happened to my sister Mairead?'

He looked thoughtful for a moment before he answered that he did not.

'She went to the lowlands, I think, to Glasgow I suppose.'

'I haven't seen her since that first time I saw you, *ban-righ*.'

'I thought you'd know where she was.'

He smiled slowly. 'I'll try to find out, *ban-righ*, but the city's a big place, it's easy to get lost here, specially if getting lost is what she wanted to do.'

'What d'you mean, Marcus?'

He thought for a while before he answered. 'Sometimes people do,' he said slowly. 'Sometimes they want to make a new beginning. Sometimes they just want to be free of their past.'

She felt fearful somehow; she did not know why but she shivered fleetingly before he pulled her to him and held her tight.

Winter came then, the trees were stripped bare of leaves by the driving winds and the puddles on the pavement bore icy crusts in the early morning, which crunched as Tia walked over them on the way to her job.

Her work became easier as she got used to it; the cuts on her hands from the vegetable knife healed and the constant routine made the days pass more quickly than they would have done if she had nothing to do. Once or twice she thought of applying for another post, but Miss Thompson had kept her reference and she did not want to risk her wrath by asking for it back. She overheard two girls talking in the street one day and learned that other households paid only a few pennies more each week; the money did not seem worth it for the trouble it could cause.

She worked and was satisfied if a day passed without a sharp reprimand from Miss Thompson; she was very proud of the florin she received in return for Marcus's reference and even prouder when she earned another at the end of the next week.

She was mortally embarrassed one day when the son of the house, a student actuary, touched her as he passed her on the stairs; horrified when he did it again the next time she saw him. In her arms she held a bundle of freshly aired linen for the cupboard at the top of the stairs; she nearly dropped it with the shock and once she had put it all away she ran downstairs, careless of the noise she made.

'How many times do I have to tell you, girl,' Miss Thompson demanded petulantly, 'to go about your work quietly? If the mistress had been in, that bell would be ringing and you would have some explaining to do. Well?'

Tia said nothing, but went into the scullery to peel vegetables for the midday meal. The kitchen produced a never-ending relay of meals, each one more lavish than the last. There was breakfast with kippers, bacon and eggs and kidneys, fresh-baked bread with rolls, coffee, chocolate and tea, and porridge for the men, while the women had prunes and freshly squeezed orange juice. Lunch followed with soup, a meat course and a pudding, then dinner with all that and fish as well, and usually game too. The food alone wouldn't have worried Tia, it was the sight of so much coming back from the dining room uneaten, when some-times her own stomach was crying out for food. The staff meal, as Miss Thompson called it, was served twice a day, in the mornings after breakfast and then at four in the afternoon. The servings were small and she looked askance at Tia if she helped herself to more than one slice of bread, though she indulged the chauffeur and the carriage boy, who were allowed to eat as much as they liked.

'I'm waiting,' she said, as Tia picked up a potato and began to work.

'I slipped, Miss Thompson,' she said quietly.

'Don't make it worse by lying, girl.'

She was standing threateningly at the threshold of the scullery, blocking the light.

Tia sighed and put down the knife. 'It was the lad, Miss Thompson, the son of the house. He touched me on the stairs.'

'What nonsense, girl! I've a mind to make you wash your mouth out with soap. Don't make it any worse than it is by lying.'

Tia thought for a moment. 'I'm not lying, Miss Thompson,' she said flatly.

The housekeeper stared at her, only turning away when she saw that Tia would not flinch. 'Get on with your work,' she snapped. 'I haven't got time to listen to your tales.'

After the staff meal, though, the housekeeper's manner softened and she offered Tia a second cup of tea. 'You know,' she said, 'I'm sure you're imagining things. I doubt the young master would do something like that.'

Tia said nothing.

'It was surely an accident. Don't you agree?'

Tia shrugged. 'It could have been. But it would have to have been two.'

'What on earth d'you mean by that, girl?'

'He rubbed against me twice, Miss Thompson. So it'd've had to be two accidents, if you see what I mean.'

'I do not, but never mind,' the housekeeper said tartly, 'but I'll make sure he knows you're just a girl. That'll put a stop to it. The Baillie's a trustee of the Vigilance Society, you know. He won't have that sort of thing going on in his house.'

Tia forgot the incident after that, because by then Marcus was on his way home from America and Mrs Anderson told her that although the weather in the city was dreadful, the weather out in the Atlantic wasn't so bad.

Marcus came home one Thursday night and set off again the

next morning on another trip, to Charleston this time, to pick up tobacco for the Wills Brothers.

'It won't be like this for ever,' he said, when he left, while she was still in the sated aftermath of love. 'Just this one last trip, and then we'll be off to America, you and me.' She wanted to hold him to her, to tell him how much she missed him, but she did not because she did not want him to feel bad.

His absence didn't seem so cruel when she reminded herself that they would have the rest of their lives together, once they set sail for America.

After weeks when no housemaid applied for the job that Betty had left, Miss Thompson sullenly took on a young girl straight from school and gave her Tia's work to do, telling Tia that she was lucky because she now had a proper job and was not just daily help. 'You'll have to live in now,' she said.

'Oh, no,' Tia said.

'What do you mean, "no"?'

'Well, I live at home. I help there, as well.'

'Don't be daft, girl. You start at six and finish at ten, or later. You won't have time to go home.

Tia's eyes dropped. 'My father, he won't let me live in.'

'What nonsense is that? This is a decent house.'

Tia realised she had made a mistake. 'My mother's poorly,' she said quickly, 'I have to cook and get my brothers and sisters up.'

Miss Thompson's face softened. 'Oh dear, I didn't realise. But you won't have time, girl. You've to be here at six.'

'I'll make time,' Tia said.

'Well, there's no extra in your wages. Ten shillings a month all found, live in or not.'

'That's fine,' Tia said happily. It seemed like a fortune to her.

The new job made little difference at first, because the work, though different, was just as hard, but it was fascinating to see the house and something of the lives the family led. The gentleman of the house prided himself on being an early riser, he was always in the breakfast room reading his paper when she took the serving dishes in, but his wife often stayed in bed until mid morning or even later, when she would ring the maid's bell and ask Tia to run a bath and lay out her clothes. The bathroom intrigued Tia, and its enamel tub surrounded by an oak cabin, the shower control which gave a choice of spray and temperature; it was much more elaborate than the bathroom at the Muirs'. Madam liked just a warm bath scented with Parisian oils which smelt of lavender, but Tia would have loved to stand underneath the shower and be cleansed from head to foot and then to drench herself in talcum powder which was kept in a glass jar over the washhand basin. In her employer's presence, Tia was nervous, anxious to avoid the sharp rebuke that came with every tiny infraction of the rules.

'Your bath is ready now, Mrs Baillie,' she had said, on the first day she was sent upstairs.

The woman's face had soured. 'You must call me "Madam" if you want to work for me,' she said sharply. 'Over-familiarity is not a trait that I like to encourage in our staff. In any case, it's my husband who's the Baillie. It's a title, you see. Not a name.'

Tia was ashamed of her ignorance.

After her bath Madam dressed herself in just a towelling robe which she shrugged off without embarrassment as Tia helped her into her camisole and bloomers and pulled the ties of her corset tight. The corset was a strange shape, padded below the breasts and tight over the waist, emphasising the shape of her generous buttocks and extravagant thighs.

'The Baillie likes me to be *svelte*, you see,' Madam said one day as she studied her reflection of the full-length mirror in her dressing room. 'I keep on telling him the S-shape's yesterday, but he says that it flatters me. Don't you think?' She lifted the fullness of her bosom, then ran her hands over her nether regions. 'Well, girl?'

'Oh, yes, Madam. Very,' Tia mumbled humbly.

The clothes she wore over the corset were soft and rich to the touch, lavishly adorned with lace and embroidery. 'I know it's not in vogue this year,' she would say as she put on an outfit and then turned this way and that to study her reflection, 'but the Baillie, he likes me to look like a woman. The new styles, you know, they're so strict. So severe. The skirts are so narrow and the Baillie says, next thing women will be wearing trousers. Can you believe it?' Her eyes would roll then and she would smile coquettishly, pat Tia's hand as if she had forgotten for a moment that she was just a maid and was treating her as a friend instead.

Madam was a woman who had ripened into age as a rose smells sweetest just before it withers and dies. The plumpness of her face softened features that would otherwise have been too angular for a woman dressed in frills and flounces. Her long hair was still auburn, and she made Tia brush it every morning and then twist it into a tight knot that she pinned on top of her head; letting it loose again in the evening when she readied herself for bed. 'It's such a nuisance that you don't live in,' she said one day, just before Tia left. 'I have to get Miss Thompson to help me and she's not really of a mind to. Her *forte* is the kitchen. I don't think she knows what to do with a hairbrush. Honestly! When she did my hair last night, it felt like she was scrambling eggs and it looked like it, too. I just don't understand why we've all this trouble finding staff. You'd think any girl would be proud to work for a house like this.'

'I could stay later,' Tia said, feeling sorry for her for some reason that she did not understand. There was something a little pathetic about Madam, despite her airs and graces, her lavender-sweetened smell and her wealth. It was in spite of, or perhaps of, the clothes she wore, richly adorned as a christening robe, or even a doll's dress. Sometimes, when the light caught her in a certain way, Madam did not look like a woman in the prime of her life, but one trapped in effigy, doomed to a state of eternal bereavement because the season of her youth had long passed.

'Oh, could you?' Madam said. 'It would help so much. In fact, if you live in I would take you on as lady's maid happily. It would make such a difference, you know.'

'I'm afraid I can't live in,' Tia said.

'Ohh,' she said, 'you live at home, don't you? That's right. I remember Miss Thompson said that you wanted Christmas off. It's the Baillie, you know. He says we mustn't be selfish and keep the staff. But I don't understand. You'd get a lovely meal if you stayed with us.'

Marcus was waiting for her when she arrived home on Christmas Eve. She felt guilty because she had wanted to be in before him but the docks were quiet, for once, and his ship had found a berth immediately.

'I'm so sorry,' she whispered.

'Don't be.' Standing just inside the door, he did not move aside to let her enter and she wondered why, until she saw the grin on his face.

'It was supposed to be a surprise,' he said, when she saw the new enamel tub in the middle of the floor and the small box on the chair beside it from Gimpel Fils of New York. When she opened the box the smell of roses and spice drifted out; there was soap and oil, a box of talcum, a bottle of eau-de-cologne, and pot-pourri in a little earthenware pot with holes in it to let the scent out.

'Oh, Marcus . .'

'I know it's not a proper bath, but it's a bath all the same. I even started boiling the water.'

'It is a proper bath. It's a wonderful bath. It'll be the best bath I've ever had.'

'How many baths have you had, *ban-righ*?'

'Marcus . . .' She hugged him tight.

'I've got other news,' he said as he gently eased her away.

She saw his face had changed. 'What's that?' she asked carefully.

He sat her down by the fire before he sat down in the chair opposite.

'The old man's asked me to do one last favour, *ban-righ*. One of his ships, *My Lady Eilean*, the new owner put her into dry dock and he's not happy with the way she's come out. He's made all sorts of complaints to the old man and she's stuck at Cork because his captain's saying she's not seaworthy. That's bollocks, *ban-righ*, if you'll excuse my language. She's as sound as a bell. I was a mate on her, then first officer in the days when the old man was sailing. She's his ship you see. The new owner's stopped payment and he's threatening the old man with lawyers.' Marcus stopped talking and sighed. Suddenly, she felt the chill in the room; she had banked the coals in the range carefully before she left and she hadn't had time to attend to it yet. She got up and threw on more coals, then used the bellows until warmth and light spread into the room from the open door; she hadn't yet put the gas lamps on either, but as she struck a match Marcus put a hand up to stop her.

'There's enough light for the moment, *ban-righ*.'

Quickly, she took the meal she had prepared early in the morning and put it into the oven to heat.

Marcus's lips formed a hard line; as she sat down he reached for her hand, touching it to his lips before he held it between his.

'Thing is, *ban-righ* . . .'

'Marcus, I . . .'

'Let me finish, *ban-righ*.'

'No, Marcus.' She smiled, though she was aching inside. 'I know what Allan Rankine means to you. If he's asked you to help him, then do. You wouldn't be able to forgive yourself if you didn't.'

'I booked us on the first Cunard.'

She grinned. 'We can wait for the second.'

He shook his head. '*Ban-righ*, how can I ever tell you how much I love you?'

'You don't have to. I know.'

He got up and took her into his arms. 'He wants me to go over there, see what the matter is, She's carrying cargo due in Kingston next month, and she's contracted to Charleston and then New York. I'll take her, if the new man's captain won't.'

She looked up, straight into his eyes.

'Is she sound, Marcus?'

'Like I said, *ban-righ*. I'd stake my life on her.'

'You must be hungry,' she said. 'I'll get you something to eat.'

Marcus was troubled. She sensed that by the look on his face when he thought she wasn't looking, the way he seemed to be struggling when he smiled. She was glad that he was leaving the Rankine Line; glad that soon its troubles would be behind them. Something had happened during the trip, or perhaps afterwards; she sensed that from the distracted way he toyed with the beer she had poured for him and sat staring ahead, as if to see what the future would bring. Always before, when he got back from sea he would reach for her and would not let her go until he had loved her thoroughly; she felt vaguely sad that he had let her go so easily when she stood up to bring his meal.

His breath on her neck startled her at first; she gasped when he kissed her gently and then more insistently as his hand moved to undo her skirt and then her blouse. Tenderly he pried her hands away from the pots and pans and turned her round to face him.

'Marcus . . .'

He told her to hush as he carried her to bed and shrugged his own clothes off, surging into her with an urgency that took her breath away. She felt her body take fire then, the heat tore at her soul as she grabbed him and clung to him and cried out her love and need and confusion.

It was so strange, the feeling afterwards, the sensation that told her he had left something there. She felt a flowering inside, a brief fluttering that made her sure. She heard the clock chime the hour and knew then that she would remember the very minute of the hour of the day when the new life started within her, the new life that would become his, their, child.

She lay sprawled against his chest, listening to the beat of his heart, as he idly toyed with the strands of her hair. After a while, he moved.

'What is it?' she asked.

He went to the dresser and picked up his brush, then came back to the bed and began to ease the knots out of her hair.

'You're worried. I can tell,' she said, once he had done and she had wrapped her robe around her as she went to finish the meal.

'It's nothing, *ban-righ*. After this trip it'll all be over. It's just a bloody shame, you know, that these two scoundrels are destroying everything the old man's worked for. But they're his sons, like he says. It's a pity they've fallen in with a gang of thieves.'

On Christmas morning he took her to the bank, where he put some money into his account and asked the clerk to tally the balance and add the interest for the year, because in February he would be closing it.

Tia was astounded that he had nearly two hundred pounds.

'It's a fortune,' she said.

He shook his head. 'To you, maybe. To the man you work for, it's only small change. But it's enough to make a start over there.'

Her half crown a week, so hard earned, seemed like nothing in comparison.

'You know, maybe you shouldn't go to that job of yours this week. Maybe you should stay home and wait for me.' He grinned. 'Maybe that'd be cheaper.' When he had seen her boots that morning, he had gone to the cobbler's and got some thick leather, then soled them for her because they were almost worn through.

She smiled to herself, then told him how the woman she worked for had asked her to be her lady's maid, and had seemed insulted when Tia had not jumped at the chance.

# Chapter Six

*T*he cutting edge of winter closed in on Tia, once Marcus was back at sea and the Baillie's household had settled into the monotony of the season. The lady of the house had her ironing endlessly, when she discovered that Tia could wield an iron better than the young girl Miss Thompson had hired for the job, who sometimes left tiny stray creases in the flounces and frills of the white lawn blouses she changed two or three times a day.

Each blouse that she ironed, each frill she smoothed to a ripple as soft as the eddies of a wave made a little more time pass; brought closer the time when Marcus would be home again. He had already booked their tickets and given Mrs Anderson notice that they would be leaving. The bank had given him a little calendar, which she set on the dresser, marking each day off in the evening, before she fell asleep. She had circled the date of his return, the 25th of February, and the 10th of March, when their ship would sail to America.

She wanted to write to Eunice to tell her but Marcus told her not to bother, there was plenty of time yet to tell her, to go home to see her, in fact, as they had promised to. She found his nonchalance strange, until she realised that he crossed the Atlantic with the same ease that she walked over the causeway to Benbecula. Because in his life there had been so many leavings, perhaps this last departure did not seem as final to him as it did to her.

The month of January passed and Madam set pots of crocuses in the conservatory, where she checked them daily for any signs of growth. Tia scored the month out on her calendar, knowing that Marcus was on his way home now, he would have already left Kingston, Jamaica and be heading for Charleston and then New York. She had worried about him sailing in the depths of winter, until he told her that in the tropics the weather was balmy all year round, especially in the Caribbean the danger time for storms was the autumn, which had already passed.

In the Baillie's library, there was a wooden globe, where she tracked his journey daily, if she had a moment to spare.

She was certain that she was carrying his child now that more than a month had passed without her bleeding, and her breasts felt heavy and tender. She noticed the change one day when she was dressing, that the aureolae were bigger and the tissue around them sore to the touch; she thrilled to the thought of the growing life inside her who as a baby would suckle there. Marcus wanted a child, she knew; he had asked her just before she left, but she kept the secret to herself because she was not certain and she did not want to disappoint him.

Even Madam knew that something had changed; Tia's attention drifted sometimes when she was working and Madam was always quick to chide her. Tia sometimes resented her employer's assumption that because she engaged her to labour for twelve hours every day, she had the right to her mind as well.

One day early in February, when she had helped Madam get ready for a reception at City Hall and there was fifteen minutes to spare before she left, she sat down and said firmly that they must have a talk, indicating that Tia should sit too.

Tia sat carefully – she had never sat down with the mistress before, she was always on her feet doing something.

'I've been thinking,' Madam said, 'this arrangement really is inadequate, for you as well as for me.' Inadequate was one of her favourite words; it cropped up often in her remarks, so much that Tia had looked it up in Reid's Dictionary and found herself looking up *defective* and *insufficient* until she was certain that she knew what Madam meant. To her, anything could be and usually was inadequate, from a meal to a dress to the whole of her wardrobe. As Tia was putting something away in her dressing room, she would come and look around and then with a sweeping gesture say that it was all quite inadequate, fashion had changed and she would have to get some new things, else people would be saying that the Baillie's wife was a frump – worse, that the Baillie did not clothe her properly. That puzzled Tia, because Madam often went into the town in the Argyle, to have lunch with her friends and usually came home followed by mounds of boxes from MacDonald's or Daly's, Copland's or Treron's. Occasionally, too, she would confide that Miss Thompson was inadequate, that the meals she prepared, though tasty, lacked *finesse*. 'She is a good housekeeper,' she would say, 'but I really think we should take on a chef. It's the Baillie, you see. He's so unadventurous. A man of habit, so he is. Habits make for boredom sometimes, don't you think, Tia?'

She had let her cheeks dimple, but she did not reply, fearing some *faux-pas* that might make Madam mad.

Tia waited patiently, hoping that the woman who faced her would not divulge any more of her secrets, because such confidences embarrassed her.

'It is ridiculous, is it not, for you to be struggling home in this weather, Tia, when there's a room free for you here? You really must live in. It's for your own good and mine as well. I've become used to you, you see. It's very inconvenient when I need something done and you are not here.'

'I'm almost always here,' Tia said softly.

'Nonsense, girl. You are never here to help if we go out at night. The arrangement's hardly adequate, you know, with me having to come in and sort myself out.'

'I could wait for you,' Tia said, 'if it would help.'

'What, and have you walking home in the early hours of the morning? Don't be ridiculous, girl. Talk sense! The Baillie and I agree that you must live in. You'll get a salary of twelve shillings a month all found. That's sixpence more a week than you get at the moment, on top of your board, which you get as well. You can go home tonight and pack your things and we'll start our new arrangement tomorrow. Miss Thompson will sort your money out.'

Tia thought of Marcus, three weeks or less from home.

'Well, girl?' Madam had stood up and was glaring at her.

'I'm afraid I can't, Madam.'

The mistress's face twisted into a scowl, her expression midway between anger and disbelief. 'What on earth do you mean, Tia? "Can't" doesn't come into it. It's what you must do, if you want to keep your position here. You're not thinking of leaving us, are you?'

'Well, yes,' Tia confessed. She wasn't scared of Madam really, with Marcus she laughed at her, but in her presence she was cautious of the advantages her mistress had. Even in her wildest dreams, Tia had never imagined having another human being to tend to her as she tended Madam; the thought appalled her, when she considered it. Left alone, Madam couldn't manage to do her hair properly, never mind dress or even run herself a bath. In many ways she was like a baby; what confused Tia was the air of utter superiority that she assumed as she gave her commands. Herself, she would be ashamed of being as clumsy and helpless as that.

'You see,' she went on, gaining strength from her thought of Marcus and the knowledge that they would soon be together. 'I'm getting married soon. We're emigrating. At the end of this month.'

It was as if a rain cloud had settled directly over Madam's head, hovering ominously until it sensed the best moment to burst upon her.

*'You're leaving at the end of the month and you don't even have the decency to hand in your notice?' she howled. 'You can't do that, girl. You simply can't. Don't you understand how difficult it is to get good staff these days?'*

Tia got up from the chair and stood mute, head down, hands folded.

'I tell you, girl, you'll give three months, like all the other staff. And you won't get a penny piece out of us unless you do.'

Sensing that she was dismissed, Tia walked downstairs slowly, feeling her anger rising because of the unfairness of it all.

'What on earth was all that about?' Miss Thompson asked.

'I'm getting married,' Tia said. 'Madam doesn't want me to leave.'

The housekeeper kept on stirring the beef broth she was cooking for her and Farquharson's supper. 'Don't mind her, girl. Just come back tomorrow as usual.'

Tia shook her head. 'It isn't worth it, Miss Thompson. She says I've got to give three month's notice and I won't get a penny piece if I don't.'

The housekeeper's face hardened. 'You come back tomorrow, girl. She could sue you for breach of contract if you don't.'

Tia walked home in driving snow, thinking that it did not

matter whether she went to work or not, the few days left made no difference. Marcus would be back by the end of the month. Until then, she had nothing better to do.

The feeling of dread struck her the next day, as she was polishing the silver tops of the crystal scent bottles that adorned Madam's dressing table. The mistress was in the drawing room, having coffee with a friend; Tia was alone upstairs doing work that she usually enjoyed because she loved to watch the changing colours when light split into its spectrum as it struck the angled edge, almost like a diamond but not quite so bright. Madam had a matching suite of diamond earrings and a brooch that sparkled with a fire all of their own; she had told Marcus how pretty they were and he had said, '*Galach* diamonds, *ban-righ*, there isn't a diamond that's anywhere as near as beautiful as you.'

She was smiling to herself as she worked, humming a tune as she buffed the metal to a bright shine. Then, all of a sudden, the bottle was on the floor and a shock as sharp as lightning ran through her from head to foot. For a moment she did not move as the perfume spilled on to the carpet; with the fire blazing in the hearth, the air became thick and smelt sickly. Bile rose into her throat; she did not swallow until its bitter taste suffused her mouth and threatened to spill out.

*If someone you love dies, you know it in your soul.*

In that moment she knew that Marcus was gone.

Within another she was cursing herself for a superstitious fool, opening the window to rid the room of the perfume smell and beating the air to make it clear more quickly.

She remembered the terror of the fishermen's wives from her childhood; the fear that shadowed the whole island when a bad storm struck while the boats were out. Many years before, a storm had taken all the men of a village in South Uist; in the islands, memories were long and imagination vivid, there were wives who had lost their minds during the wait to find out if their men were dead or alive.

Marcus could not die; he was much too alive to die.

Fleetingly she wondered if she and Marcus were being greedy, if it was sinful to want enough to make a comfortable start in their new life together before the bell rang downstairs and she closed the windows quickly and hurried down to see what it was that the mistress wanted next.

As she crept silently down the stairs in Mrs Anderson's the next morning she noticed that the landlady's light was on, though it was before five o'clock and she was not usually up by then. When she reached the door it opened wide and the landlady beckoned her inside.

'Sit down, lass,' she said, pressing a glass into her hands.

There was a man standing before the fire in a uniform just like Marcus's.

'Take a sip, Tia,' Mrs Anderson urged her.

Tia drank and gagged at once; though she had tasted whisky before she did not like it.

'Mrs Cameron,' the man said, 'I'm so very sorry. . .'

'This is Hector MacKenzie,' Mrs Anderson said, 'He works with Marcus, ye ken.'

'No,' Tia said.

'I'm sorry, Mrs Cameron,' he said, 'but I have to tell you that your husband is dead.'

'How can he be?' she asked him. 'He's on his way home. I know his route. He was due to leave New York this morning.'

'Mrs Cameron, he was killed in an accident at the pier in New York.'

'How do you know that? You can't know that.'

He squatted down on his haunches and took her hand.

'Mrs Cameron, you've heard of the telegraph. We got a cable last night. I was on duty myself. I sent one back for confirmation and that came just an hour ago. I made certain myself. I wish to God I was wrong.'

'He said *Lady Eilean* was sound. He gave me his word.'

'Mrs Cameron, Tia, the *Lady* is sound. It was an accident at the quayside that killed him, nothing at all to do with the ship.'

Tia snatched her hand away. 'How dare you touch me? *Don't you dare touch me!*'

She began to cry then, but the tears would not come so she could not weep; she just sat there rocking in her chair, making a sound like an animal in pain.

'Take a drink, lass,' Mrs Anderson urged her.

Hector MacKenzie looked away; when he spoke there was

grief in his voice too. 'I knew Marcus well,' he said, 'I knew him very well. There was no man finer.'

Irrationally, she was thinking of Marcus as she had seen him last, early in the morning when she woke up to find him watching her, not wanting to wake her until he had to because he hated to disturb her sleep. He was naked and his skin smelled of his sweat and her body and, faintly, of the soap that she used to wash the sheets. His chest was covered finely with hairs that crunched slightly as she ran her fingers through them; she made circles on his stomach for a moment before she moved on top of him and kissed the tip of his nose as she felt him tense to her. He sighed deeply as she arranged her body on top of his. They had made love quickly, too quickly, because he had to rise as soon as it was over. She wanted to get up too, to make a breakfast for him or at least a pot of tea, but it was very, very early and he made her stay abed. She had fallen asleep again, just as he left; he had almost, but not quite, broken his promise never to leave her sleeping, to always wake her to say goodbye.

'I'll take you home,' Hector MacKenzie said.

She shook her head; she had no home, beyond the room she shared with Marcus.

'Lass's shocked,' Mrs Anderson said.

'I've to get to work,' she murmured.

'Nay, lass. I'll go around, tell 'em ye've been bereaved. Home's the best place fir ye, at a time like this.'

'You don't understand,' she said, 'I'm having a baby.'

'Oh, lassie, lassie. Time'll come when ye'll be glad o' a wean.'

She raised her head and looked at the landlady. 'How can I be, when Marcus is dead?'

Mrs Anderson bit her lip so hard that it bled, then went to Tia and tried to hold her, but she pushed her away. 'Home's the best place fir ye,' she said again; Tia was wondering how to explain to them about her father when she remembered her grandmother and realised that she could go there. Her thoughts were not formed but jagged, little stab wounds inside her head. She did not have the will to argue or to explain.

'Yes,' she said. She could go to her grandmother's; she would understand.

'I'll pack a bag fir ye,' Mrs Anderson said.

She turned to Hector MacKenzie. 'How did Marcus die?'

'In an accident at the quayside.'

'But how?'

'That's all I know, Mrs Cameron. There was an accident and he was killed.'

'I need to know how.'

He turned away. Tia began to sob quietly; an image of Marcus's body flitted across her mind and she shook with shock as she imagined his injuries. Hector MacKenzie coughed and handed her a handerchief, which she brushed away. The tears felt warm against her skin. In her mind she was peeling the hours back until yesterday, the moment she had sensed his death, wishing that she could go back to before the accident happened, wishing that she could make it not have happened. There was a clock in the room which ticked endlessly, seconds that seemed to fly away with her love. At that moment she did not care for herself or for her unborn child, only for Marcus.

As if in a waking dream she went with Hector MacKenzie to the docks and boarded a ferry with him. He booked a cabin for her, but she stood on deck gazing at the grey of the River Clyde. She did not cry. Inside her was a yawning emptiness that soaked up her tears. She did not believe it yet. Marcus's death seemed like a bad dream; she would wake up from it in a moment. Hector tried to talk to her, but in a very small voice she told him she had nothing to say.

When the ferry reached the open sea MacKenzie threw a blanket around her shoulders and then, very gently led her to the cabin below decks where she fell into a deep sleep, after she drank a little of the sleeping draught that he got from the ferry captain.

When she came to, she saw the islands coming closer. It was as if the dream that had started when she left with Marcus was unwinding itself; that the months of her marriage had never been.

The ferry drifted into Lochmaddy harbour, the sea quiet all of a sudden.

'No,' she said, 'I must go to Benbecula.'

Hector MacKenzie had been talking to the ferry captain, who turned away as MacKenzie spoke to her. 'Mrs Cameron, Tia, I'm sorry, but your grandmother's dead.'

She shook herself and shrugged, made no move to argue when he asked directions at the pier and then paid a man who had a cart to take her to her village.

'Mr McKenzie . . .' she said, when the cart stopped outside her cottage.

'You'll be all right now,' he said.

The door opened and her mother took her into her arms.

Tia tried to speak, but could only manage a murmur.

'Hush, pet,' her mother said, as she led her in and settled her in a chair by the fire.

'Marcus is dead,' she said.

'I know, pet. The line sent a telegram to his folks,' Tia's mother said, as she wrapped a blanket around her. 'You sleep now, don't worry about a thing.'

She sensed her father's presence as she woke up. He was standing there, glowering over her. Her mother was cooking; the smell of bread filled the cottage.

'The prodigal has returned,' he said gruffly.

'Sorley . . .' Her mother touched his arm and whispered something; he turned away and went to the basin to wash his hands.

When the meal was served her mother led Tia to the table like a child. She sat down and stared at the food before her as her father said a prayer of thanks. There was a plate of potatoes with a little salt herring, a slice of bread with a little precious butter. Her mother was looking at her anxiously. 'Try to eat something, pet.'

Tia picked up the bread, but as it touched her lips she gagged. She was still exhausted; too tired and too shocked to eat.

Her father glared at her.

'Never mind, pet.' Her mother lifted the plate to take the food away, but her father stopped her. 'Janet . . .'

'Can you not see the girl's ill, Sorley?'

'It is no wonder, the things she has done.'

'There's time enough to talk about it tomorrow.'

'*This is my house, woman! I will talk when I want to.*'

Janet looked at Tia, as if beseeching her not to argue with him. Sorley MacIain got up and put his hands in his pockets, began to pace the length of the room. 'Do not ever think,' he said, 'that you are not welcome in this house. The prodigal is aye welcome, as Our Father says. But you have to repent, my girl. You had the chance of a good man and you refused him on a whim to run away with a papist. You will not get the chance again and you have yourself to thank for it. You must beg the forgiveness of Our Lord for what you have done.'

Tia's head began to swim, the figure of her father blurred and wavered.

'You will stay within the village, from now on. There will be no gallivanting for you, my girl. Mary is dead now, bless her soul; it was not her that led you astray but, by God, she took the blame herself . . .'

'Father, Mary liked Marcus. She said he was a good man.'

'*How dare you make it worse by lying!*'

'I'm not lying, Father.'

'Silence!' he roared. 'You will not speak until you are spoken to, girl. Not until you learn the difference between the truth and a lie. You will stay here with us and follow our bidding. You will never leave this village. If you so much as set foot on that causeway to the south, I will drive you out myself, God forgive me for it.'

'I do know the difference between the truth and a lie,' she said quietly.

'You will ask the forgiveness of our parish, and particularly the Reverend. He is a good man, but you tested him sorely.'

'That is a lie . . .'

'Silence, girl! You are ignorant, still a child. You ignored the commandments of Our Lord, and look where it got you. A fine mess it is that you are in now. No good man would take on a wife like you, a fornicator and a blasphemer and God knows what else . . .'

'I do not want another man . . .'

'Silence!'

'You see, I loved, I love Marcus. I am his wife.'

'*You are nothing, girl. In this household, the man of that name does not exist. You are the wife of no one; you are just a foolish girl who has sinned and who now must pay the price for it.*'

'Father, I am going to have Marcus's baby.'

His eyes narrowed. 'No bastard child will disgrace this house.'

Tia got up shakily. 'To hell with you and your house, Father.'

She did not see the blow coming until it was too late and she was reeling and her mother was clutching at her father's arm and begging him not to hit her again. He struggled with Janet, tried to throw her off so that he could take off his belt and give Tia the beating she deserved. She lay on the earthen floor, stunned for a moment before her mother's screams got through to her and she struggled out of the house and ran into the biting wind. 'That is the trouble with her,' Sorley was roaring, 'there is nothing wrong with the brat that a good beating would not put right.'

Tia leaned against the outer wall to catch her breath as a sharp pain tore at her side. Crazily, her childhood flashed before her, the time when she was very young, too young for a beating, but her brothers were beaten when they had been late for church because a ship had been wrecked up the coast and they had gone beachcombing with some friends. Donald was beaten first, until he wept, but afterwards he could stand up straight as her mother led him away to clean the weals on his back; her father turned on Hugh next and beat him senseless. Her mother came back and fell on Hugh, weeping, then told Sorley MacIain that she swore to God she would leave him if he did that again. 'Ach, woman, hold your tongue,' Sorley had said then. 'You have nowhere to go so do not even be thinking it.' Her mother shook her head. 'I have, too, Sorley, and don't you ever forget it. *If you ever do anything like that again I'll go to my sister Anna's and you'll never see me again.*'

It had meant nothing to Tia at the time, but it meant something now as she listened to her father's rage and her mother's soft voice trying to coax him back to sanity.

She understood now the harried look that constantly shaded her mother's face, the despondent fall of her shoulders; there was no love in their marriage and there hadn't been for years. The only tie left was one of obligation, and convenience on her father's part.

The wind cut into her tears, stinging her skin. She shivered and drew her shawl around her to begin the long walk to Lochmaddy.

Her mother caught up with her at the lazy beds, just beyond

the village boundaries. The storms had been bad that year, there was hardly any soil left and for a moment she wavered when she thought of her mother carrying creel after creel of peat and seaweed to replenish the earth.

'Tia,' her mother said, and then she stopped.

'Don't worry, Mama,' she said softly.

'He wouldn't hit you again. I wouldn't let him. He would have to kill me first. I told him that.'

'You know I can't stay, though.'

Janet nodded. 'I'd come with you, pet.'

Tia shook her head. 'You've things to do here.'

She rubbed her hands together. 'There's always something to do.'

'Mama, I . . .'

'What, dearest?'

'Mama, why didn't you leave him?'

Janet shook her head, bewildered.

'Why didn't you go to Anna's, like you said you would when he beat the boys?'

Janet smiled sadly. 'I haven't her address, Tia. I lost touch with her years back. She was in Perth, but she moved south. She never wrote after that. Your father didn't know, so I used that. But I never did because I never could, and even if I could've done I'm not sure that I would've. You see, there was you, and there was the boys, and the girls were at school . . .'

Tia shook her head.

'God bless, Tia.'

'God bless, Mama.'

'Don't lose touch. Send a note to Mistress McKie at Lochmaddy Post, she'll keep it for me.'

Tia walked on through the storm as the ache in her stomach subsided, but did not quite go away. Luckily, the ferry was still there and Hector MacKenzie on board with the captain as the boilers were stoked for the voyage south. MacKenzie took one look at her and then found her a cabin, where he told her to try to sleep once he had fed her a draught of rum. She did not come to again until she was back in the city, in a taxi-cab with Hector MacKenzie on her way back to Mrs Anderson's.

The next morning she awoke as if still in a dream, until reality hit her with a shock as cold as ice. For a long while she lay in the cold room, not thinking, but letting her mind drift over the past two days.

Although Marcus was dead, she could not believe it, could not believe that he would never walk in through the door again to fold her into his arms and make her world like a fairytale brought to life by his presence.

For a moment, she felt the thought of him recede until she remembered his baby, knew that Marcus would live on through her child.

She got up, shivering, and opened the oven flue to draw heat into the room, adding some coal and then fanning the fire to bring it into flame.

She had to get on, she thought, she had to live for the child inside her. As the room warmed she rubbed her hands and then washed and dressed quickly, combing the knots out of her hair and pinning it into a chignon.

After a while Mrs Anderson knocked at her door, coming in unbidden before Tia could open it. 'I didn't mean to disturb you, lass,' she said, 'I was africht for you, you see.'

Tia smiled thinly and asked her to sit down.

'It's the room y'see,' Mrs Anderson said. 'When Marcus said ye was leaving it, I promised it to anither lad. Not that it matters, lass, I can tell them ye'll be staying on. But it's another young couple and they're with her folks the now. I'll have to tell 'em soon's I can.'

Tia thought briefly, then took her shawl from the hook. 'I'll go round to the Baillie's, Mrs Anderson, and see if I can get my job back.'

'Ach, lass, it's a bit soon yet tae be doin' that.'

'It's what I'd best do, with the baby coming. It'll mean I have a bit saved by the time it's born.'

'Ach, lass, it's the shock, but, it's such a cruel shock. I was just telling Jeannie, that's her in the next close, I was saying I was fair vexed about it, acos the two of you, you only had such a wee while thegither afore he died. Only a few days. It disnae seem right.'

'I know,' Tia said, too sharply, not that she meant to be unkind.

Mrs Anderson shook her head. 'I'm sorry, lass. I wasna thinking.'

'I'll go round to the Baillie's now, and I'll tell you what they say.'

'Aye, lass. There's no rush. It's just I've to tell they ithers.'

Miss Thompson looked stern when she opened the kitchen door to Tia's diffident knock, telling her to come in with a gesture as she went back to the bowl on the kitchen table.

'Your landlady sent a message,' she said, as Tia stood there, damp with the morning fog. 'Your father died, or something like that.'

Tia looked down. Her wedding ring was still on her finger, where it had been when MacKenzie arrived; she always kept it on her finger until just before she reached the Baillie's, pulling it off and putting it into her pocket the moment before she walked through the door. She eased it off and hid it without the housekeeper noticing.

'I'm not sure what Madam will say,' she was saying, 'I mean, you've put us all to great inconvenience by going off like that without a by-your-leave, but maybe in the circumstances she will overlook it. I don't know. I'll go and ask her once I've finished these scones.'

Tia stood still, feeling the cold seep into her bones.

Miss Thompson put down the spoon with an impatient gesture. 'Oh, for pity's sake, girl, don't stand there like that. Sit yourself down and have a cup of tea while I speak to Madam. I'll be back in a trice.'

Tia sat as bidden, but she did not drink anything.

Within moments the housekeeper returned. 'Madam's prepared to indulge you this once, she says, but you've not to do it again. She wants you to go on up now. There's a lunch today and she's getting ready for it.'

'Can I live in?' Tia blurted, thinking of the rent she would have to pay on her own and the room at Mrs Anderson's that the other couple had already been given.

Miss Thompson looked at her sharply. 'If Madam agrees, but you'll have to ask her yourself.'

Her employer welcomed her back with a smile so faint that it was almost a scowl. 'Do get a move on now, Tia. I have to leave by midday and my hair's still a mess.'

She said not a word about Tia's bereavement; Tia felt

grateful for that, because she thought if she had to deny Marcus's existence once more she would scream aloud.

Mrs Anderson started wringing her hands that evening when Tia told her that she would be living at the Baillie's household until she left to have the baby.

'Ach, lass, stay on wi' me and I'll keep an eye on ye. You shouldn't be biding with strangers, not at a time like this.'

'It's for the best,' Tia said thinly. 'I won't have to pay rent. I can save my wages.'

'But Marcus left ye provided fir, lass.'

She couldn't even bear to think of him in terms like that. 'I want to work for a bit,' she said quickly. 'It uses up the time, you see.'

'Ach, lass, ye'll stay in touch, mind? Come roun' when ye've time aff? I've a wee room ahind the stairs, ye kin hae that when the bairn comes.'

Tia smiled thinly. 'I've a while to wait yet.'


It was the following morning when she realised that the pain in her stomach had not gone, that it was getting worse rather, drumming at her insides with a pulsing intensity. She was in the bathroom, clearing the washhand basin of its debris of scum and strands of hair. For a moment, she felt quite faint, then she regained her balance and carried on.

'You look very white,' Madam said as Tia struggled with the stays of her corset. 'I hope you're not sickening for something. Mind you, I suppose you've had a bit of a shock.'

Tia pursed her lips tightly. 'I'm fine, Madam. It's a very cold day.'

The Baillie's wife looked at the blazing fire in the hearth and shrugged.

By early afternoon the ache had become a pain that stopped her from eating the meal Miss Thompson had cooked. Just as the housekeeper opened her mouth to chide her, Tia stood up, clutched her stomach and raced for the staff privy set into the wall just outside the kitchen door. When she lifted her skirts she saw the blood rushing down her legs. As she lost consciousness and sank to the tiled floor she wondered if anyone would find her before she bled to death.

'My God,' the housekeeper said a few minutes later, when

she had come to look for Tia and saw the blood seeping from under the door that was wedged tightly shut.

'Oot the way, Jessie,' the chauffeur said, as he sent the lad for the jemmy he kept in the garage.

She rung her hands as he began to pummel the door, hitting it several times with a sickening thud before it gave way and they saw Tia lying there, as white as the winter sky.

'Jaisus,' the chauffeur said.

'The mess,' Miss Thompson said, 'oh, my goodness, what am I to do with the mess?'

'Ring the bluidy doctor, for God's sake, Jessie. An' tell him to ca' the hospital. Puir wee lass's bleeding. Can ye no see, she's bleeding tae death?'

A few hours later, in a side room of the Rottenrow Hospital, a doctor looked at the pasty figure of the woman in the bed before him. Two nurses were clearing up his instruments; the sister stood beside him as, very slowly, he shook his head.

'I'm afraid,' he said, carefully, 'she's lost too much blood.'

The sister raised her eyebrows. 'I've seen worse bleeds than this survive, Doctor.' She had many years' experience on him and was a hospital legend in her own way.

'Well, yes,' the doctor said, thinking of the way the patient had struggled when he had begun to examine her, scratched at him like a wildcat until a nurse had grabbed each hand and held her down whilst another cut her clothes off. It wasn't the struggling that worried him, but rather the way she had given in so easily, the way she suddenly seemed to give up as a vacant look came into her eyes. A woman who haemorrhaged usually didn't know where she was and often struggled like that; in a way, it was better to struggle and survive than meekly give in. The doctor had become used to examining women but he knew that the women he examined were not used to him; he understood that and sometimes hated the things he had to do to help women like this, who came into hospital suddenly in the throes of a miscarriage that was more usually the result of a botched abortion. 'I think,' he said, 'we should get in touch with her relatives.'

'If we can,' the sister said. 'She was working as a maid. They didn't seem to know much about her.'

'Get in touch with them,' he said, 'find out as much as you can.'

The sister went into her office and rang the Baillie's household, where a shocked Miss Thompson answered the phone.

'I really don't know very much about her,' she said, when the sister asked about Tia's family. 'She lived locally, but I'm not sure exactly where.'

'You must have her address,' the sister said.

'What is it that's wrong?' Miss Thompson asked.

'She's very ill. We need to reach her family.'

'Well, I don't know about that. She was just back after someone had died, her father, I think. The doctor said it was a miscarriage. He was asking her if she'd tried to do something but she didn't say. She was that sick, you see.'

'She's very ill,' the sister said again. 'We need to get her family to her, if we can find them.'

'Well, you see, this is a good household. The Baillie's got a position, as you know. It wouldn't do for there to be any scandal.'

'There is no scandal,' the sister said, impatiently, 'just a young girl who's very close to death.'

'Oh, I see. Well, I don't know how I can help you. She did tell me where she lived, but I've forgotten. She just came in to help out, you see. It was Madam who took her on.'

'You must know something,' the sister persisted.

'Well, yes, I'm just trying to think. Her name's Tia MacLeod and she's sixteen years old. She lives in the tenements along the road, I could send the chauffeur round there to try to find out.'

'If you could,' the sister said, 'but please hurry.'

'Oh, wait a minute,' Miss Thompson said, 'I have her reference, of course. You could contact them. If I remember, it was a good house where she worked last.'

The sister waited as the housekeeper hunted through the kitchen drawer for Tia's reference, then she carefully took down the name and address read out to her.

# *Chapter Seven*

*T*ia perceived the sun first of all, the vigorous energy with which it pierced the clouds, so bright that it burned her eyes; she blinked several times before her pupils adjusted and she could keep her eyes open and watch the specks of dust trapped in the glare.

She felt light, so light that she could have been floating on the air herself. It was a strange feeling, neither well nor unwell, but somewhere in between, without pain, but without feeling either.

For a moment her mind hovered, before it settled on the memory of her blood on the privy floor, the wailing of Miss Thompson as the chauffeur hammered at the door and the wood splintered. After that, she remembered moving or being moved as a bell rang sharply, then the terrible sensation of assault as her legs were roughly prised apart and a stranger's hands started to prod her there. She had screamed then, struck out until strong hands had clasped her limbs and a kind voice explained that they would not hurt her, that they were only trying to help. The same voice had asked her if she had tried to abort her baby; appalled, she had screamed that she wanted her baby, that her baby was the only thing she had left. She became still when the voice told her that she would have to if she did not want to lose her child, herself as well.

Tia knew nothing of the lowland doctors; she was as scared of them as she had been of the old woman in the next village who cast healing spells (who the other children said was a witch as well), yet she heard that they could achieve great things, miracles even. Her last thought was no more formed than a simple prayer that they would work a miracle on her child.

The dreams started then, the strange, vivid images that ran through her mind like a cinema film replayed constantly, jaggedly, from beginning to end and then back again. At first, the dreams frightened her, until she met Marcus again, and Mary. They were standing together on the other side of a river as she was struggling in the shallow waters just beyond the bank. She had been drowning but then she surfaced and caught her breath again and began to strike out towards Marcus when he shouted and waved her back to the safety of the land, where she lay, exhausted, as he called out to her and wished her farewell. Her own voice screamed 'no!' as his insisted, then Mary's gentle call rang out over his, telling her that she had life yet to live, that she could not choose to leave it. His image faded then, but his voice stayed with her, at the edge of her dreams, easing her through the hinterland between death and life. Now she remembered the dream that had ended with her waking, in which he told her that he had to leave her now, but he would never leave her really, that he would be with her always, even if she could not see or feel him.

'You must promise,' he said.

'Promise what?' she whispered.

'Never mourn me,' he said, 'You must not mourn me. You have your life still. You must go on living and you must go on loving. If you stop living, I will not forgive you.'

'But I love you,' she murmured. 'I only love you.'

'As I love you, *ban-righ*. My love is yours forever. I promise you, we will meet again.'

'*Marcus, I love you,*' she screamed. '*I am going to have your child.*'

He shook his head slowly, kindly, as he touched her brow. 'Our child has to come with me, *ban-righ*. So it is written. But you must promise me.'

'What?' she asked thickly.

'To let yourself heal. You can grieve, but not forever. Do not mourn me. Never mourn me. Just thank God for being able to give me what you did.'

'I promise,' she said.

The dream had faded then; try as she might she could bring neither the sound of his voice nor his image back.

Tia sensed the sister's kindness as she finished washing her face and dried it gently with a touch so light that it felt like being brushed with a feather. She opened her mouth to say something. Sister Aitken put her finger to her lips.

'Don't try to talk yet, Miss MacLeod. It'll be a while before you're able.'

'Tia,' she croaked in Gaelic, 'my name's Tia.'

'Lass, you'll have to try and remember you're in the lowlands now,' Sister Aitken said, 'I'm afraid the Gaelic means nothing to most of us.'

Tia smiled weakly.

'You've been in hospital for over three months, Tia. You've been very ill, but you're going to get better now.'

A nurse brought a tray of malted milk and toast as the sister settled her in a valley she made of the pillows and told her gently that she must try to drink and eat.

It was only afterwards, when the nurse was brushing the crumbs from the bedsheets, that she felt the hollowness inside her. 'My baby,' she whimpered, as the nurse pursed her lips and went to fetch the sister.

The sister grasped her hand firmly. 'I'm afraid you lost your child, my dear.'

'No . . .' Tia murmured.

'There was nothing to be done. You had already lost it by the time you reached us. The best we could do was to save you.'

There was a blankness in her mind then, an emptiness that went way beyond the boundaries of grief as if no pain could touch her because she no longer had the capacity to feel. Marcus was dead and so was his baby; there was no one and nothing else to be loved who would ever love her.

'Oh, Marcus,' she sobbed, 'where are you now?'

In the evening Sister Aitken came again, closing the curtains around her bed and then sitting down on the chair beside it.

'Are you able to talk, Tia?'

Tia nodded.

'I couldn't find your relatives.'

'I have none,' she said.

'You see, that reference, the reference you gave to Miss Thompson. The people there had never heard of you.'

Tia smiled weakly. 'It was my husband. He wrote it out when I needed it to get paid. They told me I wouldn't get paid without it.'

'The people you worked for, the Baillie and his wife, they got very upset when they discovered the reference was false.'

Tia turned away. 'There was nothing else I could do.'

The sister brushed her cheek gently. 'Your husband, where is he now?'

'He was killed in an accident on the quay at New York. Just before I came in here.'

'How long had you been married?'

'Nearly six months.'

Sister Aiken gasped. There was nothing else she could say.


Two weeks later, Tia was well enough physically to be moved to the hospital annexe, where recuperating patients spent a week or two before being discharged.

The sister watched her go with a heavy heart. She knew that her recovery was only superficial, that Tia had sustained a deep wound to her psyche that was still raw. The problem for the sister was that she had only so much time and so many patients; there were now two in the ward just as ill as Tia had once been.

'God bless, my dear,' she said, as Tia started shakily along the corridor on the arm of a nurse. 'I'll come to see you if I have a minute.'

Just then, a doctor called for her to help him. A patient just admitted had begun to bleed again.


Tia perceived the change of the seasons when she saw the green on the trees in the grounds and heard the cuckoo's call at dawn. She was shocked at the time that had passed, but still too weak to do anything but meekly comply with the nurses who cared for her. The patients in the annexe were fed like Christmas Geese on a daily menu that started at six in the morning when cocoa was served with toast and jam, through an enormous breakfast, dinner, tea and supper until ten at night when cocoa and more toast was served again. Tia was the only charity case amongst them, the others all had a family and a home to go to at the end of their stay and the atmosphere was of happy calm. She didn't know it then, but the only reason Tia was there at all was because Sister Aitken had adamantly refused to let her be put out on the streets.

After ten days the ward sister of the annexe decided that Tia was well enough to go home. She walked up to Tia, who was sitting in a chair in the conservatory one afternoon, lazily watching a bee dine on the flowers growing outside.

'I'm afraid, Miss MacLeod, it's time for you to leave us.'

Tia smiled vacantly.

'You have to go home.'

Tia's smile faded, replaced by a frown. 'My clothes,' she said, 'the clothes I was wearing when I came here. Can I have them please?' The thought had been gnawing at her for a while, it wasn't the clothes but the wedding ring in the pocket, she wanted that, needed to feel it on her finger again.

'Oh, dear me, I really don't know what became of them. You miscarried, didn't you? I will ask, my dear, but I fear they'll've been put in the incinerator. They would've been ruined with all the blood.'

A single tear formed and began to roll down Tia's cheek.

'You mustn't worry,' the sister said, 'I'll get you some from the hospital store. Now, your family. You must have one, though Sister Aitken didn't manage to find them.'

'My husband's dead,' Tia said.

'But you must have a family, dear. Everyone has a family.'

Tia said nothing.

After a moment the sister got up impatiently and went back to her office. 'We'll have to get Dr Gunnerson to see that one,' she said, 'I don't think she's right in the head. I don't know what Christina Aitken's playing at, sending her to me. There's no amount of convalescence that'll make a lunatic see sense.'

Tia did not even notice the change in the nurses after that, the impatience in their manner as they attended to her, the way they hardly cared when she was clad in a motley assortment of clothes from the hospital store that made her look like a scarecrow or even a witch.

Two days later she was ushered into a consulting room and seated on a chair opposite a man with a shock of untidy white hair and a penetrating gaze. Looking down at herself then, she felt emotion for the first time in ages; she was ashamed of the way she looked, the way she walked clumsily in shoes too big for her and the way the sleeves of her blouse were frayed at the cuffs.

She looked up at the man, whose expression did not falter, but who had noted every nuance of hers.

'How are you, Miss MacLeod?' he asked.

She shook her head.

'Are you well?'

Tia said nothing.

'Do you feel ill, then?'

Tia looked out of the window, saw a cloud that passed over the sun and wondered when the rain would begin to fall.

'Miss MacLeod!' The man's voice was louder this time, not a shout but one that demanded attention nonetheless. 'You can hear me, can't you? You're not deaf?'

He already knew the answer because he had watched the way she reacted when he raised his voice.

'I'm not deaf, Mister . . .'

'Dr Irvine,' he said gently. 'Well, now we've established that you can hear me, can you tell me how you feel?'

'I was thinking,' she said softly, 'when you asked me at first, I was thinking that I did not feel well, and then when you asked if I felt ill, I was thinking that I don't feel ill, either. I was just wondering how to tell you how I felt.'

He opened the folder of records, although he had already read it before she came in. 'English isn't your native language, is it? Where is it that you come from?'

'North Uist.'

'I see. And you were working as a maid before you came here. You miscarried. That's why you were brought here. You were very ill indeed and then you got a fever. All told, you've been in hospital a day or two short of five months.'

Tia shivered. He noted that, but did not acknowledge it.

'You are a single woman living away from home, that is, away from your parents' home.'

She shook her head. 'I am a married woman. Or I was a married woman. My husband was killed a few days before . . .'

The doctor sat back in his chair. After a minute of silence, he asked her if she could tell him any more.

'Marcus and I, we got married in September. My father didn't want me to marry him. So I left home.'

'There's nothing wrong with that.'

'We were living here. Marcus was at sea. I didn't need to

work but I got a job in a house. You see, he was away and I had nothing to do all day.' She smiled at the memory. 'I'd never worked before. It was very strange at first, but I got used to it. You see, we were going to emigrate. Our passage was booked. Marcus was on his last trip when he, when he . . .'

She faltered, then paused for a moment. 'One of his friends came. Hector MacKenzie. He said Marcus'd been killed. He took me home. He took me to my father's house. But I couldn't stay there, not if I was going to have Marcus's baby. My father, he hated Marcus, you see.'

'Why?'

'Because . . . My father is a Free Presbyterian. Marcus was Catholic.'

'I see.'

She shook her head, as a vacant expression came over her face again.

'So you're really Mrs MacLeod.'

'No, I'm Mrs Cameron.'

The doctor pulled a sheet of paper from his folder. 'You gave a reference to the household where you worked.'

Tia had to think for a moment before she realised what he was talking about, and then she became animated again. 'Oh, yes. When I went to see about the job, they asked me for this and that and I was just new to the lowlands, you see, I didn't know what they were talking about. I said I'd worked before, but I'd only worked with my mother on the croft and on the weaving. Then they gave me the job so long as I gave them the reference; they wouldn't give me my wages until I'd given it to them. Marcus wrote it for me.'

'Did you know that a reference is supposed to be from your last employer?'

She blushed. 'I realised that later. I wasn't sure at the time.'

A nurse opened the door. 'Dr Irvine, Dr Arthur told me to remind you you're due at the meeting.'

'I know,' he said tersely.

'It's already begun,' she said.

'I know that, Nurse. You can tell them I'll be with them momentarily.'

The door closed again.

'Mrs Cameron,' he said, 'can you give me the address where

you lived with your husband? You see, all we have is the address of the house where you were working.'

'It's just round the corner from there.'

'You don't know the address?'

'It's Mrs Anderson's.'

'And the name of the shipping line your husband worked for?'

Tia thought for a moment; the name had escaped her. 'It's the one that has blue and green funnels. It used to be Rankine's but Allan Rankine sold it. I don't know what it's called now.'

'I know the one you mean,' he said. 'I'm afraid we'll have to finish for now, Mrs Cameron. I'll come to see you again in a day or two.'

He watched the way she walked back to the ward, so slow that she seemed like an old woman.

'You'll take her off our hands then?' the sister asked him.

He shook his head adamantly. 'There's nothing wrong with her beyond grief and the kind of shock that follows an illness like hers. She is suffering from mild memory loss because of it. Her memory will return in a while, with care.'

'But she can't stay here for ever.'

'I'll not admit her to the asylum, Sister Smith. If I did, she'd never recover at all.'

'What do I do, then?'

'Give her another day or two. She'll begin to get her memory back if she's allowed peace and quiet. Her husband was a sailor, chances are he left her well provided for. I'll get my clerk to find out the details.'

The sister's eyes narrowed as she watched the doctor stride along the path to the main block. When she had called the asylum, she'd asked for Dr Gunnerson; Dr Gunnerson, the deputy superintendent, would not have made trouble like that. He would have taken the girl in without troubling himself with her nonsense. The problem was, now that Dr Irvine had seen her, the chance was gone. Irvine, pedantic and prosaic, was younger than Gunnerson but the trouble was, he was Gunnerson's boss. The sister turned away, pursing her lips tightly.

A little while later, a nurse came from Sister Aitken's ward. 'I'm very sorry, Sister Smith, but Miss MacLeod's skirt had to be cut off her and so were her bloomers. They were ruined. But I've got her blouse and shawl and the boots she was wearing.'

'I suppose it's better than nothing,' the sister said tersely.

She stood watching as the nurse gave the things to Tia, shaking her head when Tia burst into tears when she saw her old boots.

A few days later Sister Smith was sitting in her office when the telephone rang. She did not catch the name, but her interest quickened when she realised that the caller was Tia's former employer.

'You see,' the voice said, 'I was talking to the Baillie the other night about it, and he was saying that despite what she did it really would not be Christian for us to desert her. No doubt, the girl had her reasons after all, and she was a willing worker during the time she was with us.'

'You'll take her back, then?'

'Oh, no, I . . .'

'There's absolutely no reason why she cannot return to work. She has been ill, but she's perfectly well now. In fact, she would be a better worker now, because she's been chastened by the experience. We see a lot of her type here. Once they learn their lesson, they usually learn it well.'

'Oh, no, you don't understand. You see, the child she was carrying, the bastard that she had aborted, she tried to pin the blame on our son! I mean, I was outraged when I heard about it from the housekeeper, mortified isn't the word for it, I was appalled! And she was so sly the way she went about it, she didn't actually say that he had, you know, interfered with her, just that he had touched her when he passed her on the stairs. I mean, really! No, we certainly can't have her back, definitely not. It would be a most inadequate arrangement. But the Baillie suggested that we could hand her over to the Society and let them take care of her.'

'The Society?'

'The Vigilance Society. The Baillie's a trustee, you know. He's prepared to make the arrangements. Indeed, he insists that we help you out. There is a woman with a house in the Gorbals who takes these girls in and makes sure they don't get themselves into any more trouble.'

'Oh, well, that would be very good. We would be very grateful to you for all your trouble.'

'Oh, dear me, it's no trouble at all.'

'Who shall I contact to make the arrangements?'

'The Baillie will do that. I'll talk to him now and he will arrange to have her collected. I take it the city will pay her hospital fees?'

'I imagine so. The girl's penniless, herself.'

It was strange, the way Tia felt when she saw her old boots, the boots that Marcus had given her, and her own blouse and the shawl her mother had crocheted in the winter as they sat by the fire. At first she was speechless; as the nurse gave them to her she tried to thank her but could only manage a sob. 'Sister sends her good wishes,' the nurse said, 'she'll try to come to see you when she's got a minute, but we've been very busy on the ward.'

Tia smiled through her tears.

'I'm sorry,' the nurse said, 'your skirt was ruined. We had to burn it.'

'My wedding ring,' she murmured.

The nurse frowned. 'There's nothing in the safe. I didn't think you had one.'

'It was in the pocket. The pocket of the skirt. You see, the people, they didn't know I was married. I used to put it in my pocket at work.'

'I'm so sorry,' the nurse said.

'Don't be.' Tia managed to smile. 'You see, my husband bought these boots for me. They mean more to me than the ring.'

'I'll ask, but I doubt it's melted down to nothing.'

'It doesn't matter, really,' Tia said, 'you weren't to know.'

She spent the rest of the day sitting in the conservatory in an easy chair, clutching the boots to her chest as she rocked gently. In a way, she was almost happy, though she knew that she had no reason to be happy, that she might never have a reason to be happy again. It was enough to have her boots, to have something to remind her that Marcus had loved her. She had first to remember him before she could grieve for him; since she had come back to full consciousness she had been afraid that he had never existed at all.

*

The lady from the Vigilance Society came to collect Tia in the middle of the next morning, just after elevenses had been served. With her was the minister of her church, who knew of the good work Mrs Gordon did with fallen women and had volunteered to drive her to and from the hospital. He was concerned sometimes for her safety, what with her taking in the dregs from the streets, but she was a hardy soul and a staunch Christian so instead of persuading her to take on less trying works, he gave her all the help he could. He waited in an anteroom as the sister led her onto the ward, catching a glimpse as the door opened of a woman in a scandalous state of undress. He closed his eyes reflexively, opening them again only after he heard the door closing and muttered a quick prayer to the Lord to shield him from the Devil's temptation, a temptation he too often felt.

For a moment Mrs Gordon stood gazing at Tia, who was sitting in a chair apart from the others, gazing into the distance with a pair of boots on her knee.

'She seems strange,' she said.

'Oh, she's been fully examined. There's nothing wrong with her that time won't heal, the doctor says. She certainly isn't an asylum case.'

'She's fully fit?'

The sister hesitated. 'She's still very weak. She lost a lot of blood with the miscarriage and afterwards she had a fever.'

'Did she abort herself?'

'Apparently not. Apparently she wanted the child, though only the Lord knows why.'

'I don't take in girls who abort themselves. I made that quite clear to the Baillie.'

'I think you can be assured that she didn't.'

'You *think*?'

'You can never be sure of these things. The doctor said there was no sign at all that she had tampered with herself in any way.'

'I would want to be sure.'

The sister bridled. 'You can be sure, Madam. We have a legal responsibility to make a report in these circumstances if there's any suspicion at all. There is none. Her demeanour is not that of a girl who aborted herself.'

'Very well then. I suppose we had better get on with it.'

They walked over to Tia, who took a moment or two to notice them.

'Come on now,' the sister said, 'get your boots on. They're not ornaments, you know.'

Tia hesitated.

'You're leaving us,' the sister explained. 'This kind lady's agreed to take you in.'

'But Dr Irvine said I had to see him again.'

'Tush, girl, you'd best not bother with Dr Irvine. Spend too much time with him and you'd go mad in the head. You just get your boots on and go with this lady, now.'

'But I haven't seen Sister Aitken . . .'

The sister braced her hands on her waist. 'Look here, girl, you've been in this hospital long enough. Much longer than necessary. If it wasn't for Sister Aitken, you'd have been on the streets days ago.'

Mrs Gordon had been standing aloof from this exchange until tiredly Tia put on her boots and then stood shakily, wrapping her shawl around her shoulders.

'Hello, my dear,' she said, briskly. 'I'm Mrs Gordon. If you come home with me, I'll sort you out.'

Tia looked into a face as cragged as Lochmaddy bay, and eyes as blank as an eagle's.

# Chapter Eight

*T*ia hardly noticed the journey. The road was bumpy and the carriage window ajar so that wind blew in her eyes; Mrs Gordon sat talking to the minister as if she was not there. They drove through George Square and then Argyle street, which she recognised when she noticed the subway station at St Enoch's. A speck of grit blew into one eye then, forcing her to close both eyes tightly. She did not open them again until the grit was gone and they had stopped in a street of terraced houses, each smaller than the average tenement with a front door in place of the close.

'Home' Mrs Gordon said brightly. 'Well, girl, get a move on.'

'Has she aucht for me to help wi?' the minister asked.

'The girl's only got what she's standing up in, Willie.'

'I'll be off then,' he said, with a cheery wave, as Tia struggled to close the carriage door.

Mrs Gordon took out a key-ring, opening the door with one of the many keys that jangled from it, striking a discord that sounded harsh to Tia's ears, sensitised by so many months of hospital murmurs.

Throwing the door open, she barred Tia's way for a moment. 'This is a good house, girl. A Christian home for the likes of you. It's up to you what you make of it, but, mind, it's the last chance you'll get.'

Tia said nothing. She was wondering why she had been brought to this place.

'Well, girl?'

Tia sensed she had done something wrong. Deep inside, the loss of her child hurt like a knife wound, hurt beyond her grief for Marcus. She thought of Mrs Anderson, so near, yet so far away. For a moment, she hesitated, tried to find the strength to protest, but inside she was shaking. A wave of dizziness swept through her, she shivered, despite the warm air. 'I'll do my best,' she said. She would go along with this woman for a while, until she found herself again.

'I'll see you will, girl. Now, let's get you inside.'

The house was cold. Tia caught the hint of beeswax and lavender before Mrs Gordon led her into a huge kitchen, mercifully heated by an iron range.

'Seeing as you're new, I'll make the tea' Mrs Gordon said, waving her to a hard chair by the stove. 'The hospital tell me you're recovered, though I suppose it'll be a while before you're back to your best.'

Tia felt the wood of the chair cut into her bottom. Dimly, she realised that she must have lost weight; looking at her hands, she saw how pale her skin was and how the bones showed through.

'Now, they didn't tell me your first name at the hospital.'

'Tia,' she said, in a small voice.

'Tia? What sort of a name is that?'

'Tia Cameron,' she said, 'Mrs Tia Cameron.'

Mrs Gordon swung round. 'Don't you dare come like that with me, girl! They told me at the hospital your name's MacLeod.'

'I'm a widow,' Tia said, in a voice so low that the landlady did not hear her.

Mrs Gordon poured the tea into cups and then spread some bread thinly with dripping. Tia waited for her to add milk, and drank only when she realised that there would be none, nor sugar either.

'I'll just explain what's what,' Mrs Gordon said. 'In this house, you work in return for your keep. A girl's just left, so you're lucky there's a place for you. I doubt you'd get a job elsewhere, not with your record. There's another girl with me at the moment, so it won't be too hard on you. I'll keep you clad and fed. I usually let my girls have a half day off a month, but at first I like you to stay in until I know you're trustworthy. You can have the back room with Marie. She'll tell you anything else you need to know.'

'Don't I get paid?' Tia blurted.

'Paid? Of course you get paid girl. Your keep *is* your pay. Beggars can't be choosers, mind. The way you are, you're lucky to have a roof over your head at all.'

Mrs Gordon led her through to her room then, leaving the tea undrunk and the bread curling on the plate. Tia had turned very pale all of a sudden, her skin the colour and texture of tissue paper. 'I have to go to Mrs Anderson's,' she said.

'What on earth do you mean by that?'

'My things are there. Marcus's . . . my husband's things. Our marriage certificate.'

'And where is this Mrs Anderson's?'

'Not far from the Baillie's.'

'The address, girl?'

Tia though for a moment before she murmured that she did not know.

Mrs Gordon folded her arms and fixed her with a steely glare. 'You narrowly escaped being committed to the lunatic asylum, my girl, and that's where you'll go if you come with any more stories.'

'It's the truth.'

'It's all too convenient, girl. You are just old enough to be wed, but you're a widow. You have a certificate, but you don't know where. The lies trip easily off your tongue.'

Tia opened her mouth to argue, but her dizziness became worse. She leant back and steadied herself on the bed post. She was not sure what a lunatic asylum was, but she sensed that it would be dreadful. The months of illness had robbed her of her strength; she was not strong enough to argue, or to insist. She felt as if she was drifting, like a feather on the wind. Her mind felt fuzzy; she was sure that once she had known the name of the street where Mrs Anderson's was, but she could not remember it now.

Mrs Gordon simpered. 'That's right, girl. Best keep silent rather than repeat a lie.'

Tia waited until she had gone, then sank down on the bed and stared at the ceiling, wondering what on earth was going to happen next. She tried to focus her thoughts, but she felt nothing beyond the dull weight of grief. She wondered absently when her strength would return. This place would have to do until it did.

The voice punctured her dream just as it was beginning; she had only just begun to experience the warm, floating sensation of falling asleep when she was forced to wake again.

'I sez, are ye the new girl?' the girl said, as she stood at the end of the bed staring at her. 'Mind ye, ah suppose ye must be, acos you wouldn'a be here otherwise. Stupit, amn't I? Mibbe the auld bugger's richt when she sez I'm daft.' She was more of a child than a girl, stick thin and pale with dark eyes that were like sunken pools on her taut stretched skin. Her eyes were open wide, questioning, almost surprised as they stared at Tia, but they were not unkind. 'Dinny mind me,' she said after a moment, 'ah shouldn'a ask a' they questions. It's jis' the missus says ye wis tae help me wi' the tea, an' I thocht I'd best wake ye up, acos she'll be fashed wi' us both if I didna.'

Tia sat up and waited for the dizziness to cease.

'I'll put the kettle on,' the girl said. 'If ye come through when ye're ready, I'll gie ye a cup o'tea. The missus's in the front room, so the coast's clear.'

Tia shuffled through to the kitchen. 'I'm Marie,' the girl said, 'I suppose the missus telt ye a' about me.'

'Only your name,' Tia said, blowing on the mug of tea. 'My name's Tia.'

'Tia? That's pretty. I was christened Maria, but I aye git called Marie,' she said, as she finished scouring a pot.

'Are ye up tae daeing the spuds?' she asked a moment later and then, seeing the look of incomprehension on Tia's face, 'The tatties, I mean. See if ye put yer tea ahind the basin, the auld yin'll no see it if she comes ben.'

The potatoes were in a bowl on the ledge beside the sink. Tia picked up a knife and began to peel, before Marie grabbed the knife from her hands. 'Ye must'a been working wi' toffs afore. We dinna peel the tatties here. Ye jist clean 'em an' cut oot the bad bits.'

Tia smiled weakly. 'That's what we did at home.'

Marie was chopping onions and carrots to add to the mince that was searing in a pan. 'Ye see, Tia, the auld wumman, she taks in lodgers, girls fra the teaching college an' that. We does the work, cook an' keep the place clean an' the like. I wis run raggit on my own, but it'll no be sae bad, wi' the two of us.'

'Mrs Gordon said another girl just left.'

'Left? Is that whit she said? Oh, aye.' Marie's eyes turned in an expression of disbelief, but she said no more.

Once the food was cooking they laid the table in the dining

room and Marie lit the fire. 'The girls eat wi' the missus,' she said in a whisper, 'we eat in the kitchen. We dinna get meat, but we get soup an' tatties. It's no that bad.'

Tia fell into bed exhausted that night, but she could not sleep. She had no night clothes, so she went to bed in her blouse and the bloomers the hospital had given her.

'I'll see ye richt the morn,' Marie said. 'Thae girls that stay here, they're that rich, they leave guid claithes ahind. There's a chest o' stuff up the stair.'

Tia was so tired she could hardly think.

'I dinna want tae be nosy, like, but I heard the missus say ye wis in the hospital,' Marie said.

Tia was watching a sliver of street light that breached the curtains and danced like a will-o'-the-wisp against the wall. The shaft of light twisted and turned, as the curtains lifted and then settled again, moving in time with the breath of the wind. The rest of the room was dark and in the distance were the sounds of the city, the clank of the trams and the shrill whistle of boats on the river. She had not seen the river during her journey to Mrs Gordon's; she was surprised that it was close by.

'I'm sorry, I didna mean to pry.'

She looked over and saw Marie's face, her skin glowing yellow in the shadows.

'I was in the hospital. I lost my child. My husband, he died a few days before that.'

The facts of her life sounded so simple, tiny little insignificant words like 'loss' and 'death'. Though she shuddered slightly when she heard her own voice, it did not feel enough to tell it like that, she felt she should say more to fill the space left by the stark sentences that lingered like smoke in the air. She was surprised by the feeling of detachment her revelation left her with, as if she had not experienced these things but had rather observed them from a distance and felt no more than the fleeting sympathy of a stranger who watches a toddler tumble and begin to cry.

Just as she was about to fill the void, Marie's shrill voice smashed the silence into fragments that tore her quiet thoughts into tatters.

'I'm gey sorry, Tia. But why on earth did ye come here?'

Tia was thinking of her home and her father, her other home that she had shared with Marcus, of the room that Mrs Anderson had promised to keep for her when she had to give up work to care for her child. Suddenly she realised that she could not face seeing Marcus's things, the room they had shared, not yet, not now when his death seemed so unreal, so near that if she hoped and prayed hard she might wind time back like you can wind the hands of a clock back and bring him to life again. It would be so much easier if she could do that, if she could unlive the months in the hospital that seemed only moments, wake up from the bad dream that her life had become. There was too much life in Marcus for him to be truly dead.

'I mean, this is a place fir bad girls,' Marie said, 'the likes o' me. I wis bad, see?'

Tia shook her head and sighed deeply. She had felt blame ooze from the very pores of the sister in the hospital, not Sister Aitken but Sister Smith, from some of the nurses as well. To her father, sickness was a punishment for sin, yet a punishment that brought with it hope because if sin was assuaged in life it would not have to be paid for in the after life. Yet she had not sinned; the only thing that she was sure of was that. It had not been a sin to love Marcus, or to want to bear his child.

'See, I wis livin' wi' my ma,' Marie was saying, 'there wis ten o' us bairns and my da says he'd never feed us aw' here, sae he went tae Canada five years ago, wi twa o' my brithers, and he wis sending money back fir the rest o' us tae jine him. It wis only me an' my ma left when my ma died. I never kent whit tae dae, I never kent at all. I didna go tae the school, ye see, my ma took in washin' an' I used tae bide at hame tae help her or I'd gang wi' her if she went tae the houses o' the folk she wirked fir. The public health, they came and took her awa', said there wis fever but it wisnae the fever that kilt her, it wis only the flu. An efter a' that, I telt the priest I'd gang tae Canada tae my faither, but I'd no money like, so he sent me up the Magdalen to wait 'til he got it sortit. See, ye dinna hae to sin an gae to hell, ye only hae to gae tae the Magdalen. Richt bluidy hell on earth, that place.'

The word triggered something in Tia's memory; she did not know what. Her voice cut into Marie's shrill whisper. 'The Magdalen. What's that?'

Marie snorted at her ignorance. 'The Magdalen *Laundry*.

The place whaur the nuns tak' the lasses wha've been bad. Tae dae the laundry. Tae wash oot wur sin, like. Ye throw yer sin oot wi' the dirty water, ye ken?'

Tia did not answer as Marie went on: 'Ony case, I waited a while an' then when I didn' hear fra' him, I decided tae run mysel'. The polis caught me doon the docks wi'oot any money. They wis gonny send me back tae the Magdalen, but I sez I wisna a papist. Mother of God forgive me, I sez I wis a prod. Sae the polis sent me here. The polis sez I can run when I'm aulder, but ye canna let a wee lass like me oot on the streets.' She snorted again. 'I'm fifteen last April. D'ye reckon that's auld enough?'

'I don't know,' Tia said softly. 'Can't you write to your father?'

'I canna write, Tia. I canna read either. Like I sez, I bided hame tae help my ma. Never got mair'n a week at school at the time. I ken whaur my fither is, but.'

'Do you?'

'Aye. I've a wee bit paper wi' his address. I got it aff an envelope he sent tae my ma.'

'I can read, Marie,' she said slowly. 'I can write as well.'

Marie suddenly jumped out of bed and began to ease it aside, holding her fingers to her lips. Once that was done, she knelt down on the floor and began to claw at a plank of wood that after a moment squeaked and gave away. 'Thaur ye are, Tia. That's my my faither's address.'

Tia looked at the scrap of paper, then got up and pulled the curtain aside for more light. The paper was frayed, rubbed thin from being handled; it was damp as well. The writing had faded to a blur, only two lines were visible, written in a spidery, childish hand. 'Manitoba, Canada,' Tia said slowly.

Marie whooped silently and hugged her with glee.

Very gently, Tia eased her away. 'Marie, Manitoba's a big part of Canada.'

'Bit I ken whaur he is, Tia.'

'Canada's a very big country. Manitoba's the size of Scotland, maybe more.'

'But his address is there, Tia. That's the bit of paper the priest read it fra. I grabbed it back fra him when he wisna looking.'

Tia showed her the paper and pointed to the place where the writing had been. 'You can't even see the town, Marie.'

'Ach, ye kin aye find the Donnellys, Tia. At least, I ken whaur tae start.'

Tia stared at the paper for a long time, finding the outline of a W then an I and an N, the rest so blurred that no more could be read. 'Winnipeg,' she said, remembering the name from the islands, because so many emigrants had gone there. 'Or at least, somewhere with a name that begins "Win" and's in Manitoba. Winnipeg is the likeliest place.'

'See?' Marie said exultantly. 'If I ken whaur he is, I can find my da.'

'You can try,' Tia said slowly, remembering the way Marcus had teased her about her confusion in the city, thinking of the irony of her helping Marie to find her father's home.

'See,' Marie said, 'when the polis caught me at the docks, I wis nearly awa'. I didn' hae my fare, lik', I wis jis' goin' tae get on a ship and I found yin that was fir Halifax and I thocht, at least it was goin' the richt way.'

Tia smiled, remembering Marcus's stories of stowaways.

'I mean, see the yin' wi' red an' yellow funnels, they all go tae Canada. Ye jis' hide, like. Yin o'my brithers did it. It's easy.'

'You could ask the sailors.'

'That's jis' whit I did. But somebody cliped, like, and they sent fir the polis. And now I'm here, but I'll no be here for long.'

'No?'

'I'll run again, Tia. This time I willna get caught. You'll no clipe on me, Tia, will ye?'

'What?'

'Ye'll no' tell the missus whaur I've gone. Ye'll no' betray me, I mean. See, the ither girl who wis here, Ellen her name wis, she ran an' a', and she got clean awa'. I kent whaur she was headed, but I didn' tell the auld yin.'

'I won't betray you, Marie. But the priest, the priest who wrote to your father. You could ask him again.'

'Naw, I couldn'a, Tia. See, that's another bad thing I did, I stole fra' the Magdalen. Two loaves o'bread an a sack o' currants fir the cake fir the nuns' tea. I needed somethin' tae eat on the ship, see? It wis enough tae steal my food fra' them. I didn' want tae steal thaur money as well.'

Tia smiled in the darkness; Marie's hope had infected her, driven away for a while the canker of her despair.

'See when I dae run,' Marie said, 'I'll steal the auld besom's cherry cake. An' meat, if there's any tae take. It's mines, onyway. I wirk like a bluidy slave fir nigh a year, and I've no e'en had a farthing frae the auld bitch.'

Still smiling, Tia closed her eyes and drifted into a dreamless sleep.

The following morning she woke groggily before dawn to see Marie struggling into her clothes.

'Are you leaving now?' she asked, thinking of what Marie had said last night.

'Whit? Nae fear. I'll bide my time. I dinna want tae git caught again. Naw, Tia, ye've tae git up the now, acos ye've tae dae the fires and see tae the range afore breakfast at seven. I'll dae the fires if ye dae the range and see tae the hens. Ye feed them and git the eggs. The auld besom sells the eggs.' She snorted. 'She's that mean.'

Tia got up slowly and went over to the washbasin which Marie had filled with water.

'Ye're a'richt, Tia? Ye seem a bit slow.'

Tia splashed cold water on her face. 'I'm fine,' she said.

'Ye look gey wan tae me.'

The work started in earnest when Mrs Gordon came into the kitchen just after breakfast was finished, when Tia and Maria were eating their own meal of a small bowl of porridge and a wedge of bread each.

'It's time to give the house a good clean,' she said, reaching up and drawing her finger along the top of the kitchen dresser and then peering at it and wiping away the dust on her apron. 'The state of the place is disgraceful. We'll start at the top and work our way down to the bottom.'

Marie had taken Tia's bowl of porridge away, though it was only half eaten. Mrs Gordon glowered at her until she got up.

'I want every carpet in the house out and beaten,' she said, 'and once they're airing, you can start scrubbing the walls.'

Marie had filled the kettle and set it to boil. 'It'll be a minute afore the water's ready, Missus Gordon.'

'Well, while you're waiting, get up those stairs and start on the carpets.'

Sullenly, Maria walked out of the kitchen, as Tia followed her tiredly. She still had the heavy feeling that she had not quite woken from sleep.

'Auld bitch,' Marie spat, 'the place's clean's a pin.'

'Why does she want us to clean it again?'

'Acos ye're here. Cleanliness is next tae godliness an' idle hands dae the Devil's wirk. Some such guff, onyway.'

By the end of the day, though they had beaten each carpet and scrubbed the floor underneath and washed the walls also, Mrs Gordon was only partly satisfied.

'We'll do the brasses and grates tomorrow,' she said, 'and once they're done, there's the windows as well.'

Tia was too exhausted to eat the cold potatoes and bread they had been left for their evening meal. She fell asleep at the table, letting the fork drop on to her plate; she would have fallen off her chair if Marie had not been there to catch her and help her to bed.

The next morning Marie looked at her anxiously. 'Tia, ye look like a ghost. I'll tell the missus ye're ill.'

Tia pushed herself out of bed, stumbling before she managed to balance on the cold linoleum-covered floor. With an effort she smiled and said that she would manage; she had fine skin, she always looked pale.

Just after ten that morning she fainted and fell from the ladder as she was washing the windows under Mrs Gordon's demanding gaze. She had already washed them once but the landlady ordered her to do them again because of a smudge at the top.

'Get up, girl' she shrieked. 'Don't you dare start pulling your tricks on me!'

Tia heard her only dimly; with terror she realised that she could not move.

Marie rushed into the room. 'Mrs Gordon, can ye no see, the lass's ill?'

'The Devil she's ill! She's malingering, that's what!'

'Mrs Gordon, jis' look at her. There's no colour in her face, no colour at a'.'

'If she doesn't pull herself out of it in a minute, she's out of the door.'

Dimly, Tia perceived Marie facing the landlady. 'Mrs Gordon, she's sick! If ye don't ca' the doctor, I'll report ye fir cruelty!'

'You ungrateful brat! You'll do no such thing.'

'I will tae, Mrs Gordon.'

The landlady said nothing for a moment, then turned and stalked out of the room.

Marie knelt down beside Tia. 'Can ye hear me?' she whispered. 'See if ye can get yersel' tae yer feet, I'll get ye tae yer bed.'

Woozily, Tia managed to sit.

'Jis' tak yer time, Tia,' Marie said. 'An' dinna worry about aucht.'

Shortly afterwards the doctor visited and prescribed an iron tonic and a week's bed rest.

After the rest Tia did not feel well, but she felt less ill.

'I've been thinking,' Marie said, 'it's about time I wis leavin'. That is, if ye kin git by wi'oot me.'

Tia said nothing for a moment, thinking how Marie's company and constant chatter had soothed the raw edge of her pain.

'If ye canna, I can wait another year, I suppose,' Marie said.

'What will you do for money?' Tia asked her.

'Ach, I've a sixpence I found on the floor o' the kirk last Sunday. I'll manage.'

Tia was thinking of the money she had left in a box at Mrs Anderson's, that if she went to collect it then she could give Marie enough to buy some food and perhaps a few Canadian dollars as well. 'I have some, you see,' she said.

'Whit, here?'

Tia shook her head. 'At the place where I was staying. I was going to go back there and the landlady's kept my things.

'Ha! Ye'll be lucky.'

'She isn't like that,' Tia said quickly.

'What were ye thinking of, leaving money around the place?'

'I didn't need it where I was going. I lived in at the house where I worked, you see. I packed up our things and left them there. I didn't even remember it until now. You see, my husband, Marcus, he always left me a few pounds in case I needed it.'

'He wis a guid man, that Marcus of yours. Did ye no get ony money fra' the folks he worked fir?'

'I . . . I don't know, Marie. But I'll give you some money. You can't go all that way with only a sixpence.'

'Where is it, the place whaur ye lived, Tia?'

Tia stared into the darkness. 'I . . . I can't remember the address, Marie. But it's not far from here.'

'Whaur?'

Tia cleared her throat. 'It's close. It's close to the river. You could hear the river sounds at night, like you can hear them here.'

'Is it this side o' the river?'

'The other side, I think,' she said tremulously.

'That'd be Hillhead way, or Partick, mibbe. The house whaur ye wirked, that'd be Kelvinside. That'll be richt, Tia. Kelvinside's whaur a' the nobs bide.'

'It was the Baillie's house. The Baillie of the city corporation.'

'Ach, Tia, thaur's hundreds o' thae buggers. Dozens an' dozens o' them.'

Tia shivered so hard that her bed shook. 'If. . . I'll go soon's I get an hour off, Marie. I'll see you have your fare at least.'

'Ach, Tia, dinna fashe yersel' wi' me. I'll manage ma'sel'. I allus have, an' I allus will. Ye dinna mind, dae ye? Me leavin' that is?'

Tia smiled in the darkness. 'I don't mind, Marie. But I'll miss you.'

'Ach, awa' wi ye.'

Though Tia could not see her face, she sensed in the darkness that Marie was blushing.

'I'll miss ye tae, Tia. I ken ye'd no betray me.'

In the morning when she woke up, Tia sensed that Marie was gone. After checking the scullery and the outside privy, she felt Marie's bed and found it was cold. Marie must have climbed out of the window just after she fell asleep. Tia sat down on the edge of the bed; tears came to her eyes because she would miss Marie, and worry about her. She was hurt that the girl had not said goodbye; then she realised that she could honestly say that she knew nothing about it. She brushed the tears from her eye, and prayed briefly that Marie would find her family, wherever they were.

It was mid morning when Mrs Gordon found out. By rushing everything Tia had managed herself until the landlady told her to take out the coal box from the drawing room to scrub it; the box was so big that it took two to move it. Tia had to take out the coal and stack it in the grate before she managed to maneouvre it out to the yard. Mrs Gordon was in the drawing room when she got back, puffing and panting, edging the ugly big box over the floor. Mrs Gordon watched until she had it perfectly in position before she demanded to know where Marie was.

'I have to wash,' Tia said, starting for the kitchen. 'I'm sorry, but I have coal dust in my eyes.'

'Well?' Mrs Gordon demanded, as Tia splashed water on to her face from the sink. 'I asked you a question,' she said, when Tia did not answer.

Tia paused. 'She was here this morning, Mrs Gordon.'

'When?'

Tia doused her face in water.

'I'm waiting, girl.'

Tia reached for a towel to dry her eyes but Mrs Gordon grabbed her by the back of the neck and pushed her face into the sink of water, shaking her vigorously before she let go. Stunned, Tia stood for a moment as water dripped down her neck.

'*I asked you a question, MacLeod! Answer me now, or, by God, I'll have you in jail as well.*'

'Mrs Gordon, we did the breakfast. I washed up while she polished the table. We had our own food, then I said I'd go and see to the coal box. I waited a moment, then realised I could manage myself if I took the coal out first.'

'She was here a moment ago, you say. Are you sure of that?'

Tia took a deep breath. 'Quite sure, Mrs Gordon. You know yourself how long it takes to clear up after breakfast. I'd still be at it now if she hadn't helped.'

Mrs Gordon stared at her for a long time. 'Well, she can't have gone far,' she said determinedly, taking her coat from the hook just outside the kitchen door. 'Don't you set so much as a foot outside this house, girl. Mind now, you'll make it worse for her if you're disobedient as well.'

Tia waited until the door had closed and then sank down in the kitchen chair. She had already checked the cake box and found the cherry genoa that Mrs Gordon served to her lady guests, as she called the lodgers, but Marie had taken a couple of loaves and a slab of cheese. Tia had sliced the bread for breakfast very thinly, but nobody had said a word.

For a moment, she thought of running herself, until she realised that she believed Mrs Gordon's threat of jail if she did. Living in this house, she felt trapped in the lie that she had never been married, and that Marcus had never been. She was scared of confronting the lie for fear that it would triumph and the truth never come out. That would be too painful for her to face. In the strange world of the lowlands, she knew that a woman like Mrs Gordon was respected, that her word would be taken and believed against a girl like her's. Until she could find Mrs Anderson, Tia had no proof that she had ever been married, no proof that Marcus had lived. But Marie had given her hope, hope that in time she would find herself again, that her strength would return and she would be able to put things right.

Mrs Gordon came back with two policemen. 'This is the girl who shared a room with the thief,' she said.

In front of the landlady, Tia repeated her story; when they asked to speak to her alone she stood mutely in front of them, her hands nervously clasped together.

'It's nothing to us if a lass that age runs away,' one said, 'but theft's a different matter.'

'She stole nothing,' Tia said.

'Maybe you didn't see her,' the other policeman said, 'but the landlady says she's lost ten shillings from her purse.'

For a moment Tia believed them, until she realised that since Marie had left late at night she could not possibly have taken anything from Mrs Gordon's purse, which she kept in the pocket of her pinafore. The landlady had already been out that morning to buy the paper and take her eggs to the dairy where she sold them for three pence the dozen. Tia had seen her paying the baker's boy for the bread when he came to the front door as she was laying the table for breakfast. If there had been money missing, the landlady would have realised it then.

'She must be mistaken,' she said quickly.

'What makes you say that?'

Tia shook her head; if she told them she would betray the trust that Marie had put in her. 'I know Marie, you see. She wouldn't do anything like that.'

The policemen looked at each other. 'If you know where she is . . .' one said.

'Ask her to come to see us,' the other said. 'If there's no more proof than what Mrs Gordon says, and she comes voluntarily, that's in her favour. If she doesn't . . . see, it looks bad, doesn't it? She runs away, and the landlady finds money missing. It'd be easier if she turned herself in.'

'I don't know where she is,' Tia said, 'but if I do see her, I'll tell her.'

That evening, as she was washing the supper dishes, Mrs Gordon came into the kitchen. 'I think you should know,' she said, 'Marie Donnelly's been arrested and charged with theft.'

Tia stiffened.

'You can count yourself lucky you're not being charged as well.'

That night, Tia cried herself to sleep. 'Oh, Marie, Marie,' she sobbed, 'I didn't betray you.'

She knew that most of the North Atlantic ships left early in the morning; she had been so sure that Marie had managed to get away.

She could not help thinking of the girl, just a year or two younger than she was, whose growth had been so stunted by poverty that she had the body of a child, who had done nothing wrong in her wretched life, but who had been first sent to Magdalen Laundry and then to Mrs Gordon's. Of the two, Tia did not know which was worse. Marie had been branded a thief, but it was not she who had stolen: the things she should have had, the things that every child had a right to, food and shelter, love and innocence; these things had been stolen from Marie when she was still too young to protest her loss.

If only she could remember Mrs Anderson's address, or even how to get there, she would be safe. But she couldn't; she did not understand the ways of the lowlands, she believed that if she left she would go to jail, or the lunatic asylum. She did not know which one of the two was worse, but if Mrs Gordon used them as a threat, they had to be worse than where she was now.

She began to feel her own bereavement then; the depth of her pain, which Marie's companionship had filled with gentle banter, began to haunt her. Though she had told herself that Marcus was dead, she could not accept it; they had been so close and she was so used to being parted from him that she found her thoughts drifting towards the hope that he would come back to her, and she let herself believe he might. In that way she had drifted through the days by living within her imagination; she was quiet and compliant and willing, she worked diligently and tirelessly so that Mrs Gordon never had reason to chide her and even grudgingly admitted that she was satisfied with her work.

'I knew that Marie was a bad one,' the landlady said one day, after inspecting the kitchen that Tia had cleaned so thoroughly that there was not a speck of dust to be found anywhere. 'You see, you manage the work alone without any bother. She was obviously a bad influence on you. Maybe it's a blessing she's gone.'

'Is she still in jail?' Tia blurted, emboldened by the mention of her name.

'Where she is is no concern of yours,' Mrs Gordon replied sharply.

Tia looked away, to hide the pain on her face. She wanted to help Marie, wherever she was, but she did not know how or where to begin. The only time she left the house was to go to church on Sunday, and then Mrs Gordon took her there and back again.

She woke up one bright summer morning to the stark realisation that Marcus was dead, gone for ever; her pain then was so real that it was physical. Her head throbbed, her stomach ached; her legs, when she got out of bed, felt like rubber, not flesh.

Somehow, she got through the day; she ate nothing, nor did she drink, she did not even speak because she had nothing to say and no one to talk to.

Mrs Gordon dismissed her just before nine in the evening;

Tia went to her room then and lay upon her bed with her clothes still on, staring at the sky as the light of day faded.

She did not want to undress, to catch even a glimpse of her naked body because that reminded her of Marcus and the way he had loved her. He had soothed her shyness, blunted the shame she felt at the taking of pleasure (her father's faith held that all enjoyment was inherently sinful); Marcus made her feel joyful to be herself. The knowledge that he loved her gave her the power to love herself; now that he was gone she cared about nothing, believed that she would never care again.

The clock counted the hours; so many hours that she wondered when the noise would stop. It was strange, the way that time in the city couldn't drift as it could in the islands, that every quarter hour was marked, every hour rang out with a repetition funereal in its monotony that reminded her only that she was alive and Marcus was dead. Distantly she wondered how he had spent the last moments of his life; whether he had had time to think or even to know. She did not know how he died, only that it had been an accident at the quayside. She glimpsed him in torment, in agony, screaming for help and then in rage at the knowledge that no help would come.

Once she heard midnight she rose and put on her boots, threw her shawl around her shoulders and crept through the kitchen and out of the back door, past the sleeping hens and into the passageway that ran behind the yards. She had never been out this way before; she knew about it only because of the rattle of carts that she heard through the day. At night, all was still; her footsteps threw up gravel that grated against the silence.

Having broken one of Mrs Gordon's cardinal rules, she knew that she could never return to the lodging house again.

The lane met a road; for a moment she listened, then turned and walked on. She found the river easily; the sound that she had heard, the faint lapping and the hollow echo, grew louder until, suddenly, she was there.

The bridge was lit by gaslight; down river she could see other bridges, the railway bridge and the road bridge, the suspension bridge lit by electricity. Tia walked to its middle and then, leaning on the railings, gazed at the oily water that pulsed below. The play of light on the water, the shifting images of reflection and refraction made shapes that took on meaning after a while. She saw the shadow of herself and, far below, amidst a miasma of curving images, Marcus's face, deep below the surface. He seemed to be calling out to her; she could not see all of him, just the outline of his features, as indistinct as a faded photograph, as if his memory was blurring in her mind. For a while she watched, mesmerised, and then opened her mouth to tell him to speak louder because she could not hear what he was trying to say.

The police sergeant, walking home from the late shift at the police office in Jail Square, was on the bridge before he saw her. At first he did not consider the image; it was only when he got closer that he saw a young woman, sensed the danger she was in. His first instinct was to grab her; thinking carefully, not wanting to startle her, he decided against that and walked back over the bridge to the coffee stall at the city end, where he had his flask refilled.

'It's a nice nicht,' the woman said, as she handed it back to him.

'It is that,' he said, handing her a coin.

'I thocht ye wis awa' hame.'

'I am that, Aggie.'

She looked at him questioningly.

'There's a lass on the bridge. She doesn't look too happy.'

'Aye? I didna see anbdy. Mind ye, I'm that blind, hauf the time I cannae e'en see my customers. I'm gettin' gey auld fir this racket, Jock.'

'Ach, you'll still be here when all the rest of us are pushing up the daisies.'

'I'm awa' at the year end, soon's' get my pension!'

He thanked her and walked slowly away.

Jock Patterson had been forty years a policeman; when he had started the sight of a constable was a rarity in most parts of the city, common only in the old Trongate, the network of alleyways at the eastern end of Argyle Street that had once been as lawless as the Wild West. He had learnt his trade there, amongst the shebeeners and the prostitutes, the thieves and the pickpockets. When the old *North British Daily Mail* had run a series of articles on the squalor, he had gained fame of sorts as the police constable who had caught the drunken woman thrown out of a second-floor window by her merciless husband, infuriated that his wages had been spent on drink.

Acceptance came after the shock had worn off, compassion years later as he watched children grow into effigies of their parents, unable to change because they knew of nothing to aspire to. The city fathers, spurred by public outrage, had knocked down the worst of the slums and replaced them with pristine tenements that bore the legend City Improvement Trust. The people of the old Trongate did not live there; they had moved further along the Gallowgate, the problem was not addressed but merely dispersed in such a way as to be less noticeable.

The strange thing was that these people had become his friends over the years.

Very slowly, silently, he walked towards Tia, not saying anything until he was within arm's reach, if need be.

'You look cold,' he said, tensed to catch her arm if she moved suddenly.

She turned towards him and he saw that her face was soaked in tears. He recognised grief; he had seen it before.

He opened the flask and poured steaming coffee into a mug. 'Here.'

She stared at the mug for a long time before she reached for it.

'It's very kind of you,' she said, her teeth chattering.

The policeman set another mug on the parapet and poured a coffee for himself too.

'It's a warm night,' he said, 'you must have been out a while.'

Tia said nothing.

'I mean, it's none of my business.'

She looked at him.

He paused for a moment, praying that his guess was the right one. 'You know,' he said, 'my wife died a while ago. For a long time, I didn't take it in, I just went on as usual. Then one day, all of a sudden, it hit me. I was angry with myself for being alive. I wanted to die too. There was nothing left, you see, or so I thought. We never did have children, we only had each other. I thought I would be better dead then I started thinking how easy it would be to kill myself.'

She was staring at him, her face a blank.

'Then, I thought, if I had been the one to die, I wouldn't've wanted Margaret to die just for me. I would've wanted her to live on. I knew that she would be angry if. . . I knew she'd never forgive me if I died like that. You see.'

Tia took a sip of the coffee.

'I don't know you,' he said, 'but I know this. No matter how bad you feel now, no matter how hopeless everything seems, if you can survive this things will never be so bad again.'

She shook her head. 'There's nothing left.'

'There is. You are left.'

She smiled bitterly. 'I am nothing.'

'You are not.' He grinned. 'Else I've gone mad and I'm standing here talking to myself.'

She winced. 'I have nowhere to go back to. I've left the place where I was.'

'Do they know you're gone yet?'

Her face told him that she did not know.

'How will they ever know, if you go back the way you came?'

She shrugged.

'Let me walk you home.'

Her shoulders slumped as he took her arm.

'You know, the dawn will come soon.'

She began to think of the hens, laying eggs everyday yet never rearing chicks.

As they reached the lane that led back to Mrs Gordon's, the sun transcended the eastern horizon, casting an aura that made the sky come alive. The birdsong rose to a crescendo and in the windowboxes the dew on the leaves of flowers made jewel colours that radiated brilliance.

'It's just along here,' she said.

'I'm Sergeant Patterson. I work at the police office in Jail Square. I live just along the road, the first house above the dairy. They all know me around here. Just ask for Sergeant Jock.'

There was something about his concern that had shocked her back to life again.

'He made me promise,' she said slowly.

'Promise what?'

'Not to mourn him. He made me promise that.'

The policeman winced with pain of his own, because his wife had extracted the same promise from him.

'Well then,' he said. 'A promise is something that should be kept.'

Tia gazed at him for a long time before she turned to walk away.

'Mind you come to see me, if you get a chance,' he said to the silence.

As she opened the gate to the yard she looked down at the gravel, the mess of stones and dirt, and saw a daisy trying to bloom there, the petals huddled tight against the chill of the dawn, so that only the pink underside showed.

She ran back to the road. 'Sergeant Jock?'

He turned to face her.

'Was a girl called Marie Donnelly arrested for stealing from Mrs Gordon?'

'Not that I know of. I know she made a complaint, but there was no trace of the girl.'

'Would you know if she had been arrested?'

'I would. What's it to you?'

'I know she didn't steal any money. All she did was run away with some bread and cheese.'

'Well, she wasn't arrested. You can be sure of that.'

Tia walked slowly along the lane and then into the house, vaguely relieved that she had not been missed.


That evening, after she had made the cocoa, she went into the drawing room as usual, to ask Mrs Gordon if she wanted anything else done before she went to bed.

'I don't think so,' the landlady said.

'I have decided to leave,' Tia said.

'What?' Mrs Gordon spat.

'I'm going to leave, Mrs Gordon.'

'Leave? Where on earth are you going to go?'

Tia bridled. 'There's plenty of jobs advertised in the paper. I'm a good worker. Even you admit that.'

'Good worker you may be, but you can't leave yet. Oh, no. If you do, I'll put the police on to you, same way as I put them on to that Marie.'

Tia felt anger for the first time since Marcus died. 'You can't stop me, Mrs Gordon.'

'You're in debt, girl.'

'I am not, Mrs Gordon.'

'You are so, you hussy, you! You owe me a pound or two at least.'

'You haven't paid me a penny since I started.'

'Of course not! I paid the doctor and I gave you these clothes and your food, put a roof over your head, then there's the hospital bill to consider. Let me see now, that iron tonic was one and thruppence, and the doctor's fee, and then there was your keep when you were in bed. I don't even remember what the hospital bills were, I'll have to look it up in the Society's books but it was at least five guineas if it was a penny. It'll have to be paid back, girl, every penny. You can leave then, but not a moment before. If you do, I'll have you jailed for debt. Hah! I was beginning to think you'd put your past behind you. I never dreamed for a moment you were so ungrateful for what I've done.'

Tia was struggling to think. She hardly remembered the doctor's visit, but she remembered afterwards Marie telling her that the doctor was a good man, that he hadn't charged a penny for visiting her.

'Mrs Gordon, don't I earn anything for all the work I do here?'

'Of course you do, girl. Don't be stupid!'

'How much do I earn?'

The landlady's eyes narrowed. 'Eight shillings a month.'

'Mrs Gordon, I do the work of two maids and a maid gets ten shillings a month living in and that's just to start.'

'Get out of here, you ungrateful girl,' the landlady roared. 'How dare you ask for ten shillings a month, after all I've done for you? I've never heard such cheek, not in my life. Such cheek. Get out of here. Go on, get out of my sight!'

Tia went through to her room, where she flung herself down on her bed and sobbed.

The next morning the atmosphere in the dining room was different when she served breakfast to the lodgers. One pressed a shilling into her hand, and wished her good luck.

'What?' Tia fumbled.

'We're leaving,' the girl said. 'It's the end of term, and we've finished our course. Hurrah! Next term, we start as teachers. No more studying for us.'

Tia looked at the shilling, smiling at them because they were smiling at her.

'Did you ever hear what happened to wee Marie?' one of the others asked.

She had to think a moment before she realised who they were talking about. 'I haven't,' she said.

'Mrs Gordon said she vanished off the face of the earth. She had the police out looking for her for some unknown reason.'

'Mrs Gordon told me she'd been arrested.'

'Really?' The girl looked puzzled. 'I asked her yesterday, and she said she had no idea.'

Tia walked out of the room, trying to hide her glee.

Mrs Gordon came into the kitchen just as Tia was finishing the supper dishes. Because the lodgers were gone, there was little to do.

'I've been thinking, MacLeod,' the landlady said, carefully, 'perhaps I was slightly hasty yesterday. I've had a word with my friend Miss Collins from the Kirk. She's head seamstress at Daly's and she said she could use a girl like you there. You would get paid three and six a week, which is more than I could reasonably be expected to give you here. I would only charge two shillings for your board, if you would help with the housework. You see, there's always girls from the Society needing to be taken in, and it would be silly to keep you on as a maid when there won't be the work because my guests are away.'

Tia was thinking that it would mean she would be free to leave the house; to begin to pay off her debt to the landlady. Her pride would not allow her to run away from a debt, even though she knew it was not as much as Mrs Gordon said.

'Well, girl?' the landlady asked her sharply.

'Yes, Mrs Gordon.'

'Well, then, that's sorted. I'll take you there on Monday morning. It'll keep you busy, if nothing else. Idle hands do the Devil's work. You know that.'

'Yes,' Tia said quietly, thinking that if she got out of the house she could begin to look for Mrs Anderson to find her way back to the life she used to have. Marcus had left money for her there, more than enough to pay Mrs Gordon back.

Her eyes closed, she knew sleep would not come, but she prayed to God to let her have at least a little rest. She had the briefest sensation of the storm abating, that, far over the horizon, a faint glow of hope was rising in the east.

And then she slept.

# Chapter Nine

*T*he only thought that kept Tia going was the memory of the brief elation she had experienced that morning when she woke up. It was the feeling she'd had in her married days, her first waking thought the recollection of the pleasures past, and the next thought the anticipation of those to come. For just a moment she had relished the dawn, before her pain came again with the portrait of Marcus that occupied centre space in her mind. He seemed to smile then, and she knew that he would not forgive her if she gave up, that his soul still shadowed hers, sharing her tears and her sorrows, the rare and fleeting joys.

Daly's was one of the best stores in the city, though she did not know that when Mrs Gordon took her there and handed her over to the grim and forbidding Miss Collins, head of the workroom – the alteration charge hand, as she was known in the parlance of the trade. They went into the trades entrance at the back of the store in a dank little alleyway off Sauchiehall Street and waited in a grubby hall as the doorman shouted for a boy to take them up to the workrooms. The stairway was an endless spiral that climbed five floors before it ended in a corridor lit by a skylight.

'I'll jist let the missus know ye're here,' the boy said, flitting away as Mrs Gordon struggled to regain her breath. The air smelt crisply of starch and linen; there was the sound of machinery and the subdued hum of women at work. Miss Collins came out and scanned Tia from head to toe before she turned to Mrs Gordon. 'As I said, Mrs Gordon, I'll give her a try but I can't promise anything. We work to very high standards here.'

Mrs Gordan bridled. 'She's willing and a good worker.'

'We'll see about that.'

She turned away and Tia sensed that she should follow her as the landlady began to clump back down the stairs.

'You haven't done this sort of work before,' Miss Collins said, making a statement, not asking a question.

Tia was angry at her presumption, at the condescending tone of her voice.

'I used to launder all the mistress's clothes. I've done sewing as well.'

The workroom door swung open and the hum amplified. Tia noticed that the chatter fell to nothing as Miss Collins walked in, her eyes sweeping the room. She was not yet old, her pepperish hair twisted tightly into a knot pinned on top of her head, but her face was deeply lined, a sombre expression etched on to the bland mask of her features. Tia sensed that she rarely smiled, never laughed.

'Ha!' Miss Collins arched her eyebrows arrogantly. 'Our workroom is the best in the city. We are every bit as good as Paris. Some of our staff were trained there. There is a world of difference between the work you might have done elsewhere and the type of work we do here.'

Tia demurred. She had caught a glimpse of a waterfall of silk being draped around a dummy: one woman holding the material, another pinning it into place, and a third watching and giving commands. At first the garment was shapeless, an untidy tumble that had grace only because of the richness of the cloth, but as the women worked it took on form and quickly became exquisite even though no seams had yet been sewn and the whole was kept in place by pins. The transformation fascinated her; she wondered how the women had gained their skill, whether she could learn it too.

Miss Collins nodded briskly and strode to the back of the room. 'You say you can launder, Miss MacLeod. We'll see about that. Mrs Hendry, give her an iron. Start her on lingerie first.'

A woman lifted her head from her work and brushed a wisp of hair from her face. 'Aye,' she said, sullenly, indicating a board beside hers and a stand where irons heated on the stove. 'If you do the bloomers, I'll finish the camisoles.'

Tia lifted a pair of bloomers from the pile and spread them carefully on the board. The linen was fine, snowy white edged with embroidery and little satin ribbons that tied around the legs. She began to iron carefully, folding them once she had finished and then taking another pair before the woman stopped her. 'That's no' richt, hen. There shouldna be creases anywhere, and you've made creases down the side.'

'But it'll crease when it's folded,' Tia said.

'No, hen. Yon's packed in tissue and then in a box. See?' She took the bloomers and damped them slightly, then pulled one of the legs over the board so that she could iron out the creases. Once they were done, she checked that the cloth was dry and then laid the bloomers on a sheet of tissue paper, which she folded carefully and then placed in a box with another sheet of tissue paper on top. 'That's the way to do it, hen. Do it ony other way and the missus'd mak ye stay on efter to do it all again.'

Tia ironed all morning, feeling a quiet sense of satisfaction when Miss Collins checked her work without comment.

At midday there was a fifteen-minute break for dinner, when the worktops were cleared and the women ate sandwiches and tea brewed in a big pot on the stove. Tia had no sandwiches, but Mrs Hendry gave her a buttered scone. 'Ma name's Jeannie,' she whispered, 'ca' me that 'cept when the missus's listening.'

Tia smiled for the first time that day.

Afterwards there were more underthings to iron, a never-ending pile replenished from time to time by the message boy who brought up boxes from the basement storeroom, who winked at the women and made ribald comments when Miss Collins was out of earshot. The garments fascinated Tia, the frilled bloomers and lacy camisoles, the nightgowns of silk and satin so soft that touching them felt like dipping her hand in flowing water. The corsets were long and straight, not at all like the padded, whaleboned contraption that Madam had worn.

'Yon's out o' fashion,' Jeannie told her when she asked about it. 'The waist's out. The dresses jist hang; there's hardly any shape at all. Hobble skirts an' that. Daft, so it is.'

The clothes were sold with seams unsewn, so that dresses and suits were then made to fit the customer. On the other side of the workroom teams of seamstresses were working at dummys, each laboriously altered to the customer's measurements. 'See,' Jeannie said, as two girls pulled a skirt tight while a third tacked a seam that fell straight from hip to hem. 'How the Devil will she ever walk in that?'

Tia thought of the suit Marcus had bought her, the memory of pleasure changing sharply to pain, guilt even when she realised that he would never be able to share her happiness again. She returned to her work, sinking her grief in the frippery of ribbons and lace, feeling sorrow renewed when Jeannie whispered that the reason they were so busy was to get trousseaux ready for girls marrying that spring.

'Ye've no done bad,' Jeannie said at the end of the day.

Tia was looking at the burns on her hands, the callous forming on her palm where she held the handle. Her arms ached and her eyes stung, yet the older woman seemed scarcely touched by the work she had done.

Jeannie laughed when she saw her expression. 'I've been ironing thirty year, hen, since I was twelve years auld. Dinna fashe yersel', ye'll get used tae it in time.'

The clock was ringing six when she left the store by the back door; she remembered Mrs Gordon's admonishment to be back by 6.30 and began to walk quickly, grateful that the route was easy, straightforward to the riverside and then across the bridge where she had met the policeman only a few nights before.

Her evening meal was the soup she had prepared the previous day, a pot of potatoes and bread, which she ate in the kitchen alone after she had served Mrs Gordon in the dining room.

'I've had word from the Baillie,' Mrs Gordon told her as she cleared the dishes. 'There's a pair of Irish girls coming. I'll put them in your room and you can move upstairs.'

Tia thought of the perishing cold of the rooms that were let to boarders; the room beyond the kitchen was always warm.

She was paid her first week's wage at the end of a fortnight; her first week's money was 'lying in'; paid to her only when she left the job. She handed the entire sum over to the landlady, who marked it down in the rent book. 'Exactly how much do I owe you, Mrs Gordon?' Tia asked.

'I dread to think,' the landlady said grimly. 'It's several guineas, what with the hospital bills and everything.'

Tia bit her lip and swallowed the impulse to remind her again of the work she had done.

'And there's sixpense you owe on rent, no one and six

because you have cocoa at supper, don't you? You see, the rate I charge for lodgers is two shillings a week, two and six with cocoa at supper. But don't worry, you'll pay that off next week.'

'But how long will it take to pay you everything?'

The landlady shook her head. 'You really are ungrateful, girl. I took you in, fed you, cared for you when you were sick. If not for the Society, you'd be on the streets, you know. Even dead, maybe.'

'The thing is, Mrs Gordon, I hate to be in debt.'

'Ha, my girl, you'll be in eternal debt, so you'd best get used to it.'

'I would like to try to repay it,' she said carefully.

'And not a word of thanks. All you want to know is how much you owe. I tell you, girl, charity is not a matter of pounds and pence. Charity comes from the heart, from the grace of Our Lord. You can never repay Him. Or me, for that matter.'

Tia thought of the Lord's Prayer, the words that tripped so easily from her father's lips: 'Forgive us our debts, as we forgive our debtors . . .'

She smiled to herself.

In the height of summer, when the sun shone golden overhead and the sky was a flawless blue, the city streets were like canyons, always cool, untouched by the sun. As Tia walked to work in the mornings along Buchanan Street she passed MacDonalds' and Wylie & Lochhead, Ferguson's the grocers, Miss Cranston's Tea Rooms and the Old Waverley Hotel, then after she turned into Sauchiehall Street Copland & Lye and Pettigrew & Stephens before she reached the Daly's building, marked by the clock at the corner and the flag flying from the pole on the roof. The electric arc lights were not lit, but trams trundled past in the centre of the street from dawn to dusk, their roll a constant thunder that ebbed and surged throughout the working day.

The workroom girls were not allowed into the store itself; they were kept hidden from public view, entering and leaving as surreptitiously as kitchen mice by the alleyway at the back, as if the clothes they made were not perfected laboriously under Miss Collins' vulture gaze but conjured up effortlessly by the haughty, elegant sales assistants. Pomanders hung below the fans to dissipate sweetness in the area where money changed hands. No customer was allowed beyond the door at the back of the sales area that led to the rabbits' hutch of the workrooms and the maze of storerooms beyond. The gilt and flock ended abruptly where the smell of sweat began. If she was a moment early in the morning, Tia used to walk around to the front of the store to gaze into the windows and wonder at the riches that she sensed beyond. Heavy canvas awnings shaded the windows; it was difficult to see anything, when the lights were not on.

At Mrs Gordon's Tia felt lonely in the top room where she had one of the three beds, and two drawers in a chest for her things. She had so little, only a change of underwear, a nightgown, and a spare blouse, all of which Marie had given her from those that the boarders left behind. They looked pathetic, just a tiny bundle in the corner of one drawer. She had worn her boots almost constantly since she left the hospital; when she saw wear on the soles she saved pennies from her wages until she had enough to buy a new pair at the discount rate for Dalys' employees. It was her only extravagance and one about which she had no choice.

The boots were all she had left of the man she had loved. Sometimes, at night, she cried so hard that she felt herself choking, stopped only when she remembered the promise she'd made and how close she had come to breaking it.

When the rush of wedding orders was over, Miss Collins started her on sewing, nothing complex, just tacking seams for the machinist and hand finishing the seam once it had been stitched; the work was repetitive and tiring but not nearly so bad as ironing. She learned how a seam must be sewn neatly and evenly or the finished dress would not hang properly, how to hem a skirt with invisible stitches and how to hand sew a collar so that it sat perfectly straight.

She missed Jeannie's chatter, being a part of the little enclave that the older woman had marked out for herself in a corner of the workroom. The seamstresses sat hunched over their machines, their brows furrowed because they had to strain their eyes to check the tiny stitches. When they handed Tia something to do, they indicated by gesture what it was as the noise of the treadles made it impossible to talk. Even after work was over and the machines silenced, it took a while for her hearing to return to normal; her ears still rang with the mechanical noise.

'That's richt,' Jeannie said one evening, as she followed Tia out of the back door, 'jist walk past me wi' yer nose in the air.' There was a hierachy in the workroom; Miss Collins was the pinnacle and Jeannie contentedly at the bottom, where she good-naturedly derided everyone else. Tia knew that in Jeannie's estimation she had moved up a place in the world since she started sewing; she did not understand why because she was the same person she had always been.

Tia turned round, grinning. 'I didn't hear you.'

'I've been efter ye all the way doon the stairs, telling ye there'll be overtime the morn, if we're lucky.'

Tia smiled.

'Ye see' – Jeannie leaned closer, after looking around to make sure that no one was listening – 'the girl Hamilton, yon that's merryin' the laddie Fraser, she's put on weight.' She nudged Tia, winked knowingly. 'The dress, the gowns, everything's tae be let oot two inches, apart fra' the mantle. I heard the missus on the phone about it, it's a' tae be ready by the end o' the week.'

Tia's puzzlement showed on her face.

'Ach,' Jeannie grunted, exasperated, 'd'ye no get it? Lassie's got a bun in the oven. She's expectin'! They bloody nobs, yon's no fit fir the gutter, the way they carry on.' Jeannie turned towards Cowcaddens, still muttering to herself.

Tia walked on towards the river as the hum in her ears faded to a whisper and then vanished entirely, as the city sounds of trams, cars and carts roared in its place, punctuated by the chattering of starlings. She often wondered why the little birds bothered with the city, when there were open fields, running water and trees only a few miles away, where they could fly free of the noise, the grime and the soot. To her the city was a contradiction of nature; the layers of sewers, drains, roads and buildings on top of the soil suppressed its energy and subdued the will of the people who had no choice but to live there. As she walked to work over paths crusted with stones she longed to feel the earth under her feet again, to experience the tender comfort of growing grass. Towards the end of the day, when the air became so heavy that she could hardly breathe she yearned for the breezes and open spaces of the island, to hear the song of the land again, the rhythm of the wind as it swept through the grass. As she paused on the bridge over the river where the air was cool and moist, she watched the faces of passers-by and saw that their skin was pasty and grey, that in living in this place they had become submerged in its colour. She was shocked when she caught her reflection in the hall mirror and saw that her skin was the same colour, that her once golden hair had become tarnished, like an ornament left uncared for accumulates filth. For a moment she stared and then she patted her cheeks until they were rosy again.

Mrs Gordon came into the hall from the living room and glared at her. 'The new girls are here,' she said, 'they'll serve the meals from now on.'

Tia went to go to the kitchen, but the landlady stopped her. 'You can eat in the dining room now, like the other lodgers.'

Tia hesitated.

'Well, girl, away up to your room. Mind and keep it tidy now, because the other lodgers are coming at the end of the week. Dinner's at six thirty. I'll ring the bell.'

'I might be late tomorrow,' Tia said. 'I might have to do overtime at work.'

The landlady's lips pursed. 'It's of no concern to me what you do. Your meal'll be ready at six thirty. If you're not here it's kept 'til eight thirty. If you're not in by then it's thrown out.'

'But I thought, but you said I'd to come straight back after work.'

Mrs Gordon sighed. 'You're a lodger now, MacLeod. The front door is open between six in the morning and nine at night. Your time is your own, to do with what you will. In your case, you will almost certainly waste it.'

Tia climbed the stairs, filled the washhand basin in the bathroom and soaked her hair, scrubbing it with soap and rinsing it several times until the water ran clear. Afterwards, her hair was damp and dark, but she felt better because it was clean.

Jeannie was right about the overtime, wrong in the assumption that they would be paid for the extra work. Once the trousseau was finished Miss Collins clapped her hands for attention and then told the workroom that the girls who had stayed late to do the work could have Saturday afternoon off.

'Crabbit auld hag,' Jeannie said as they left work at midday on Saturday. 'I coulda done wi' an extra bob or twa.'

Tia stopped on the corner of Buchanan Street, looking at the shoppers milling around her.

'What's the matter?' Jeannie asked.

'Nothing,' Tia said. 'Where's the nearest subway station?'

'Are ye blind? It's richt there, see?'

Very slowly, Tia walked to the entrance, bought a ticket and went down the escalator.

When Marcus first took her to Mrs Anderson's, it was on the subway. She decided to take the subway again, and look for Mrs Anderson's. With her marriage certificate, Mrs Gordon could not bully her any longer and the money she had there would pay off her debt. She felt sick at the thought of the debt she had accumulated; at the unfairness of it all. She wanted to have her own things again to bring substance to her memories – not that Marcus was fading in her mind but she could face the past now, face the fact that he was dead.

For so long she had been drifting; she wanted to anchor her life again, to try to keep her promise not to mourn.

All of a sudden she felt terribly alone, waiting in the cool of the platform, listening to the fading rumble of a departing train as its wake frilled the hem of her skirt and wafted a breeze around her legs. The station was deserted momentarily, though a moment later other passengers appeared, their voices echoing emptily along the void. She remembered her fear the first time on the subway, the thrill of descending on the escalator and the frisson of excitement when Marcus grasped her arm tightly to reassure her, the overwhelming feeling of safety through being with him. The fear returned now, the claustrophobia of being in an enclosed place deep underneath the city streets where the sound was amplified and distorted; she began to shiver and almost turned back before she remembered the way he had begun whistling non-chalantly, grinning gleefully at the echo and telling her not to be daft when she asked him if there was a risk that the tunnel walls would collapse; like almost everything else in the city the subway had been constructed by highlanders, strong, skilful men who took pride in their work.

The train arrived then, the noise a crescendo that dulled her thoughts and made her reach for her skirts to steady them against the gust. The door opened and she got in, taking a seat by the window and smiling to herself, taking pleasure from the thought that she was going home again. Once the train moved, her fear faded, replaced by anticipation tinged by apprehension. She wondered what Mrs Anderson would say, how to explain her absence over the months, how she would cope with the pain that repeating her story would surely bring. The stations passed quickly, all the same except for the names painted in stark black letters on the tiles; she rose when the train started out of Kelvinbridge, not wanting to miss Hillhead, her stop; thinking suddenly of Marie and whispering to God to give her some luck.

Climbing the stairway to the street, she looked for the newsvendor and heard an unfamiliar voice heralding the Late Special; on the level she turned around, looking for a landmark in the busy thoroughfare. She remembered Marcus teasing her about the mystery tours he took her on and wished suddenly that he hadn't been so flippant always, so quick to make fun of the things she did not know. Yet he hadn't, she remembered; he made a point of telling her about it all, painstakingly pointing out where they were; she had been so happy, so much in love, that she had paid more attention to him than to what he had said.

'*The trains run in circles on the subway,* ban-righ. *You could stay on one for ever and never go anywhere at all.*'

'Why, Marcus?'

'*Why not? The subways's easy,* ban-righ. *It's much easier than the tram. You just get on the train, on any train. It'll take you wherever you want to go, sooner or later. You just have to wait and then get off at the right stop.*'

Smiling at the memory, she hugged herself and walked down the street, looking for the grocer, the butcher's, Miss McCafferty's Haberdashery, the little booth where Jock sold his newspapers.

An hour later she realised that she was lost, or in the wrong place. She had walked the road from end to end, seen nothing familiar beyond the dull monotony of the Glasgow tenement, the red sandstone buildings that lined the street, four storeys tall from pavement to roof. Though there was a grocer and a butcher, the shops were different from those she remembered and there were others as well, a haberdasher with a different name painted on the window and an ironmonger's, a stall where a woman sold fresh-cut flowers. The seasons had changed since she had been to Mrs Anderson's; she had thought of that and taken account of it, but she was sure now that the boarding house was nowhere near. The afternoon sun was strong, sweat wreathed her brow; she felt herself wilt, momentarily sway until she steadied herself by clutching a lamp post.

'Are ye a'richt, hen?' a woman asked, a washerwoman by the look of her because her hands were red and rough and she carried a sack of laundry slung over her shoulder.

'I'm just a little hot,' Tia said.

'Ye look as if ye're lost, hen.'

'The docks,' Tia said, suddenly inspired, 'are the docks anywhere round here?'

'They're the other side o' Partick Cross,' the woman said, 'if ye walk down there, o'er the bridge an' then take the ferry road, ye canna miss the docks. The Queen's Dock is down that way, an' the Broomielaw's alang fra that, but see once ye reach the river, ye canna miss the Broomielaw.'

'Th . . .thanks,' Tia murmured, thinking she might have been right after all, that her mistake might have been to get off at the wrong subway station. It was Marie, after all, who had told her that it was Hillhead; for the life of her she could not remember the name of the station Marcus had used, if she had ever known it.

'Are ye sure ye're a'richt?' the woman asked again.

'I am now,' Tia said.

'Ye can tak' a tram. A green tram goes doon that way.'

'I can walk it,' Tia said, as she struggled to smile.

'Aye, hen, ye kin, but it's aucht but a ha'penny fare, if ye git tired.'

Tia began to walk, hopeful at first, smiling at the kindness of strangers. It took her a while to walk to the docks, and to realise that on the way she had passed nothing familiar, nothing at all. After another hour she stood at the Broomielaw, staring at the passenger bills for MacBrayne's and MacCallum Orme, the Clyde Steam Packet Co. Suddenly she had a vision of Marcus, his arms folded as he stood at Oban Harbour, telling the MacCallums' captain, whoever would listen, what he thought of old David MacBrayne. The tears came then; she began to walk aimlessly, crying with relief when eventually the road led her back to the familiarity of St Enoch's, the crush of the afternoon crowds. Passing a clock, she glanced at it and realised that her free afternoon was gone; tiredly she walked back over the river to Mrs Gordon's.

The landlady was in her salon, as she called the front room which was stuffed with furniture and damask curtains and a bewildering array of ornaments that covered every surface, including the walls.

'Ah, Miss MacLeod,' she said, 'I see you've returned.'

Tia blushed, hoping she would not see the traces of her tears. She stood hesitantly at the open door, as Mrs Gordon introduced her to the three young women sitting there. 'I've put Beth in the room with you,' she said; 'she's from the north as well.'

Tia said 'hello' quietly, then hurried away, though not before she heard Mrs Gordon telling the girls that although she worked for her living, she did have a respectable job in a most respectable store.

When Beth came up to the room, Tia perceived a distance in her manner, that she had hardly noticed at first in her distress.

She was thinking of what the doctor had said, that mild memory loss in the circumstances was common, even normal, that her memory would come back if she gave it a chance.

The bell rang for dinner; she went down with the other girls, not caring that they excluded her from the conversation, not minding even when she heard Beth telling the others that it was an outrage that she, a trainee teacher, was expected to share with a common shop girl.

Tia did not eat; she went back to her room as soon as she could, and lay upon her bed, staring at the cracks on the ceiling. Though tears gathered at the edge of her vision, she did not cry, but blinked them back again and again. Because she was no longer alone in the room, she did not even have the privacy to be sad.

She was changed and in bed by the time Beth came upstairs; she feigned sleep to preclude the embarrassment of the companionship that had been forced upon her.

It was only as she was falling asleep that she thought again about what Marcus had said: '*You just get on the train, on any train. It'll take you to wherever you want to go, sooner or later. You just have to wait and then get off at the right stop*.

'*The subway's easy*, ban-righ.'

All she had to do to find Mrs Anderson's was to keep on travelling the subway, alighting each time at a different station. The more she thought, the more she remembered of the station Marcus had used; she had only to find the station and then she could find Mrs Anderson's. She fell asleep at last, thinking of the map of the subway she had seen hanging in the ticket office; there were only fifteen or so stations, she would find her old lodgings; it would only take time.

In the morning she felt ashamed of herself; of her stupidity and also her fear.

Another girl came the following week, a girl from Skye called Catriona Nicholson; she wasn't patronising like the trainee teachers but there was something reserved in her manner, that made her pull back from the kind of confidences that move towards friendship. Tia saw the state that her feet were in and lent her Marcus's boots without thinking, apologising profusely the next week when Catriona wanted to buy them and she had explained that they were not for sale. Catriona seemed hurt, though she said she understood; Tia remembered the way she had suddenly stopped talking about her family and wondered what her own secret was. There was something about city life that made secrets of things that otherwise would be normal, of the tragedy of her widowhood, twisted into shame by the constructions of others, that had made her afraid to talk about herself. In a flash one day, as she listened to Catriona talking about school, she realised that the girl had not finished to her certificate, that she must be younger than herself; realising then that Catriona was still a child, she did not want to burden her with the sorrows of adulthood.

In September the pace of work at Daly's changed. The tailors were busy making wool coats and capes that were sold ready made, and huge bolts of satin and silk lined the shelves to be made into gowns for the winter dances. Tia remembered the Baillie's wife lashing herself into a corset fit for a woman half her size, ignoring the change of fashion. That year, the tango drove a raucous wedge through the last restraints of Victoriana, the mood in society was wild and free, and even dour Calvinist Glasgow began to dance at tea-time and continued to dance until dawn. The dresses were slim in silhouette with a tunic to the knees but a flounced skirt beneath which permitted movement and ruffled engagingly about the ankles. Seeing the drawings tacked to the wall by the cutting table, Tia flinched, thinking of her own wedding suit that had been high fashion before she'd even known what that was. The ladies' gowns buyer and Miss Collins shamelessly copied Lucille's designs; before long the cutting tables and every surface were covered with yards and yards of chiffon silk, carefully matched to brocade and damask. When the orders came in by the hundred they were quietly satisfied.

Tia began to work on finishing, tying threads and pressing seams and sewing backing on to embroidered bodices to keep the decoration perfectly in place. It was close, detailed work but her eyes were young and her vision perfect; she gained confidence when Miss Collins stopped apportioning work equally between the assistants and instead gave the most important orders to her. She loved the feel of silk, took pleasure in the perfect finished article, folded gently into its tissue swathing; sometimes hours passed before she felt a stab of grief or of the more familiar guilt. In the empty hours after work was over, when she was walking home or waiting for sleep to come, her thoughts of Marcus were tinged now with regret that his death had not been marked by ritual. At the time she had been too confused to ask Hector MacKenzie; now she blamed herself. She was – had been – his wife, after all.

Now that the nights were drawing in her free time was curtailed by her fear of the city in darkness and the winter rule at Mrs Gordon's that the front door was locked at seven each evening, to be opened later only by prior arrangement. It was not like the island, when night brought only a lessening of colour, when the familiar shapes became shadows and the stillness was reassurance that no danger threatened. The city streets were ominous after nightfall, the noise of the traffic merged with man-made sounds of mirth and joy and sometimes pain. Though she had intended to ride the subway after work, once a drunk man approached her in an empty station she changed her mind and instead went only on Sunday afternoons, using a civic transport guide to travel the train route methodically. She was certain that she would find the boarding house by Christmas; she had already marked off four of the fifteen stations.

In October Miss Collins gave her an hour's overtime each night after the store closed at five-thirty; she was paid a shilling extra each week and there were still enough people on the streets to make her feel safe walking home through the darkness. She did not hand the money over to Mrs Gordon; until she was sure how much she owed, the landlady's ledger was as dark and deep as Hades, her debt as interminable as hell.

One day Catriona Nicholson announced that she had found another room, a cheaper room in a nicer house; she asked Tia to share it with her. Tia wanted to, but could not, dare not face Mrs Gordon's wrath. Catriona said she would be leaving at the end of the week and though she had not been a friend, Tia thought she would miss her.

Workmen were painting the pedestrian bridge that week, so instead of using it Tia crossed the river by Glasgow Bridge, the big road bridge beside the railway bridge. On Friday there was an accident on Clyde Place and the traffic stopped in an angry chorus of horns and carters' whistles. Just as she was about to turn towards Mrs Gordon's, Tia saw something familiar in a car waiting in the line. Rain was falling; her vision blurred and shifted, she blinked against a speck of mud then opened her eyes and saw the Baillie sitting there in his black Argyle with Farquharson at the wheel. Disbelieving, she shook her head then looked again. The car was so close that if she reached out she could touch it.

It was just before seven o'clock, the street lights cast dim pools of light that made the way ahead a sequence of static images suspended in the darkness. Tia pulled her jacket tight and walked on, not turning into Norfolk Street but following the road ahead. After a minute or two the Baillie's Argyle passed, throwing up a plume of water in its wake; she began to run crazily, terrified it would disappear before she saw the direction it was going in. A policeman's whistle blew; the traffic juddered to a halt again, a tram stopping just beside her; she jumped on, pushing thruppence into the conductor's hand and ignoring his protests that she couldn't board, not until they reached the stop. Gasping for breath she ran up the stairs and sat down at the front, her eyes fixed on the car a little way ahead. The conductor followed, shaking his head, telling her that there were seats below, she did not have to sit in the rain. Tia smiled at him, told him it didn't matter. 'Where're ye going, lass?' he asked, shaking his head again when she told him she didn't know.

He gave her a penny ticket, telling her that it would be a penny more if she stayed on beyond Eglinton Toll.

The traffic moved in fits and starts; Tia gripped the rail tightly, her eyes on the Argyle, ignoring the downpour matting her hair to her brow and soaking her jacket and the carefully ironed blouse that had to do another day because she had been too late to use the iron at Mrs Gordon's on Tuesday and her other blouse was clean but still creased. The tram stopped and passengers got off and on as the Argyle pulled away; progress was torturously slow, ahead the lights of the car merged and mingled with others as she screwed her eyes tightly to try to keep track of it. Above her head, the tram line crackled and spluttered. She saw the Argyle pull into the middle of the road to make a turn, and put her head in her hands and sobbed. The tram was moving and she could not jump off.

Some schoolboys had come upstairs, the conductor took their fare and then came to ask her if she knew where she was going yet, because Eglinton Toll was just coming up.

She looked up, caught a glance of the car turning away in the distance.

'That car,' she said, clutching the conductor's arm, 'where's it going to?'

He glanced at her then followed her pointing finger.

'Yon's Ballie Cuthbert going home,' he said, 'he'll be turning into Maxwell Road, then Albert Drive. Pollokshields, ye ken. Whaur aw' the nobs live.'

Sobbing, she thanked him and hurried off the tram as it drew up, then crossed the road, careless of the cacophony of horns that rose in protest. She could still see the Argyle in the distance and followed, careering blindly along until she found the turning, slipping and nearly falling as she turned into it and saw the long parade of shops that stretched ahead.

Suddenly she saw Jock's newsvending stall, its boards up and locked for the night, and the grocer's, and the butcher's where she had bought the joint of beef for Marcus's dinner.

There was Miss McCafferty's Haberdashery, the coloured cottons faded in the reflection of the gas lights.

For a long time she stood staring at it, tears falling helplessly until she trusted herself to go on.

It felt so strange now to see the street, so familiar in detail yet so similar to so many others, the same arrangement of tenements drawn together, the front windows lit and the little shops at the corner. The differences were almost imperceptible, in the shade of the paving stones, the peculiar smell of coffee and tea that still seeped past the shuttered grocer's windows, the peeling paint of the butcher's pole. Shaking her head, brushing the tears from her eyes, she walked down the road and turned towards Mrs Anderson's, almost crying for joy when she saw the lit window and the landlady looking out.

Knocking at the door, she held her breath until it opened and then she collapsed into Mrs Anderson's arms.

# Chapter Ten

$M$rs Anderson eased off Tia's sodden jacket, led her into the living room and helped her into her own chair, set tight by the fire. Tia, sobbing uncontrollably, clung to her for a long time before her grip loosened and the landlady sat back on her haunches and wiped the tears from her eyes.

'Ach, lassie, lassie, whaur e'er wis ye?'

Tia began to cry again, folding herself around the cushions of Mrs Anderson's generous chest, the loose flesh encased in layers of vests and jumpers and two pinnies over that, the one that she always wore and the other on top for baking, to shield the first. There was a veneer of flower crusted on to the cloth that softened with her tears, became soggy and smudged, smearing against her skin, getting into her eyes. The smell was of nurture; for the first time in ages, Tia felt safe.

Mrs Anderson waited until her sobbing had quieted to a whimper and then, very gently, she took Tia's hands from around her shoulders and rested them in her lap. 'I'm jis' ganging ben, pet, tae take the kettle aff the fire. I put it oan the minute I seen ye beltin' up the street, lass. Ye'd the look o' wan wha needit a cuppa.'

The kettle had boiled dry.

She heard the fizzle as the landlady poured cold water into it, saw the cloud of angry steam that rose to the ceiling and surged through the kitchen door.

Unsteadily, on legs that felt like blades of grass, she got up, found her balance and walked to the doorway. The kettle was on the plate again, hissing merrily, as Mrs Anderson opened the oven and, wrapping a rag around her hand, pulled out a tray of burnt scones.

'Ach,' she said, picking one up and scraping the charcoal off, then flaking it into crumbs and flinging a handful out of the back door, 'the birds'll thank ye, lass. It's that hard fir 'em tae get enough tae eat in winter.'

The cold draught freshened her face, dried the vestiges of tears and, after a while, brought a quaint little smile to her lips.

'You know,' Tia said, as Mrs Anderson carried a tray of tea and buttered bread through, 'I was afraid of you when I met you at first.'

Mrs Anderson poured the tea and handed her the milk and sugar. 'Ach, I kenned that, a wee bit, thing is, I didna ken why. Ye wis sae young then, like a puppydog, jumpin' aw' o'er the place then scamperin' fir shelter when ye thocht ye might pit a fit wrang. I tried tae tell ye, I'm no yin fir giein' onyyin a tellin' aff.'

'I couldn't understand what you were saying,' Tia said, as she blew on the surface of the tea to cool it, 'I was always scared that I'd do the wrong thing and you'd think I was daft.'

'There wis ne'er ony chance o' that, lass. Ach, ye young yins are aw' alike. Ye come doon fra' the islands and there's a look about ye, aw' precious an' fresh, like a blossomin' bud, but then Glesca gits tae ye and ye harden up an' efter that, ye git the look o'lead. Mind ye, it'd tak' mair'n this place tae make ye ugly, lass. Ye're as bonny as e'er. But ye've got tae toughen up, see, tak' the rough wi' the smooth. See if life gies ye a belter, lass, ye jis' gie it yin back.'

Tia watched the ripples her breath made in the tea in her cup, the spreading rings that expanded to hit the rim and then bounced back, making diagonal checks where the eddies met. She had the feeling that she had travelled a very long way to get here, to get back to where she'd been.

'See, pet,' Mrs Anderson said, 'ye don't mind me ca'in' ye pet, dae ye?'

She shook her head vigorously.

'I wis jis' waitin' fir ye. That first Sunday, I put a pot on, tae mak' a meal fir ye, and then one o' the lads said the lasses in service dinna git evry Sunday, they jis' git yin Sunday a month. But I was frettin', mind, I'd this feeling, see? I'd the thocht that there wis somethin' the matter wi' ye an' it jis' widna leave me.' She pursed her lips and shook her head, took a sip of tea before she continued: 'Sae the second week, the second Sunday, I went roun' tae the hoose tae' esk fir ye; I was that feart I'd git ye intae trouble I didna chap the door, I jis' waited ootside till I saw the wee lad that helps the gaffer an' I esked him and he telt me ye'd been taken tae the hospital.

'I went richt there, pet. I goes straight tae the Royal an' they say they didn' hae ye, I went to the Bella an' the Rottenrow an' e'en the Southern Institute, an' they aw' say the same thing. Sae I goes back tae the hoose the morn and I tells the missus that, the housekeeper like, and she says there's aucht the metter wi' ye, that ye've been healt and sent hame, like. Well I didna belie' that either, but I couldna say aucht. I mean, when I esked whaur ye wis she jis' slammed the door in ma face. I chappit agin, but she didna reply. I thocht tae ma'sel', the rude besum, whit the bluidy hell's she daein' in a job like that?'

The landlady was angry, her face had gone red and her big brown spaniel's eyes flashed fire for a moment before they quiesced to the sadness she had borne through life. Her body was taut, like a spring poised to recoil until with a giant shrug her posture loosened and she sat back and swept the air with her hands in a gesture of helplessness.

'I didna ken whit tae dae efter that, pet.'

Tia dipped her head; she understood how she felt.

'I'd been tae the hospitals an' I goes back, wi yin o' the lads, and got telt the same thing, 'cept he says I shouda wrote tae them. Weel, ye ken, I'm no muckle guid wi' a pen, Tia, but that's whit I did. I went and got some paper an' I sat ma'sel' doon, an' wrote tae the lot o' 'em. I esked if they kent a young lass ca'ed Mrs Tia Cameron, an' the blighters wrote back an' said they did not.'

Tia cut in suddenly. 'They had me down as Tia MacLeod.'

'They shoulda kenned, lass. I mean, how mony lasses did they hae fra' the Baillie's hoose in Pollokshields? I telt them that an' aw'.'

'You see,' Tia said slowly, 'when I went for the job, they asked me for a reference. I didn't know what it was but I said I'd give it to them later. Marcus wrote it. He used my maiden name because I didn't think I was supposed to be married.'

'Ach.' Mrs Anderson shook her head again. 'You shouldn' 'a done it, lass. Ye shouldn' e'er tell a lie. I coulda written ye a line if ye'd esked. I've done it of'en fir the lads. But that's no excuse fir thae bastirts. They said they didn' ken whaur ye wis, and they kenned fine weel the whole o' the time.'

Outside, the rain had stopped its insistent battering at the window.

The tea in Tia's cup was drunk; the landlady got up to pour her another, and then went into the kitchen to make her a ham sandwich.

'It's no much, pet, but it's better than aucht.' She grinned. 'If ye'd telt me ye wis coming, I'd'a put a spread on.'

'Next time, I'll give you some warning,' Tia replied. The food tasted of that; not the sawdust and cardboard she had been eating for months.

'Ye kin stay if ye like. Sleep in here for the nicht, an' I'll dae the room out fir ye the morn. Room?' She looked up at the ceiling. 'Whit am I telling ye? It's jis' a cupboard, lass, wi' a wee window out the back. It's shelter though.'

'I don't need it,' Tia said firmly, 'yet.'

Mrs Anderson was surprised.

'I've been staying in this place, you see. I'm in debt to the landlady, or so she says.'

Eyes narrowed, she looked at Tia askance.

She smiled slowly. 'I will come, though, if you'll have me. I just want to make sure that my debts are paid first.

'There'll aye be a place fir ye here, lass.'

Tia got up and stretched, then took her plate and cup through to the kitchen where she rinsed them and put them on the rack to drain.

'Ye're no' awa' yet, pet?' Mrs Anderson said, as she dried them.

'I'm tired,' Tia said.

The look on the landlady's face was understanding.

'I'll come back on Sunday.'

'Ye kin move in then. I'll put the room tae richts.'

'Thank you,' Tia said, as she took her jacket from the hanger by the range and put it on, felt its crisp dryness.

'Ach, I mind now, lass. There's a letter for ye fra the line, ye ken. Marcus's line. It's ahind the clock on the mantle, pet.' She had to search through a bundle before she handed it to her. 'I git that mony letters fir abdy. I dinna ken whit tae dae wi' them hauf the time.'

Tia stared at the writing on the envelope. She hesitated for a moment before she opened it. The letter expressed the line's condolences and asked her to visit a Captain Douglas in the line's offices at the docks. She trembled slightly.

'Is there aucht wrong, lass?'

'The line want to see me.'

'That's because Marcus left ye provided for. There's nowt to fret about.' The landlady's brow furrowed. 'There wis a lad called fir ye, an aw. Ken, he was called, or sommat. I dinna ken, pet. I wisna here. It wis yin o' the lads wha ansirt the door.'

Tia thought for a moment, before she remembered the Reverend and scowled.

'Ye're no here if he comes agin?'

She smiled. 'Not if it's who I think it is.'

'A young lad, he was, tall and dark.'

'That'd be the minister from home. He's a friend of my father's. Not of mine.'

The landlady smiled. 'Whit about yer things, pet? Shall I put them in the room fir ye?'

Tia shook her head. 'I . . ' She took a breath and swallowed. 'I'd rather not see them just yet.' Her strength had ebbed a little, with the shock of finding Mrs Anderson's; she needed time to adjust to being herself again. Now that she had found the boarding house, she no longer felt the need to vindicate herself with Mrs Gordon; she just wanted to pay her dues and leave.

'Dinna you fret, pet. Thaur's plenty time yit.'

Walking home in the rain that seeped again from the oily sky, Tia caught her reflection in a shop window. Her shoulders were upright and her stance straight; she had cast off the harried, hunted look that she had worn for so long. She walked blithely along the route that she had travelled by tram, her dignity restored now that she knew where she was.

Her old pride had returned, the same pride that would not allow her to give in to her father. She wanted to stand up to Mrs Gordon, she would pay her due but not the massive debt the landlady had concocted out of her plight.

The bells of the Gorbals Church rang ten times as she walked up to the front door, and then waited for an answer.

The strange thing was that she was no longer afraid of the landlady's wrath, or even of the dark. One of the Irish girls let her in, saying that the missus was at a prayer meeting, so she hadn't been missed.

'I don't care if I am,' Tia said, nonchalantly folding her arms. 'In fact, I might just wait for her.'

'I wouldn't,' the Irish girl said, 'the other girl left, the girl in your room, and the aud yin's that mad, she'd take on a bull.'

She went upstairs and took of her wet clothes; too tired to be angry any longer, she went to sleep instead.

Tia went to the shipping line offices at the Prince's Docks on Saturday morning, having written a note to Miss Collins to say that she would be late for work. The workroom was quiet at that time of year; the supervisor herself was not due in until ten. The torrents of ball gowns and dinner gowns, tea gowns and day wear, as the sales girls called the plainer dresses worn by the poorer rich, were ready, so most of the work was over; all that remained were a few alterations and the odd repair.

Once she found the office, the new name Pacific Hunter painted over the Rankine Line of yore, she had to wait before the man who had written the letter was ready to see her.

'You should have made an appointment,' his clerk told her pedantically.

'I have the letter here,' Tia replied. 'It says at my earliest convenience. It says nothing about an appointment. You can read it, if you like.'

'I know what it says.'

'It'd've helped if you'd said.'

The clerk sniffed. 'Company wives should know the procedure.'

'I'm not a wife. I'm a widow.' It hurt her to use the word; she turned away briefly before she looked up again to find him staring at her, so she stared back.

They glowered at each other until the bell on the clerk's desk rang and he grudgingly led her into the manager's office.

'Mrs Cameron,' the man said, rising and extending his hand, 'I'm Captain Douglas. Captain, retired, that is. I'm based ashore now. I'm so sorry that we have to meet in these tragic circumstances.'

She nodded in acknowledgement; there was nothing that she could say. His handshake was limp and cold and so were his eyes beyond the false bonhomie of the smile he wore.

'I've had the papers brought up from the archives. I was expecting you some time ago, I feared we'd lost you when you didn't come at once.'

Tia met his interest steadily. 'I was away for a while. My landlady kept the letter for me.'

The Captain (retd) pursed his lips as if her explanation did not fit, somehow. 'Let's deal with your husband's effects first; those that we were able to recover, that is. We can deal with the policies afterwards.'

He opened a manila envelope, shook out the signet ring that Marcus always wore, that had been his father's before him, that he had wanted to leave with her for safekeeping in case he lost it; then his wallet, some stained and folded papers. Captain Douglas lined them up on the desk as he consulted a list, then nodded. 'This is it all, you see. There's the police docket.'

She gasped when she saw these things, so familiar yet so distant, as if they had tried to run from her but had been captured and brought back. She was frightened to touch them at first; her hand, which had been resting on the edge of the desk shrank back like a tormented sea anemone.

A bit of paper fluttered across her vision, headed State of New Jersey.

'But I thought . . .' she murmured.

'Mrs Cameron, I thought you had been told. Captain Cameron's body was recovered three days later, a few miles up stream.'

The signet ring gleamed in the gas light, she saw a stain on it, reflexively she picked it up and blew, began to rub at it with the cuff of her jacket and then held it between her fingers, staring at the circle of gold that had been so very slightly marked with salt.

'He was identified by his uniform and some papers that he had in his possession. They're hardly legible now, I'm afraid.'

'Where did you bury my husband?'

'If you just sign here, Mrs Cameron, so that I can keep my records straight.'

She scribbled her name with the pen that he proffered.

'Where did you bury my husband, Captain Douglas?'

Hurriedly he replaced the wallet and papers in the envelope which he handed to her before he turned to a folder. 'Now, the Captain was a member of the Seaman's Union, and the line has a scheme to safeguard the dependants of our officers.'

'Captain Douglas, where did you bury my husband?'

He paused. He was avoiding her eyes.

'Why didn't you bring him home to me?'

'Regulations. Health regulations. He'd . . . the body had been in the water for a while.'

'Marcus was Catholic. He would have wanted a funeral.'

'Mrs Cameron, the matter was out of our hands.'

'I would've buried him.' There was a tremor in her voice; she felt her temper quicken for the first time since he had died. The shipping line's official began to tap the holder of his pen against his desk; the sound calmed her slightly, though she did not know why.

'Mrs Cameron, I knew your husband well. He was one of old Mr Rankine's most valued employees. Believe me. I regret the circumstances of his death. We all do. If it was possible, we would have brought him back, but we could not.'

'I want to go there. I want to see his grave.'

'Mrs Cameron . . .'

'I must go . . .' Her voice cracked then and she paused trying to get a grip of herself.

The official sighed. 'If you want to, the line will make the arrangements. It's the least we can do. Mrs Cameron . . .'

She turned away, wiping her eyes quickly with the back of her hand.

'Here is his death certificate. His Seaman's Policy was made out to his mother, but we can have that changed.'

'No, don't change it.'

'Mrs Cameron, the money is yours by right.'

'I don't want it.'

'The company benefit is payable to you. If you sign this form.'

The words wavered and blurred; she read something about a final settlement. 'What does it mean?'

'It's standard, in the circumstances. It means that you accept this money from the line in final settlement.'

'Captain Douglas, I did not come here for money.'

'Mrs Cameron, like the Seaman's Policy, it's yours by right.'

She scribbled her name, then took the paper he handed to her. 'What's this?'

He sighed. 'A cheque. You deposit it in your bank. I can give you cash if you'd rather.'

She said nothing so he rose to call the clerk then told him to get the cheque cashed at the Purser's office.

'I'm so sorry,' he said, as he handed her the money a few minutes later. 'So very, very sorry.'

She did not even count the notes that she put hurriedly in her purse.

Outside, the chill of the morning surrounded her. Though it felt as if a long time had passed, it was still early in the morning. Tia stood for a while, thinking, then began to walk determinedly towards the Women's Hospital in Rottenrow. Wise to the ways of the city now, she stopped to buy a transport map at St Enoch's so that she knew how to get there.

The building was old, scarred with decades of grime that blackened the sandstone. It had been an almshouse once, the stigma of poverty was etched into the brickwork and carried within the smell of wax polish tinged with carbolic that assailed her as she walked into the foyer and asked the way to Sister Aitken's ward and then, before the clerk had a chance to answer, turned and walked out again.

Marcus had gone to Catholic Mass on Christmas Day, in a church somewhere close to here; she wasn't sure where but she remembered now, she had waited outside for him when they were on their way to the bank. The service had been a short one, just twenty minutes or so, not even the length of the Bible reading in her father's Free Church. He had asked, begged her to go with him, but, through a brief resurgence of obstinacy, she had refused. They had jested for a few moments on the church steps before he had gone in and she had stayed outside, telling him that she would remain under God's sky, praying for the soul he was intent upong giving up to idolatry.

She had laughed then, but the memory made her cry now over the loss of the simple pleasures they had shared, of the tolerance of, even capacity to revel in the difference that was supposed to separate them but that had actually bound them tighter than a fly caught in a spider's web. She wished now that she had gone, but she had been so sure of herself then that she had denied him what he had wanted, of allowing her to see what his faith was about. It was strange that the memory of that moment, so long forgotten, came back now.

The clerk left her desk and came to where she stood on the hospital steps.'

'Madam, the sisters're at the Matron's meeting now, but they'll be back on the wards at eleven.'

'It doesn't matter,' Tia said, rubbing at the corner of her eye as she turned away.

'If you come back, I'm sure Sister Aitken will see you then.'

'Thank you,' she said, neutrally.

'Is anything the matter, Madam, anything I can help you with?'

Tia turned to face her again. 'Is there a Roman church anywhere near here?'

Briskly, the clerk told her where it was.

She stood staring at the door for ages, then knocked once, and again when it did not open. She was walking away when she heard the creak of timber, and turned to see a man in a priest's robe looking this way and that.

'Whas it you who whas knacking?' he asked, in a deep brogue.

'I didn't think you were open.'

'The door of Our Lord's Howsse is neffer cloh-ssed. Come away in, Mizzus, if you want to ssay owt.'

She followed him slowly, scared now to face the dim and the smell of burning candles, the effigy of Our Lady in an alcove by the door over a little vial of Holy Water.

'Iss it the confesshunal you'll be needing, or whas it chust a wee chat?'

The priest spoke very slowly, stretching each word.

She swallowed nervously. 'I'd like to talk, if you have a moment.'

'Och, awway in, womman, while I poot the kettle onn.'

He walked into the church, dipping briskly before the altar as she shifted on her feet, then led her through to a little room just beyond, where he seated her in a little chair close to a stove as he fiddled with a pot and cups.

'What iss the matter, can you tell me now?' he asked, after he had given her a cup and taken one of his own.

She told him quickly, in a string of words that sounded hardly long enough when she realised that she had told him it all.

He nodded, the bald patch at the top of his hair catching he light and glowing dully.

'I ssseee. And what iss it that you would like mee to doo?'

She folded her hands in her lap. 'I would like him to have a decent funeral. He would have wanted that. I would like some prayers to be said. If you could.'

The priest got up and lit a lamp, throwing a pool of light over the little room. 'You haff to understand, Mizzus, the Holy Church has been in bussyness effer since the death of Our Lord. It wass the Apostle Peter who wass the first of our Popes.'

'I know that.'

'I dare ssay you do, but do you know that the Holy Church was around to watch ovver the end of the Roman Empire? We went through the Dark Ages, the plagues and the Crusades, all the wars and all the peaces since the day Our Lord was rissen again. Tanks be to God, we were around when Columbus discovered America. The fate that you think hass befallen your Marcus has befallen many before.'

'I don't think, I know,' she said.

'What do you know?'

'I know . . .' She blinked and turned away for a moment. 'I know that he died alone. That there was nobody there to comfort him and nobody was there to speak of him – for him – at the burying.'

'Comfort in death is a luxury oft denied, lass. Death is more often uncomfortable, iss it not?'

She turned away.

'My dear,' he said slowly, 'I know you think little of our Holy Church, but what I wass trying to tell you iss that, whatever our failings, we haff a ritual for everything. Everything on God's earth that can happen, we have a rite of prayer to mark it. What do you suposse happened to all the voyagers who neffer returned? We haff a ritual, oh, yes. A Requiem Mass. I can say one for your Marcus and I can also ask Our Lord to bless your union, howeffer brief it was. I can do that, if it would be off comfort.'

'I would be very grateful if you could,' she said in a small voice.

He led her through to the church and after leaving her standing in a pew at the front he turned to the altar and began to speak in a language she did not understand. Every so often he would pause and beckon to her; she knelt in prayer then, trying to follow his words but uttering ones of her own when she realised how pointless it was just to mime.

After reading a passage from the Bible, he took Communion himself, then knelt in prayer. 'Gloria Patri et Filio et Spiritui Sancto. Sic erat in principio, et nunc, et semper, et in saecula saeculorum. Amen.' He rose, came to her and touched her brow. 'The mass for the soul of your beloved husband is over, my child. Go in peace.'

Her eyes matted with tears as he led her towards the daylight. She opened her purse and handed him one of the notes Captain Douglas had given her; he said it was too much, that he wanted nothing but she begged him to keep it. He told her he would give it to the poor of the parish. She said that Marcus would have wanted that. He told her that the candle he had lit would burn its way out, but that he would remember Marcus at prayers that Sunday, and for a year afterwards.

When she left the church the morning had been freshened by rain, the streets were slick and slippery. A sense of peace came over her as she walked back to the hospital and was shown the way to Sister Aitken's ward, where she waited in the corridor whilst a nurse went to fetch her.

The sister strode towards her, puzzled at first until she recognized her visitor. A smile lit her face as she took Tia into her office and asked the maid to fetch some tea.

'I wanted to say thank you,' Tia said, 'I would've before, but I didn't get the chance.'

'It's nothing,' the sister said. 'Healing your body was the smallest part of the process.'

'It was you who did that.'

'I gave you the chance.'

They drank the tea the maid brought as Tia wondered at the vagaries of life, at how easy it was to incur a debt that was impossible to repay because its worth could never be counted in terms of money. She was angry at the hospital, angry because they had denied having her when Mrs Anderson had asked for her and had then given her over to a woman who would be quite happy to accept payment of her dues in blood, but she sensed that the sister had nothing to do with that. It was the sister's anxious, tender care that had made her live when there was nothing to live for.

'I just wanted you to know that I am grateful,' she said.

Sister Aitken smiled. 'It's nice to see you now that you really are getting better. We don't often know, you see.'

After they finished the tea, the sister led her quickly through the labyrinth of passages to the outside world.

'What are you going to do now?' she asked at the front door.

'I'd like to go to the office and find out about my bill. It's been paid, I know, but I'd like to know how much it is.'

She frowned. 'But, Miss MacLeod, I'm sorry, I mean, Mrs Cameron – '

'Tia,' she smiled.

'Tia. You were a city case. The corporation gives us money to care for the sick. I'm pretty sure about that. There was no bill.'

'But Mrs Gordon, the woman who took me in, she said the Vigilance Society paid it.'

The sister's frown deepened. 'If you'll give me a minute, I'll go to the office and ask about that. But I'm sure there was no bill. There never is, 'lest I'm going daft.'

'There's something else,' Tia said quickly, 'Mrs Anderson, that's the landlady Marcus and I stayed with, she tried to find me and she wrote to all the hospitals and they all wrote back and told her they did not have any patients of that name.'

The sister nodded. 'Well, they would, you see. It's a standard letter. Confidentiality. We're not allowed to release the information unless they're your next of kin, and in your case we could find no next of kin.'

'But she was a friend,' Tia said.

'We weren't to know that. All letters like that go to Matron's office, and the same reply goes to everyone. There's sixteen hundred beds here, that's as many people. They wouldn't even've checked the name, beyond that there was no Mrs Cameron registered. I registered you myself, Miss MacLeod, no known relatives, all enquiries to be addressed to me. I thought it was best, you see. I didn't want that curmudgeon, your employer, getting at you.'

'I see.'

She went off briskly, softened shoes brushing the polished passageway, coming back later with a slip of paper.

'I was right, Tia. You were a public case. Here's a note from Matron to prove it.'

Tia took the paper and folded it carefully into the pocket of her skirt.

'I'm sorry about your friend, I really am, but I thought I was doing the best, you see.'

'Thank you,' she said, 'I understand.'


She arrived at Daly's workroom moments before the lunch break ended; she took her jacket off quickly then went to her work bench to find an empty space where her scissors, threads and needles had been. Two of the seamstresses who had been nonchalantly eating biscuits stopped chatting and glared at her.

'Miss Collins wants to see you right away,' one of them said, the dark one with the pinched face who usually ignored her.

Tia stopped midway; she had been about to sit down on her stool.

'Where is she?'

'I don't know,' the other said.

Tia sat down. 'I'll wait here.'

They looked at each other and shrugged. 'As I was saying,' the dark one said, 'I went down to Candleriggs to see him . . .' 'See who?' the other asked. 'Weinstock, Molly, I don't know, you're so glaikit, in any case, as I was saying, I went to see him but it was pandemonium, garments and pieces all over the place, and all machined too, no hand work at all. I thought, this isn't right, this isn't the place for me. I mean, Daly's quality is second to none.' They both nodded vigorously. 'But the advertisement did say garment maker and not just machine hand and the pay is supposed to be very good. Well! I waited, Molly, I waited and I waited. I must've waited thirty minutes for the man before he eventually notices me and asks me what I want. So I say, a job of course, the paper did say you're looking and he just stands there and stares at me as if I'm mad. Well!' 'I'd've walked out if I were you, Agnes. I mean, if he treats an applicant like that, how will he treat a worker?' 'You're right there, Molly, right you are. I'd best done that, but I was there and I'd done the waiting, I thought I might as well see what he had to say . . .' 'It was that place on Candleriggs, Agnes? Weinstock's Haute Couture? I thought it was a good place. I mean, there's no couture houses in Glasgow these days.' 'You're right there, Molly, but then there never was. . .'

*'Miss MacLeod! My office now. This instant!'* Miss Collins roared, cutting into Tia's thoughts. She had been fascinated by the seamstresses' chatter; she was sitting listening with her chin cupped in her hand as they carried on oblivious.

'What is the meaning of this, girl?' the supervisor raved, waving her note, as Tia hurried into the glass-panelled booth at the corner of the workroom.

'It was about my husband, Miss Collins. It was urgent that I see to it.'

'Husband?' she frowned. 'You have no husband, girl. That's why Francis Gordon took you in.'

Tia looked down at the floorboards as her face flushed. 'I don't have a husband now, Miss Collins. I did have once. I was married a few weeks after my sixteenth birthday. My husband was at sea. He was killed in an accident at New York docks.'

'Oh.' Lips tightly wedged, for a moment the supervisor considered what she had said. 'If you had said there had been a bereavement, it would've been a different matter.'

Tia looked up at her. 'Would have been?'

'It's the rules, you see. Didn't you ever read them?'

The rules were posted all around the workroom; Tia had glanced at them but she had never learned them. There was only one that she had really noted, that the staff were not allowed to take home anything, even a scrap of thread, without the supervisor's permission. It was Jeannie who doled out the remnants swept up from the floor at the end of the day under Miss Collins' keen eye. Over the months, Tia had collected enough for a pair of bloomers and then a blouse, each patched from several different remnants. Even then, she had never worn the blouse to work, for fear that Miss Collins would see in it a piece she hadn't meant to be thrown out.

'I did,' she said.

'Well, girl?'

She took a breath. 'Miss Collins, I'm not sure what I'm

supposed to have done. Whatever it is, I'm very sorry. I'll make the hours up. You know I will.'

'You will not, girl, at least, I doubt it. Mr Hendry made an inspection today . . .'

'Mr Hendry?'

'How dare you interrupt me when I'm speaking, girl? Disobeying the rules's bad enough without adding insolence. Mr Hendry is the director in charge of the workrooms, as you well know.'

Tia had never heard the name in her life before.

'. . .And when he saw the empty space at your bench, I had to tell him you were absent without leave.'

'But I left a note for you at the door.'

*'A note's not enough, girl. You have to have my permission and you just went off without a by-your-leave to anyone. Mr Hendry asked me for an explanation and when I was unable to give him a satisfactory one he insisted that you be dismissed.'*

Tears welled in Tia's eyes, despite her anger. The job wasn't much but it had kept her going through the dark days, in the cold dawn of the hinterland of her grief when it seemed to her that day would never truly come again. The work, the transitory custody of the riches that passed through her hands, even gave her the odd flash of pleasure now and then.

'As I said, I'm very sorry,' she said, helplessly, 'But I got a letter and I had to go.'

'Get back to your place,' the supervisor told her abruptly. 'I will go to see Mr Hendry now, but I am not promising anything. You'll have to explain to Mrs Gordon yourself.'

'Explain?'

'Yes. I wrote to her and told her what had happened. I had to. It was our agreement, you see, that I would inform her if you tried anything.'

'You had no right, Miss Collins . . '

'Don't you tell me what's right and what isn't. Just get back to your work now and be thankful that you're not out on your ear.'

It was after eight o'clock when she got back to the boarding house. Mr Hendry had agreed not to dismiss her, but then Miss Colins had given her some work to do and she did not finish until well after closing, when the night watchman was beginning his rounds. The work had been to fix a panel on an evening dress, the stitches were so fine that she had to use a magnifying glass.

One of the Irish girls opened the door to her and told her to wait for the landlady in the dining room.

'What's the matter?' Tia asked her.

She shrugged.

'Please,' Tia said.

The girl made to move away, but Tia caught her arm. 'Please,' she said again, 'just listen to me for a moment. The Vigilance Society brought me here too. I know what you're going through.'

The face that stared back at her was cynical and also old.

'I was married, you see, and I had a miscarriage. But I was working as a maid, and I had pretended that I was single. When I told them I was married they didn't believe me.'

The girl shook off her grip roughly. 'Let me alowyn,' she murmured thickly, 'if ye've got a smidgen guid in ye, let me well alowyn.'

'But I know,' Tia insisted. 'I know what you're going through. I'll help, if you let me.'

'Will ye?' Her eyes had rimmed with tears.

Tia shuddered inside. 'I will, I can honestly.'

'Can ye?' There was anger there, too, deep below the pain.

'You see, it happened to me too. Just the same. I know what you're going through.'

'Ye do, do ye?'

'I do.'

Their eyes met for a moment, then the girl shook her off more roughly than before. 'I do,' she mimicked bitterly, shaking her head. 'Well, Miss, Missis, wha'er ye are, I haff news fir 'ee. I wisny wed, I've ne'er wed, I wis a maiden, y'see? I was a maiden and so was Briege, we're sisters, ye'see, I'm fourteen, she's jis' twelve. We wis raped, y'see, the taw o'us. Me first, then her. It wis the son o' the house an' a friend, home from some school they go to in Edinbra. Me first, then her. I begged him t'leave her, I told him to have me instead, I said they both could, but they laughed, see? They raped me first. That night, and then each night till they went back tae school. I didna protest or aucht, I was that feart they wid rape her. They saved that fir last. They tied me and gagged me sae I widna scream. They made me watch, but. I didna miscarry, Missus. I kilt it ma'sel, acos I couldna stand it. Briege helped me. We wis caught. An' thrown out. An' sent here. No' acos we wis raped, see, but fir leadin' the son o' the house astray. Ye ken whit I'm going thru, Miss, Missus? Don't make me laugh.'

She turned away, ignoring Mrs Gordon, who had been standing listening. 'I'll have a word with you later, girl,' she said, before she turned to Tia.

'I just want to collect my things.'

'What things?' Mrs Gordon folded her arms.

'My clothes.'

'When you came you only had what you stood up in. Much less even that you have on now.'

Tia tried to get past her but she moved to block the passageway. 'You owe me money, don't forget, MacLeod.'

'I just want to take my things, Mrs Gordon.'

'When you've paid what you owe, MacLeod.'

Tia stepped back. 'I owe you nothing, Mrs Gordon.'

The landlady began to count off debts on her fingers. 'Hospital bills, doctor's bills, the cost of your iron tonic. Clothes and shelter when you were too sick to work.'

'What does it all come to?'

'I don't know. I will count it all up.'

Tia shook her head. 'The hospital didn't charge anything. I have a letter from the matron. The work I did paid for everything else. And more besides. You owe me, Mrs Gordon.'

'Say that again and I'll have you for slander.'

'Mrs Gordon, if you say one more word to me about debt, I swear to God, I'll kill you for it. Now let me get my things.'

They faced each other for a moment longer before the landlady saw the fire in her eyes and let her past. Tia ran up the stairs and tied her things in a bundle, changed from her shoes to her old boots and left the room as she had found it all those months ago.

The corridor at the front of the house was silent and empty. Just a glimmer of light seeped from the tightly closed door of the landlady's salon.

'I have it all here. Every penny,' Mrs Gordon roared,

from the safety behind it. 'It's all written down in my books.'

Tia threw the door open with her shoulders, then grabbed the ledgers from the table, ripping the covers from them before she tore up the paper and tossed it onto the fire, poking the ashes dementedly before she added the covers and watched them burn.

'The police,' the landlady spat. 'I'll have the police on you, girl. Just you wait.'

'Wait is the one thing I am not going to do,' Tia yelled as she strode out of the house, slamming the door behind her and then kicking it savagely, just in case she had not made herself clear.

Once she had turned the corner, the safety of the night closed around her, its sounds amplified but no longer threatening. Rain was falling, making the road glitter in the reflection of the gaslights. She looked up to the sky and breathed deeply, felt a great weight lift from her shoulders.

Without looking back, she headed for Mrs Anderson's.

# Chapter Eleven

*H*esitantly, she walked into the building in Candleriggs and up the stairs, past the Deco tiles of lilies lining the walls, the flowers miraculous in the hostile medium of institutional ivory, the textured border chipped and stained. Though the plate at the entrance grandly said Weinstock's Haute Couture the workrooms were on the top floor, the floors below layered with an accountant and an insurance broker, a jeweller and a silversmith, all of whose names had the same elongated endings, the same cacophony of consonants. There was a Halbesohn and a Wicniesky, a Wallechinsky and a Grutschkopf. Of them all, Weinstock was the most comprehensible, the others just long lines of letters that suggested no sound that Tia recognised at all.

The thrum of the machinery started on the street, becoming louder as she climbed the stairs until the crescendo at the top drowned all but itself.

There was no point in knocking on the door, no one would hear; so she opened it and waited, in the hope that someone would notice her.

The workroom was unlike any she had imagined – long and low, it was lit on two sides by windows and also by rows of skylights. Electric lamps strung from lines of cable battled with the stronger light of day that tumbled in from above. There were sewing machines in a line by the windows, and the middle of the room was filled by a huge table covered with bolts of cloth, with more stored on racks by the door. Women and men sat huddled over the machines, cutters in the middle sliced cloth like butter, tossing pieces at the boys who ran in between. At the far end were racks full of garments beside a row of dummies draped with that season's styles, with notes pinned on to them to explain the trim.

To watch, it was a human beehive, the activity a pattern almost like a reel with the message boys moving in time with the thrum of the machines. Occasionally, one would stop and the machinist would yell 'thread' and hold his or her hand up for a replacement, or 'finish' and the garment would be taken from them and added to the pile awaiting the women who wielded steam pressers like cutlasses.

A small man scampered through the throng, stopping here and there to peer and to check, to say something in a yell that came out as hardly a whisper, gesticulating wildly to get his message across.

His movements were constant and regular as the ticking of a clock. She watched him for a while, then beckoned to him when she caught his eye. He smiled broadly, gesturing for her to follow him through the workroom and then to an office hidden behind the racks of finished clothes.

The noise dropped a decibel or two once he had manoeuvred the racks back into place and closed the door firmly.

'I'm Tia Cameron, Mrs Cameron,' she told him. He looked bewildered, but his smile did not falter. 'I wrote you a note,' she said, 'last week. I said I hoped that it would be convenient if I came in today.'

'Letter, letter, *schmetter* letter.' He prodded a pile of papers on his desk, peered over his glasses at the one on top, holding it up to get the light. 'Ach, *nein* letter. That is a bill.' He flicked through another layer or two of the file, becoming more earnest as his search continued, until the whole structure tumbled over on to the floor and he followed it on hands and knees, peering this way and that.

Tia bent down to join him. 'What are you looking for?'

'Bills, bills. If letter not answered . . .' He sat back and gave a careless shrug. 'If bills not paid it's a different matter. They not supply materials, they close me down. Weinstock Haute Couture? Kaput!'

He scanned the papers randomly, picking up a bundle at a time and leafing through it, putting the headed invoices to one side as he discarded the others on the original tumble. Tia began to help, gathering the papers all together and quickly sorting through them as he paused and peered at something written in a strange, ornate script, pulling at his glasses to focus them. Once she had put the bills carefully on a space she cleared on the desk, she hunted the discards and found her letter.

Mr Weinstock was still reading, shaking his head and smiling to himself.

'Mein cousin. A musician. Vienna. The price of chocolate cake. Is nonsense. Music is the food of love, so they say. I write my cousin, tell him to eat his wife. Weinstock Haute Couture cannot support the Vienna Opera.'

He smiled at her. 'Now, my dear, what can I do for you?'

She handed him the letter, which he glanced at briefly before he put it to one side: 'One thing about letters, my dear, is if they are important, the writer himself will come, if you wait. If not . . .' He gave another helpless shrug.

'It was about the job, Mr Weinstock. I heard you were looking for workers. I'm at Daly's now, just an assistant, but I can finish and I can press. I haven't got a reference, though.'

'Reference? I've never read a reference yet that was not nonsense. If the worker is good, what employer in his right mind vould let the worker go? Is rubbish, this reference. I get a reference once, it says, Meezes Ross is an excellent machinist. Meezes Ross is *Maestro*.' He threw his arms wide. 'Meezes Ross, she did not know one end of a sewing machine from the other. I sack Meezes Ross. I never sack anyone before, but I sack Meezes Ross. If I didn't sack Meezes Ross, I go *pphhhht*. Weinstock Haute Couture totally kaput.'

He got up and went to an urn perched precariously on a table slumped against the wall. 'We will take tea, Meezes Cameron, and you tell me why you would like a job.'

'Well,' she began slowly, 'at Daly's I'm an assistant and I'll never be anything else. I want to learn, and to be able to use what I learn.'

'Do you want to be a machinist?'

'What I really want to do is design, but I'd like to be able to machine too. I can handsew very well.'

He beamed broadly and told her she could start whenever she wanted. He had decided to give her a job when he saw how quickly she got his papers in order, he said.

'It's not Daly's', she said that evening to Mrs Anderson, 'but it seems a nicer place.'

'I'd be canny, if I wis ye, pet. Ye've tae watch thae Yids, so they say. They'd skin ye alive as soon as look at ye, they say.

Mind ye . . .' She cocked her head to one side for a moment, as if she was thinking. 'I suppose yon Missus Gordon alriddy did, an' yon bluidy Baillie afore her.'

'Marcus said that people are the same the world over, some are good and some are bad, but mostly they're just foolish.'

'Thon maks sense, I s'pose, pet. It's jis' it taks a while tae git to ken onyyin. It's hard enou' tae get tae ken yer ain folk, wi'oot e'en botherin' wi' folks fra' onyplace else. Ye kin say this an' that abou' the al' o' us, pet. Dinna pay no mind tae an' auld wumman like me.'

'I liked him,' Tia said.

'Well, s'long's ye dae, it disna matter whit abdy says.'

The room she had was under the stairs; as Mrs Anderson said, it was a cupboard really, long and thin and for the most part slant-ceilinged, as if it had been cut like a wedge of cheese. She put her bed up against the lowest stair, and the first few mornings bumped her head when she woke up before she got used to it and remembered not to sit up suddenly with the shock of waking, but to ease herself out of bed carefully, aware of the precipice just above her head. Apart from that, there was one window that let in the morning light, a chest and a table, a little chair for her to sit and hooks on the wall to hang her clothes. She wanted or needed no more than that. Her things were still in the hall cupboard; a week had passed before she even dared look into it and then the shock of the familiar but forgotten was so great that she slammed the door immediately and then cried herself to sleep. Mrs Anderson was understanding; she seemed to sense Tia's moods, when she wanted to talk and when she wanted to be quiet, when to comfort her when she cried and when to let her cry alone.

It was only on Christmas Day that she opened the door and pulled out Marcus's chest and opened it to find the photograph taken outside the Registry Office in Oban, which she hugged tight to her chest for a long time before she carefully put it in a frame Mrs Anderson gave her and hung it on the wall beside her bed, where she could see it at night when she went to sleep and again in the morning.

This Marcus never changed, he never looked away from her.

For a long time she had suppressed her memories of him, of the way she had thrilled to him when she had first known him and he had lifted her in his boy's arms and helped her into his rowboat to check the lobster pots that Mary kept in the bay, and he teased her and talked to her as a friend and not in the distant tone of command her father used. Sorley MacIain was the only man she had known well before that, though she saw the other village men, as grim as her father, during the endless church service on Sunday morning when even a baby's cries were subdued by a sermon so long that sometimes the congregation seemed to be in a trance. There was only the minister's words, the phrases, the clauses, the paragraphs punctuated by the prophecy of damnation and the absolute silence that segregated each threat. To a child, it was frightening. The first time she took it all in, actually listened as opposed to waiting, her thoughts drifting, for this divine torment to be at an end, she said nothing for the rest of the day, not during the cold food cooked the previous evening that Janet served on Sunday, nor in the afternoon when with her sisters and brothers she was allowed to take a walk on the sands, nor after the evening Bible reading when her mother put her to bed and then knelt beside her to listen to her prayers. When Janet prompted her, she paused for an eternity before at last she whimpered her only hope, a brief invocation that God would let her live despite the hellish morass of sin into which she had tumbled, unaware of what she was doing or even of what, exactly, sin was. To Tia, sin was any word or action which displeased her father; which more or less meant anything at all. Sorley MacIain's temper was not short fused so much as pure dynamite, instantly ignited by the slightest spark.

In the morning Janet took her for a long walk across the causeway to Baleshare, and to the endless, pristine sands that rimmed the edge of the island, where the birds called and the seals played and the pounding of the ocean was as immortal as time itself.

Way out to sea, a school of dolphins leaped and dived like ebony scythes, flashing blue-black curves through the water that glittered like onyx in the light of the sun. An old man took her out a little way in his boat and she laughed as the dolphins saw her and came closer, saw that if she reached out with her hand she could almost touch them. For a while she drew circles in the air with her hands as they dived and soared; she was so happy then, as they let her join their game, that, for a moment, she had danced with them.

On the way back to her cottage Janet recited the third chapter of Ecclesiastes and Tia listened to the words that drifted so softly around her and knew that the God of her father was not all there was to Him.

When, in the rage of the March tides, a whale was beached at Baleshare, abandoned by the ocean where she had danced with dolphins landed high and dry and left on the scrub to choke, she knew it was not the will of God that the animal died that way, but rather a matter of nature and chance.

To her father the death of the whale was an act of God; the will of God was omnipotent and ever-present; nothing happened that was not ordained and arranged by Him.

It was in January that she took Marcus's clothes, those he wore when ashore, out of the chest and put mothballs into them before she wrapped them in ticking she had brought home from Weinstock's and packed them again. She kept his sweater, the Eriskay sweater, and rolled it up underneath her pillow where its aroma wafted around her as she slept. That comforted her through the depths of winter; in spring she folded it carefully in a pillowslip and put it away again. There was still a trace of him in the fabric and she wanted to save it carefully.

The sight of her wedding suit made her sob; Mrs Anderson took it to hang in her own wardrobe, clucking and muttering that if she did not the fine cloth would be ruined.

To Tia, the memory was enough.

She went just once to remind herself and found the embroidered label inside which read *Pacquin, Paris at **Bergdorf Goodman, New York***. She knew what it meant now and cried again.

Amongst Marcus's papers she found a notebook with a list of addresses after her sister Mairead's name, the last address being an alley in the Gallowgate; she went there one evening after work when the sky was light enough to see her way along the road where the gas lamps were habitually out. The alley was filled with children, an old woman on a stool watching over them all.

'Excuse me,' Tia said, 'd'you know where Mairead lives? Mairead MacLeod she was, I don't know her married name.'

'Wha's that, hen?' She cupped her hand to her ear as if she was deaf.

'Mairead,' Tia said. 'She's my sister. She looks like me, 'cept her hair's darker and she's a few years older.'

The woman looked her up and down. 'There's naebdy aroun' like that, hen.'

Relieved secretly, Tia walked out of the alley quickly; Marcus must have been wrong, she thought, or maybe it was just that someone there would have known of Mairead.

At work Mr Weinstock gave her another job, that of checking the completed order against the order slip, and then the garments themselves, the sizes and the trimmings, that the buttons were secured and the seams to be finished to the customer's fit were neatly tacked. She did some of the finishing herself and watched the work of the other girls.

'You have an eye for detail,' Mr Weinstock said, when she told him she had never done work like that before and was not sure if she could. 'It does not matter that you are not sure. I am sure. I am the boss.'

After her first few months, when she was paid ten shillings a week, he offered her fifteen if she would take charge of the invoices as well. It meant extra work; she arrived at eight in the morning and rarely left before nine at night, but she was glad of it.

She sent the bills out promptly when the goods were despatched and a polite little reminder note two weeks later, then a copy of the invoice and another letter if a second fortnight went by and the money had not come in yet. If the bill was not paid withing six weeks, she would go to the customer and ask if anything was the matter, if there was any reason why not. The bill was always paid when the customers realised that no more orders would be delivered until it was.

She kept the cheques in the safe during the week, listing them for Mr Weinstock to take to the bank each Friday before dusk, when Mr and Mrs Weinstock left the workroom in the charge of Alice, the workroom chargehand, as they went home to celebrate *shabbat*.

As much as a hundred pounds went in every week, though almost as much went out again to pay Weinstock's costs and the staff wages.

'Doesn't it worry you?' she asked Mr Weinstock one day. 'All that money being in the bank?'

'Haven't I enough to worry about without worrying about the bank as well? The Bank of Scotland is solid. Sound as a bell. It not go kaput else Scotland kaput. If country kaput . . .' He shrugged enigmatically, as if unable to consider any more of a consequence than that.

She smiled at his expression. 'I meant,' she began, very slowly, 'I meant, if . . . if anything happened to you . . . I mean, my husband, he had money in the bank.' She shook her head. 'I can't ever get it out.'

'What?' He frowned, his whole face twisted into confusion. 'Get it out. Of couse, you can. The husband's money belongs to the wife. They will give it to you, every penny. You see. We go there Monday, you and me. They will give it then, you see.'

Tia looked out of the window and saw a finger of darkness coming in from the east; she completed the deposit slip quickly because he was already late for *Shabbat*.

On Monday, at noon, they went together to the Ba    of Scotland in Argyle Street, where Marcus had held an accou nt.

'You have the papers?' Mr Weinstock asked.

She took an envelope from her pocket and handed him her marriage certificate and also the certificate of Marcus's death. She hated even to look at it, to touch it made her fingers hurt.

He marched boldly up to the counter and asked to see the manager at once.

Tia watched, ashamed, guilty that she was not as astute or as able to deal with things as her employer was. He had told her once that they were both immigrants, the difference was just that he had come a little further.

Within a moment she was ushered into the manager's office, given tea as Mr Weinstock shook his hand vigorously and left, after gesticulating wildly and telling him volubly to sort it all out.

'Mrs Cameron,' the manager said, 'I am so sorry, so very, very sorry.'

She nodded briefly; she did not want his sympathy, only his help.

'Your husband, Mr Cameron, Captain Cameron, he had an

account with us all of his working life. He started it when he was just a lad. We thought, we wondered when he didn't come back, but he told us he was going to close the account when you moved to New York. He had funds there too, I believe. We have the deeds of a property in Montauk. I'm pretty certain that he had a local account—'

'Please,' she said, lifting her hand to stop him. 'I don't want it.'

'But Mrs Cameron, it's yours.'

'I don't want it,' she said again.

He sighed and looked over her shoulder through a window on to the street.

'You see,' she said, after a time. 'He died there. In New York. In New Jersey, I should say. In an accident. I would've gone, but by the time I knew there was nothing to go to. I thought . . .' Her voice trailed off.

He waited.

'I thought it wouldn't help,' she said. 'It wouldn't help him and it wouldn't help me. I wanted to go, but there was nothing to go to. I had a requiem mass said here instead.'

Her eyes glittered with tears.

The bank manager coughed and then reached into a drawer and handed her a paper to sign.

She picked up the pen thoughtlessly before he stopped her and told her that she must read it first, that if it would help he would read it to her.

She nodded and he did, enunciating each word carefully, keeping track with a blunt pencil that hovered just above the form itself. She did not understand what it meant, so he went through it again, explaining every phrase carefully. The form was merely an agreement that the bank retain the deeds and the account in her name as opposed to Marcus's.

'It's so complicated.' She smiled thinly.

'Mrs Cameron.' The manager folded his hands pedanti-cally. 'You must never, ever sign anything without reading it first. You must always read it and ask if there is something you don't understand. Do not believe the person who is asking you to sign it. Sign it yourself only if you are certain. If not, ask a lawyer first.'

She signed the form then blotted it and handed it back to him.

'There is just one other thing,' he said, rising to indicate that the meeting was over. He handed her an envelope with her name on it in Marcus's writing. She took it and folded it quickly into her pocket and then she thanked him and left, walking fast down the street towards Weinstock's in the hope that the breeze would dry her eyes before she arrived.

'Ban-righ, mo cèile annsachd,
    'Tha gaol agam ort . . .

Later that day, in the dim of her room, lit gently by the window, it was easier to read the only letter her husband had ever written to her. There was something about her language that was not in accord with the stridency of electricity, or even the softer glare that came from a gas lamp. The words were natural, unenhanced, they did not need to be emphasised or restated.

Queen, my darling wife,
I love you. I know that if you are reading this, then something has happened to me. As I said, the ocean will never be your friend, the best you can hope for is her tolerance. It seems that she has had enough of me.

I will not be lonely. It was the ocean that took my father and his father before him. In my life, I have loved and been loved; that is the greatest gift that any man could have, or woman, come to that. And it is a gift, because you cannot learn it or make it or earn it. It is a gift that can only be received.

Please know that, above anything else, you are loved now as you were when I was by your side, as you always will be. You must be angry at my passing; forgive me please, it was not my intention to leave you. Forgive me please and live your life with my love beside you. I talked to you once, on the morning of the first day we were wed. You were asleep and I was awake, but I made you promise not to mourn me and you promised that you would not.

Never doubt that we will meet again, nor doubt that I will love you still, despite the years apart. I could ask you to do things, like I would want you to see my mother again, because she loves you too, and my brothers and sisters, to understand Bridie's bitterness, for it is her who has taught me more than anyone that to mourn is to choose death, not life, that while grief is healing, to mourn is to allow death to seep into the soul. I know that you will do these things in time, because I know

213

*the woman you are. There is one apology that I have to make, and that is that I didn't have time to find Mairead. I found an address for her in Partick, which you'll find in my book, but when I went there I got another and then another and in the end the trail ended with nobody knowing where she had gone next. I did the best I could in the few hours I wasn't with you, when you were out earning my keep.*

*Most of all, take a little of the love you gave to me and use it to love yourself. There is money – not that you care, I know, I guess you won't touch it, but I hope that you do. I hope that you will use it to do anything that would make you happy, to love yourself a little in the certainty that, in time, someone else will as I already do.*

*Forever,*
*Marcus*

For a long time after she read the letter she did not want to go out, did not want to do anything but stare at the great grey world hinted at beyond the mist that clung to her window. At some time during that long evening she took some of the notes from her purse and put them in an envelope then sealed it and addressed it to Eunice.

It was late spring that she decided to try again to find her sister. She took her old shawl from the island to work one morning, and wrapped it around her jacket when she left that night. The sky then was tincture of iodine, blue and clear above the hard edges of the tenements' remorseless grey. The children at play did not notice her this time when she went into the alley and waited in the courtyard, her shawl tightly wrapped against the evening chill.

After a while the yard cleared of children, and a woman came out to take in the washing cursing at the dust that streaked the sheets, the grubby finger marks where the children had brushed against them, caught up in the urgency of their game.

Tia went up to her when she had finished folding and the bundle was neatly packed in a basket at her feet.

'Excuse me,' she said, 'but I'm looking for someone called Mairead. She comes from North Uist, though she's been here a while. She's my sister, but she's a bit older than me.'

'Come ben wi' me, hen, an we'll ask auld Meg. If it's onyyin, she'll ken.'

Tia followed her into a close that stank of urine, sharpened with the sting of bleach. The woman went up a flight of stairs, then kicked a door open, bringing Tia into a room just ten feet or so square that was full of mattresses and children asleep.

'Ye'll no disturb 'em,' the woman said. 'They're that used tae the racket o' folks comin' and goin'.'

She hauled down a pulley and laid the dried sheets over it to air.

'Meg's at the back doon the stairs,' she said, as she left again and pulled the door to.

There was another stair, leading down from the main one, that Tia hadn't noticed when she went in. The passageway beyond was filled by shadows that wavered in time with the echo of their steps. The woman stopped at a door and put her fingers to her lips. 'She sells ale, like. She africht o' the polis. Ye hae tae chap the door lichtly afore ye go in. She's got a stoatin' dog that wid kill ye soon's look at ye.'

'Meg,' she called, raising her voice a little, 'Meg? It's only me, Ishbel fra' up the stair. I've a wuman wi' me wha's eskin' fir someyin', an' I wunnert if ye'd ken.'

The door creaked then opened slowly, as a dog's head, tongue lolling, strained to get out, held back by a leash.

'Come awa in, Ishbel,' a voice said, 'dinna mind the dug. He's haud his dinner.'

She laughed, and the sound touched a chord in Tia's memory.

She pushed open the door and looked into her sister's eyes.

Tia stifled the gasp that rose in her throat. Mairead had aged terribly in her years in the city. Her hair was flecked with white and her face serrated by lines. Time had not been kind to her.

Feeling sorrow and a little pain, Tia went to her, knelt by her chair and hugged her. The woman called Ishbel closed the door and went away. Mairead swallowed a sob. 'It's been so long.'

For a long time they held each other without talking. Tia was thinking of her early childhood, of how familiar her sister felt. The loneliness that had haunted her for so long ebbed away. She wanted to tell Mairead about Marcus, to tell her everything. She opened her mouth to talk, but Mairead held a finger to it. 'I'll put the kettle on.'

She shuffled around inside the room, finding the matches then lighting the gas, jumping back when the lamp flared angrily. It was a room and kitchen, and they were in the kitchen, sitting at the fireside with the alcove for the bed behind them. Once the lamps were lit Tia saw that it was unmade, that Mairead had been sitting by the fire with a mug beside her chair. The whole of the room at the front by the sink was filled with barrels and stone gallon jars.

Mairead brushed at the hair that matted her brow and then sat down, blowing hard.

'Why didn't you come sooner?'

'I couldn't,' Tia said quickly. 'I didn't have your address.'

Mairead frowned and drank from the mug, jumping up when she realised she had not made tea for Tia yet. She swore when she discovered that the milk in the larder had turned, but Tia told her it didn't matter, she was not thirsty.

She was still trying to hide her shock, her anger that the sister who had left her little more than a decade before had turned into a woman who was haggard, even old. The skin of Mairead's face had the sheen of an apple, dimpled by little currant eyes, over cheeks that sagged past the corners of her mouth. Her chin had receded and her smile was split by gaps.

'Tam *beag*,' she said, lasping into her native Gaelic, 'do you remember Tam *beag*?'

Tia shook her head.

'Tam was Tam *mor*'s son. If you remember, Tam *mor* was about five feet nothing, and Tam *beag* was hitting six feet by the time he left school.'

'Was he from our village?'

Mairead shook her head. 'Paible. Any case, Tam and I felt the same way about things, so we run off together and got wed. He was in the shipyards, Tam, a good job he had. But he wanted a better one. He wanted to save his pay and we'd be off to America.' She winced and sighed. 'He used to brew ale, he had his mother's recipe, just a sideline, like. I used to watch over it when he was at work.'

Her face had turned wistful; she took a sip of ale from her mug by her chair and then she gagged and threw it down the drain. 'I'll jis away and get some milk, pet. You make yourself at home now.'

Tia looked around at the bare floorboards, the frayed cloth that covered the chairs, the unmade bed. Briskly, she got up and made it, then took the dishes from the table and rinsed them in the water from the kettle.

'The state of the place,' Mairead said when she got back with a full jug. 'Do you want to stay, pet? I'd've put the place to rights if I'd known.' She smiled. 'But it's home, pet. If you need one.'

Tia turned away, too numb to voice her gratitude or her shock. 'I have a place,' she said slowly, after a while.

The door opened and two boys came in, each as tall as their father had been. Mairead opened the oven door and handed them a plate of food each. 'This is your Aunt Tia, my sister,' she said.

They glared at her then turned away. When Mairead caught their indifference, she chided them. One looked up at her while the other poured two glasses of beer from one of the jars.

'I'll not stand for it,' she said, 'not from you, Tam, nor from Willie either. Tia was just toddling when I left. She was two or three, no older than that.'

They ate on, ignoring her.

'The pair of you,' Mairead said threateningly, 'now . . .'

They looked at each other and then at Tia, smiled grudgingly before they went back to their food.

Mairead made the tea and sat down again. 'Don't mind them,' she said, 'they don't mean it.'

'Why are they angry with me?'

Mairead hunched her shoulders and took on a haunted cast that sat uneasily on the laughing girl of Tia's memory. 'There was an accident. At the docks.'

Tia's face flashed sympathy. 'Tam was killed?'

'No, worst luck. I shouldn't say that, but. His legs were crushed and his back was broken. He was a complete cripple from a healthy young man. His life was over the moment the pallet landed on him, but he lived on.'

She paused to take some tea and sighed. 'He was in the hospital then they brought him home. The twins were just eighteen months. I'd another on the way, but I lost her with all the lifting I'd to do. Poor wee thing, she lived just an hour or two. Premature. I buried her the day I bore her. Tam said to

217

keep the ale going, that'd keep the money coming in. It did, for a while, till the polis found us. They took us to the workhouse, the Southern Institute. Tam's still there, but they care for him, like. I got the boys out myself.'

Tia said nothing.

'I wrote again and again. I asked if we could come home. Tam wouldn't let me write to his folks, he said he didn't want to tell them, but I wrote to mine. Christian charity . . .' She snorted derisively. 'That's why they're angry. I told them Ma would help, but I never even heard from her.'

Tia looked away.

'But you were too young to know.'

She stood up. It was dark outside.

'I can make a bed up for you, Tia. Stay the night.'

'I'd best get back. I married Marcus,' she said, almost as an afterthought. Mairead's story made hers easy by comparison.

Mairead smiled. 'How is he?'

'Dead.'

Mairead wrapped her arms around Tia and for a long time they sobbed.

'He was killed in an accident in New York on his last trip. I . . . I was pregnant. I didn't know what I was doing. I let one of his workmates take me home. Father threw me out. When I got back here, I lost the baby. I was in hospital for months. They didn't believe I was married.'

Mairead's grip tightened. 'At least I have the boys.'

'Why does it have to be so hard, Mairead?'

'It won't be so hard, now we have each other.'

'My landlady, she's good to me, but it's not the same.'

'You can come to me, pet. You can always come to me.'

'Mairead, I can help you. I have money that Marcus left me. Will you let me help you?'

She shook her head. 'No, pet. I can manage fine. If you come to see me every now and then, that's all the help I need.'

They walked out together on to the Gallowgate.

'Mairead,' Tia said as they waited for the tram, 'Mother never got your letters. She cared for you. She still does. It was Father. He would've destroyed them. He must have.'

'I guessed that.'

'It broke Ma's heart. She told me so.'

'Are you in touch with her?'

'I write, every so often. I send them to the Post at Lochmaddy so Father doesn't get them. But she never writes back. I don't think she can find the money for a stamp. I sent her one a while ago, but I've heard nothing yet.'

Mairead shivered. 'It's better, sometimes, isn't it, to leave things the way they are? It's not changed, pet. It'll never change. Best to leave it alone, and get on with the life you have.'

Tia remembered the grey sky on the day in August in 1914 when the war began, the relentless lack of colour, the way that rain fell with the dusk, darkening the paving stones, streaking them as if with blood.

When the cry of victory rose a short while later, she knew that it was hollow, the news it promised false.

Mr Weinstock fretted about his cousin, the violinist, drafted into the Kaiser's army, last heard of digging trenches on the rim of France. 'I worry about him,' he said once, 'why not make up the row? These threats, this bloodshed, it only makes things worse.'

She had been working at Weinstock's for nearly a year now; beyond the administrative work that she had taken on she had begun to design blouses and learn how to cut a pattern. When she noticed from the paper that women were being employed to examine the tram switching boxes and also the gas mains, she went to the tram company and got an order for a uniform she designed herself, but the gas company refused to deal with a company that bore a foreign name.

Mr Weinstock gave her thruppence commission on every uniform sold.

She was walking home one evening when she heard a cry behind her; she turned and saw Marcus waving at her, but not the Marcus she had married, Marcus as the boy who had rowed the little boat.

The shock made her faint clean away.

She came to in a stranger's arms, with the same familiar but subtly different face peering at her. 'She'll be all right now, laddie,' a voice said, as the arms gently lifted her upright. The speaker walked away; she was still so shocked that she did not think to thank him.

Marcus was in soldier's uniform, that of the Scots Guard, so tall and straight, but his laughter lines had deepened somehow and his eyes were a shade darker, his hair bleached a lighter brown. The whiskers on his upper lip were not quite right; when he was ashore he shaved daily but at sea he grew a moustache and a beard; he only had a moustache now and it sat at a slant so she reached out to straighten it.

Her gesture seemed to puzzle him; when she saw his hesitancy her hand recoiled as if scalded.

'Tia, Tia?' he asked. 'D'you not know me? I'm Cal. Cal Cameron. Marcus's brother. The youngest. The runt of the litter.' He grinned. 'I was training to be a priest, but . . .' He shrugged.

For a moment she could not speak as the sounds and the people whirled around her and the whole world blurred into a carousel that unwound itself as she waited, swaying, for its maddened gyrations to ease. For a while she was afraid that she would faint again and then, slowly, tentatively, when she could breathe again, she tried to smile, but stopped when she knew it was just a wince.

'Marcus said he didn't know if you'd go through with it. He said it was what your mother wanted.'

'Marcus . . .' he said, shaking his head.

'What is it?' she asked.

He looked down. 'I can't believe he's dead.'

She waited until his eyes met hers again. 'Nor can I, Cal.'

'*Galach!* These bloody bastards he worked for.'

'The ship was sound, he said. I mean, Marcus told me that before he left. It was an accident, an accident at the quay, Cal. The line said they were very sorry about it.'

'I bet they were,' he said grimly.

She waited, but he said nothing as he took her arm and they walked along Argyle Street to Buchanan Street, where he led her into Miss Cranston's Tearoom, ordering high tea for two before she had a chance to stop him. She doubted if her mouth could bear the taste of food.

'I wish you'd tell me,' she said carefully.

He shook his head. 'There's nothing to tell.'

She would have argued, but his expression had gone blank. 'I wrote to your mother,' she said, 'I wrote twice . . .'

He nodded. 'They got a telegram from the line. You sent the letter to the priest and he died.'

Her face fell.

'Don't be sad. He was old enough.' He grinned, reached out and tickled her chin. 'They grind slowly. The wheels of God, you know.'

'I thought . . . Marcus said that Eunice couldn't see to read, and I thought Bridie would . . . I thought it'd be better to write to the priest. I didn't want to cause trouble.'

He looked upwards in exasperation, then blinked when he saw the fantasy of the sun and the elements etched in gold and green. 'I suppose they have to paint the ceilings. You can't see the sky in this place for fog.' His emotions crossed his face as easily as scudding clouds; he could be serious, funny, then serious again in an instant, just as Marcus was. 'The father died just before the first letter arrived. It got sent to Dalibrog and the father there sent it to the Bishop in Oban. He did the same with the next one. The Bishop kept it until a new father had taken the parish. By then . . . Mother got the letter, but you didn't give a return address.'

'Are you still going to be a priest, Cal?'

'My mother thinks so. I went to the College, but . . '

'Marcus said you'd not make it.'

'He was right. Marcus was always right.' Pain passed over his face like lightning; he slammed his hand sharply against the emerald linen tablecloth, sending the crystal salt and pepper cellars a-tinkle before he remembered himself and smoothed the ripple in the cloth. 'I was there with a bunch of do-gooders and demagogues. We weren't supposed to talk to each other, just to listen to the voice of God. Thing was, God didn't want to speak to me.' He smiled broadly. 'I felt left out. One morning, just after the war started, I had a flash of inspiration. I told the Abbot I'd heard the voice of God calling me to fight for my country. I got sent home to think about it. I did and I told them I'm not going back. So there you are.'

At long last she managed to smile back at him. 'Marcus thought you'd be better at university.'

Cal cocked his head and rubbed the side of his neck vigorously.

'He left money, Cal. I could help pay your fees.'

'Why is it every woman I've ever had anything to do with wants to plan my life for me?'

'I don't. I just wanted you to know the money's there if you need it.'

A waitress brought their teas; Cal ate, Tia pushed the food around her plate. Marcus had taken her to the Willow Tearoom just once; she had been appalled by the prices and had refused to go inside. She had a sensation of history repeating itself, that the clock had been turned back as she'd so often wished it could be. If she closed her eyes and peered at Cal through the shadows cast by her eyelashes, he was Cal no longer, but Marcus come to life again. The brothers had the same way of looking at life at a slight distance faintly sceptical, a little quizzical; to them the world was neither smooth nor round but rather asymmetrical. They had the capacity to laugh at life's vagaries, most of all to laugh at themselves.

'That's sixpence,' Cal said, his meal finished.

She had a little breast of chicken poised on the end of her fork, midway between the plate and her lips.

'Might as well,' Cal said, when she bit into it. 'They won't give me the money back, you know. At least, I doubt it. I can always ask.' He made a play of turning to look for a waitress as she blushed furiously and tugged his arm, vigorously shaking her head.

'They bloody well should,' he said. He lifted one of the knives and gazed at the shaft of bronze topped by a green-enamelled handle with a motif that Tia thought was meant to be a copy of the mural of the sun goddess on the wall, but was so small and stylised that it could have been anything. Cal looked around again, making a play of pocketing it. 'D'you think the knives are thrown in as well?'

'Put it back!' she hissed furiously.

His face broke into a broad grin and he moved his plate to show her that he had just hidden the knife behind it. 'The Scots College. The ghost of Abbot Ignatius. They haven't given up on me yet. They would if I got caught stealing Miss Cranston's cutlery.'

'You'd go to jail, you mean.'

'The sinner would be forgiven, chances are, with my luck. Ach, to hell with it.'

'Cal, I . . .'

He put his hand over hers. 'Tia. Don't worry. Marcus took good care of us. That money you sent, we didn't need it. You shouldn't've. Ma gave it to me, told me to bring it right back to you. I went to Mrs Anderson's, but they said you weren't there. They didn't know where you were. I went again, and got a flea in my ear till I managed to convince the old witch I wasn't a Presbyterian Minister from North Uist, but a failed student Catholic priest from South Uist. She told me I might meet you on your way home from work.'

She laughed.

'Ma put the money in the bank in Boisdale. It's yours.'

She shook her head. 'I don't need it.'

'Tia, when I saw Marcus last, a couple of years ago on my way to Rome, he put some money in the bank for me. I haven't touched it.'

'Cal . . .'

'Tia, if you say another word about money, I'll get up and leave you now. I won't even pay the bill. Mind you, I might not pay it anyway.'

The waitress came with a trolley of cakes, he chose chocolate, she a spiced fruit tart.

'Cal, I wish you weren't going to war.'

One end of his mouth lifted into a smile of irony. 'I had to escape from the priesthood somehow.'

'You don't have to go, Cal.'

'*Ach, is moisa an t'eagal na'n cogadh.*' (Fear is worse than war.)

'You will come back, Cal.' She was surprised at the tone of her voice; it was a command, not a question.

'I will,' he affirmed, serious for a moment before his habitual, rakish smile came back. 'I'd better. I'd have too much explaining to my brother to do if I end up in heaven.'

She smiled.

'I promise you,' he said, 'on the day of peace, on the day the war ends, we'll meet here again. And you can buy me tea.'

'I will, Cal.'

He touched her hand briefly. 'That's a promise. I always keep a promise.'

His expression was serious for a moment, before he caught an early bluebottle diving for the cake stand, and a waitress's frantic efforts to head it off. 'There goes the Kaiser,' he joked, as he threw down a handful of coins, more than enough.

# Chapter Twelve

*F*or a long time after Cal left, Tia bought the paper to check the casualty list. In the evening, when she went back to Mrs Anderson's, she would study them in the solitude of her room, coming out to eat only after she had made sure that Cal was not listed.

'Laddie had the look o' a survivor to me,' Mrs Anderson said one night in 1915. 'Ye're jist tormenting yersel wi' these lists, lassie.'

The city was a grim place to be in wartime. After the phony peace of Christmas 1914, the battles started in earnest and women wore bleak faces; the papers carried scant news of progress juxtaposed with endless lists of the dead. There was money to be made, though. Women were recruited to do the work once done by men; Mairead earned 25 shillings a week at a munitions works near Parkhead.

'It's an ill wind,' Mrs Anderson said, when Tia told her how she felt seeing the uniform she designed on the tram box-junction checkers.

'I'd rather it wasn't because of the war,' Tia replied. Now Samuel Weinstock let her design blouses, suits and dresses as well. The concentration took her mind off Cal. In the summer of 1915 she wrote to Eunice; she was surprised when Bridie replied, saying that Cal had asked her to tell Tia that they were to meet in Miss Cranston's the week after the war ended, to give him time to get back from the front in France.

Mairead no longer brewed beer. The men who had drunk it had gone to the front, and she no longer needed the money, since she was working in munitions. In the close, some lads had joined up as young as fourteen, and she was worried about her boys.

'Mrs Anderson keeps telling me that I should buy a place of my own,' Tia said. 'She says it isn't right, me living in a sailors' boarding house.'

Mairead smiled. 'You have the money.'

Tia wanted to explain that her life felt as if she was living in limbo, waiting for the end of the war to meet Cal again. The feeling was too fragile to put into words. She had spent only a few minutes with him before he had left for the front.

'It would help me,' Mairead said.

'How?'

'If you got some place away from here, away from the temptation to join up, the boys could stay with you.'

'They don't have to join up till they're nineteen.'

'Try telling them that, when some of their friends are already in, under age or no. The army doesn't care, as long as they're strong enough to hold a gun.'

'Would they stay with me?'

'They would, if I told them they had to.'

Tia looked at Mairead. The worry lines were etched deep into her face, the smile she always wore on top like an afterthought. They were close again, as close as they had been on the island, when Mairead the oldest took care of Tia, the youngest. Even now, she took care of Tia in a sense. She listened when Tia talked about Marcus; she never said she talked too much.

'You have to start living again,' Mairead said.

'I'm living now.'

'No. You're just existing, apart from your job. Marcus only expected you to stay with Mrs Anderson for a few months, and you've been there for years.'

Tia shivered. She did not like to be reminded of how long she had been a widow.

She asked Samuel Weinstock what he thought. 'Of course,' he said, 'it is the right thing to do. Buy now, before all the troops come home when the war is over.'

'Will the war ever be over?'

'All wars end. At least, every war has ended up till now. This one will be no different.'

She began to look in the papers, but everywhere seemed too expensive, or not in the right place. The money Marcus had left her was untouched in the bank; spending some of it would be like severing her links with him. If she bought a home of her own, she was acknowledging that he was dead, and in her dreams he still lived on. In quiet moments, when she had time to herself, she lived a fantasy life in which he was still alive, just away for a day or two. She still remembered the way her body felt when he touched her, the frisson of excitement when he began to love her. The feeling came back through her dreams; in a way, it made reality easier to deal with.

At the end of the year she found a place, two rooms and a kitchen in a little back street in Hyndland; it was a tidy place, a nice respectable close and far enough away from the Gallowgate to make Tam and Willie safe from the army recruiters. It cost £125.00, about half of the money she had in the bank, and she had to spend a bit more to furnish it.

Mrs Anderson came with her to see it, and took her to a lawyer who did the conveyancing.

'I'm richt glad ye're settled, pet,' she said. 'Marcus would no forgive me if he kent ye were still biding by me.'

Tam and Willie came; Willie put on a gruff face and hardly spoke to her, but Tam chattered away, as he always did. Mairead had made them promise not to join up; it had been a hard job. She worked twelve hours a day at the munitions works, sometimes seven days a week; they had a family meal together every Sunday evening, but Mairead was so tired that she sometimes fell asleep. She told Tia that it was the sense of relief that her boys were safe at last.


Tia went to see Mrs Anderson on Saturdays after work. The landlady was grieving continually now; she'd had so many lodgers over the years and almost every casualty list carried the name of a man she had known. The war had aged her, shrivelled the skin of her face and made her stoop-backed, though her eyes still sparkled when Tia managed to make her laugh.

She had a hacking cough which worried Tia, but she said she would throw it off when the winter came to an end.

Summer came, with news of the Battle of the Somme and endless casualty lists. One day, at lunchtime, a young lad came to Weinstock's to see Tia.

'The missus is asking fir ye, Missus Anderson, that is.'

Before she could ask, Samuel Weinstock gave her the rest of the day off.

Mrs Anderson was in her bed, pasty grey. 'I hope ye dinna mind, precious, but I doubt I'll make the weekend.'

Tia felt a mist cover her eyes.

'I'll get the doctor.'

'No, pet, he's been already. I've a tumour, he says.'

'What can I do for you?'

Mrs Anderson shifted on the pillow; Tia went to help her sit up. The landlady grasped her hand. 'That time, that time ye wis in the hospital, wi' a miscarriage, I should've tried harder to find ye.'

'How could you, when they were calling me by my maiden name?'

'I should've tried, I could've done. See, I thocht, I thocht maybe yer folks had taken ye, I didna ken. I never dreamed you'd forgotten how to get here.'

Tia blinked. 'That's all over now. Do you know what?'

'What?'

'Mr Weinstock, the man I work for, he's sending me to Paris, soon's the war's over.'

'I doubt the war'll ever be over, no till aw the men are deid.'

Mrs Anderson began to cough. Tia took the jug by her bedside, poured a little water and tried to help her drink it. After a long time, the coughing eased and she managed to drink the water then.

'I wanted ye tae forgie me, pet.'

'There was never anything to forgive.'

Mrs Anderson's eyes closed; her breath came in short, sharp gasps. Tia scribbled a brief note to Tam and Willie to tell them that she would be home late, if at all, and asked the young lad to take it round to her place in Hyndland.

Mrs Anderson's eyes opened briefly.

'You know,' Tia said, 'it was you who helped me. You helped me grieve for Marcus. You brought me back to life again.'

'Ye're still mourning,' Mrs Anderson gasped.

Tia closed her eyes against the tears.

'Dinna mourn me, pet.'

Tia shook her head. 'But I will always miss you.'

The world felt a colder place when the landlady died later that night. Tia walked home, through the darkness, her tears mingling with a soft rain. She did not have the patience to wait for a tram.

She reached home in the early hours, long after the boys had gone to bed. In the morning Tam found her sitting by the range, staring listlessly at the grey day that had dawned through the window.

'Are ye a'richt?' he asked.

'Yes, no,' she said. 'A friend died last night. The landlady whose house we stayed at when Marcus and I came here after we were married.'

Listlessly, she went to wash and change and get ready to face the new day.

Bridie's letter came after the funeral, with the news that Cal had survived the battle of the Somme and even won a medal. Tia stared at the letter for so long that her tears dissolved the ink and all that was left was a blot.

'Oh, God,' she murmured, 'how much longer with it go on?

'How much longer?'

She threw herself into work, working all the hours of the day, so that she had no time to worry, or to fret.

# *Chapter Thirteen*

Paris, 1918

*T*ia rose early, with the first birdsong. She went to the french
windows that led on to a precipitous balcony and opened them
wide. Paris floated eerily against the dawn, the rise of
Montmartre only a shadow against the veil of the sky. To the
east, the Eiffel Tower was a tumbled spider's web caught on a
needle-point, Les Invalides a chubby thumb, topped by a spire
like the Kaiser's hat. In between the rooftops floated, undefined
at first until the rising sun marked the edges, made the city like
a stage set, brightly painted and cut out of wood.

The plumbing in her room did not work. The tap, turned on,
sounded like a fog-horn, so she turned it off and crept down the
stairs with her coat thrown over her nightgown and searched
until she found a bathroom on the first floor where she washed
in water that was brackish and cold. She dressed quickly in her
utility suit, the jacket severely cut from charcoal grey serge, the
skirt straight and so tight that it made her walk like a mouse,
taking mincing, nervous, steps lest the seams burst, and that
despite her having added splits between the gores. Underneath
it she wore a rayon blouse of black shot with amber, a mistake
that had arisen at the dye works but she had used it for herself
because there could be no waste during the war. There was a big,
floppy scarf at the neck that she tied loosely, like a cravat. Her
hat was a beret of the same material, stiffened by tacking, with a
single ostrich feather that she had found in the storeroom and
dyed with *crotal* to match.

In the mirror she looked this way and that. She was wary of
Paris, scared to face the Mecca of style that had defined fashion
for so long from a distance, through the pages of *Vogue*.
Weinstock's Haute Couture had given up fashion in the
autumn of 1915, turning to austerity and uniforms instead. The
clothes they created were functional, made to wear easily and

made to last. Skirts had crept up to beyond the ankle and then mid calf, blouses and dresses were made in artificial silk that did not dye like the real thing but in colours that were garish and harsh. Eunice had sent her some nettles and irises, lichens and mosses, but the only thing that had any impact on the cloth was *crotal*.

After her success with uniforms, Samual Weinstock had given her more designing to do, until designing used up most of her time at work. Tia had a natural sense of style and colour which he recognised; a talent that proved itself with everything she did. As the war seemed finally to be drawing to an end, he sent her to Paris ostensibly to buy trims and to pick up a Fortuny dress, but really so she could see new looks evolving in the city that still defined style.

She had designed her suit herself and made it from remnants of the tram box-checker's outfit. It had taken two years to gather enough; she had intended the jacket to be military style (with epaulettes and patch pockets, a wide leather-backed belt) but in the end had just made a simple high-necked cardigan shape, cut in panels like the skirt, which had splits between the gores to enable her to walk. There had not been enough cloth for pleats. The war regulations prohibited more than four and a half yards of wool being used for an outfit; her suit took less than three. She had prided herself on that for a time, thinking of it as a prototype for the autumn lines, until Alice, one of the machinists, had pointed out that it was indecent when she sat down carelessly, because the splits between the gores would ride up and reveal a flash of thigh. Weinstock's autumn line that year had been built around an elaboration of the pattern, with black and white checked rayon trim on the jackets and pleats in the skirts and dresses. No style used more than four yards in a small woman's size, but the hefty dowagers of Glasgow needed five at least, and their lust for embellishment made her add sash belts and covered buttons, bows and facings which, she felt, ruined the simplicity of the look.

She had tried to substitute *simplicity* for *austerity*; Sam Weinstock insisted that in the Glasgow of Miss Cranston and Rennie Mackintosh it would never catch on, ignoring that Rennie Mackintosh's lines were the simplest and straightest of all. The problem was that Miss Cranston, with her motifs and murals, her silvered mirrors and penchant for lavender-tinted glass, cast a rosy glow over the architectural lines that blunted their impact, made the style seem not of itself but as a mere backdrop for a mode of decor that passed itself off as art.

She put on the short American boots that ended just above her ankle, gathered her papers together in the leather clutch bag she had bought in MacDonald's sale and walked briskly down the stairs, nodding to the *concierge* on the way out. The woman had booked her in amidst a flood of voluble French, too many instructions at once for Tia even to take in one of them. Miriam, Sam's wife, who had lived in Paris as a child, had carefully taught her some phrases; they flew out of her mind under the verbal assault, left her mumbling, '*d'accord, d'accord*' as the concierge launched another salvo and led her up to the room at the top of the stair.

'*Madame, Madame,*' she now cried after her, '*je vous dites, c'est interdit à utiliser l'eau avant l'après midi. Je vous rappelle, l'eau pour le lavage est dans la boîte sur le sol, et l'eau potable est en le bouteille sur la table. C'est vraiment interdit à utiliser! C'est le regulations de guerre! Arrêtez vous tout suite, Madame! Madame?*'

'*D'accord, d'accord,*' Tia muttered as she hurried up the street, the iron tips of her heels clattering against the cobblestones, the soles swishing as she slipped and nearly tumbled when she reached the corner of the *boulevard*. She walked briskly until she was halfway along the thoroughfare, then turned around cautiously, relieved to see that no demented Frenchwoman was in pursuit.

It was still very early, the rain-slicked streets quiet with only a street cleaner half-heartedly sweeping the pavement outside a café and a newsvendor roaring '*Paix! Paix! L'accord Versailles est complet. La guerre est finis!*'

'*Madame, Madame. C'est historique!*' He followed her, thrusting a paper into her hand as she tried to explain that she could not understand a word of it then gave up and handed him a coin from her purse.

'*Paix! Paix! L'accord Austro–Hungarien etait signé aujourdhui! Les bataillons allemandes sont en retraite! Paix! Paix!*'

Tia walked on before she found a café with doors open wide on a smell of freshly baked bread and coffee, she went inside, gingerly taking a table by the window where she could see the street. The bar was lined with men, toasting each other with little glasses, tossing down a liquid that looked like whale oil and smelt strongly of liquorice.

A woman came over, smiling broadly as Tia asked carefully for a *café* and a *croissant*. She bustled away shaking her head, as a waiter came over with a dim, dusty bottle and a glass which he set down before her. The champagne was a cascade, a torrent of bubbles that did not settle but bounced over the rim of the glass, fizzing and popping like a Atlantic breaker until its energy was exhausted and it settled into a little puddle that rolled to the table edge and slowly dripped off.

Tia smiled uncertainly.

'*Anglaise?*' the waiter asked.

'*Non. Ecossaise.*'

An old man peeled off from the group at the bar and, holding his arms up, began to dance a variant of a jig, turning and twisting, carousing a tune that was somewhere between the 'Marseillaise' and 'The Dashing White Sergeant'. He grabbed Tia's hand and pulled her towards him, then hooked his arm through hers and began to spin her around. The interior moved and began to blur, she had a sensation of a stool toppling drunkenly in their wake; the old man doggedly ignored her protestations, dragging her like a carthorse, stomping insistently until she gave up resistance and moved with him as his fellows lined up, whistling and clapping madly. The dance was nonsensical, the old man moving like the piston of a crank shaft, so many steps this way then a military turn and the same again that way. His movements were abbreviated by salutes and calls of *Olé*, the rhythm modulated by the onlookers' claps. It went on for a long time until at last he collapsed against the bar, amidst more cheers and calls for *viskee*.

An amber liquid was poured from a lableless bottle; he poured another glass which he handed to her and then raised his: '*Salut*,' he said, seriously. '*A L'Ecosse.*'

Everyone drank.

He raised his glass again. '*L'alliance vieux.*'

They drank again.

Tia got a glimpse of the headline written across the first page of the paper; the meaning clearer now that she saw the words.

'*La Guerre*,' she stumbled. 'The war is over?'

The old men looked at each other and shrugged. '*La bataille dernière est fini*,' one said.

Head reeling, she took the glass of champagne and drank with them, waited shakily as the woman saw her pallor and brought, at last, the coffee and croissant and also an omelette, miraculously light and smelling of herbs.

She ate hungrily, balanced on a bar stool as the old men jabbered away.

The woman leaned over the bar and smiled at her. 'You are a nurse?'

Tia shook her head. 'No. Fashion. I work in fashion.'

'Ahhh, *couture*,' she nodded, as if she understood.

'*Oui*,' Tia said.

'Now the war is over, *l'haute couture* will begin again.'

'We've been making uniforms,' Tia said, gesticulating. 'My boss, my employer, he sent me over to see the new styles.'

'And where you go?'

She took a sip of coffee. 'Worth. Chanel.'

'Chanel.' The woman shrugged. 'Chanel is not *l'haute couture*. Chanel is making women dress like men.'

The men murmured in agreement.

'The cut? Chanel's cut is too severe. Like a uniform. No one will wear it, once the Armistice is signed. *Les maisons haute couture* are closed anyway.'

Tia had some addresses that Miriam's sister had given her, and a pass from the military that Sam Weinstock had obtained by bribery. The wife of an officer in the Highland Light was a customer; the pass given in exchange for a bill conveniently forgotten. The pass permitted her to travel on military trains and to pass through the fortifications on the city rim. Sam had told the woman that if he did not manage to get to Paris soon, his line for the few private customers he had would be forever as boring as it now was.

'They will *stay* closed,' a young man said darkly. He had been sitting in the corner, hunched over a coffee that had been long drunk. Tia had not even noticed him before, but there was something about him which made her feel cold.

'The bourgeoisie is the enemy of the proletariat. They are the heritors of Shylock and Robespierre. The war was not fought for freedom; it was fought to fuel the gold lust of the bourgeoisie.

Who took the money that paid for the weapons? Who sold the proletariat down the river to line his pockets? The bourgeoisie, that's who. The bourgeoisie is the enemy of the people.' He sneered, his lips curved into an ugly twist. '*Les couturiers* exist only to beautify the ugly. The barbarian becomes civilised.' He spat, *phahh*! – a streak of phlegm that stained the sawdust floor like venom.

The older men huffed and hummed. 'You are young,' one said, 'not yet old enough to have learnt your lesson.'

'Education is the instrument of the ruling class.'

'Would you rather we had laid down and lived under the Kaiser?'

'One of his kind is much the same as any other.'

The older men began to thrum with anger. 'You child, you boy,' said the one who spoke in English. 'You know nothing of history, nothing of the past.'

'All that is holy is profaned,' the young man mocked.

'We have fought and won our revolution many years ago, and many times since,' the old one said.

'Then why are you so scared of fighting again, but fighting this time for ourselves? The revolution only substituted bourgeois property for feudal property.'

The man who had danced with Tia filled glasses all round, even giving one to the man who had started the argument.

'Proudhon,' he yelled, raising his glass.

They all smiled as the young man shook his head.

Tia looked at him.

'All property is theft.' He grinned broadly, lifting his glass to his elder in a gesture of capitulation. They all laughed uproariously, gesturing and clapping each other upon the back. Tia stumbled out to the mechanics of the morning rush hour, the roaring trams and the marching crowds of office workers, dizzily wondering where on earth to begin to look for the addresses of the man who had Mr Weinstock's Fortuny dress and the workshop where she had to buy the trimmings.

The tide swept her along, oblivious of her destination, through the Bastille then along the Rue Rivoli, past the spires of Notre Dame on one side and the rise of the Sacre Coeur, then Les Jardins des Tuileries, where she realised in passing just how great an insult Treron's in Sauchiehall Street was, to the

Place de la Concorde which led to the expanse of the Champs Elyssee, where the true grandeur of the city made her stop to catch her breath and wonder at it all.

She stood for a long time, drinking it all in, the monuments and the gardens, the palaces and the arches, the Arc de Triomphe in the distance like a full stop to the sentence written first of all by the kings and then finished by Napoleon. She sensed that the kingdom sat uneasily with the republic, as if the successor was determined to top the splendour of its predecessor; Paris was never truly a republican capital and it never could be; it was too proud of its majesty and the echoes of its vainglorious past. The republic she had heard the young man and the old men argue about had only existed briefly, a passing dream that had worked its way into the soul of the people along with the knowledge that as an art form their city was supreme. Miriam Wienstock had told her that for two hundred years Paris had straddled the schism between republic and empire, had been one or the other so often that the traditional opposites had become an alliance of sorts. The nature of the city was neither one nor the other but somewhere in between.

On that day, though, when the news came that the Austro-Hungarians had surrendered and the Kaiser's troops were at last in retreat, the city was as much at peace with itself as it ever could be, the mood on the streets restrained joy that gave rise to cheers when a military truck trundled past, flying the tricolore jauntily from a pole haphazardly attached to its flank.

Le Magasin Brillot, the shop owned by Samuel Weinstock's friend, was in Montparnasse. She walked along, drinking in the air and the sensation, the style of the women who despite the war or perhaps because of it had made an asset of austerity, who wore military berets at a raffish angle, tailored jackets slung negligently around their shoulders, walked in their stern shoes with a wide stride that kicked the deep twin pleats at the front and back of their skirts in a gesture that was more sexual, more abandoned than anything she had ever seen before. Their scarves were not arranged, but trailed anarchically, sometimes with the smoke from cigarettes that dripped from their lips at the end of long ivory or ebony holders. The war had cast off some of the inhibitions of femininity; they were not afraid of standing at street corners chatting, gesticulating, or to catch their reflections in a window and then pause, smiling coquettishly at themselves.

In her stern suit and sensible boots Tia felt dowdy, her reflection was pallid beside theirs, her hair cut in a style that was too long and her features vapid. Though she had bought lipstick once as an experiment, she had never worn it outside the confines of her room. The mores in Glasgow still held that there was something indecent in women who wore make-up; they were whores or tarts or at best artists at several removes from respectable. In Paris, virtually every woman she saw wore make-up; lips were sharply defined in red, eyes emphasised with Kohl in a face made peach-skin perfect by powder and cheeks were struck with a rosy blush. Some, only a few, wore too much and looked like caricatures; most looked just a little more beautiful than God had intended them to be. For a while she pondered it until she decided that make-up was like the trim on a suit, necessary embellishment that made the whole work.

She smiled at herself when she crossed the Boulevard du Montparnasse, and walked with a lift in her step along to the little shop with sky-blue cloud-painted awning streaked by the dropings of philistine birds.

Inside, the light was low, spilled by lamps arranged on tables beneath posters of dancers and cinema films. There were no rails of garments, just two plaster models draped with crushed silk that shimmered like butterfly wings, a floating display of scarves that moved with the breeze from the street.

There was a woman, older, with eyes painted like a car's headlamps and semicircular eyebrows that made her look permanently shocked, who sat at a table with a cigarette in an ashtray that gave off a spiral of smoke.

'*Bonjour, Madame,*' she said carelessly, turning a page in the book she was reading as if she did not care whether Tia was a customer or not.

'*Je veaux parler avec Monsieur Kassinsky,*' Tia said, stringing out the syllables as Miriam Weinstock had told her to.

'*Ah, le monsieur est dans le bureau à bas. Attendez une minute, Madame, il serait ici tout suite.*'

Tia shifted nervously as the woman went through a door at the back of the shop, calling out something in French that sounded like a reprimand. A moment later a little man appeared, smiling and grabbing her hand and shaking it as if she were a long-awaited guest, and not just on an errand. He led her through to a room at the back, where he swept aside piles of papers to give her a seat whilst the woman served coffee in tiny porcelain cups.

'And how is Miriam?' he asked, in English that was almost without an accent.

'She is well,' Tia said. 'So is Mr Weinstock.'

'Have they heard any news of his family?'

She shook her head briskly. 'Only that his cousing Chaim will never play the violin again. Mr Weinstock had a letter from the Red Cross last year, but he must have told you that.'

Mr Kassinsky looked away. 'My son was killed at Passchendaele,' he said slowly. 'It seems, I mean, we should have reached peace sooner. It is the law of God, a life for a life, but will it ever end, I ask myself?'

'They say so,' she said.

'Ach, a life for a life, if we do not stop the whole world will be dead.'

For a moment they sat in silence, until he slammed his desk with the palm of his hand. 'Forgive me, my dear, I should have asked about you. Did you have a safe journey?'

She told him that she had, trembling slightly with guilt at the use of the black-market pass.

'This war has been cruel to everybody, but I hope it is not too cruel for you.'

She could not tell him that her brothers, the brothers she had not seen for years, had been killed by U-boat in the Atlantic, that she had not been given the news by her family but by Marcus's sister Bridie, who had written to her through all the years of the war. Or that she had bought a flat in Hyndland and taken in Mairead's twins because they were so tall at sixteen that their mother was terrified they would be tempted or coerced into joining one of the regiments that checked birth-dates rarely and of poor people not at all. Or that, at last, in the terror of the Somme, when the whole city had been poised on a knife edge awaiting the full casualty list – in fact never published because in the confused aftermath it was impossible to list the dead and those missing – she had been glad that Marcus was dead because she doubted he would have been able to live with the guilt of survival. So many of her generation were dead that life was no longer a certainty but rather a trick of fate. There was no reason to it, there never could be; the papers spoke of the valorous and the brave, the heroes whose heroism was to kill more Germans than their fellows. She hated the Germans and she always would, but with her hatred she felt sympathy for the foot soldiers who had no say in the war, only the duty to follow orders.

But Cal had become a hero too and that troubled her. Bridie had written that Eunice had received a telegram saying he had been awarded the Victoria Cross, though later he ended up only with the Military Medal because he had walked all the way home from the Somme to give the good news himself.

She did not understand how that could have been. Cal had been at the front for most of the war, from his regiment he had been posted to the Machine Gun Corps and she had passed messages to him through Bridie. Bridie had sent her his letters from Ypres, to remind Tia that he had a date with her at Miss Cranston's Room de Luxe but that she would have to wait for a week once the war was over, to give him time to get back from France.

'Business,' Mr Kassinsky said, pulling a sheath from a shelf. 'This is the Mariano Fortuny dress Sam asked for.'

Unwound from its wrap, the dress was a torrent of silk in all the colours of a sunset, from the palest peach to burnished amber, streaked with fingers of brilliant grey blue. It looked like nothing so much as a rag, a hank of wool untidily dyed. A scarf with it was marked in a pattern on a dinner service called The Glory of Greece, which she had seen displayed in one of Wylie and Lochhead's windows.

'Is that it?' she mumbled.

Mr Kassinsky laughed. 'Sam, Sam, Sam will never give up. He went to Mariano, you know. He went to his palazzo in Venice years ago, begged him to give up his secret or at least to share it with him, but Mariano wouldn't. Ever since, Sam's been buying Mariano's dresses and picking them apart, trying to discover his secret. He was buying them from your Liberty's in London, but Mariano said that Sam was such a philistine, he shouldn't be allowed to, so Sam had to ask me.' He beamed. 'I told him, "Your customers, Sam, the Glasgow matrons, they are far too fat. They are not Rubensesque so much as overgrown cherubs." Sam says to me, "They slim down if I make them dresses like this. You and me, we be millionaires if we make this up and sell it to the mass market." You know, that is not the rich, but the shopkeeper's wife, the wife of the accountant and bank manager, the doctor and the lawyer.'

Tia nodded. Mr Weinstock was always talking like that, when she mentioned an idea from *Vogue* or one of the great designers. 'Forget the wealthy,' he would say, 'our customer is not wealthy. She is Meesus Average. The wealthy are not worth the trouble. They are too fickle, too quick to change. You make a dress, a nice dress, for Meesus Average, she never forget you. She remember always. And the next time she look for a new outfit, she look for Weinstock label, Weinstock name.'

The only word that he ever pronounced properly was his own name.

She smiled, shaking her head, as she handed over the envelope Sam had given her.

'You laugh,' said Mr Kassinsky.

'It's madness, Mr Kassinsky. It looks like a rag to me.'

'Come,' he said, taking her hand and leading her through to the shop. 'Madeleine, *chéri*, can I have a Delphos for Madam?' He turned to look at Tia, flicking her hair gently and gazing at the colour of her eyes, before he told her to try the blue one first. The assistant brought the cotton tube that held the dress, then pulled open the door of the changing room.

'You try it,' Mr Kassinsky said. 'Just try it.'

Diffidently Tia peeled off her jacket and skirt, then the blouse, leaving her standing in her cotton underthings, clean but coloured ivory from so many washings. She was still as slim and lithe as the girl who had married Marcus; she had no need of a corset or a brassiere.

The dress slipped out of its tube like liquid in her hands. There seemed to be nothing to it as she held it up, only a shirred wisp of silk that jangled slightly with the glass beads sewn around the neck and then at the hem. She stared at it for a moment before she put it on; felt the feather-light cloth like the gossamer of a moth's wing. She turned this way and that, to be sure that it was on properly, then looked in the mirror and gasped. From a workaday woman in a functional, austere suit she had been transformed to a nymph or a goddess of some sort. Fearing indecency, she stood against the lamp and peered anxiously at her reflection to see if it was transparent. It was not; the illusion came from the movement of the cloth as she moved, the colour as motile and changing as the surface of the ocean. The line was perfectly simple, drapped from the neck over a high waist, then falling to the floor; there were sleeves slit at the shoulders that fluttered like the wings of a bird. The glass beads kept it perfectly in place like the stars on a clouded night.

She walked out into the shop and gave a little pirouette.

'Well,' he said.

'Oh, Mr Kassinsky.'

'You see what I mean now? Why Sam will spend his life trying to discover the secret of Mariano Fortuny.'

'Oh, Mr Kassinsky.' In that moment, she remembered Marcus's last words in his letter to her, she heard his voice repeating them in fact. 'Mr Kassinsky, I have only a few francs and five Scottish pounds, but can I buy it please? I'll send you the money as soon as I get home and you can post it to me.'

He turned to the assistant. 'Bring me that scarf from the window, Madeleine. And the cape that matches it.'

The scarf was the same colour, almost as long as the dress and printed with Cycladic motifs. The cape was a swirl of darkest blue, lined softly with deep crimson that became purple and then midnight as it caught the shifting pattern of light from the window.

'May I?'

She stood perfectly still as he twisted the scarf into a roll that he wound around her brow before letting it fall loosely from her neck, then put the cape around her arms so that it wrapped about her like apple peel.

'Oh, Mr Kassinsky, how much does it cost?'

He laughed. 'If you like it, you shouldn't have to ask.'

'I love it,' she said sincerely. 'Its . . . it's the second most beautiful thing I've ever seen.'

He tickled his chin. 'Tell me, what was the most beautiful?'

Her eyes fell slightly. 'The suit my husband bought me. The suit I wore on my wedding day.'

He nodded slowly. 'If you change again, my dear, I'll take you round to Gulbin's, where you can get Sam his bits and pieces.'

'That would be very kind,' she said.

She took the dress off carefully, putting it back in its slip before she quickly put on her own clothes again, biting her lip to brighten it. She thanked Madeleine as she handed the dress back to her, sad that she had to leave it.

'I mean it,' she said to Mr Kassinsky. 'I will send you a money order.'

The assistant was fiddling with tissue and paper.

'*Rien du tout*, my dear. It is already yours. The cape and the scarf and the dress. Fortuny made his clothes for a woman who looks like you. It is only right that you must have it.'

She blanched. 'I couldn't.'

'You can. If you do not, I shall write to Sam and report that you came to my premises drunk in the company of an American soldier. Or, worse, a French one.'

She laughed as he took her arm and led her out into the light of the noon.

'I'm happy,' she said, as they walked along. 'I feel guilty.'

'Guilty? Why?'

'Because of the war. Because of all of the men who are dead.'

'That is life,' he said.

'They were fighting for a better world, Mr Kassinsky.'

'In France, we fought because we had no choice.' He shrugged. 'I have another two sons, both doctors. They fought.'

'Did they survive?'

'They did. But one of them, he is not so good. The war gave him the appetite to fight another. He's going with Herzl's lot, with the Zionists. They are sailing for Palestine as soon as they can. They will settle there, in *yeretz Isroel*. Our promised land. We Jews, he says, there is no place in Europe that is safe for us. We must go and take our Israel again. I say, we've been here since before the time of your Christ. We may as well stay.'

'Palestine is British, is it not?'

'They have conquered the land. Whether they remain, I

don't know. But your Balfour, he declares that the Jews shall have a home in the Holy Land. That is enough for David. Jacob, he settle down in Paris. He works in the Institut Pasteur. He wants to study life now. Not death.'

They turned off the street into a little alleyway that led to a courtyard, where he knocked at a door and then opened it. The din was awesome.

He took her hand. 'Come and see me again, Mrs Cameron.'

'I will.'

'If you weren't leaving on the night train, you could dine with us. Meet Kitty and David, if he isn't out at one of those meetings of his.'

'Next time,' she said. 'And thank you.'

He waved his hand dismissively.

In the *atelier* she took the swatches of cloth from her bag. The *vendeuse* studied them briefly, then went through to a backroom, returning with a tray of buttons and buckles, another of trims and another of belts.

Tia had the drawings of Murielle's order for the spring, the simple sheath she had designed that was cut in layers to give it shape and buttoned simply at the back. Murielle Hyman who owned the most exclusive dress shop in Glasgow, had glanced at it briefly and ordered it in a half a dozen shades of wool crêpe. The order from her guaranteed that at least one of the big stores would order as well. But there had been no wool crêpe in Glasgow for months; Tia was wondering if she could make it in cotton serge instead, and if she did whether Murielle, with her eye for detail, would cancel the order.

The *Vendeuse* had matched trims and buttons soberly to the cloth; Tia glanced at her choice and then thought for a moment.

'May I?'

The *vendeuse* nodded.

Taking the charcoal gabardine, she put the matching buttons to one side and tried first a vibrant yellow and then an almost luminous pink. The yellow looked cold, but the pink lifted the cloth and made it glow. She stood back to study the effect.

'*Bon*,' the *vendeuse* said, 'but zat ees Parees and not Glazgow. M' Weinstock has always been conservative in 'is choice.'

'But the war is over, nearly,' Tia said.

'Ow about jet? We 'ave some jet from years ago. Special price.'

She clipped through to the store and came back with a dusty box. The buttons were dull, but when she wiped one Tia saw the glittery effect when the light hit the bevelled edges.

'I'll have these,' she said slowly. Some of the buttons were huge and she was thinking of Murielle's order made up in stiff white cotton dupion with big black buttons for contrast. Or pale grey. Murielle had asked for navy and black, slate grey and light grey, beige and ivory.

'Some people will be in mourning,' the *vendeuse* said.

Tia flinched. 'How much are the coloured buttons?'

'They are not expensive, but I don't zink M'Weinstock will like.'

Tia thought for a moment longer, then decided to compromise. The coloured buttons could be used for summer dresses if Mr Weinstock insisted. If she used jet instead of black, she would be well within the budget he had given her; the cotton braid for the trim was not as expensive as the silk.

'No calf,' the *vendeuse* said apologetically, picking up a bundle of belts. 'All calf gone for zee ovvizers' boots. Kid, suede, buckskin and sciver. But we 'av flower in sciver. Is *bon*.'

The flower was a dainty bud of shaved leather, with one perfect snakeskin leaf. The petals were bronze, the stem black.

'I'll take four dozen,' Tia said quickly.

'I don't know 'ow many left. I see.'

She waited for her order to be wrapped and totalled. When the *vendeuse* told her how much it was in francs, Tia leaned towards her and whispered that she would pay in American Dollars, as Mr Weinstock had told her to. The *vendeuse* nodded and gave her another price. Tia quickly handed the notes over wondering why the transaction felt so tainted. As she turned to leave with her order, she noticed for the first time a man who had been standing at the workroom door. He smiled at her as he opened the door; she nodded briskly, suddenly anxious to be out in daylight once more.

'Forgive me,' he said, 'but I recognise you.'

She did not pause. 'I am sorry, but I do not recognise you.'

'That surprises me,' he said. His voice had turned cold. She turned to look at him.

244

'I am Haldane Brodie, the accountant for Stewart and MacDonald's. I'm the man who pays your bills, Mrs Cameron.'

She relaxed. 'I'm sorry, Mr Brodie. I would have recognised you in Glasgow, I think. I didn't expect to bump into you in Paris.'

He smiled again. 'I understand. I don't believe we've ever been formally introduced, but I've seen you in my office several times.'

She blushed slightly. Stewart and Macdonald's were a big customer of Weinstock's for their wholesale warehouse in Buchanan Street, but they never paid on time. The accounts clerk had incurred her anger once when she had said that it was enough to be at war with Germany without having to pay the Germans who had settled in Scotland.

'What brings you to Paris, Mr Brodie?'

'We carry a lot of lines from Paris. I'm here to pay the bills. The franc is so weak that we're paying in sterling.'

'I see.'

'If you remember, I hardly did business with Weinstock at all until I found he'd taken on a competent manager in yourself.'

Her mouth opened to tell him that she wasn't a manager, just an assistant who helped with the designing. She had never really had a title at all, but over the years she had done more or less everything, from designing to making sure that the bills were paid.

'I did wonder about the ethics of trading with him at all. He is German, I believe.'

'Actually, he isn't,' she said quickly. 'He's Russian by birth but his parents were killed when he was young and his cousins in Vienna took him in.'

He shook his head as if the information meant nothing to him, then peered at his fob-watch. 'We're a shade late for lunch, Mrs Cameron, but perhaps you would care to join me for a coffee.'

'Of course,' she said, thinking of business. 'It would be my pleasure.'

Although his manner was friendly, there was something about Haldane Brodie that made Tia wary. She detected arrogance in the way he introduced himself, disdain in the way he assumed Samuel Weinstock to be of German origin. Though she had been too busy to eat lunch, she would have turned down his invitation if she had a choice.

He took her arm, holding it gingerly as he led her across the road, then dropping it the moment they reached the pavement. Though it was late in the year, the air was warm and smelt of food. They passed one café where diners were having coffee on the pavement, several others with doors open wide to let in the breeze. The aura of war had faded quickly; there was an exuberance around that spilled out with the accordion music and the scent of liqueurs. A woman who sashayed up the street to a chorus of catcalls from a patrol of soldiers was not annoyed or even offended, she turned and waved at them and they waved back.

Haldane Brodie led her into a café on the Boulevard St Germain, past an organ grinder playing merrily at the door. Though there was a table outside, he said he'd rather find one indoors.

The interior was cool and quiet, with the endless mirrors on the walls holding the reflections of women talking, men smoking. Haldane Brodie gestured at a banquette, waited for her to sit before he sat himself, ordering two coffees and brandies from a circulating waiter. Tia caught the bored look of the man opposite as a woman talked earnestly; the gesture as he flicked ash from his cigarette and called the waiter for another drink before he silenced her with a menacing look and she sat back, slightly caricatured by her heavy make-up. Two wooden Chinese mandarins squatted slightly above, surveying the scene with oriental inscrutability.

She was drinking in the smell, the taste of the air, the insouciance of the women so carefully, carelessly, dressed, the loose drape of their scarves and the tilted berets, fur jackets haphazardly abandoned on the backs of chairs. For ever more, Paris woud be this to her, style considered but never contrived, as if women were born to look the way they did. Two women who had the poise of models rose and strolled to the door, proud as stallions of their limbs tight against the cut of their skirts. She envied them for their assurance and for the easy way they adjusted their monkey-fur-trimmed hats, hugging their velvet coat-jackets to their chest when they saw a light rain had begun to fall outside and sending a waiter to call a cab, which swerved to a halt at the door. When, the next month, *Vogue* reported the trend, she smiled to herself because she had been there and seen it first. She was already thinking of new designs.

'These dashed Bolshevists,' Haldane Brodie spat sud-denly, interrupting her reverie.

She looked at him questioningly.

'I mean, every damned cab in Paris is driven by a Russian prince,' he said, 'if you'll excuse my language. 'The Revolution, you know. Most of them escaped with just the clothes they stood up in and a Fabergé piece or two. Last night, one offered to sell me an emerald if I'd get him a ticket to New York on the first ship out once the war is over.'

'And did you?'

'Gracious no, Mrs Cameron. I paid the man cash. It'll come in useful for Mother's Christmas.'

Tia smiled to herself.

'I would have asked you to dine with me, but I fear it would be improper.'

'It would also be impossible. I am leaving on the evening train.'

He cleared his throat. 'Mrs Cameron, I do hope you do not mind me asking, but I have heard that you are a widow.'

She stiffened imperceptibly. 'That is true.'

He smiled. 'Then that is another thing we share.'

Her eyes rose in question.

'My dear Louisa passed away at the start of the war.' He looked away and for a moment his face settled into a mask as the waiter served their coffee in thick white cups.

'I'm sorry, Mr Brodie. I didn't mean to pry.'

'Oh, absolutely not, Mrs Cameron. You did not pry. I raised the subject myself.'

She took the cup, wincing slightly at the bitterness. 'And the other thing, Mr Brodie?'

He looked confused.

'You said that was another thing we shared.'

'I meant, apart from our business.'

'Ohh.'

She did not know what to say to him after that, except to tell him about the new lines she was planning for the spring, how hard she was working to find cloth to make up for the shortage of wool. She finished by assuring him that the price would not rise on any of Weinstock's lines. She was glad when she heard a clock chiming four; that it was time to collect her things from the boarding house and make for the station.

'You must let me escort you,' he said.

'Please, I wouldn't dream of letting you. You must be very busy, Mr Brodie.'

He frowned and consulted his fob-watch again. 'I have an appointment soon at the hotel, I'm afraid, but I can ask my driver to take you to the station.'

'Please do not, she said again. 'I have to collect my things first.'

As they walked out of the café he asked her where she was staying she told him that it was just off the Champs-Elysées, praying he would never know the lie. After the time in Glasgow when she did not know Mrs Anderson's address, she always kept a careful track of herself; she would never be lost again.

They walked over the bridge in silence and stopped outside the Hôtel George V.

'It has been a most pleasant interlude, Mrs Cameron,' he said.

She smiled politely but did not say anything.

'I would be most grateful if I could perhaps enjoy your company again.'

She smiled again.

'There is a vacancy at the store, MacDonald's that is.' He reached into his wallet and took out a card. 'Perhaps we could meet and talk about it.'

'I have no experience of retailing, Mr Brodie, but it is nice of you to think of me.'

'The pleasure is mine, Mrs Cameron. If I might say so, you are wasted working for that Jew.'

Her lips met thinly; she bit back a retort, thinking of the September bill, seven weeks outstanding and still unpaid.

She extended her hand. 'I will be in touch, Mr Brodie.'

'I will look forward to it.'

# Chapter Fourteen

*T*ia opened the door of her flat in Hyndland; the hallway was dark and quiet, the air stale. She walked through to the kitchen and opened the window wide, then knelt at the door of the range and saw that the ashes were cold. Tiredly, she took off her jacket, then rolled up the sleeves of her blouse before she cleared the ashes and filled with space with paper and kindling and a few chips of coal to start the fire again.

The room was cold. She shivered and went through to her bedroom, where she put on her nightclothes and a dressing gown and then returned to the kitchen to wait for the water in the kettle to heat.

Tam's and Willie's clothes were all over the kitchen, along with newspapers, dirty dishes and general debris. Tia began to fold their clothes, then gave up, gathering them into a bundle which she carried through and dumped on their tousled bedclothes. They resented her, she knew, resented their mother sending them to stay with her, resented most of all not being allowed to join the army and go to the war. Their friends from the Gallowgate had gone, most of them at the age of fourteen or fifteen; the Highland Light Infantry regiment that recruited so many from Glasgow was careless of the ages of the lads who signed on.

At first Tia had not understood Mairead's hysteria, her utter terror at the thought that her sons might join the army. They had left school the year the war began, and were fine, strapping young men, both of them, with a keen wit and an easy smile for their friends, but they had never quite forgiven Tia for being a part of the family that had betrayed their mother. Though Mairead had often told them that Tia had been but a child herself when it all happened, she sensed that they blamed her, in some way, for their mother's predicament, for the years they had spent in the workhouse while their mother worked her hands to the bone to get them out of that purgatory into the comparative ease of the slum in the Gallowgate.

Over the years Mairead had told Tia about some of it, and she had listened and kept her tears to herself until she left their room and walked through the dark back to her home. Only Tia knew how Mairead detested having to brew ale to make a living, making pennies off the drunks, the men who beat their wives and spent the tail end of their wages on beer that she sold for tuppence a pint. Mairead had come to hate her life; it was all Tia could do to stop her from hating herself.

The front door slammed and Tam and Willie came in together, their dusty boots marking a track over the linoleum that was already layered with a week's worth of muddy footprints. They nodded to Tia, who was still waiting for the kettle to boil, before they threw their jackets down and then opened the bags of chips they had bought on the way home.

She had picked up a tin of meat and some stale bread from the corner shop; there were still three precious eggs in the larder and she was going to try to make a meal once the oven was warm.

She told them that.

'Disna matter,' Willie said, through a mouthful of chips. 'We got a week's work today and we wis paid already.'

The kettle groaned, seeping steam that seemed weak. She poured water into the pot, stirring it to eke the last of the strength from the flakes of tea. They boys liked tea to be like treacle, strong, thick and sweet. The sugar she had managed to beg or buy was finished, so she went to fetch the jar of honey that she had hidden underneath her bed. She added a spoonful to each of their mugs, none at all to her own.

'Did ye hae a guid time, Auntie Tia?' Tam asked. He was the more open of the two and did not seem to resent her as Willie did. When she took them to the pictures for a treat, Tam laughed through *A Dog's Life* whereas Willie just scowled at the screen.

She pushed her hair back and rested her elbows on the table. Since the boys had come in, the room had warmed itself.

'I wasn't there for long enough,' she replied.

'Did you see any Germans?'

She smiled. 'No, they've gone back to Germany. I think. The armistice is to be signed this week.'

Willie's face twisted into a bitter mask. 'Bastirts,' he spat.

She knew he wanted to avenge his dead friends, share the triumph of the live ones. Impulsively, she reached for his hand and grasped it. 'It was what your mother wanted, Willie, keeping you out of the war.'

For just a moment he softened, then he pulled his hand away angrily. 'I'd've belted them, Auntie Tia, sae I wid. I'd'a been there in another month or twa.'

He wore his agression as armour against the world, as if there was another completely different person beneath the young man who raged at the injustice of his hurt. Mairead had told her that the boys had just had time to know their father before the accident had left him to face the world as immobile as a statue. For some reason Willie's anger was greater than Tam's or even than her own, which had faded over the years into a dull acquiescence that was almost acceptance. Tia tried hard to love him, in fact she did, but he was so gruff to her that it was difficult to keep a hold on her frustration.

'I'm glad you didn't,' she said, 'but then I suppose it's selfish to say that.'

He got up abruptly. 'I'm awa' tae the pub.'

The wake of his departure drove a chill through the room.

'We're aye gettin' called fearties,' Tam said, to fill the gap.

Tia knew that. She got up and cleared the paper from the table, then Willie's mug, refilling Tam's and her own before she poured the rest of the hot water into the sink to wash the accumulated dishes.

She was thinking of Cal, of the way she had spent the entire journey back to Glasgow hoping that he might already be there. His letter about their meeting at Miss Cranston's was in a drawer in her room, beside the box in which she kept Marcus's papers.

She read in the *Herald* that the guns on the Western Front were silent at last. There was, as yet, no news of the returning soldiers; at the station she had overheard a woman saying that each regiment would be disbanded in turn, with the first soldiers to join being the first to come home. Cal had been one of the first, he had joined up in 1914 long before conscription and won his medal at the Somme in 1916.

'Willie's no a fearty,' Tam said.

She finished the dishes and sat down to join him, smiling gently. 'I know he's not, nor you.'

'Aye, but it's being *called* that. If ye say ye've no jined acos o' yer ma, it's worse.'

She laughed. Mairead could be as hard as nails when she wanted to.

'I mean, if they'd sent Ma tae fight the Germans, they'd'a gone packing richt at the start o' it.' Tam grinned and she grinned back at him.

'Used tae curse the bullets, so she did. Used to say yin o' thae curses yous yell when ye're fashed.'

Mr Weinstock grabbed her by both hands when she walked into the workroom to show him the trimmings she had bought in Paris, offering him the change from the money he had given her in an envelope.

He waved away the money generously. 'Keep it, Tia. Is a bonus for good work.'

She had made some sketches of how the braid trim would look on that season's jacket and of Murielle's order made up in cotton piqué if there was still no wool at the beginning of the year.

'I 'ave the address of a firm in Rutherglen who 'ave wool,' he said. 'You go see them on Monday.'

'Monday's my day for chasing the accounts,' she reminded him.

Again, he waved his hand over her drawings. 'With a new collection like this we do not 'ave to worry about these crooks. Stewart and MacDonald? Stewart and MacDonald will wait in line for this. They will pay *on order!*'

She laughed. 'I'd be happy if they pay us the £859 they owe from September.'

'Ach, I worry about that. You, Tia, you concentrate on the design and the cut and getting the girls working again. 'Ow many times I tell you, you are a designer, Tia. You make the garments. I worry about the bills.'

Flustered, she went into the cramped little office and rang the shop in Sauchiehall Street, where she managed to make an appointment to see Murielle herself on Monday afternoon. She spent the weekend on a *toile* of her design in cotton piqué, to show Murielle that the design would work as well in cotton as it would in wool crêpe.

Tia spent Armistice Thursday at work alone in the workroom, while all around the joy on the streets rang out. Even Mr Weinstock had taken the day off, to spend with his wife and family in celebration not only of the end of the war but also the bills that Stewart and MacDonald had paid on Monday, sending a message girl round with a cheque not only for the outstanding September bill, but the October one as well. Haldane Brodie had enclosed a note addressed to Mrs Cameron in which he apologised profusely for the 'oversight'.

At the Avonbank Mill in Rutherglen Tia had found yards and yards of a wool weave that was supposed to be the tartan of the Argyle Regiment, which she bought cheap because of a mistake in the dye. She quickly substituted the check on jacket facings for the spring lines, due to be delivered to the shops in December, to add piquancy to the austerity of the gabardine they had been forced to use by the war. There was rumoured to be no more wool in the city, and even Stewart's buyer had been on the phone to ask if Weinstock's had anything in stock.

She left the workroom at eight in the evening, not because she was finished but because she heard a lull in the racket from the streets just then and thought she would be able to walk home through the crowds. The trams had stopped at eleven in the morning and she did not think that the subway would be running at all.

As she turned into Argyle Street, though, she ran into a crowd of jubilant City Chambers workers on their way to a dance in the City Halls and when a drunk man grabbed her and began to dance in the street she fled in the other direction, heading for Mairead's instead, thinking that the boys might have gone there when the papers said all the factories were closed.

Mairead was sitting in her kitchen, the room unlit despite the dark. There was a pot of tea on the table; when Tia walked in she got up and filled the kettle again, pulling a chair close to the range for her sister.

'The lads've gone up the Green,' she said tiredly. 'There's bands playing and dancing up there.'

'Why didn't you go yourself?'

Mairead shook her head. 'I took a tram first thing this morning. I went down to see Tam.'

'Oh.' Mairead usually visited her husband on Sunday morning; she loved the man who had become an invalid as she had loved him when they were both young. During the war she had saved as much as she could of her salary in the hope that she might manage to find a little bungalow somewhere that she could rent for them both. The boys had promised to help her with their wages.

She filled the teapot and stirred the leaves mechanically.

'I get laid off at the year end.'

Tia frowned. 'So soon?'

'There's no more need for bullets since the war's done.'

They drank their tea in silence. When Tia had finished, she put her cup down and looked at Mairead. The sadness was sunken in the pools of her sister's eyes, she had that whipped look again, like a bitch whose pups have been drowned. Mairead's dog had died years before and she had not got another because she had the munitions job by then, but she had kept her sons throughout the war, spending money on food and clothes for them that she would have been better to spend on herself. In the years that Tia had been in Glasgow, she had never seen Mairead spend anything on herself; everything she did was for her husband or her sons. She even paid for Tam's hospital room because she could not bear to think of him in the pauper's ward that his paid up National Insurance allowed for. She was so bitterly proud that she would take no more of charity than she had been given in the time she had spent in the workhouse.

'You know,' Tia began, 'you remember, that idea I had.'

'What idea?' Mairead asked listlessly.

'To take a stall at the Barras and sell Weinstock's unsold stock. I was thinking, we could do it now.'

Mairead shook her head. 'I haven't got that much saved, Tia. Only fifty pounds or so.'

'That would be enough. We can rent a barrow from Maggie McIver for ten shillings a week.'

'How d'you know?'

'I asked her. Mr Weinstock said I could have the stock on sale or return.'

'I thought you said you'd nothing because of the war.'

'We've got some rayon blouses from that bad dye run. I could get the girls to run up some skirts and I've got some cotton dresses I made myself .'

Mairead began to think. 'There's a wee shop on Moncur Street right next to Marshall Lane. It's for rent, I know. I saw the sign from the tram today.'

'Let's do it, then.'

Mairead smiled. 'I'll put in ten pounds and you do the same. The rent can't be that much. It's not even a proper shop. It used to be a paper booth, but the man that had it died a while back.'

Tia spent the night at Mairead's, huddled in the same bed with her, and felt almost as if she was at home on North Uist where she had fallen asleep in her sister's arms most days, when her mother was too busy with her father and brothers and sisters to give her more than a peck on the cheek.

She thought of Cal as she went to sleep. He had been in her mind during all of the war years; she had prayed for him; the odd certainty that he would survive had comforted her and spared her the torment of her casualty lists. She realised that she wanted to see him for his own sake and not just because he was Marcus's brother. Cal made her laugh; it was a long time since she had laughed at anything.

On Tuesday she called at the City Chambers and heard from a sergeant in the Machine Gun Corps that Cal had been among the first to be demobbed and was expected home soon, but not within the week. The sergeant said that the trains in France were terrible and it would take two weeks at least.

Even so, she took an hour off from work to wait outside Miss Cranston's.

The returning troops began to arrive in the city at the weekend; the station was thronged, the streets virtually impassable.

It took two more weeks before she managed to find the same sergeant again, who looked at a list and then told her that Cal would be back in Glasgow on the first Tuesday in December. She left a message for him with the RVS at the station, another at the regimental office and a third at the pier where the Hebridean boats docked. Mr Weinstock told her to take the afternoon off work; she raced home and changed, then got back to the station in time to meet the train, but she could not find Cal anywhere.

The whole concourse was thronged with soldiers, hundreds of solders in uniform, and thousands of milling women, children and older men, wives and mothers, sisters and daughters, veterans of lesser wars, all come to welcome them home.

Tia waited until late, then decided to go to the Willow Rooms on Thursdays, because Cal had said, if he did not make it back in time, she should try the next week and then the one after that.

She was so sure he would come then that she took another half day off work, and was waiting nervously from noon, when she took a table in the Room de Luxe that overlooked Sauchiehall Street so that she would be able to see Cal before he even walked in the door.

The waitress asked her if she would be having lunch; she asked just for tea because she was waiting for her brother-in-law, who had just come home from the war. The waitress smiled knowingly and left her with a glass of lemon tea for more than an hour until she came back at the height of the lunchtime rush to ask her with slightly less understanding if she would like to order now because the tearoom was very busy.

'I wanted to sit at the window,' Tia said.

The waitress glanced down and pointed out that there was a free table in the room below. Tia gathered up her clutch bag and walked down the stairs, ordering a lunch that she did not want so that she would be able to wait there.

She left at half past three, suddenly angered by the stencilled walls and the poise of the cashier in the booth by the door who asked her in an over-loud voice if she was the lady who had eaten lunch alone. For a while, just after one, she had felt Cal so close that every moment she expected him to walk in the door, had watched it so intently that she developed a painful twinge along the side of her neck. At one point, she had even gone to the door and looked out, so convinced that he was coming, feeling a sensation so strong that it was almost like the way she knew that Marcus had turned the corner into Mrs Anderson's street long before he reached the front door.

She walked back to the workroom the long way, pausing when she passed the Buchanan Street Tearooms, going in there on impulse just in case she had been mistaken or that during the war he had forgotten the arrangement to meet in the Room de Luxe.

The tea room was quiet, almost, after the hum of the streets, the joy and relief that throbbed through the crowds of relatives meeting the men come home from the war. There was even an empty table by the side of the room, in between two of the murals that Cal had found disturbing before the war. She sat down and loosened the Delphos scarf that she had slung around her neck when she had dressed so carefully in a deep emerald suit she had made herself, trimmed with matching velvet embossed with a Deco motif. Ordering a pot of tea, she chose a scone from the trolley so that she could linger a while longer. Women went to tearooms together, but it was not the done thing to go alone and she was very aware of her solitude as the waitress put down the pot of tea and a single cup and saucer.

'I'm . . . I'm waiting for a friend,' she explained hesitantly. 'I thought, we made the arrangement a while ago and I thought we arranged to meet at the Willow Rooms and I went there and then I remembered it was probably here. So I've missed my friend. I think.' Her voice trailed off into a nervous laugh; the waitress smiled sympathetically.

'Don't worry, Madam. We're quiet now.'

'Did you . . . was there anyone waiting?'

'I'm not sure, Madam. We were very busy during lunchtime. If you give me your name, I'll see if anyone's left a message.'

'Really, it doesn't matter,' Tia demurred.

She poured tea into her cup, but not milk. In the sugar bowl there were two lumps, which she pocketed furtively to give to the boys later. Looking around, she saw two women on the other side of the room huddled in a secret chat, a man, a woman and a girl who had been shopping; the man looked bored. The subdued hum of male voices came from the Smoking Room upstairs; two businessmen walked down towards the door, pausing to leave some money with the cashier.

The murals seemed to have faded since she had seen them last, the gold aurora of the sun had darkened and the white of the women's gowns was stained ivory. The tangled cage of leaves and twigs around them was scarred and chipped in places.

Mrs Cranston, in real life Mrs John Cochrane, had been widowed almost exactly a year before. She had been devastated by grief and although she was still seen occasionally in her tearooms clad as always in long black skirts, cape and sombrero, she did not have the heart to carry on her business alone. She had announced her retirement at the age of sixty-eight; Tia had heard that she was putting her tearooms up for sale, with the exception of the Willow Rooms, which she was giving to her friend Miss Drummond.

She poured milk into her tea and then added one, then both of the purloined sugar lumps because she felt in need of comfort. The scone tasted dry; she washed the crumbs down with tea and then sat, staring into space.

The gossiping women quieted for a moment and turned to stare at her openly before turning their attention again to each other and a new round of confidences. She imagined that they were talked about her, speculating what she might be doing in a tearoom on her own. It was clear now that nobody would join her and her isolation made her ache inside.

Hating to waste anything, she poured the dregs of the tea into her cup and drank the bitter liquid before she hunted in her purse for a penny to leave the waitress who had been so fleetingly kind to her.

When she heard the sound of a masculine step on the stair she looked up expectantly, hoping finally that Cal had arrived and had perhaps waited for her in the Smoking Room because he had picked up the habit in the war. Seeing just a pair of dark trousers she turned away hurriedly and stared at the women on the walls again, remembering what he had said about them being in cages, almost like doves, that no being on God's earth should be caged like that.

'Mrs Cameron!' the voice rang out over the almost empty tearoom. 'What a surprise! I had almost given up hope that you would appear. I was quite hurt, you know.'

Haldane Brodie was striding towards her in his crisp business suit, with a broad smile on his face.

She stood up suddenly, flustered. 'Mr Brodie, really, I was about to leave.'

'Please don't, Mrs Cameron.' He sat down at the table as if it was his by right and beckoned the waitress, ordering coffee for himself and another pot of tea for Tia, asking her in passing if she would like some of the salmon mayonnaise sandwiches that they were serving for tea and perhaps a slice of cinnamon cake as well and ordering that as well before she had a chance to answer.

'Really,' she said again, 'I was just about to leave.'

Very briefly, he put his hand over hers, smiling fleetingly. 'You'll have to stay, now. It would be too great a pity, wouldn't it, to waste one of Miss Cranston's delicious high teas?'

She smiled politely, grateful that by his presence he had brought her back to respectability again. She no longer felt the scrutiny of the women who had stared at her; when they rose to leave she even returned their smile of farewell.

Haldane Brodie took in the room at a glance. 'A little *de trop*, don't you think? I usually have lunch upstairs and a game of billiards afterwards. I use the demon weed, you see.'

She smiled again as he took a cigarette from his pocket and lit it, sending the waitress scurrying in search of an ashtray. The lighting in the room was low; as she studied his features she realised that he was really quite handsome, in a rather cold way. His eyes were dark and hooded, his nose fine and straight, his dark hair swept back with Brylcreem greying at the sides in a way that added poise and wisdom to an otherwise undistinguished face. His profile was so angled that it was almost Roman; topped with a wreath of leaves he could have been Caesar, or even Brutus, come to that. She smiled to herself as she wondered what he would look like in a toga. During the war, she had whiled away the empty hours in the Kelvingrove Gallery and the Hunterian, and so become *au fait* with culture of a sort. She had even been to Rennie Mackintosh's art school for the summer exhibition and shed bitter tears for the artists who could paint no longer because they were obliged to fight in the war.

The sandwiches came; she took one through obligation and then another when she realised that she was still hungry. Haldane Brodie watched her with a wry little expression upon his face, pouring her tea for her when she finished eating. He had stubbed his cigarette out when the food came; he lit another hurriedly, sucking in the smoke like a drowning man would gasp for air.

'I was waiting for your call,' he said.

'I beg your pardon?'

'In my note, I suggested that we take tea one afternoon. There is something luxurious about afternoon tea, don't you think? Lunch on a business day is always such a hurried affair.'

She looked away guiltily; she had not even read all of his note, just the apology for not paying the Weinstock bill sooner. 'This is the busiest time of the year for us, Mr Brodie.'

'There is usually a good income from the ladies' department in the months leading up to Christmas.'

'We get repeat orders for gowns, if we're lucky. And we've the spring collection to do as well. It isn't easy, when you can't get wool.'

'Mr Hugh said that only the other day at the board meeting –there wasn't a yard of serge to be had in the whole of Glasgow.'

'I managed to,' she began, then pursed her lips because she did not want to reveal the secret of the Avonbank Mill. The manager had promised her twenty bolts of tan that had been ordered for offiers' coats, if the regiment no longer needed the cloth. She had agreed eagerly, even offering to leave a deposit, though she wasn't quite sure what she would do with that colour. The mill was not sure what would happen if the cloth was put through a second dye bath.

'You found some, did you? That was always Samuel Weinstock's forte. When he started, nobody could deal with him, but then he began to import French lace at a price that was so good we didn't have a choice.'

'I've always enjoyed working with him, Mr Brodie.'

'I imagine the experience is mutual, Mrs Cameron. His garments have improved immeasurably since he took you on board. Before that, our buyer tells me that it was chaos.'

She said nothing.

'Give a dog a bad name,' he said, 'he will never get over the United States Guitar Zither Company scandal. You know all about that, of course.'

She nodded noncommittally.

'It was a bunch of Jews from Roumania. They got some guitar zithers from Germany and took on a lot of their own as agents to sell the things. The agents offered a hundred free lessons as well, at a place in St Vincent Street. They were selling the instruments for between two and four guineas, whereas the wholesale price was only five shillings or so. I can't remember. Dallas's stocked them as well, but they were selling them for the right price without the lessons. Of course, the United States Guitar Zither Company did quite well, with gullible widows and grandparents and the like. I think half the city bought a zither for a child or a grandchild. There was only one problem. There were no lessons after the first one or two. The scoundrels fled. The agents were left to face the music, as it were.' He paused and grinned wryly at his own joke. 'Weinstock was one of them. He wasn't prosecuted, but he was taken to the civil court and made a bankrupt.'

Tia winced, because she did know that. Mr Weinstock had told her about it one day, when a ladies' shop in Paisley wanted to open an account without a banker's reference. He insisted that they pay cash until their credit was established and Tia was afraid that if they thought she did not trust them they would cancel their order. She had protested that the lady who owned the shop had a husband who was well dressed and looked like a gentleman, but Sam replied that sometimes a thief wore the best clothes of all. He told her then that he had fallen in with some scoundrels, and ended up having to pay their debts himself. It was the hardest lesson he had ever learned in his life, but also the best.

'He paid his debts,' she said quietly.

'Oh, yes, every penny. But he didn't have a choice really. He would have been jailed otherwise. Severals others were.'

*I worked my fingers to the bone as a tailor, Tia. Miriam, she take in sewing. I work nights at Geneen's. Clean dishes. Miriam, she do laundry. Sophie, she feed the children. Without Sophie, I starve. Sophie lend me money for this lease. But I pay back. I pay her every penny. And the others also. Weinstock honourable man, Tia. Always pays 'is debts.'*

'I am not a friend of the race, you see. The Jews help each other and to hell with anyone else. I think Delaval's right. Let the lion follow the example of the bear and give the sea another opportunity of parting its waters and letting them through with dry feet.'

'I could'av gone to United States, Tia. Miriam's brother, he say, you go. Debts are not your own. Is debts of the scoundrel. But I stay, Tia. I stay and pay. I not want to run away and people think bad of Weinstock name.'

She was so angry that for a moment, she did not trust herself to speak.

'I do hope I haven't upset you, Mrs Cameron.'

'No, no,' she said, thinking of the order she would get for the spring collection if Weinstock were the only garment-maker in the city to have wool cloth. Stewart and McDonald's would pay through the nose for it, and she would make a point of giving Murielle a discount for her loyalty over the years.

'Certainly not, Mr Brodie. I was thinking only that I will look forward to doing business with you.'

'I was hoping,' he said, 'that you might consider the position I mentioned to you. I hear the buyer in the ladies' department is leaving us.'

'I will think carefully about it,' she said, as she picked up her bag and watched the hurried way that he rose to help her out of her seat.

She looked away as he paid her bill. The waitress was arranging some dried flowers in a vase by the entrance, and she asked her if the rumour was true, if the tearooms were being sold.

'It has already been sold, Madam. The new management are going to run it as a club.'

'Oh, well, I suppose I will still be able to have tea here now and again, if someone invites me,' she said brightly.

'I believe it will be a gentlemen's dining club, Madam.'

'Oh.'

'We're closing at the end of the month.'

'Oh. I did like looking at the murals. But I suppose they will too.'

'No, Madam. They have already been in. The walls are going to be stripped and panelled over.'

She walked out with Haldane Brodie to the drizzle of the late Glasgow afternoon as the trams rumbled down the streets, sending sparks like dragonflies that streaked against the grey of the sky, flaring briefly before they were devoured by the gloom.

'That will be a pity, don't you think?' she said to him.

'What will be a pity?'

'The murals. They are going to panel them over.'

'I never liked them much myself.'

'Nor did my brother-in-law. He didn't like the image of women in cages.'

Haldane Brodie laughed. 'I've always thought that was just the place for them. A woman's place is in the house. Of course, the war's changed all that. Or so they say. You have the vote now, don't forget. Pankhurst and her gang needn't have bothered.'

She felt the chill suddenly and thanked him profusely when he hailed a passing cab and gave Weinstock's address to the driver, with some money to pay her fare. She did not tell him that she would have to wait another eight years before she could exercise the right the suffragettes had fought for.

The workroom was quiet when she got back. Though it was just after five, only a few of the machines were going, and the cutting table cleared of cloth. Archie, the boy soldier who had lost an arm at the Somme, was sweeping up with the other one. She smiled at the machinists, who were chatting as one filed the nicks out of her nails.

'Is it true, Tia?' one asked, as she walked past.

'Is what true, Peggy?'

'Will we git laid aff wi' the end o' the war? Some o' the mill girls in Paisley 'a been sent hame already.'

'I don't think so,' she said. She had not thought about it; there would be less work without the gas company's inspectors' uniforms and and the soldier's shirts, but more from the fashion trade that had been hit so hard with the shortage of cloth.

Peggy jerked her head towards the office. 'He's no said a word a' day.'

'It's the end of the month,' Tia said, 'he's getting the bills ready to send out.'

Kathleen, the little Irish machinist whose work was so perfect that a garment she machined could almost be made by hand, looked at her. 'Will it be me, Missus? I've not been here as long as the other girls.'

'I need you for the spring, Kathleen. You're the only one who's been getting the suit trims right.'

Tia could have bitten back her words when she saw the hurt spread over the other women's faces.

'I meant,' she said, 'your hands are so small that you can get the turns right. I was thinking of trying a line, you know. Peggy, Elsbeth, Maureen and Jenny on the seams, Kathleen and Sheena on that cord trim on the facings and lapels. Kathleen and Sheena aren't nearly as quick on the seams as the rest of you are.'

They were all watching her anxiously.

'What about the men?' Jenny asked.

Tia looked at her.

'I mean, the men that wirked here afore the war. Yous are supposed tae gie them the jobs back.'

'I don't know,' Tia said quickly. 'He will if he can.'

'D'ye no ken yersel', Tia?' Jenny asked.

'I don't,' she said, shaking her head.

Sam Weinstock was shouting into the phone in Yiddish, a string of anger interspersed by the odd pause when he listened intently. The language sounded quaint to her, as she supposed her Gaelic did to him, but she could never quite understand how Samuel Weinstock could switch so easily from Yiddish to German to English almost in the same breath. He spoke Hebrew as well, though he said he only used it when he went to the synagogue at Garnethill.

She waited until he banged the phone down, shaking his head. 'My cousin in Vienna, my cousin in New York will take him but only if I pay fare for family. The children from 'Ungary, orphans of the war, they go to Sinclair Drive but, *but*, only if we bring them from Vienna also. Is Rabbi on phone. I tell 'im, is business here, not benevolent society.' He threw his arms up in a gesture of helplessness. 'I azk you, Tia, 'ow can you say "No" to orphans? I cannot say "No" to my cousin. In Vienna, he will never work again. In New York, maybe Juilliard take him as teacher of composition. So the Rabbi say.'

She smiled and sat down.

'Did you meet your brother-in-law?'

She shook her head quickly; he did not question her about it, but simply nodded at the information, as if he had expected that.

'The girls are worried,' she said, when he got up to pour some tea from the samovar in the corner of the office.

'Why?'

'They are scared you will lay them off.'

'I 'ope not.'

'Is there any chance that you might?'

He shrugged. 'Maybe, but I 'ope not.'

Suddenly, her anger flared. 'Mr Weinstock, you cannot.'

'Why not?'

'Mr Weinstock, they've worked for us right through the war. They worked through the night sometimes, you know that.'

'They were paid, weren't they?'

'Yes, but they stayed with us when they could have gone off to munitions works. They were loyal. We can't discard them just like that.'

'As I say to Rabbi, is business, Weinstock's Haute Couture. 'Ere, I talk business talk. At orphanage and *Bikur Cholim* it's different, but 'ere, always is business talk.'

They memory of what Haldane Brodie said flared briefly before she looked him in the eye and asked him if he could really do that, if he could really lay off the women just like that.

'Of course not,' he said, smiling at last. 'You know that, Tia. Not if there is a choice. You 'ave my word. No lay-offs unless the orders 're cancelled. If the orders are confirmed, there is enough work for all the girls.'

# Chapter Fifteen

*B*ridie's letter came from South Uist the day after Christmas. 'I wrote to the regiment,' she told Tia, 'and they wrote back and said Cal was demobbed at the end of November. They say he arrived in Glasgow on the 23rd of the month. We have not heard anything. Mother is almost mad with the worry. Can you find what has happened to him, please, Tia? Can you try?'

She put the letter down on the plant stand in the little hallway, empty since Willie had fallen over the aspidistra when he came home drunk on Armistice Day. She had gone to her flat only to find her secret hoard of sugar so her sister could make a pudding for Hogmanay; Mairead had used her own to hasten the fermentation of the hootch she made so that everyone in the close would be able to toast the New Year. Tia had saved the cubes and grains in a paper bag, wrapped in cotton and hidden in her pillow. She rarely took sugar herself, but saved it for the boys; Mairead had saved quite a bit herself but would not ask the other women in the close for money or sugar and Tia knew precisely why. The family dined well on Christmas Day because Samuel Weinstock always gave his Christian workers a food parcel of a chicken and some *Stollen* that his wife Miriam made for everyone. Others in Mairead's building were not so fortunate.

Their shop, Meg's Pegs, had opened in the booth in Moncur Street during the first week in December. Though they had cut their prices back to the bone, Mairead had to let her customers pay their bills at a shilling a week; they could not afford to buy otherwise. Meg's Pegs sold new blouses starting from 3/6 for the amber-streaked black rayon, end-of-lines and returns from Weinstock's for sixpence more than Samuel Weinstock charged Tia, and a few shillings each for the skirts and dresses that she and the machinists ran up in their spare time.

The Gallowgate was a different world from the stores of Buchanan Street and Sauchiehall Street; the women who had worked so hard during the war were out of work and poor again as soon as peace came and the demobbed soldiers began to flock back to the city in search of work. The only way they could buy anything for themselves was to pay a little every week. Mairead herself made only shillings after the rent had been paid; in time, she said, she would build up a good trade. Of the two hundred women she had in her book, none had defaulted so far.

It worried Tia, though, because although she paid for the stock out of her wages she had been using her savings to buy food for the boys on the black market. She had very little left in her savings account, and she was still keeping the rest of Marcus's money in case Cal or his family needed it. The fishing boat Marcus had bought for his brothers had been commandeered by the Navy and sunk not long afterwards; although they had been promised compensation not a single penny had been paid yet.

The sugar was hard, crusted into the shape of her head. She pummelled it several times and then slipped it into her bag, turning the hall gas light off on her way out.

In the daylight, as she waited for a tram, she read the letter again. Bridie's handwriting was careful, her English precise, as she had learned it at school a dozen years before.

The thought of Cal brought an ache to her heart. That day when she had waited, she had been so sure that she felt his presence, but when she looked nobody was there. When she read Bridie's letter she realised that he had arrived in the city the day before. She knew by instinct that he *had* been outside the Willow Rooms, but for some reason he had not come in. She had been looking forward to meeting him for four years, and she was sure that he had wanted to see her too. Something had prevented him; she was certain of that. She sensed that he was hurt.

Mairead noticed the morose look on Tia's face as she mixed the sugar with meal and flour, some peel that she had saved and half a pound of black-market currants.

'What's the matter?'

'It's Cal,' Tia said. 'Marcus's brother. I think something terrible's happened to him.'

'He survived the war,' Mairead said, 'surely there's nothing as bad as the war.'

Tia glanced out of the window that looked up to the yard where the children played. A pair of spindly legs flashed past in shorts, then chubby ones beneath a skirt. 'Come here, ye wee blighter,' a woman yelled. 'See if ye're no up thae bluidy stairs in two minutes, I'll skelp yer arse fir ye, an' sae will yer faither.'

Mairead smiled, shaking her head. 'I mind when I used to do that.'

Tia frowned. 'Tam couldn't've.'

'He didn't, Tia.' She stopped mixing and flexed her right arm. 'When they needed skelped, I skelped them myself.'

Tia smiled wistfully.

'This Cal,' Mairead said, 'he's like Marcus, is he?'

'A bit, but he's different as well.'

'Look alike when your eyes're half shut?'

'Yes.' She smiled again.

'Careful,' Mairead said.

Tia cocked her head to one side as she inhaled the aroma of the hootch that Mairead was adding to the pudding mixture. 'Why?'

'Because you could fall for him, pet. Happen you already have.'

'I could never do that,' she said sharply. 'He's Marcus's brother. I like him. That's all.'

Mairead looked at her, but she said nothing more.


The Regimental Sergeant Major glared at her. She had written three letters to the regiment's headquarters in Stirling and then come herself when she received no reply. It was January and the winds were icy, the hills and the castle draped in a frosting of lacy snow.

'Mrs Cameron,' he said gruffly. 'Although the war is over we are still very busy here. We have men in France still. We don't have time to drop everything to hunt for one soldier we have already discharged. It is not the regiment's fault that former Private Cameron does not have the decency to contact his family himself.'

The air in the anteroom of the castle was almost as cold as the RSM's manner. She shivered reflexively, inwardly cursing herself for her lack of strength. Though there was a chair where she could have sat, he had not invited her to do so. He had seen her only because she told the soldier on the gate that she would not leave until she saw someone who could tell her about Cal.

She cleared her throat, stifled a sneeze. She wore a jacket she had tailored herself from some left-over charcoal serge and black velvet with a high collar of seal cut from a coat she had found at the Barras. The style was Parisian, the execution Glaswegian. In Sauchiehall Street she had bumped into Mrs Hymans, who had promised her an order for six dozen if she could make any more but she had to turn down the request with regret because she could never find enough identical scraps.

Remembering Murielle's effusive admiration, she raised her head haughtily and met the glare of the Sergeant Major, then sat down without being asked. For a moment he frowned and then, failing to quail her, pulled back a chair and sat down himself.

Tia folded her hands and rested them on the edge of the desk, glancing in passing at a tumble of papers and requisition forms.

'Mr MacMillan . . .' she began.

'*SERGEANT MAJOR MACMILLAN!*' he roared.

'Sergeant Major MacMillan,' she repeated, in a voice that was soft anyway but then also shaky with shock. 'I do not expect you to keep track of a soldier once he has been discharged. I understand that you are busy. Cal's mother and I are both certain that something has happened to him and I wondered if you know what.'

He shrugged. 'He was but a private soldier, Mrs Cameron. One of many thousands.'

'He might have been, but he's also his mother's beloved youngest son.'

'Might I ask what relationship you have to him?'

'He is my brother-in-law.'

He stood abruptly. 'Mrs Cameron, I am afraid I must ask you to leave. I saw you only on the understanding that you were his wife. I cannot divulge any information to anyone with as remote a relationship to the soldier as you have. If you ask your husband or preferably his mother to get in touch with me, I will see if there is anything, but I must warn you again that I do not believe that there is.'

The Sergeant Major knew something; she sensed that from his manner, from the look of relief in his face once he found a reason not to speak to her.

'I am a widow,' she said tersely. 'My mother-in-law is also a widow. In addition she is nigh blind. She lives in Iochdar in South Uist. I really don't think that she could manage to travel to Stirling with the weather as it is. It took me most of the day to reach you from Glasgow.'

His lips tightened and his glance flew out of the window to the grey sky before he sat down again and looked back at her. He slammed a bell on his desk, bringing a lad who looked almost too young to wear long trousers rushing to the office, clicking his heels smartly when the Sergeant Major ordered a pot of tea.

'I am very sorry,' he said. 'But you must understand, we cannot possibly know everything about each individual soldier. The war has hit everyone hard.' His eyes drifted again and his face turned into an expressionless mask. 'There are more than a million Allied dead, Mrs Cameron. In a way, their families are the lucky ones. At least they know their loved one has been accounted for and identified and given as much of a burial as we could manage in the circumstances.'

The youth brought a tray of tea and biscuits and two cups and saucers embossed with the regimental crest. The Sergeant Major waved him away, pouring the tea himself when the door was closed.

Tia drank her tea before she spoke again. 'I am afraid that I don't understand, Sergeant Major,' she said.

'I will try to explain, Mrs Cameron. The official toll of dead at the moment is just over half a million but that figure is by no means complete, simply because there are many, many confirmed dead who simply have not been counted yet. I imagine that the figure will be revised upwards at some time in the future. Beyond that there are the wounded and those taken prisoners of war and also a very large number who have been simply reported missing.'

He poured some more tea and she used the pause to think.

'I don't understand,' she said finally. She had seen that phrase 'reported missing' in the papers and had never understood what it meant.

'Be glad of that, Mrs Cameron,' he said, 'and pray to God that you never do.'

Their eyes met and held for what seemed like an eternity.

'I wish you would explain,' she said.

'Mrs Cameron, I cannot.'

She opened her bag and took out Bridie's last letter, fumbling with it although she did not need to remind herself of the details. 'Cal joined your regiment a few months after the war began, Sergeant Major. He didn't get home leave, or if he got it he did not take it. The first his mother saw of him was when he got home the day after she got a telegram telling her that he had won the VC at the Somme in 1916. She hasn't heard from him since then. The only reason she knows he isn't dead is that another lad from Uist saw Cal in Etaples in October. Eunice is out of her mind with worry.'

The Sergeant Major steepled his fingers. 'Mrs Cameron, I'm an army man. My duty is first of all to the regiment. All I can say is that I know Cal and I made sure he got home safely. I saw him off the train in Glasgow myself.'

Her eyes narrowed. 'He wasn't wounded, was he? Is he hurt?'

The Sergeant Major looked away. 'He sustained a bullet wound a while back, but it was a flesh wound. Superficial.'

'But is he hurt?' she asked him again.

'As I said the wound was superficial, Mrs Cameron.'

'What does that mean, Sergeant Major MacMillan?'

He did not answer.

'His family need to know,' she said.

Still he ignored her.

'*I have to know*,' she yelled.

He stood up and for a moment his face radiated pain as acutely as if he had taken Cal's bullet himself. He flinched and then trembled briefly under the assault of her anger. His face went as white as a newspaper. He was human no longer, but bones covered by a mere parchment of skin.

The walls of the room reverberated with the echoes of her voice until the air settled again and silence fell like a shroud.

'I . . . I'm sorry,' she said. 'But you must be able to tell me about his VC at least.'

He sat down and opened a drawer, taking a metal flask from which he poured something into his tea. The aura of *uiske beatha baul* drifted into her nostrils and she sniffed and swallowed; shook her head when he offered the flask to her.

'He was not awarded the VC. He got the Military Medal'

'Why?'

He looked away. 'Cal decided that he had had enough of the war. He did not get home leave during the Somme. He simply left. Once he was over the Channel he walked all the way home. He was lucky not to have been shot as a deserter.'

'Cal was not a deserter.'

'He was, Mrs Cameron. Had he not saved an officer's life he would have been shot after he returned to his regiment. The officer intervened and he was given another chance.'

'But the war's over now. Why doesn't he come home?'

'Mrs Cameron,' he said, 'I do not know. I do not even know where he is now. All I can say is that of the wounds of this war, not all are physical.'

As her eyes misted with tears, she looked out of the window and saw snowflakes falling, drifting as tumbled eiderdown through the air that was the texture of gauze. She blinked. 'Are you telling me that he's gone mad, Sergeant Major?'

'A man like Cameron would never go mad.'

She got up abruptly and ran from the office, not saying anything and not pausing even when the guard on the gate cocked his rifle and shouted out an order to halt. She dimly heard the footsteps of the Sergeant Major following her and a counter instruction that in the future she would remember with gratitude because his two sharp words saved her life.

At that precise moment, though, she did not care, and nor did she know that troops throughout the country were on alert because of the rebellion the government feared would break out in the lowland cities.

The soldiers who had survived the trenches had come back to a land that did not care, or even appear to want them.

Early the following morning Tia walked up Sauchiehall Street towards the statuesque red stone building that faced Lyons Stationery Shop. When she reached the block she slowed down and looked in Miss Jay's and Miss Stirling's windows before she rang the bell of Murielle's at number 432 and waited for the assistant to answer the door.

'I'm Mrs Cameron from Weinstock's,' she said, 'I've an appointment with Mrs Hymans.'

'If you wait, Madam,' the girl said carefully, the syllables stretched over the raw Glaswegian growl beneath, 'I'll tell Madam that you are here.'

She was led to a room in the basement beyond the fitting rooms where the walls were covered with sketches by Pacquin and Worth, Molyneux and Premet. In a glass frame over the fireplace was a colourful cartoon, walking towards it she saw the harlequin cast of a clown and the scrawled signature of Robert Delaunay. The room, though just an office with all the clutter of the trade, reeked style. She had never met Murielle Hymans at her shop before, only in Samuel's work room. Now that Tia had her full attention, she wanted to sell her not only the dress, but a suit that she had designed in island tweed.

'It's so very kind of you to come to see me,' Mrs Hymans drawled.

'It's very kind of you to see me,' Tia replied.

'Please . . .' She pulled out a chair by a little table, where one of her assistants was setting out cups of tea. She poured carefully and the delicate scent of Earl Grey rose in twisting spirals. 'It's so much more civilised,' she said, handing Tia a perfect little porcelain cup, 'to do business over tea, is it not?' She smiled tactfully. 'That is, if we are to do business at all. As I explained to Samuel, the orders I gave you during the war were one-offs. I usually buy in Paris or London. I've never bought locally before because my own girls can run up anything we need from the *toile*. But your designs intrigued me, Mrs Cameron. As I said to Samuel, if you can get the wool, why not?'

Tia smiled discreetly again. 'As you know, Mrs Hymans, there's hardly any wool to be found in Glasgow.'

Murielle waved her hand dismissively. 'Shortages, shortages. I went to Paris last month and believe me, my dear, *they* will have wool for the spring. Wars come and go, my dear, but fashion goes on for ever. Austerity? Pah! There's been enough austerity for the last four years. My clientele wants style! Why, I had Lady Haig in yesterday, for an outfit for the unveiling of the memorial to her husband, you know. I showed her a little jacket with a seal trim, and do you know, she would not hear of it! She wanted sable. Sable! I told her, "My Lady," I said, "there has been no sable since the Revolution," but she just patted my hand and said, "Murielle, I know there is some sable somewhere. You must find it for me." ' She shrugged. 'I will. I already have. I had a little bit which I was saving for a certain client, a lady of the most exquisite taste but if Lady Haig wants it?' Her mouth twisted down at the corners. 'If the Field Marshal's wife wants to look more like a gutter rat than she already does, what am I to do?' Her disdain was so sharp that it could have cut crystal.

Tia's smiled was fixed. 'I was thinking, Mrs Hymans, though I accept everything you say about austerity, the war has also brought us a little liberty, has it not? When I was in Paris in November I saw the way the women walked there, the length of their skirts and the kick pleats to enable them to walk and not just totter. I really don't think the pre-war shapes will ever return. We've had orders for hobble skirts and a gown we did in the S-shape, but I really don't think these styles will sell very well. Floor-length skirts are dead, and so are those dreadful corsets. The matrons, certainly, will not suddenly cut a yard off their skirts, but the younger women, there is a great deal for the younger woman in the tailored outfit, especially if the cut is slim but also allows her the freedom to walk in comfort and to dance if she wants to.'

Mrs Hymans was looking at her acutely as she paused to take another sip of her tea. The taste did not appeal to her but she wanted to make sure she finished it rather than leave it to congeal in the cup.

'Don't you think?'

'Do carry on, my dear. You have me intrigued.'

Tia opened her bag and took out a sheaf of drawings that she had perfected in her spare time. 'You see, we've gained two expert cutters as a result of the war, and our seamstresses are good at tailored garments. I think there's going to be a lot of interest in sportswear. Maybe not tennis, but golf and walking. This suit, for example, this suit would be made up in Hebridean tweed.'

Mrs Hymans picked up her half-moon glasses and perched them on the end of her nose as she took the drawing and peered at it.

'Still rather severe, I think, my dear.'

Tia delved deeper into her bag and took out a tiny square of tweed and a twist of very fine silk cord, which she put beside the drawing.

'It is pure wool, Mrs Hymans.'

'Lucille did some styles in Home Industry Tweeds, you know. She took a terrible loss, I heard. It's so difficult to work with, you see.'

For a moment, Tia heard her grandmother's voice: *'Clo mor is clo mor. Best to be honest and sell if for what it is rather than what it is not.'*

'I did not order anything myself. I was never a fan of hers. Too derivative, you see. Her designs were not originals, but copies of Paris. You might as well have the real thing.'

Tia nodded. 'It is pure new wool, Mrs Hymans.'

'But could you get enough for a decent order, my dear?'

'I could have two dozen made up for finishing delivered by the end of February.'

Mrs Hymans' eyes narrowed and she turned her head slightly as she glared at Tia over the top of her glasses. 'You see, my dear, that is where Samuel and I get into arguments. I want an exclusive and Samuel sells to the first person who walks in the door with the money. I want repeats and Samuel tells me I must wait in line. Well, my dear, during the war, as you know, I did. The quality of some of the lines you made was superb, despite the restrictions. But I was not happy, not happy at all when one of my best customers complained that an acquaintence of hers, the wife of her husband's lawyer in fact, bought virtually the same garment at MacDonald's. Only the good Lord knows what she would have done if she had discovered that the garment was on sale at MacDonald's at a guinea and a half less than I was charging.'

Though she was inwardly laughing, Tia's smiled faded. 'I'm so sorry, Mrs Hymans. Before the war, we could hardly sell all our output, never mind get the bills paid. During, it, when the stores discovered our lines were just as good as anyone's, better in fact, we were overwhelmed. Our first priority was the uniforms, of course . . .'

Mrs Hymans cut in. 'Now that is where Samuel did our community a great service, my dear. The shirts you made were of excellent quality and so were the tunics. I was talking to a client the other day who says a Weinstock's greatcoat saved her son's life.'

Tia blushed demurely.

'I mean it, my dear.'

'I doubt it. We only had one order for greatcoats. The Yorkshire Mills made most of them.'

'My client told me that when your order arrived it was supposed to be for the NCOs but the officers were queuing up to get their hands on the garments. Apparently you had a cloak or something that kept the worst of the rain out and the lining was so warm that you could sleep in it.'

Tia's flush deepened. 'I changed the style a little, you see. I made a dolman sleeve that didn't have a top seam to leak and we put a cotton cape collar around the neck as added protection. We lined it with blanketing with an interlining of cotton. We did the best we could.'

'That's what I mean, my dear. That's why I rethought my policy of not doing business with Samuel. So many just profiteered, you see; some of the coats they sent weren't fit for a tramp.'

Tia blinked briefly, remembering the day she had got the order by phone late in the autumn of 1917. The warrant officer from the Highland Light Infantry had asked briskly if there was any chance that they could supply a gross of coats for his soldiers by the end of November. Though the workroom was busy with an order for gas company uniforms she had managed to get the delivery date deferred and taken the HLI job on in its place. When the wool arrived from the military store it had been so thin that they had used the gas company's cloth instead, and lined the coats with blankets and sheets the women brought from their own homes and the contents of Miriam Weinstock's linen cupboards. The whole workroom had worked overnight until the order was completed; Mr Weinstock and Tia cutting and finishing, the sewing machines working around the clock in shifts as the seamstresses took turns to rest for an hour or two in the office where Tia had made up a couple of beds from bolts of cloth.

Murielle Hymans' expression was bitter fleetingly. 'Memories are long here, my dear. Samuel is still associated with that guitar zither scandal, despite everything he has done since.'

'He was just a boy himself then, Mrs Hymans. How can they blame him for that?'

'They blame us all, my dear. It wasn't anyone from Glasgow who started it. It was a rogue called Beitan who passed through on his way to America. He was long gone by the time we discovered what a crook he was. But you know what they say. One bad apple spoils the barrel. Because of Beitan, every Jew in the country was called a thief. It's twenty years ago now, but when they think of us they think of Beitan and not of Himmelweiss and his orphanage or Dr Stockman in the Gorbals who has spent forty years tending the sick and hardly making a penny piece out of it.'

Tia opened her mouth to say something but Mrs Hymans held up her hand to stop her.

'Don't you tell me you care, my dear. Don't insult my intelligence by telling me you don't hate me deep inside, because I know you do. I've yet to meet a *goy* who doesn't, who doesn't blame us for killing your Christ. Our dead don't matter. You've been hating Jews and killing Jews for nigh two thousand years for the death of one man who got a trial as fair as anyone did at the time.'

'Mrs Hymans, I . . .'

'I was born here, My dear. I have lived in this city all my life but to them I am still a stranger, still a filthy Jew. They will do business with me, even take tea if I offer it politely, but they would never invite me into their homes and if I were to dare invite them to mine I would be snubbed as surely as a washerwoman. Don't tell me it's different, my dear, because it is not and never will be. It will always be this way because that is the way it is.'

'Mrs Hymans, really, I come from the islands myself. What we call the *gaidhealtach* and you call the Hebrides. My native language is Gaelic. I was sixteen and married before I heard English spoken anywhere but in the schoolroom. I don't know anything about the guitar zither company and I don't want to. I only know that I've worked for Weinstock's for five years and I have been happy there. What you say is probably true, as it's true to people who were born here that I come from a different world, that I'm a teuchter, as they call us. Teuchters are romantic and foolish and rather stupid. Our fathers went to jail to give us the privilege to graze a cow. That is what the lowlands think of us. But we distil good whisky and we weave

277

good tweed. The reasons Lucille's designs did not sell was that she cut the cloth to the garment whereas the cloth is made in such a way that it has to be the other way around. That is why my designs will work whereas hers did not.'

Murielle looked at the scrap of tweed closely. 'The colour,' she murmured, 'the shade is so perfect. Is it a fluke?'

Tia shook her head. 'My mother can dye wool to any colour in the rainbow so long as it is natural.'

'Peach, I would say,' she said, getting up and walking to the window where she held it up to the light. 'Are you sure the trim isn't too dark, my dear? Maybe something nearer to cream would be kinder.'

'The contrast is not so harsh when you see the finished garment.' Tia took the sample from her bag and joined Mrs Hymans at the window, holding the softly tailored sports suit with a cardigan jacket and four-gored skirt with kick pleats against herself. 'I could put it on, if you like.'

'No, dear. I'd rather my own girl did that.' She rang the bell and handed the suit to a maid, telling her to tell Catherine to put it on.

'The other thing is the dress,' Tia said, taking the other sample from her bag. 'As you can see, piqué holds the cut very well.'

'But it creases so.' She grabbed the cloth and crushed it between her fingers. 'See?'

Tia took the cloth and smoothed it. 'This is top quality, Mrs Hymans. A cancelled military order. The mill put it through a trial dye run and as you can see it is perfect.'

'*Vogue* says that muted shades are in.'

Tia smiled. The neutral khaki over which her dyes had been added gave a subdued cast to the bronze she had tried to achieve, and made the navy the shade of the sky as a storm breaks. She held a button of similar shade against the dress, and then an alternate contrasting one. 'I was thinking of doing some with self buttons and others with bright ones. I ran up another sample in three different shades of cotton. I thought the younger women would find it intriguing.'

Mrs Hymans squinted at the dress she held up.

'Too brazen for my clientele, my dear, far too brazen. I will take two dozen in taupe, two dozen in grey and two dozen in navy. I want the taupe and the grey with jet buttons and the navy with a self button.'

Tia scribbled the order down on her pad.

The model came in wearing the suit, pirouetting in front of Mrs Hymans and then standing before her nonchalantly with one hand on hip.

Mrs Hymans frowned and then turned to Tia. 'I want an exclusive on the dress.'

Tia smiled. 'The MacDonald's buyer came in yesterday. She wanted a gross.'

'Let her have them, but not in my colours. Let her have the harlequin if she wants it, but not the self.'

'I will have to charge three guineas a garment.'

Mrs Hymans shrugged, then turned back to the suit. 'I will take half a gross, but I do not like the syle of the trim. The key pattern is too angular. I would rather it was softer and more discreet.'

Tia inclined her head. Samuel Weinstock had told her that Murielle Hymans would not order anything exactly as it was shown, would want to make some changes of her own. For that reason Tia had deliberately made the trim too precisely angled for the casual cut of the suit.

She scrawl-sketched an alternative. 'Would this suit, Mrs Hymans?'

'Perfectly, my dear. The colours, I would like two dozen in that peach.'

'I have to explain,' Tia said. 'The tweed is made in lengths. I get two suits from a length. So these two will be the same, but the others will vary slightly. It is inevitable with a natural dye. The variation will be slight, though.'

Mrs Hymans peered at Tia and then at the card she handed her with the different dye strands of wool. 'That, that and that. The yellow is far too bright.'

'It can be delightful on a sunny day.'

'Well, only half a dozen, my dear. The others a dozen of each and half a dozen in the bronze.'

Tia handed her the order slip to sign and then shook her hand and thanked her.

Samuel Weinstock was poring over the books as she

returned. 'I have an order for six dozen suits and six dozen dresses for Murielle's.'

He looked up at her. 'That's not enough, Tia.'

The machines in the workroom were almost all silent, the seamstresses finishing an order of blouses.

'It will help.'

'For how long? There is not enough work around, Tia.'

Her eyes narrowed. 'You promised then you wouldn't lay them off.'

'Only if I have work. Without work, no money. Without money, no wages. Miriam, her brother has come. He wants work too.' He shrugged. 'I try, Tia. That's the only promise I can make. I try.'


At the end of the month, she took a bundle of blouses around to Meg's Pegs for Mairead to sell, but found her sister padlocking the shutters of the shop in the street near the Gallowgate.

'It's only Thursday,' Tia said.

Mairead shrugged. 'I'm not going to risk it. There's another rally in George Square today. Mannie Shinwell's been stirring it for weeks.'

'Are the boys all right?'

'I don't know,' Mairead said. 'They've gone already.'

Tia hugged her sister, then walked back to Candleriggs. Samuel Weinstock was standing at the window overlooking the street. The workroom was working, but not busy. The Hebridean tweed, neatly packed and with a bill written out in Ceit's careful hand, had arrived on the same boat that had delivered Tia's letter to Ceit. When she unpacked them, Tia smiled. They were the tweeds that had been woven for Lucille before the war, the order cancelled and the surplus never used. Ceit had even charged the same price. She took the bill to the office and took out cash to pay it, marking the entry carefully in the bought ledger.

Samuel Weinstock nodded when she told him what she was doing. She sent the messenger along to the boat with the envelope for Ceit; it would reach her late the next evening.

Tia took the tweeds into the workroom and laid the first one on the cutting table. The touch of the cloth, the very smell of it, triggered long-forgotten memories that surged with the insistence of the tide. She remembered the feel of sand underfoot, the scent of salt and weed, sometimes the staleness when a high tide left fish stranded or a sheep broke its legs on the rocks above the beach and died there; the faces of the men determinedly peeing into a bucket for the urine in which the Duchess's tweed was soaked. Bunching up the cloth, she held it to her face and inhaled the eddy of peat and sharpness of ammonia, remembering the concentration on her mother's face as she mixed and fixed her dyes, the way her father took Janet's work for granted, labour was his by right.

She had not heard from Janet all these years, only once when her brothers had been killed, and although she had been away for four years by then she felt the loss so keenly that it cut like glass and she felt a warm trickle of blood running down her arm. Only later did she realise that when she read the letter she had clenched her fist so tightly that she had bled.

'I am so sorry for this scribble,' Janet had written; looking at the spidery writing Tia knew that something was wrong.

A veil has fallen over my eyes, you see, the doctor said it was the cataracts but your father said it was the Will of Our Lord and chased him away. He says it is not a bad thing for a woman to be blinded because then she cannot see temptation's way and it is the Lord's way of reminding me that He will call me to him, but, Tia dearest, I know you will understand this, I miss the joy of the rising sun and the glory of its set when it gilds the ocean and I miss the sight of the birds and watching the way hair grows as gently as down on a baby's head. I miss all of these things, but I will not miss the sight of the world that took my sons when they were young and strong. I will not miss sight of the evil men who made this war.

That is why I have not written to you for so long, but I think of you each day and I keep your letters carefully in a safe place. Christina, Ealasaid's mother, she reads them to me. She had not heard from Ealasaid since the start of the war, but she asks me to remember her to you and give her your love.

Tia had crumpled the letter into an angry little ball through rage at the loss, but she had folded it out again and now kept it in the bottom of her bag together with her photograph of Marcus and his letter to her.

As she smoothed out the tweed and chalked the cutting marks she remembered Janet and the smell of the cottage when Janet was dyeing; only she, with a fistful of *crotal*, could turn wool into the texture and shade of a ripening peach.

The cloth resisted the blades for just a moment and then cut crisply, cleanly, shedding little tendrils of fibre that drifted in the breeze and caught in her throat. She worked steadily through the day; by the afternoon, when she took a break for tea, the machinists had already finished the first few jackets.

She was standing at the window when the crowds began to run down Candleriggs towards the Trongate, pursued by a detachment of police on horseback. She watched distantly at first, her interest rising when she saw a white on red banner headed Discharged Soldier's Society, the legend demanding Justice for All.

Two men carried the banner and would not allow it to fall in the rush to get away from the police, rather they held it high above their heads and were guarded by dozens of their comrades who formed a ring about them. The banner danced its way down the street, jogged and jostled like the marchers but standing straight and standing tall and for a moment her heart went out to them, to all of the men who had fought so hard for nothing at all but a moment's glory at the end of the war.

She saw Mr Dysart, who sold papers on the corner, emptying his pockets and then running over and handing the coins to them. Impulsively, she grabbed her own purse, took some money and raced down the stairs to give it to them.

Though she had little left over each week, she had much more than so many of them.

When she reached the street, the crowd had moved on and she began to run along the Trongate after them; when she saw the banner again just below Glasgow Cross she pushed her way through the crowd, nearly reaching the soldiers before all of a sudden the police charged and she was trampled under in the rush of the men trying to get away.

She floated for a moment like a leaf on a river, but caught her ankle and tumbled, for a horrifying moment losing her breath as a man fell on top of her and she saw the sparks of a horse shoe as it scraped the cobblestones just inches away from her head.

She screamed and closed her eyes as the world turned ugly and streaked with blood.

A voice rang out over the crowds. 'Remember the Somme, lads. We charged them once. Let's charge them again.'

The tide turned as the discharged soldiers soldiers broke through the fleeing crowds, charging the police with a roar like a lion's.

The voice rang through Tia's head again and again.

'*Let's charge them, lads!*'

It was Cal.

For a moment she bobbed on the surface like a cork and then she was running with them, her fists flailing, shrieking at everyone to let her past. The crowds reared and then parted, stunned by the sight of the warrior woman. Cal was six men away from her, then five, then four, then she reached for him, touched the back of his neck, grabbed for the collar of his coat. 'Cal!' she screamed. 'It's Tia. It's me. Cal. Cal!'

He stared at her and the granite of his mask seemed to melt for a moment, then hardened again.

'Get away,' he hissed. 'Get away. This is no place for you.'

'It's me, Cal,' she screamed. 'Cal, it's me. Cal, CAL!!!'

Strong arms pulled her back and lifted and carried her to the side of the street as the men raced past, beating back the police and holding them for a moment as Cal climbed on to the ledge at the base of the clock and called for calm.

'To hell with calm,' another voice roared. 'To hell with it. I've not eaten for a week, nor drunk either.'

A window shattered somehow, not a big one but a little window of a baker's shop and they fell on it like gannets as from the front the leaders yelled and pleaded with them to be calm. The police gathered and charged again, this time breaking through as they flayed wildly with their truncheons. A glancing blow struck Tia on the side of the head and she fell, winded, to the pavement where she lay and sobbed.

'My God,' the voice said, 'it's Mrs Cameron.'

A pair of arms gathered her up and she was carried along the Trongate and shoved into a car, still dazed and bloody from the truncheon blow.

'Cal,' she said dreamily.

'You're in my car, that's right,' Haldane Brodie said. 'Don't worry, Mrs Cameron.' She opened her eyes and saw him sitting beside the chauffeur.

'I'm so sorry,' she said. She was glad to see him.

'Don't be. They were animals. You must have got trapped. Soldiers? Thugs, more like. That sort certainly didn't fight for the likes of me. I am ashamed of them.'

The car pulled into Mitchell Lane and stopped at the back entrance of MacDonald's. Haldane Brodie helped her out and then into the back lift, which took her to the suite of rooms at the top.

He told a maid to get her washed, and sent for a sales assistant to find her something to wear.

She submitted meekly to their attentions, drinking the hot sweet tea the maid brought after she had washed like an obediant child.

'I will ask Archibald to take you home,' Haldane Brodie said.

'I . . . I have to get back to work.'

'Mrs Cameron, you cannot. You have been concussed.'

She winced then forced a smile. 'Mr Brodie, I assure you, I am made of sterner stuff.'

He stared at her for a moment. 'Very well,' he said, 'but I will drive you there myself.'

'You must not.'

'Mrs Cameron, I insist.'

He drove his car, a brand new Daimler, one of the first the factory had turned out after the war, as carefully as a carriage and pair.

Tia was staring out at Argyle Street, amazed that the riot has vanished so quickly. There was nothing left now except a few stray handbills, scudding along in the eddies of trams.

'Have you considered my offer?'

The streets were empty except for a few policemen and one or two shoppers.

'I beg your pardon?'

He pulled to a stop behind a tram. 'Mrs Cameron! I asked

you if you were interested in the position of ladies' gowns buyer at MacDonald's. I wrote to you a week ago on the board's behalf, offering the post formally.'

She coughed. 'I didn't get the letter.'

'That Jewish rascal intercepted it, you mean.'

'You sent it to Weinstock's?'

'I do not have your home address. It was marked personal. He should not have opened it. You could have the law put on to him for that.'

She grinned, wincing as the tight skin around the forming bruise twinged uncomfortably. 'Mr Weinstock wouldn't do that. He's terrible with the mail. He probably hasn't even seen it yet. I do it normally but I've been busy all week, trying to get some orders.'

He turned into Candleriggs and glided to a halt, leaving the engine running as he got out and opened the door for her.

'Please think about it,' he said.

Taken aback, she nodded. 'I will. I will be in touch.'

'I look forward to it,' he said.

She walked up the stairs slowly, pushing open the door on a silent workroom. The machinists had gone, only Samuel Weinstock remained at his desk, scratching figures on a piece of paper.

'Sit down, Tia,' he said wearily.

'Where are the women?'

He got up and poured tea for both of them, putting it down and looking closely at her forehead when he saw the vivid bruises. 'What?' he asked her. 'What on earth did that?'

She pursed her lips. 'I thought I saw someone in that crowd. I got caught up in it.'

'Do you want to go home? You can, if you want.'

'I'm fine,' she said shakily.

He looked at her clothes, remarking that they were not those she had worn when she went out.

'Where are the girls?' she asked again.

He began to rub his hands as if he was washing them as he told her that the Royal Polytechnic had cancelled its spring order, as had Darlings' of Edinburgh, Stewart and MacDonald wholesale and Dallas's as well.

'They can't have,' she said.

He searched around on his desk and found the written confirmations.

'We could sue,' she said, 'they all signed. It's breach of contract.'

He shrugged and said that suing would not help if the money was not there. The management of all the big firms were moaning about the Excess Profit Tax, levied to help the government with the costs of the war.

'The girls . . .' she said again.

'I gave them a choice,' he said, 'either two laid off, or all part-time piece rate, not wage. They say they will take the piece rate, part time, five hours a day. I try. I pay sixpence an hour. It's fair. You know that.'

She hunted upon his desk, found the envelope and ripped it open. 'No, Mr Weinstock, it is not fair.'

'It *is* fair, Tia. Weinstock a fair man.'

She unfolded the letter and saw the offer of £200 a year.

'And me, Mr Weinstock. How much do I get? Sixpence an hour too?'

'No. You get your usual wage. You design, make, sell garment.'

'And you, Mr Weinstock. What will you take yourself?'

'Nothing. Miriam and I, we will live on our savings. It's more important to keep the business running.'

'And the business is yours, isn't it?'

'Yes.'

'So you get your reward anyway, Mr Weinstock, if a little later than you would like to have it.'

She got up and went to collect her bag.

He followed her.

'Tia . . .'

'You promised me.'

'I said I try.'

She shrugged. 'You didn't try hard enough. Not nearly as hard as we worked to get the orders out. You forget, Samuel, I open the mail. I saw the bank statement. You have enough to pay the women for six months.'

'No.'

'You do.'

'I need. Family need.'

'Mr Weinstock, the women who work here have families too.'

When she reached the street outside she paused for a moment, rubbing the bruise on her forehead, before she turned towards Argyle Street and the subway at St Enoch's that would take her home.

# Chapter Sixteen

$T$ia's flat was silent; since the boys had gone back to their mother it seemed too big for one person, she felt greedy at having all this space to herself.

She sat down in the cold kitchen and cried for a while; when she put her head in her hands Cal's face swam before her eyes, the bitterness of his expression, the way he told her to go. Taking a piece of paper from the drawer, she went to the table and tried to find words to tell Bridie that she had seen Cal, but he had not wanted to see her. Her soul ached, the four years of waiting were for nothing. Something had changed him, but she did not know what. For a while she wondered if it would be kinder not to tell Bridie, then she wrote a brief note saying that she had seen him, but thought he would not go home yet because he had joined the Discharged Soldier's Society and was campaigning for a better deal for the men who had won the war. She did not know how to explain the city to Bridie, how big it was, how many tramps were on the street, how the government had sent troops to keep calm for fear that the people might revolt.

In that moment when Cal had stared at her, she sensed the same longing as he felt herself. She did not know why he had pushed her away. She finished the note and then went out to post it in the box at the corner. A while later she took the letter from Haldane Brodie out of her bag and wrote a quick reply taking the job. As soon as she had posted it, she regretted it. She had taken her pain out on Samuel Weinstock. She knew he could not keep the workroom going for ever without orders.

Her only consolation was the knowledge that, as a buyer for MacDonald's, the top store in the city, she could replace at least some of the lost orders herself.

The next day she began to work there, and was amazed at the size of the departments she had to manage and the amount of money she had to spend on stock.

Two weeks later she saw Miriam Weinstock standing hesitantly at the arch that led to the ladies gowns department. Mrs Weinstock was short and squat, clad in a straight black wool coat that Tia had made for her, with a little black straw hat uneasily balanced on her head.

Tia was at her desk, the sales assistants chatting in a corner. Although the store opened at 9 a.m. they did not expect their first customer until hours later, when the ladies who lunched in the restaurant might come to have a look around. They rarely made a sale before noon.

The department was in a corner of the store overlooking Mitchell Lane. The walls were painted a bland shade of ivory, with the stucco ceiling defined in white. The gowns were arranged on rails in glass cabinets around the sides next to the fitting rooms, the only display on a model in the centre. Ladies were supposed to come in and wait for the assistants to show them something that might suit; there were dainty little chairs arranged in a conversation group where they could sit and chat as they waited. The place was as inviting as a railway station waiting room and had the same aura of listless expectancy: nothing would happen until you went somewhere else. Tia was going to change all that. The first thing she had asked from Mr William, the director in charge of the department, was a budget to redecorate and renovate the salon and displays. Nothing had changed since before the war. Mr Williams had said he would bring up her request at the board meeting that morning; Tia told him that unless the department was brought up to date, they could not compete with Daly's and Copland's, never mind the myriad small shops that served the well-to-do Glasgow women.

Until then, she had a budget only to buy; she was allocating that when she heard the level of the assistant's chatter fall a notch and looked up to see Miriam waving shyly at her.

She got up, leaving the department in the the charge of Ellen, the sales charge hand.

'Come,' she said to Miriam, 'we'll go and have a coffee upstairs.'

A waitress showed them to a table in the cavernously empty

restaurant, where the sounds of the kitchen preparing for lunch rang through the serving doors.

'I'll have a coffee,' Tia told her. 'Mrs Weinstock?'

Miriam waved her hand.

'Two coffees, please,' Tia said.

Once the waitress was gone, Miriam leaned over. 'Please, Tia, call me Miriam like you used to.'

Tia smiled at her. 'I was only being polite.'

'Ach, manners. We are friends, no?' Unlike her husband, Miriam Weinstock's English was perfect, leavened only by a slight French accent and inflection. 'Samuel doesn't know I've come to see you. I was so sad when I heard about it. Please, Tia, he does not want to be your enemy. He wants you to stay as friends.'

The waitress brought the coffee pot, cups and saucers; the women leaned back to let her serve them.

'I am not Samuel's enemy, Miriam.'

'Why leave us, then?'

A wistful expression came over her face. 'It was time for me to go, Miriam. I wanted to learn this side of the business. The orders were cancelled, you know.'

'Without you, Samuel says he doesn't know how he's going to survive.'

'Miriam, Samuel will survive. You know that.'

Miriam shook her head. Tia looked around and then leaned closer. 'I've reissued the Stewart and MacDonald order. I posted it on Friday. It'll be there today.'

Miriam frowned. 'Tia! he would not want you to do that.'

'I did it because his prices are good and his workmanship is the best. Tell him that. There is no other supplier in Glasgow who can match him with what I need for the inexpensive mantles. If they sell well, there'll be a repeat.'

Miriam pursed her lips. 'I did not come here to ask you to keep my husband in business.'

'Miriam, I left in anger.'

'He will keep the girls on as long as he can. You know that. The money he has in the bank would only pay his costs for a month or two. We cannot say no if our family needs our help.'

'Miriam, I know that. I was trying to say to you, I left in a rage, but when I got home and thought about it I realised that leaving was the right thing to do. Tell Samuel that. Tell him that we are still friends and we always will be. Tell him that Mairead will still buy from him for Meg's Pegs and so will I, so long as his standards are what they are now. Don't you see? I can do more for Samuel here than I ever could if I still worked for him.'

'He doesn't want that, Tia.'

'Miriam, he gave me a chance. He gave me a chance when nobody else would even give me the time of day. He took me on without references. He trusted me. I will never forget that.'

Miriam stifled a sob. 'Please, Tia, don't lose touch. Come on *shabbat*. Your *shabbat*, I mean. Come and eat with us.'

'I will,' she said, rising to go.

Mr William called her into his office after lunch, but the department was so busy that she had to ask him to wait until tea time.

A plump woman had come to the department to look for an outfit for a spring wedding; the assistants despaired of fitting her in the gauzy organza styles that she liked so Tia had to cajole her into a simpler silhouette which she decorated with little bunches of velvet violets that sat like pot plants on the shelf of her bosom. The woman was so pleased that she ordered another two dresses and a coat as well. Tia noted the order in her book; it came to nearly thirty guineas. She was pleased with herself.

Mr William stood up as she walked into his office, sitting down again only when she had. 'Mrs Cameron,' he said, 'the board ask me to give you their congratulations. They note that sales are up by a third even though you have only been with us for two weeks.'

Tia demurred. 'Sales always go up towards spring, Mr Williams.'

'They do, Mrs Cameron, but the board noted that last week's figure was the highest for week ten over the last five years, and they have asked me to convey to you their satisfaction. Now, as to your request for a budget for renovations . . .' He ran his finger down a column of figures and then folded his hands on top of the paper so that she could not see what it was. 'I am afraid that your success has not been matched by that of our other departments. The wholesale side is suffering a torrent of cancelled orders . . .'

'But, Mr William, MacDonald's is a separate company. We are independent of the wholesale side. Mr Brodie emphasied that when I agreed to join you.'

'Precisely, Mrs Cameron. But both the store and the wholesale business are owned by Stewart and MacDonald. If the wholesale side is not profitable, then the retail side cannot demand investment of money that the parent company simply does not have. There is talk of recession and we have been hit hard by the Excess Profit Tax . . .'

*The Excess Profit Tax is only paid on excess profits*, Tia thought, but did not say.

'The war has to be paid for and that is the way the government has chosen, so we must comply,' Mr William continued. 'It is the feeling of the board that the ladies' departments are doing well enough without the expenditure of a great deal of money on renovations. That is their sentiment at the moment, so I am afraid that your request for a budget has to be turned down. However, the departments are due to be repainted and you can of course choose the colour. You can also change the soft furnishings if you can find something suitable in the warehouse and make use of any other items there if you feel such would improve the sales environment.

Tia was responsible for all the ladies' departments, from inexpensive mantles to model gowns, including ladies' tailoring, costumes and shoes. The doughty old *corsetière* Mrs Clark was still in charge of underwear, but Tia had to oversee her buying budget. At the moment she was trying to find a source for the exquisite French lace lingerie that Caroline's of Paris were selling in their shop at 79 Buchanan Street.

'Mr William, I hate to say this, but the ladies' departments resemble nothing so much as the waiting room at Queen Street Station.'

'Mrs Cameron, as I have said the board notes your achievements and I am quite certain that if you make your request again in one year's time they will look upon it with sympathy.'

Mairead brought a steaming bucket of water to her as Tia sat by the fire. 'Jis take your stockings off and soak your feet in that.'

Tia winced as she eased off the little lizard pumps that she had bought in Daly's sale for ten shillings, because although they were a size smaller than her feet she was quite sure they would stretch in time.

'I was on my feet all day,' she said.

'I thought you had an office.'

'I have a desk in a glass booth overlooking one of the departments, Mairead. The assistants are a bunch of snooty bitches.'

Mairead got another bucket for herself and sat down on the other chair. 'It's hard work, selling, isn't it?'

They sat in companionable silence for a while, then Tia put on her shoes and stockings and got up to leave.

'I need some more stock,' Mairead said.

'Go to Weinstock's and buy it,' Tia told her.

'I might not get the right thing.'

'Mairead, you know your customers better than I do.'

'Tia,' she said, clasping her hand. 'That Cal. I know you're hurting. It's not worth it, pet. Don't get yourself any more hurt than you've already been.'

Tia winced. 'Mairead. I have to try to find him again. I have to try to help him.'

'You can't help him if he doesn't want to be helped.'

'I have to try. For Marcus's sake.'

The tram juddered through the evening air, the city misted and still. The interior smelled stale, of dampened clothes and discarded tickets, of smoke and the sweat of the men who still had work.

Tia did not like living alone, she did not want to. Since the end of the war, when the boys went back to their mother's, she would rather have gone with them but in her own rooms she had the only things she valued – Marcus's letter and his photograph, his old shirt and his chest, his clothes wrapped in sacking and mothballs; if she inhaled hard she could still catch a whiff of him, if she closed her eyes and hugged herself she could feel the touch of his skin. There was space in her bed for his body beside hers.

She could dream and think and remember and cry, and nobody would tell her not to. If anyone had accused her of mourning, she could deny that. To remember was neither to mourn nor to grieve; to remember Marcus was to love him still, and she would always do that.

Her hall was dark, distantly warm from the stove. She opened the hatch and let the warmth spread, sitting down still in her coat and hat, in the comforting dim of the moonlight that glanced over the roof outside her window. The slates glowed silver, pockmarked by starlings. She threw them scraps sometimes, when she had any to spare.

The door sounded, a dull echoing knock that for a moment seemed like the wind blowing into the close from the street.

Tia cocked her head to one side and listened before the knock came again and she went to the door, putting the safety catch on before she opened it. The catch was a gift from Mrs Anderson, who had made her promise to use it whenever she was at home alone.

In the shadow of the gas lamp that shone over the stairwell, she could see nothing but a beard and the rim of a hat.

'I'm sorry,' she said, 'but I think you have the wrong door.'

The voice was low and thick. 'You are Tia MacLeod,' it said, in Gaelic.

In shock, she swung the door open and gazed into the grey features of the Reverend Kenneth MacQuarrie.

She ushered him in, apologising in passing for the absence of light as she fumbled for matches and then lit the gas lamp in the kitchen.

He stood there, refusing the chair she offered but nodding at the offer of tea, as if he had no alternative.

'I'll not stay,' he said, 'but your mother is ill. She asked me to come to you.'

'I . . .' Tia spilled the boiling water, sending up small splashes that scalded her hands. She began again, made the tea successfully. 'I had no idea,' she said.

'I am afraid so, Miss MacLeod.'

She did not remind him that she was now Mrs Cameron.

'Is there anything I can do?'

The question sounded silly and quaint. Janet's face swam

before her inner eyes, wavered and then settled. 'I meant,' she said, 'is there anything that she needs? Can I come to see her? Does she want that?'

The minister looked away. 'That is what she wants. It was your father who sent me. There is a boat that leaves from the Broomielaw at midnight. The weather is clear.'

Tia ran into the living room and picked up the phone that MacDonald's had installed only that week because they insisted that all members of the management staff must be contactable in an emergency. She tried to remember Mr William's home number and then asked for Haldane Brodie instead, because she remembered that he lived in Rutherglen. He answered the phone on the second ring and told her without hesitation, once she had explained to him, that she must go to see her mother, that he would make her apologies to Mr William.

'It won't be for long,' she said, as a terrible dread seeped into her consciousness.

'Mrs Cameron, you must stay as long as you are needed,' he said. 'The store rules provide for compassionate leave to be given to all staff.'

'Thank you,' she said, with sincerity. 'Thank you so much.'

Kenneth MacQuarrie waited in the hallway as she threw some things into a bag and shrugged on an old coat from the war.

'We must go to Mairead's,' she said, 'that's my sister, my older sister. Mother would want to see her too.'

He coughed. 'Your father did not say so. He told me to tell *you*.'

They walked out of the close into fog so thick that it felt like rusted eiderdown. In Hyndland Road Tia saw the tail lights of a taxi and hailed it like a Valkyrie as the minister's eyes narrowed in disapproval.

The driver agreed to wait in the Gallowgate for a half-crown tip and the promise of another one when they reached the Broomielaw.

Willie and Tam were at home, stretched on the sofa in front of the fire as Mairead worked doggedly on a huge pile of socks. She looked up as Tia rushed into the room, getting up to make tea when she saw the flush on her sister's face.

'We don't have time,' Tia said breathlessly.

Mairead turned. 'Time for what?'

Tia took a deep breath. 'Mama's very sick, Mairead. She sent for me. She would want to see you too.'

Their eyes met; though Tam was dozing Willie was wide awake and alert to every nuance of emotion that passed over his mother's face.

Mairead fumbled with her apron. 'I can't go, Tia. I've the shop to see to.'

Tia looked at Tam and winked. 'Tam would keep an eye on it for you.'

Tam opened one eye. 'That'll be richt, Auntie Tia.'

She glared at him.

'I suppose I could,' he said, 'except dinna expect tae sell onythin'. I'd be feart yon biddies wid belt me if e'en suggested it.'

Willie turned to his mother. 'I'll get Bessie tae watch it, Ma.'

Mairead sat down, twisting the ties of her pinny. 'Tia, I can't.'

'She wants to see you, Mairead. She wants to put the past to rights.'

Mariead's face turned bitter. 'She didn't ask for me, did she? Did she, Tia?'

Tia shook her head.

'She knows you found me.'

'She wants to see you,' Tia said again.

'She didn't ask.'

'She wouldn't dare to, Mairead. She wouldn't want you to turn her down.'

'You don't know that, do you?'

'Please, Mairead . . .'

'No, Tia. Let the past rest. I'd rather not think of it.'

The rest of the journey to the pier passed in silence. When they reached the boat Tia asked for a single cabin, paying the fare herself. The journey to North Uist would take all of the night and most of the next day as well.

'I will have the steward wake you,' the minister said.

'Don't bother,' she said. 'I can manage myself.'

*

Janet reached out for her with a hand whose skin was parchment thin.

'Is that you, pet?'

'It is, Ma.'

'Mairead isn't with you.' Janet stifled a sob. 'I didn't dare ask, pet, but I wished you would.'

'She would've done if she could, but she has the boys.'

Janet's glassy eyes shone. 'You came, pet. That's more'n I had a right to ask.'

Tia sat up on the bed beside her, cradled her mother's frail body in her arms, felt the cold in her chicken's wing arms, the racking cough in her chest. She reached for the cloth beside the bed, dampened it and wiped Janet's fevered brow. 'You haven't been ill for long, Mama? I came as soon as I knew.'

Janet's thin lips twisted into a half smile. 'I'm not ill at all, pet, just old, that's all.'

Tia was thinking of the times she had loved her, of the times she had hated her when she had seemed powerless to stop Mairead's hurt, her own as well.

Janet clutched at her hand. 'D'you remember, pet?'

'Remember what, Mama?'

'That day, pet. That day when you told me you were frightened of God. D'you remember that day, pet?'

'I remember, Mama.'

'I mind it too, pet. I mind carrying you over to Baleshare when the tide was out, and walking along the beach with you, and then the *bodach* took you out in his boat, and you played with the dolphins. D'you mind that?'

'Hush, Mama. You don't have to talk to me. Save your breath for yourself.'

'And you came back, pet, and you said to me, "Did you see me, Mama? Did you see me dancing with the dolphins?" '

'Hush, Mama,' Tia murmured.

'I will not, pet. I saved this breath for you, you see. I've talked to the others, those that are here to listen, that is. I wanted to remind you of that day, and I wanted you to remember that there is a time to get and a time to lose, a time to keep and a time to cast away. I wanted you to remember most of all that the time to laugh comes after you have wept and the time to dance comes after you have mourned. You've mourned enough, Tia. I don't want you to go mourning me as well.'

'Mama.' Her voice cracked. 'Don't you dare tell me not to grieve, because I will grieve for you and don't you dare stop me.'

Janet's hand tightened slightly. 'Pet, I wouldn't dream of it. Not that I deserve it, mind. I don't want you to grieve, but I want you to promise to heal. I want you to promise me that you will heal and that you will laugh and that you will dance again and most of all that you will not be afraid of God.'

Tia made up a pallet beside her mother's bed, not sleeping but dozing through the night, instantly alert every time she sensed a change in the rhythm of her mother's breath. Janet's chest sounded raw, like raking coals; her breath came in little urgent gasps, liquid rales, bubbling sounds that churned like the neap tide in the base of the throat. After a time she became used to it, used to the sound of her mother fighting for life; it comforted her in a strange way and then she slept.

Sorley was sleeping in the other room, in the bed that had once been the boys'.

Just before dawn, Tia woke to silence. Distraught, she jerked up and reached for her mother's hand, expecting it to be cold and lifeless, that God had taken her when she was not watching.

She cursed herself then for succumbing to the needs of her own body.

Janet's fingers tightened slowly, returning her grasp; Tia listened again and heard not silence but her mother's breath, coming softly, gently, rhythmically. She sat up and felt Janet's brow, cool but not cold, the sheets still damp with her sweat. The fever had broken; Janet's eyes were clear again. Tia gathered her into her arms and held her for a moment, then settled her back against the pillows as she went to put a kettle on.

Her father was by the fire, squatted into a knot, his head on top of his gnarled hands over his open Bible. Tia filled the kettle carefully, not wanting to disturb him, but when she fixed it to the hook, he slowly lifted his face and looked up to her.

There was pain deep in his eyes, longing and regret. He opened his mouth to speak, but the words did not come.

She held the kettle to make sure it did not tilt, then dropped her hand to his shoulder. 'She is awake, Father. The fever has broken.'

Sorley's head fell again; his shoulders were racked with sobs.

Quickly, she fetched sheets, a rug and fresh bedding, dried sea grass that crinkled to the touch. When the kettle boiled she made tea then poured the rest into a bowl that she carried through to her mother.

Janet was struggling to sit up, weak with the shock of recovery.

Tia helped her to sit up then eased her nightgown over her head and sponged her body all over, as gentle as Janet had been with her as a baby. Janet did not have the strength to protest, she succumbed to her attentions meekly. Tia helped her to sit and then stand while she put a fresh gown on, trying not to see the ravages of time, what age had done to her mother's body.

She led her to a chair and Janet sat as Tia quickly changed the bed, then fetched a peat in the warming pan to make it comfortable for her.

Janet brushed at her hair. 'I should be getting up, pet. There's things to do today.'

'No, Mother. You must rest a day or two.'

Janet looked at her. 'I've never had a day's sickness all my life, pet. When I took the flu, I thought it was the end.'

Tia remembered what she had read in the *Scottish Women's Hospitals Bulletin*, that flu too often became pneumonia, that when the lungs filled with water death was a merciful release. Janet had had pneumonia; she had heard the racket of it herself.

'You must rest, Mama. Give your lungs a chance to heal.'

Janet rose and slowly walked to the window. During the war the old walls had been built up and a slate roof put on; her brothers had paid for the work, had insisted upon it because there was nothing else for the men to do, those who had stayed behind, that was. She braced her hands on either side and stared out towards the morning.

The dawn was fragile, the colours bland. Eaval was hidden in mist, the ocean a glassy void resting, for a moment, in the hiatus of the spent tide. For a while, she stared at it until movement came again, little shivering waves that marked the water's retreat, as the ocean's surface silvered in the sunrise.

A bird called somewhere and the wind rose to brush the land.
Tears streamed down from her eyes.

Tia found milk in the jug in the pantry, not the cheese churn
but a jug usually reserved for water. Her father was still bent
over the fire, muttering to himself. She coughed.

'You do not have to worry about the cow,' he said, 'I have
relieved her of her burden..'

Tia was too amazed to say anything. She made a mug of
milky tea, spooned honey into it and then took it to her mother
and settled her in bed again.

'Are you hungry?' she asked Janet.

Janet thought for a moment before she said that she was.

Tia found some dried carrageen, put it on to heat in milk as
she began to make porridge for her father.

'The milk is for your mother,' he said, gruffly, when he saw
her reaching again for the jug. She dropped it, scalded, and
added water, noticing that the barrel outside the door was
almost dry.

She reached for her coat, but Sorely held up his hands. 'I will
fetch the water, girl.'

'But, Father,' she murmured, 'your hands . . .'

'I am not a cripple,' he spat.

Tia stayed with her mother until the end of the week. In silence,
Sorley did the work of the house, fetching water and milking the
cow, keeping the fire on the go. Tia knew that it was time to
leave when she saw her father making boiled eggs for her
mother one day when she had slumped into a chair by the fire
and fallen asleep, exhausted. He took the eggs in to her, with a
little soda bread and a cup of sweet milky tea. Tia was worried
at first that he might chide her, for he never had any patience
with invalids, but when she went to the door of their room she
saw Janet resting against the pillow as Sorley knelt at her side,
gently smoothing the hair from her face.

'I have sinned as much as any man,' he said that night as she
did Janet's darning, 'more than most because I dared to
chastise others. I would have been better to chastise myself.'

She said nothing.

Janet had told her that Kenneth MacQuarrie was an
incendiary device to Sorley's fire, worse, much worse than her

father had ever been. He hovered over the village like a crow, alighting at random on the imperfections he perceived; his sermons were so furious that to listen was to subject yourself to a vocal assault that, if nothing else, dulled your eardrums for the week until the time came to listen to him again. The years had tempered Sorley, the years and the loss of his sons had tempered anger with compassion, rage with tolerance.

'He blames himself for you,' Janet told Tia.

'For what?' Tia asked listlessly.

'He should've taken Marcus in. He should not have hit you.'

'It's in the past, Mama,' Tia said tiredly, 'that's where it belongs.'

'He blames himself for killing your child, Tia.'

Her stomach contracted. 'How did you know that?'

Janet touched her chest. 'I knew it here, pet. I felt your pain. I hated him then. God forgive me, but I hated him.'

'You forgave him,' Tia said.

'I knew it was not his intention. I told him that. He took it for forgiveness.'

On Friday, Tia helped Janet dress warmly and they waited for the tide to recede and then walked across the causeway to Baleshare, where they stood on the pearl white sands and scoured the horizons for the sight of dolphins, but there were none that day.

Tia did not say goodbye to her father; she left on foot early the next morning, in time to catch the Lochmaddy ferry, after she has assured herself that her mother was well.

As work once again, she apologised to Mr William for her absence; he tolerated her apology briskly and then said he wanted her to go to Paris as soon as she could make appointments to see all the couturiers. When she asked him what her budget was, he mentioned a sum that made her gasp.

'We have to get things straight, you see,' he said.

'I don't understand,' she told him.

'I mean, since the war ended, the days of the working woman are over. The time to dance has come again and we can't have all this confusion, one day the chemise and the next the ball gown with a full skirt. This Sex Discrimination Removal Bill, I don't know what the government's playing at. A lady's place is in the home. It always has been and it always will be.'

'And what does that make me?' she asked him.

'Why, Mrs Cameron, you are widow. A widow's lot has never been easy. Society has long tolerated her an occupation to ease her plight.'

For a moment she looked thoughtful.

'I shall get my secretary to book your ticket,' he said.

'Mr William, I honestly think it would be a waste of money. The Paris Fashion houses are just beginning to open again. They haven't the cloth or the skilled workers they once had. I know there's plenty of Indian Silk and Egyptian cotton around, but it's not the same as the French cloth was and it will take them time to get used to it.'

'But the style, Mrs Cameron, we have to decide the style.'

'I don't think we do, Mr William. We might suggest a look but we must not dictate it. We have to offer our customers the choice.'

'Choice?'

'Choice, Mr William. We are a store. I've been watching our trade for the past few days. Our customers are not identical, far from it. We have the matrons of Pollokshields who come in to buy something for a *soirée* at the City Halls and their daughters looking for an outfit for the spring parties. They are different shapes and they have different tastes. I'm not going to tell Lady Denholm that we are no longer stocking the long skirts she favours, nor Miss Clarissa Coates that we have decided not to touch the chemise because we think it's louche and undignified. They come to us and it is our job to sell them what they want. If we can add a little flair, a touch of artistry to the accessories, maybe a hint of glamour to the trim, we will have done our job and they will come back again and again and again. If we tell them that we at MacDonald's think that the government has gone mad and we have decided to bring back the S-shape and whaleboned corsets I doubt they'll buy what we try to sell them . . .'

Mr William had folded his hands; there was a thoughtful expression on his face. 'I hope you don't want to abandon the corset entirely, Mrs Cameron. My wife had tea with Mrs Campbell yesterday and she was complaining that there isn't a good corset to be had in Glasgow for love or money.'

'But there is, Mr William. We have plenty in stock. We can fit anyone from a girl to a sixty-inch hip and we make to order to our customers' requirements.'

His face had taken on a deep flush.

'Another thing,' she went on, 'I see our clientele coming into the store every day and going up to the restaurant for lunch or tea and then leaving again without even bothering to look in on us.'

'Mrs Cameron! We cannot tell our customers what to do with their time.'

'Exactly, Mr William, but we can put word around that we serve morning coffee and afternoon tea. We can also have some of the sales staff walk around the restaurant at lunch with the latest styles on.'

'Old Mr MacDonald would be spinning in his grave if he thought we would employ mannequins.'

'We are not going to. We are just going to ask some of the sales staff to do a little more work for their money. You know as well as I do that we pay assistants to work from 9 a.m. to 6 p.m. and in that time they do an hour's selling, at the most.'

He nodded his head slowly. 'That certainly does make sense. But I would still rather you went to Paris, Mrs Cameron.'

'I would rather we make sure we can sell what we buy there first.'

'What of the new looks for the spring?'

She smiled. 'I have garments on order, Mr William. Once we see how they sell I have a provisional order for more. I have some sketches I would like you to look at that I can get made up here in Glasgow for a fraction of what Paris would cost, and the look is right, believe me.' She tapped the magazine that she had been holding in her lap. 'If you don't, I can show you what *Vogue* says. With respect, Mr William, I don't want to follow fashion. I'd like to lead it if I can, at least so far as Glasgow goes.'

He stared at her for a minute, looking down when he realised that she simply stared back. 'I hope you're right, Mrs Cameron,' he said. 'If you're wrong, it's upon your own head it'll be.'

In the comparative privacy of her glassed-in office, she closed her door and took a deep breath. She would have loved to go to

Paris, if she could have done, but she had promised herself that she would not leave Glasgow, not until she had found Cal again, and made sure that he was safe.

At night she went home and ate hurriedly, through need but not desire, then changed into an old skirt and the shawl she had brought from the islands, and walked out into the darkness, taking a tram to Argyle Street and then trawling the length of it from Anderston Cross to the Gallowgate, stopping each time she saw a tramp and pushing a farthing into his fingers.

They knew her by now, but she had not trusted her secret to them because they were mostly so sodden with drink that they would have laughed at her, perhaps asked her, if she did not find Cal, would she take one of them instead?

Drink was the only thing that kept the cold out on nights like this; the only way to reach the oblivion of sleep. She knew well enough that many hardly cared whether or not they woke again; each morning one or two did not and the police wagon would come around and collect the bodies for the mortuary and a pauper's burial. Some of the tramps had been on the streets for years, some did not even know that the war had been fought, others had been refused enlistment on medical grounds.

The discharged soldiers were a breed apart; though they begged with the others they lit a campfire each night on Glasgow Green where they cooked the food they had begged or stolen and sang songs together to ease them through the night. She had been scared to go to the green at night; it was Mairead who told her that she would be all right, that they would not harm her if she held her head upright. Mairead warned her not to offer them money, because they still had their pride. They accepted gifts of food more easily. Tia went to the baker's in the Gallowgate each evening and bought a bag of pies, then walked to the green and gave them to the man in a tattered uniform who had been a sergeant once and who still wore medals for bravery at the Somme and Third Ypres.

He thanked her without words and went away, as she shrunk into the shadows and prayed that she would see Cal.

One night, a man sang in Gaelic, a new song that she had never heard before.

For a moment the words blurred in her ears.

> *'The laird, he promised land so,*
> *I went to be a soldier . . .*
> *The laird broke his promise,*
> *I am older and wiser,*
> *No more a soldier . . .'*

'Cal?' she murmured. 'Is that you Cal?'

She walked towards the knot of men, they parted to let her but the singer was gone. 'Please tell him,' she said, 'please tell him I came to see him. Please tell him his mother wants to see him. Tell him it doesn't matter, nothing matters, s'long he's safe. Please tell him that.'

One of them gripped her arm and began to lead her away. She shrugged him off once but he grasped her again. 'If he wanted to, he'd've stayed to talk to you,' he said.

'There must be something I can do.'

The man shook his head. 'If you want to do anything for him, let him be.'

She walked all the way home, sobbing her heart out.

Her door sounded in the middle of the night. She turned over, ignoring it until she remembered that she had put the catch on because there was a lobby dosser in their close now and he sometimes came back drunk on Saturday nights and the old woman below had complained that she had found him, fast asleep, on her best antimacassar. 'I mean,' she said, 'naebdy minds him dossin' down in the lobby, acos it's cauld out and he's nay place else tae go tae, but ma best antimacassar? I wouldna hae minded if he'd the sense tae tak it aff, but thaur he wis, snorin' his head aff, draped in ma lace like a wean, sae he wis.'

Tia shouted and when the knock came again louder, stumbled up and opened the door.

It was Willie. 'Ma's not weel, Auntie Tia. She sent me tae send fir ye.'

She shook her head. 'I saw Mairead yesterday. She was fine then.'

'It's the flu, Auntie. She widna 'a esked fir ye if she wisna bad.'

She drew him into the warmth, told him to take his wet coat off and put on the greatcoat she had made for Cal but never sent because that was after he stopped writing home.

'Kin I keep it, Auntie Tia?'

She was about to say 'no', then told him that he could, but to hide it from Tam until she got cloth to make one for him as well. She struggled into her own clothes, then walked out with him, wondering if they would ever find a taxi or would they have to walk all the way. 'The late tram'll be round in a minute,' Willie said when they reached the stop, as if only a fool didn't know that.

'Don't worry,' she told him, as the tram rattled and shuddered down the Trongate. 'She'll be fine.'

'She wisna weel when I left.'

'She'll recover, Willie. Your mother's strong. Our mother had flu, and she got over it. Mairead will too.'

He glanced at her then looked away.

Tia touched his face and pulled it around. 'Don't worry, Willie. She'll get better. I'll make sure she does. I promise you.'

When they reached the close, the door was already open, Tam waiting for them. One of the women called down the hallway that the van was coming from Ruchill. She would not come closer.

Tia stopped. 'Tam,' she said.

'Ma died an hour ago, jis' efter Willie left.'

'Oh, no.' She gathered him into her arms.

Willie was staring at her with hatred in his eyes.

She walked into the room and saw her sister's body, slumped over a chair by the fire. The rug had fallen from her, and Tia bent to pick it up and wrapped her up again. Mairead's brow was damp and cold, her hair in ragged fronds. Tia got cold water and washed her sister's face, then tidied her hair, crooning to her all the while. 'Don't fret,' she said, 'we'll have you to rights in no time.'

Mairead's eyes stared back at her lifelessly. Tia put her fingers to the lids and closed them for the last time.

The fever van came then, with two grim-faced men in overalls who threw a shroud over Mairead before they lifted her up and began to carry her out like a sack full of coal.

'Careful,' Willie said, 'that's ma ye've got.'

They apologised softly, told him that it was the law, that the public health would be round to fumigate the place on Monday morning.

'Come,' Tia said to them both. 'Come with me.'

Tam went to pack his things but Willie stood there, defying her.

'It's what your mother would have wanted,' Tia said.

'Ye dinna bluidy ken whit she wanted acos she's bluidy dead,' he spat.

'Willie . . .'

'Don't "Willie" me. Don't ye bluidy "Willie" me. Ye promised me, so ye did, an' a fucking lie it wis, sae it wis. Dinna bluidy talk to me, Tia, dinna ye say a bluidy wird, acos I'll no listen, sure I won't.'

She let him rant on, work out his pain on her.

Tam waited patiently until Willie was finished and then they walked into the night together, locking the door behind them and leaving the key with the landlady who would let the fumigators in.

When Tia and Tam turned away from the landlady's door, Willie was nowhere to be seen. Tia supposed he would come eventually, to be with his brother, if not with her.

# Chapter Seventeen

$T$am MacDonald senior's eyes were the only part of him still alive. The rest of his body was emaciated and lifeless, slumped like an empty glove puppet against the pillows of the bed where he rested.

He looked at her for a long time, then looked away.

'It was swift,' she said, 'if that comforts you at all.'

There was a gurgle in his throat. His lips opened and a glob of phlegm dribbled out. Tia felt revulsion rise but ignored it and wiped Tam's lips with the face cloth from his locker. With her munitions wages, Mairead had decorated his room with pictures, bright curtains and a tapestry quilt for the bed. If Tia had ever wondered where her sister's wages went, she knew now. Tam was no longer in the public ward, but in a room of his own facing a verandah. There was a wicker chair beside his bed, filled with cushions to guard his fragile limbs and a warm blanket. He had a locker full of jumpers and a new tweed cap.

'I'll visit you,' she said.

He gurgled again. 'Don't bring the boys.'

'Why not?' She tried to smile.

'Mairead did not want them to see me like this,'

She remembered what her sister had said: *'He doesn't want to see the boys, Tia. It'd hurt them, he says. Truth is, it would hurt him more.'*

Tia put her warm, pink hand over his cold, lifeless one.

'I'll be going back,' he said, jerking his head towards the mausoleum-like building where the crippled paupers were. 'It'll not be for long.'

'No,' Tia said, 'Mairead left money.'

He spat out more phlegm. 'Use it for the boys. Use it for the living. Can you not see I'm nigh dead?'

The lie was that Mairead had left nothing but the book in which Meg's Pegs debtors were marked, the names written out carefully beside a line that was marked with a tick each time they paid her sixpence, or two ticks for a shilling. The shop had just taken a delivery from Weinstock's and Tia had paid the bill from her own wages.

The fumigators would let her take nothing from the house. All the clothing and bedding was bundled up for the Corporation Laundry, where it would be cleaned and returned. Tia was shocked when women from the close came to her and asked her to put in some of their things with Mairead's, until she realised that they were so poor and so busy that they could not manage to wash more than essentials in the washhouse each week. 'It's an ill wind,' one of them said. 'She wis a guid wumman, Meg. She'd no' mind giein' us a wee bit o' a wash.'

The old oak furniture that Tam had bought after their wedding had to be left, and Tia wept when she thought what the stream and bleach would do to it. In Mairead's bottom drawer she found a bundle of papers, letters written by Tam to her when he had been working at Greenock and couldn't get home every night, and a few from her to him when he was in hospital and she had been in the workhouse.

Tia supposed that Tam had kept them and given them back to Mairead for safe keeping.

The letters were bright and airy and audacious. Mairead did not let Tam know they were in the Southern Institute, she said that she had found a housekeeping job in Kilmalcolm and had a wee cottage for herself and the boys. Mairead wrote about the burn which ran through the garden, and the boys out trapping rabbits.

Tia had slipped them into her handbag and taken them away without the fumigators knowing about it.

She took them out of her bag now and handed them to him. Because she had worried about infection she had wrapped them in oiled paper and heated them in the oven until the paper was crisp and scorched at the edges.

Tam looked away for a long time and then, picking up the first letter, read only a few words of it before he began to cry.

'She didn't tell me,' he sobbed. 'She let me believe they were fine and they weren't. She was out of the workhouse two years before I ever knew she was in.'

The letter crinkled and flaked into fragments. Jerkily, he began to swipe them with his good arm, the one that he could move slightly at the shoudler, and pulverised them into dust that stained the clean linen sheets.

On her way out of the hospital, Tia stopped at the office and paid for Tam's bed until the end of the month.

Willie had come back to Hyndland the day after his mother died, but he had hardly spoken a word since. He was sleeping in front of the fire when she got back – he had been in the pub last night and did not come home till the early hours. Tam had cleared up the breakfast dishes in a masculine way, leaving them stacked on the table and not on the rack, the dishcloth drying on the hook above the range. He had tidied the table by shaking the cloth on the floor, so it was now covered with crumbs.

Tia took off her damp coat and hat, putting the coat on a hanger to dry and draping the hat over a jar so that the felt would keep its shape.

Tam's face was bright with hope.

She opened the oven, checking the pot roast she had put on that morning – not a real roast but a casserole of turnips and old potatoes tinged, she hoped, with the aroma of the meat bones she had bought from the butcher in Candleriggs. The war had been over for months, but nobody knew when the shortages would end.

'It's ready,' she said. The rice pudding she had made with sugar filched from MacDonald's Restaurant was brown.

Tam began to lay the table.

He did not dare to ask her, and she did not know what to say to him. She woke Willie instead, gently shaking his shoulder until his eyes opened, telling him softly that dinner was ready. 'I dinna want nuthin',' he said, turning over and snoring again. Tam shrugged an apology on his behalf.

They ate in silence and then Tia made tea and took it through to her front room, where Tam's bed was neatly made but Willie's a heap of discarded clothes.

Tam watched her as she drank her tea.

'Did ye ask him?' he asked finally.

She sighed. 'I did, Tam. It's like your mother said. He doesn't want to see you. He wants you to remember him the way he was, not the way he is now.'

For a moment Tam looked hurt, until anger spread over his features. 'He can't stop us, so he can't. We can go if we like. He can't stop us.'

Tia thought for a time. Her grief was like a shroud, black in the middle, the edges stained with the red of her anger that God had spared her mother only to take Mairead in her place. Or so she thought, she did not know for sure if God was like that, bartering one life for another; if He was, she was glad that she was no longer a believer but somewhere in the limbo between agnosticism and atheism.

In the early years of the war she had often hoped for death herself, as a way to bring her back to her Marcus, to true love again in a life where everything else was a pallid pastiche. After that one time when she had been tempted, in the first raw months of her pain, she would not have done anything to hasten her end, but she was careless if it should happen anyway. Even now she wasn't sure what had made her want to live again, whether it had been her chance meeting with Cal, or Samuel Weinstock's mercurial enthusiasm, or the realisation that she could, would be, much more in life than the young girl so unsure and afraid that she had allowed herself to be tricked first into penury and then purgatory.

Marcus had been her strength at first, but she had a strength of her own now and since she had found it she would never abandon it, she would never again let herself be swayed by the tides of chance or by people who would use her without knowing the woman she was.

The room was cold. She knelt to stoke the fire in the grate, shovelling the dead ashes away when she realised that it was out and she would have to start again. Tam began another apology but she told him to sit down; it wouldn't take her a moment to see to it herself.

She worked quickly and the new fire was lit in no time.

'You see,' she said to him, 'it's so different here from the way it is at home. Peat's slow to take flame and when a fire's started we don't let it go out. It's terrible bad luck if it does. We used to cut the peat in June or July and leave them to dry. Every so often we would go and turn it to dry it evenly, but we never quite managed it. At the end of the summer Hector would bring his cart and take the peats to each cottage and we'd stack them around the fire to dry them through before we ever put them on to burn. Even then they fizzled a little, sometimes.' She smiled and brushed her hair back, smudging her brow. 'Peat doesn't burn, really. It just glows and gives off heat. At night, the last thing you do is smoor the peats with ashes, and in the morning you add a dry peat and give it a few puffs and it's away again.'

He smiled. 'Do you miss home, Auntie Tia?'

'I miss the colours. I miss the people. Not all of them, though. I don't miss my father.'

Her face turned thoughtful.

'I was thinking, Tam,' she said, 'your father, whatever you think of him, you must know that he loves you and cares for you very much. He is not a selfish man. A selfish man wouldn't have cared whether you saw him or not, wouldn't've cared that you would've been hurt. But he loves you and he loved your mother.'

'If he loves us he would let us see him.'

'He decided a long time ago that he didn't want that, Tam. He might have been right and he might have been wrong but he did what he thought was right and if he still thinks it's right, I think you should respect him for it. It would hurt him even more if you forced his choice for him.'

Tam put his head in his hands. 'But it hurts me, Tia, I want to see him. I want to talk to him. He doesn't have the right to tell me I can't.'

Tia rose to close the curtains against the darkening sky. 'You could always write to him, Tam. There's no reason why you couldn't do that.'

'Would he read it?'

'Of course he would. He would read it. Maybe he would write back. There's a nurse that would write a letter for him.'

'Ach, I wisna much fir writin' at the school. Willie's the brainy one.'

'Well, get him to help you,' she said.

On Saturday evening a week later she ran out of the Mitchell Lane door of MacDonald's towards Argyle Street, hoping vainly that she would find a taxi despite the rain. For a week she had abandoned her hunt for Cal, going home after work each evening to make dinner for the boys. Once she had seen the old soldier who had spoken to her about Cal. She gave him ten shillings for food when she heard him begging – literally singing for his supper – under the Heilanman's Umbrella, the long tunnel where the lines into Central Station crossed Argyle Street.

The road was a glassy streak, split by the roaring trams and cars that rolled past oblivious to the soaked pedestrians they left in their wake.

She saw one taxi and began to run for it, but a man with an umbrella caught it first, leaving her cursing. A car pulled to a halt beside her and she was about to curse it for soaking her shoes when Haldane Brodie opened the passenger door and told her to jump in.

'Mrs Cameron!' he exclaimed. 'What a pleasant surprise!'

She grinned obliquely. 'More for me than for you.'

'I've been trying to see you all week,' he said, 'but each time I call you're elsewhere and when I visited the department you were at the warehouse doing a mid-season stock take.'

She blushed because she had been avoiding him. Something about his manner told her that his interest in her extended beyond the workplace, and she was not sure how to deal with him. She could not contemplate the thought of another man in her life; her interest in Cal was fraternal.

'I suppose that it's too much to hope that you are free this evening,' he said, confirming her intuition.

'I'm afraid that I'm on my way to Duke Street,' she said quickly. 'I have a relative there who's invited me for dinner.'

'What a pity,' he said, 'I was going to ask you to dinner myself.'

'That is a pity,' she said, hoping that he would not see her relief.

In a squeal of brakes he turned the car into Queen Street, then drove up to George Square where she saw a vacant taxi in the rank. 'This is fine,' she said, 'I can get a taxi here.'

'Mrs Cameron! You will not! I shall take you to Duke Street. I was on my way home anyway, and it isn't so far.'

'It's the opposite direction to Rutherglen,' she said tersely.

'That is the beauty of the motor car. It turns miles into minutes.'

Shortly they were rolling down Duke Street, behind a tram

that was sending showers of sparks like tracers against the sky. Tia was reminded of the photograph she had seen of London criss-crossed by searchlights when a zeppelin was supposed to be on its way.

'Where shall I drop you?' he asked her.

She looked around. She was well away from the Gallowgate now. 'It doesn't matter, really.'

'But the rain, Mrs Cameron, I must drop you at the door of your destination.'

'Right here,' she said, spying a likely looking close.

Haldane Brodie frowned. 'I'd best escort you. The lights are out.'

'No, really,' she said.

'But Mrs Cameron, you might be attacked.'

'I'm sure I won't be,' she said, slipping out of the car and making a run for the pavement as the car behind sounded its horn.

He leaned over and called out the window. 'I trust I will see you next week.'

'Certainly,' she said, 'I will look forward to it.' Despite her feelings, she was flattered by his interest, though his overly formal manner made her nervous. She did not know how to turn him down without insulting him.

She waited in the back close until she was sure the coast was clear and then began to walk down towards Gallowgate, praying that Mairead's customers, if they had seen her sign, would not have given up waiting and gone home instead.

She reached the little booth and unlocked the door, stepping into a small shop that smelled strongly of camphor and lavender. The sign she had posted in the window during her lunch hour on Wednesday hung at an angle: 'Meg's Pegs regrets any inconvenience to our customers, but we will be open on Saturday between 6 and 8 p.m. and all day on Sunday.'

The church bells told her that it was still only 5.45; she had fifteen minutes to go, despite the diversion she had been forced to take. Tia leaned against the wall for a moment to catch her breath before she found and lit the gas lamps, and put a match to the little wood stove that Mairead used for heat.

She noticed that the rails of clothes were drawn in from the wall, and began to push them back until she saw the condensation running down the walls. The shop was damp; there was mould growing in a corner and the staleness in the air had a fusty note, like the socks that Willie habitually dumped beneath his bed.

She shivered as she sat on the stool beside the little table, thinking that was why Mairead had taken the flu so badly that she had died. The boys told her that though Mairead had sickened during the week, she wouldn't take any time off or even let them call her until it was too late.

'It wasn't worth it, Mairead,' she said, then realised that, to Mairead, anything was worth it that would have paid Tam's hospital bills and fed and clothed her boys.

She put her head in her hands and sobbed, cursing her sister for pride, herself for lack of sensitivity. She should have known how cold it was, how damp in a little alleyway off the Gallowgate, close to the open-air Barras where stallholders always wore two coats and stood in front of a brazier filled with glowing coals. There was a drawer in the table, she opened it and pulled out a sheaf of drawings that Mairead had done in her spare time, suggestions for things she thought would sell well to her clientele. Mairead was good at drawing; the sketches were better and more precise than anything Tia could have done herself, despite her experience of designing.

She sobbed again, smearing the figures on the flimsy scrap paper, until the door rattled and brought her back to herself.

There was a line of women stretching along the alleyway, clutching their shawls around their heads against the sleety rain.

Tia fiddled with the door and opened it too quickly, with a sickly rattle that told her the hinges would have to be fixed.

'Thank God,' the first woman said, 'I was that worried, sae help ma boab. I didna ken whit tae dae, acos I owe her two an six fir that blouse fir ma lassie.'

Tia wiped her eyes as she let her in.

'Meg wis a guid wumman,' the customer said, 'I widna want thae boys o' hers to go short. I've it here, hen, every penny.'

Tia took the coins and scored a line across her name in the book and immediately another woman took her place, saying virtually the same thing as she handed over three shillings, apologising because she could not pay the other two that she owed, and promising to have the rest of it next week.

By the time she reached the end of the line, Tia had collected almost all the money that Meg's Pegs was owed; there was only a pound or two outstanding and that would be in by the end of the week. Of more than two hundred customers in Mairead's book, none had defaulted.

Tia brushed a tear from her eye; she could not find the words to thank them.

Some of the women stayed, and one went to Fat Peter's stall at the Barras and brought back mugs of steaming tea and a bag of doughnuts.

'Ye'll be Tia,' she said, as she handed her a mug. 'Mairead was that proud of ye.'

Tia felt bruised. 'I was proud of her,' she replied.

'Ye'll be closin' the wee shop now, will ye?'

She looked around at them. 'Not if you'll help me keep it open, I won't.'

'Whit d'ye mean by that?'

'I mean,' she said slowly, 'I can keep the stock up but I'll need help to keep the shop open.'

The women looked at each other.

'We've no got much time, hen. I ken Mairead wasn't paying hersel' aucht.'

'She paid herself ten shillings a week,' Tia said, 'and a two-third share of the profits. Not a store wage maybe, but it's fair enough.'

'It's mair'n that,' a woman said. 'Ye kin put me down fir a morning, hen.'

'An' me.'

'An' me.'

By the time she locked up the shop that night, she had a rota worked out to keep Meg's Pegs open seven days a week.

'I'm glad ye're bidin' wi' us,' said the woman who had been first in line to pay off her debt. 'It's that nice tae be able tae buy somethin' guid. Ma name's Peg, by the way.'

Tia grinned. 'We won't need to change the name, then.'

Peg laughed as she took the keys from her. She had offered to open the shop on Sunday to give Tia a chance to visit Tam. It was also the day when she did her and the boys' washing, the only time she had to tidy the flat.

Neither Tam nor Willie was at home when she got back to Hyndland, though the dinner she had made for them had been eaten and the plates washed and stacked.

She did not worry until the following morning, when she rose to a house resonant with silence. The boys' beds had not been slept in and the clean clothes she had laid out for them so she could wash the dirty ones were as she had left them. They were spread over the chaise longue she had bought at a junk shop in Byres Road, stripped and polished and then covered with a faded Victorian velvet curtain.

The kitchen range was nearly out, the hot plate cold.

For a while she busied herself stripping the beds and washing sheets, until the world woke up at seven o'clock and it was nearly time to go to the hospital to see Tam. Taking a brush, she decided to sweep the rooms out first, ending up with the muddle of socks under Willie's bed that were so pungent she had to open the kitchen window before she tossed them into a bucket to soak. She went back to straighten the beds, pausing when she found a torn envelope that had escaped the brush.

She could read no more than 'acdonald' and supposed that it had been sent to Tam or Willie. She wondered what it was, what could have taken them both away so suddenly. Though she gave them money to see them through the week, she doubted if they had more than ten shillings between them. Neither had had any work for months, though they had both tried. The shipyards were no longer taking on apprentices and the ranks of the navvies had been swollen to bursting point with homecoming soldiers. There was hardly any work to be had anywhere and the idleness hurt Willie, she knew that. Tam took an easier attitude to it all; he was more secure than Willie was, less prone to self doubt. He was mature enough to know that there was nothing personal in being unemployed, whereas Willie took it to mean that he was worthless.

She waited as long as she could and then went out to take the tram to Govan.

The corridor to Tam *beag's* room seemed longer and quieter than she remembered it. The nurses must have been at their

317

teabreak because there was nobody around to take her to him. She found it finally because she remembered the view from the window just before it; the crane was still perched over the docks, in exactly the same position as it had been previously.

The room was empty, the bed stripped, the locker ajar. The only sign of Tam's presence was faint margins of pale on the walls where the pictures Mairead had hung had shielded the paint from the sun.

Tia stood for a moment and closed her eyes to pray that when she opened them again she would see that she was wrong.

The room stayed solidly empty, the air smelling clean but also of death. There was a breeze; she looked up and saw the window ajar.

Far away, echoing steps led her to a sister, who looked blank when Tia asked her what had happened to Tam.

'There's a lot been sent to Erskine,' she said, 'the war wounded, that is. It's not fully open yet but they've a ward or two ready for the worst of them.'

Tia had not even known that the hospital cared for the war wounded.

'You could try Bellahouston as well,' the sister said.

'He wasn't a soldier, he was just a man. He was crippled at the docks years ago.'

The sister folded her arms. 'If you go to the office, Miss, they'll tell you what became of him.'

At the office, Tia had to wait for another nurse to be summonsed. 'I'm so sorry,' she said, 'but Tom MacDonald died on Friday. You're not his wife, are you? We sent her a letter but she hasn't come yet.'

'The letter,' Tia said, 'could you tell me where you sent it?'

The nurse frowned. 'I certainly could not. We don't give out information like that.'

Tia repeated her own address and asked if it had been there. The nurse had to check a folder before she told her that it had.

Tia shook her head and turned to leave. The boys must have opened the letter; that would explain why they had gone, but not where.

'But his effects,' the nurse said, 'who will come to collect his effects?'

It was late afternoon when she reached Glasgow Green where she stood beneath an oak tree, watching the lengthening shadows. Although it was March, there was no sign of spring yet, no hint of the growth to come. She wondered if the earth itself felt as she did, sick of war and sick of death, that there was no longer any point to procreation with the world as evil as it was, when male children grew up to die in mud and female to grieve their brothers.

The Discharged Soldiers were meeting there; a man stood on a platform to read a letter from Mannie Shinwell, who was serving a five-month prison sentence for inciting the George Square riot – the riot that had never happened, really, and not in George Square. All that had happened was that a few hungry men had come on the rampage in the Trongate; the government could have quelled the unrest with a soup kitchen but instead they sent detachments of troops to watch over the city streets the next weekend and for weeks afterwards. The only unrest they had to suppress came from sightseers interested to find out what all the hullaballoo was about.

She watched them for a while, shrinking deeper into the shadows until she saw Cal's tall head rising above the crowd. He did not speak that day, though he sometimes did. The Discharged Soldier's Society was anarchist, according to a snippet she had read in the *Herald*. They did not believe in leadership.

A letter of support was read out from John MacLean, Honorary Consul in Glasgow of the Union of Soviet Socialist Republics.

As the meeting dissolved the ex-soldiers hung about in groups clustered around the braziers; she wondered if they really had been planning the revolution the government thought it had thwarted, if their slogan *Justice for All* meant that, or the simpler demand of the Calton rent strikers for decent housings and a wage to support a family.

She did not know. In the months since she had joined MacDonald's she had toadied to the gentry and kow-towed to the wives of wartime profiteers, jested with their daughters who only wanted to let their hair down and have some fun. The spirit was there, just below the surface, to assuage grief with celebration, to forget because there was no point at all in remembering, no point in regretting the mistakes of the past. It was done now and the dead would not return to life, the emptiness throughout the land would never be filled again and nobody wanted to comfort the bereaved mothers and wives and sisters who bore the brunt of the thirst for power and money and glory and blood, knew that the price of 'victory' was too great for ever the word to be any more than a hollow joke.

As the poet asked, 'Don't you know that *Tir nan Og* (heaven) is in France?'

Tia had done her grieving before the war and, once she had begun to recover, had thought she would never grieve again, but she did, in silence, ashamed of her part in it all: instead of protesting in the streets, downing tools and making government listen for once, with all the other women she had just worked hard and long to make sure that the soldiers still alive had decent coats to put on in the winter.

That was what women did, after all. They got on with their work, with whatever men told them to. The vote would not make any difference and nor would the government's Sex Discrimination (Removal) Act. Women bred children who grew into men who learned to fight and learned to kill, and were killed because other mothers had sons who fought with them. And their mothers had not told them not to, had not counselled caution, far less peacefullness, but had knitted parcels of socks to send to the front.

There was no one to blame beyond themselves.

Cal was standing beside the brazier closest to her. He did not see her, she knew that, night had fallen and in the darkness he could not tell her from a tramp.

She waited for him to peel away, listened to him saying goodbye and watched him stick his hands in his pockets and begin to walk smartly towards her.

He was close enough to touch before she called out to him softly and watched the same mixture of shame and pleasure spread across his face.

His eyes narrowed angrily. 'I thought I told you . . .' he began, before she cut him off with a gesture and slipped her arm into his, holding fast when he tried to shake her off.

'You see, Cal,' she said, 'I need you.'

For a moment, he seemed about to argue.

'My sister Mairead, she died last week. Her man was a cripple. He was in hospital; the shock of her death killed him too. Her sons, Tam and Willie, they came to stay with me, but they're gone now. They went when they got a letter telling them their father was dead. I don't know where they've gone and I'm worried about them.'

'What can I do, Tia?'

'You could look for them. They've no place to go. If they're on the streets, you could find them. I can't.'

His face had changed, become softer. 'Why do you keep coming after me, Tia? Why do you keep on coming after me when anyone else would've given up?'

She turned away so that he did not see the pain on her face. 'You are family. I'm only doing what Marcus would have done, if he was still alive.'

'Marcus would've let me be.'

She turned to face him. 'Would he?'

Cal was silent for a long time. 'Ach, I don't know. What do these boys of yours look like?'

She described Tam and Willie as best she could.

Cal said he would try to find them; she gave him a card with her address and telephone number. He said he would come or telephone as soon as he had any news of them; she asked him to come anyway, news or no news. Curtly, he told her he would not do that.

# Chapter Eighteen

'You look as if something's worrying you, Mrs Cameron,' Haldane Brodie said. He had cornered her in MacDonald's restaurant on the Wednesday of the week after he had picked her up in the rain.

'I . . no,' Tia said. She was sitting at the table reserved for buyers behind the plant stand that separated the main room from the cacophony of the kitchen.

'Your departments are doing very well indeed.'

She rested her elbows on the table and cupped her chin in her hands. 'We do the best we can.' A waitress came to remove the soup plate and the bread she had not eaten. 'Will there be anything else, Mrs Cameron?' Tia shook her head, but Haldane Brodie ordered coffee for two.

'I ate at Lang's,' he said. 'I just dropped in here on the off chance.'

'What chance?'

'That you would be here.'

She blushed and smiled. 'I usually am at lunch times. I don't like to be away from the department in the afternoon if I can help it.'

'A pity your predecessor didn't think that way.' He frowned in a way that made her think she should know all about it, but she did not. 'I was thinking, wondering if you would like to join my family for tea on Sunday.'

'Mr Brodie, I'd love to, b . . .'

He rose abruptly, cutting her off with an apologetic wave of his hand. She thought his departure was deliberate until she saw Mr Hugh and his nephew young Mr Douglas sitting down on the other side of the room, and that Mr Hugh had waved the accountant over to join them.

The waitress brought the pot of coffee, but Tia told her she no longer wanted it, she would send up one of the assistants and have it in the department instead.

She had thrown herself into work since the boys left. Cal had made her promise not to worry about them; he had also promised that he would find them, if they could be found. Each evening she raced home, but both the door and the telephone had been stubbornly silent.

Model costumes was on the first floor, two floors down from the restaurant. She had chosen from the warehouse a sunny French chintz for the curtains and had the chairs upholstered to match. On the tables that used to hold note paper for the customers' convenience she put vases of freshly cut flowers which came from Mr MacDonald Senior's own conservatory in Kelvinside. On the walls between the rails of clothes she had hung framed illustrations from *Vogue* and *Scottish Country Life*; during lunch and afternoon tea in the restaurant sales assistants modelled garments discreetly but effectively. The first time she had done this the suit that one girl wore sold out in an afternoon; now she was careful to make models wear designs that did not sell quite so well. Mr William had been astonished that she asked one of the plump corsetry assistants to model dresses for her, until he saw the effect it had on outsize sales.

'We sell to women,' she told him, 'not plaster dummies.'

'Mrs Cameron . . .' one of the assistants, Moira Wilson, took her aside. Moira was in her late twenties, several years older than Tia; she had taken the job when her husband was killed in 1915, just months after they married. She was a music teacher by training, but she no longer had the will to play. Her sympathetic manner made her a favourite with certain customers, but others thought her taste was a shade pedestrian. Though Tia had not known her for long, she sensed that Moira would not force a sale for her commission. While the other assistants often got more than Moira, their wages went up and down like yo-yos whilst her stayed level. Instinctively, Tia liked her, though she was careful not to show favouritism.

'There's a problem,' Moira said.

Tia opened the door to her office and drew her inside. Moira stood against the window so that nobody could even lip read what she said, if anyone around had that skill. 'It's Mrs Colquihoun,' she whispered. 'She wants the coat with the Medici collar. I was about to put the sale through when I remembered that Mrs Chisholm had been on to stop her account. The last cheque bounced,' she said.

Tia mouthed an 'oh'. Then she asked if Moira had rung Accounts to see if they would clear the charge now.

'Yes,' she said. 'They asked Mr Brodie and he said "no". There's three months outstanding. It's her husband, you see. The War Office hadn't paid his compensation yet.'

Tia thought for a moment. 'Isn't Colquihoun the shipowner who lost all those ships on the last convoy?'

Moira nodded. 'Yes, he was.'

'Send Elsie up to the restaurant for coffee,' Tia directed. 'I'll deal with Mrs Colquihoun myself.'

Mrs Colquihoun was standing nervously by the desk, wringing her hands as the coat lay on the surface, not yet wrapped. Tia walked up and introduced herself, asking if she would have a cup of coffee while they waited for the message boy to bring some more boxes from the storeroom. 'We've been very busy,' she said, speaking loudly so that the cashier would understand.

They sat down at one of the side tables. 'I did want to meet you,' Tia said, 'you see, I'm trying to get to know all our customers.'

Mrs Colquihoun smiled shyly. 'I haven't been a very good customer this year. Just school uniforms, I'm afraid.'

Tia noted the slight sheen on the cloth of her suit. It was an old design, she guessed Molyneux.

'I read about your husband's ships. I'm terribly sorry.'

She pursed her lips. 'Really, the loss was a small price to pay. We were so lucky that the boys weren't old enough to go and my husband was asked to keep the Atlantic convoy on the go.'

'Did you lose all your ships?'

'It wasn't the ships, Mrs Cameron. It was the widows of the men left behind. My husband kept them on the payroll until their pensions were paid.' She winced. 'It nearly bankrupted him, but the compensation's through now. At last.'

'You'll be glad of that.'

'It seems so unfair,' she said again. She was a woman perhaps in her late thirties; but her skin was lined with worry that made her look much older. 'I mean, with the compensation paid, my husband's company has done very well out of it. But

324

money's scant reward if you've lost a friend, and the men on the ships were my husband's friends as well as his employees.'

'Did you know old Captain Jardine?'

Mrs Colquihoun smiled for the first time. 'Very well, my dear. He was one of the last of them – the small lines, I mean, a few ships with the owner in charge of the company. The lines are so big these days. There's Cunard and P&O, Pacific Hunter. They say Pacific Hunter did very well out of the war.' She shuddered again as she finished her coffee; Tia was glad that her own expression went unnoticed.

Tia gesticulated to the cashier to tell her to wrap the coat.

Mrs Colquihoun fiddled in her bag, found a purse and began to count out the money. Tia told her, not to worry, they would send the bill.

'But I'd better pay, Mrs Cameron. My husband tells me that the bank stopped a couple of his cheques last month.' She shrugged.

'Mrs Colquihoun, I'd be insulted. I can have the coat delivered, if you like.'

'Oh, no. I need it today. It's my niece, you see, she's getting wed. I wanted her to have something nice to wear and this is the nicest thing I've seen in ages. The young these days, with the war just over, they meet up again and decide to get married immediately.'

Tia signed the authorisation herself and went down to inexpensive mantles to see how the spring lines were doing, if she could order any repeats yet, if the serape she had designed for the fuller figure was selling since she had put it on display in the window.

On Sunday, Haldane Brodie collected her at 2.30 p.m. precisely. He had sent a little note through Stewart and MacDonald's internal mail to confirm the invitation; her instinct had been to cancel it but when she tried to reach him his secretary told her that he was away in Perthshire with a shooting party.

She was waiting at the window and saw the car come down the street, make a precise turn and park outside her close. Hyndland was an area of tenements that were mostly well kept and bordered on the middle class; it was considered respectable for a woman to live there on her own, so long as she was a widow or a spinster whose parents were dead. In her close were two families with children, two widows apart from her and a single man who lived in the single end on the top floor – apart from the self-invited lobby dosser who slept in the basement or hallway when he wasn't sleeping off a binge at the police office.

The lobby dosser was of Irish origin; in a good mood he would sing ballads in a rich mid brown baritone that rang out over the back close and rose tunefully over the contrapuntal rhythm of the echo. Sometimes on warm evenings he would sing outside, and all around kitchen windows would open and women throw down ha'pennies or farthings. The sound he made was at once joyful and melancholic; tears came to the eyes of his audience and rolled down his own cheeks as well.

As a drunk he was depressive, he would begin to recite the sorrowful mysteries and then would begin a dirge that rolled around the 23rd Psalm before it lapsed into a tune by Chopin.

Each evening that week, after work, Tia had rushed to the butcher's and grocer's to buy whatever they had to offer, to make a welcome-home meal for the boys. She had made soup and a stew, bread and scones, a cake with bran and raisins. In the boys continued absence, the lobby dosser had eaten well. In the morning she had left him breakfast, at night she put a meal out for him in the basement where he slept by the boiler, a plate covered by another one and wrapped in a tea towel to keep it hot. He left the plates, washed and dried, outside her door each morning, and when she went out to work he tipped his cap to her: 'Thank 'ee, Ma'am, sure an' ye'r a lady, so ye are.'

As Haldane Brodie sounded his horn, the signal he used because he felt it was not appropriate for him to come to her door, Tia picked up the pot of chicken soup and left it by the stairs that led to the back yard, where she could hear the rhythm of the lobby dosser's breathing, sleeping off the after effects of a night's carousing.

Though Tia said it wasn't necessary, he insisted upon arranging a rug over her legs to keep her warm. For a while he concentrated on the heavy traffic in the city centre, then he turned to her and smiled. 'I was so afraid that our arrangement would be thwarted, Mrs Cameron.'

'Why is that, Mr Brodie?'

'Well, we have been thwarted so many times before. I have to congratulate you,' he said, as the powerful car surged over the High Street Bridge.

'Why is that?'

'The Colquihoun woman. You authorised her charge when I had refused.'

'She offered cash. The coat was for her niece who was getting married. I decided it was worth the risk.'

'Risk, Mrs Cameron?'

'I thought we might lose her custom if we did not trust her. She seemed honest and her husband's had difficulties getting compensation for the ships he lost. She told me that.'

'Ah. You see, as an accountant, I deal in tangibles.'

'As a saleswoman, I have to make allowances. I like to think of my customers as my friends. To let Mrs Colquihoun pay cash would have betrayed that friendship.'

He smiled cynically. 'You were lucky. As it so happens, a cheque for the bill outstanding came in the afternoon post and it cleared the bank. If it had not, you could have been held liable for the cost of the coat.'

She shrugged and looked out of the window. The car was heading up the hill towards Rutherglen, leaving behind the tightly packed tenements and smoke-laden atmosphere. For a while they rode in silence, then Haldane Brodie pointed out a sign by the roadside.

'We are a borough ourselves, you know. Robert the Bruce gave Rutherglen the charter nigh eight hundred years ago. Now Glasgow wants to swallow us up.' He laughed. 'We Ruglonians are too proud for that.'

'Ruglonian?' she asked politely.

'A native of Rutherglen, born and bred. My father served on the borough council, his father before that. I am proud to continue our service. Louise, my dear late wife, she said we would have to give in sooner or later. Amalgamate, that is. Join with the City of Glasgow. It was the only note of dischord between us.' His face turned grave at the mention of her name.

Rutherglen High Street was a wide thoroughfare, lined with a church and a library, the arrogant municipal buildings on one side of the old market place that was now dissected by tram lines. Tia remembered reading somewhere that the town had been the last bastian of the home weaving industry in the Clyde Valley, the final weaver forced to abandon his work when the High Street was widened at the turn of the century. There were four machine mills now, a rope works, iron works, a pottery and a big shipyard. The omens were bad for the shipbuilding industry; the huge demand of the war years had stalled abruptly in the summer of 1918. The shipbuilders were talking of lay-offs; she had heard two wives complain that they would have to tighten their belts now.

'No more Paris, my dear,' one said to the other, 'and the accursed thing was when I had the money for Paris, I couldn't spend it there. I had to make do with Daly's or here.'

'I like Murielle's,' the other said. 'She always has something.'

'Yes, but she's a Jew. My husband wouldn't let me have anything to do with her.'

'What's it got to do with him?'

'He signs the cheques, my dear. I just sign the bills.'

Trilling with laughter, they linked arms and set off for the fur department, where Tia found out later they spent the best part of two hundred pounds.

'Here we are,' Haldane Brodie said, turning into the driveway of a Victorian villa with tired-looking ivy growing up the walls, drawing to a halt and nimbly jumping out to open the passenger door before Tia could open it herself.

She reached in her bag for the little box of candied fruits that she had bought at Malcolm Campbell's – the famous fruiterer on Sauchiehall Street who, before the war, had fascinated her with his window displays of mangos, papayas, figs and watermelons.

'I'm afraid it's the best I could do,' she said apologetically.

'Dear me, Mrs Cameron, how kind of you! There was no need to do that.'

The fruits had been intended as a treat for Cal and the boys but it would have been rude to go to tea without taking something.

The door was opened by a maid, who took her jacket and Haldane Brodie's topcoat and scurried away into the gloomy depths of the hall before Tia had a chance to thank her. 'We do not have electricity yet, alas,' he said. 'We have been promised a supply by the next year, but during the war the important thing was to keep the works going.'

'I understand.'

He swung open a door off the hallway, ushering her into a large room where his mother sat on a winged chair between twin plant stands that held urns of azaleas, the blooms past their best, looking parched and muted, though the faded colours blended with the soft chintz and heavy velvets of the upholstery and curtains.

'Mrs Cameron, what a pleasure,' Mrs Brodie said, rising and extending her hand, though the grim expression in her eyes belied the words.

Tia handed her the glacé figs apologetically.

'My dear, they are my favourite.'

Haldane sat down as she rang the bell to summons tea.

Tia looked around, noting the framed samplers, the precise arrangements of dried flowers, the handworked needle lace that covered every flat surface. By Mrs Brodie's side was a work box and a piece of lace cast aside, the silken thread glistening as the light of the fire glanced against it. The work was exquisite.

'I see you make lace,' she ventured hesitantly.

'A hobby,' Mrs Brodie replied dismissively. 'Idle hands make for mischief, as my dear husband used to say.'

The silence echoed.

'I sew myself, a little.'

'My son told me that. He tells me that you are very clever that way. In my day, women worked at home.'

The maid came with the trolley that rode like a tram over the floorboards and nearly stumbled on the rug. She put the silver tea pot by Mrs Brodie and handed around plates and napkins. Mrs Brodie poured carefully, and then the maid gave Tia her cup, holding the milk and sugar for her to serve herself. The white lumps glittered like diamonds, invitingly, but because Tia could not see how she could palm them without being caught she just added a little milk.

Mrs Brodie was clad in an ornate linen blouse and a long skirt plumped like upholstery over her solid table-legs. She took a handful of sandwiches onto her plate as Tia and her son took just one each.

The bitter taste almost made Tia wince.

'Watercress,' Mrs Brodie said, 'it grows in the garden burn. Such a blessing, with all these dreadful shortages we've had.'

There was a ginger cake, a Dundee cake and a cherry cake, all cut as thinly as boiled ham. Seeing the Dundee cake crumble as Haldane took a bit, Tia took only a biscuit when the maid offered the server to her.

Mrs Brodie took four slices of Dundee cake in all, harvesting the crumbs like a gull after she had finished the cake, eating them one by one.

At a loss for something to say, Tia asked her if she liked her emerald.

Haldane blanched as his mother snorted.

'We met in Paris, you see,' Tia said, 'and your son was kind enough to take me for a late lunch.'

'I really don't know what this world is coming to,' Mrs Brodie fumed, 'with a young woman your age travelling abroad during a war. Maude Cunninghame says the VADs were more trouble than they were worth, what with all the nonsense they got up to over there.'

'I . . . I was not a VAD,' Tia said quickly.

Haldane cut in quickly. 'Tia was working as a designer, Mother. She had to go there to make sure of her supplies. It's ladies such as her who ensure you have a choice of clothes to wear.'

'Harumph!' she coughed. 'I always managed to clothe myself, with a little help from good old Mrs Donnelly. She has done two generations of us Ruglonian women proud.'

'We must go,' her son said. 'Mrs Cameron has an evening engagement, I fear.'

Gripping her arm firmly, he led her out of the room and out of the house, where a watery sun was shining from a wintry sky. In the distance Tia could see the Campsie Hills smeared by mist.

Once in the car, Haldane turned left out of the drive away from Glasgow. 'It's a nice afternoon,' he said, 'we've time for a little drive.'

Tia sat, watched the tendrils of civilisation give way to countryside, the rich loam of the fields turned to take the early seed.

'You must call me Haldane,' he said, after a while, 'at least, when we meet socially.'

When he smiled, his whole persona changed. He was no longer grim and forbidding, but almost childlike in his delight.

They were travelling over the Ayrshire moors, bleak, high countryside under a spartan sky that bulged with rain. By the road the soil was boggy, pocked by reeds.

'It changes in the summer,' he said, 'when the wildflowers grow.'

He stopped at Fenwick, at an inn lit by a log fire where a shepherd drank Irish stout with his faithful dog folded up by his feet.

'Would you like some tea?' Haldane asked. 'Or perhaps something a little stronger?'

Tia thought for a moment. Being out of the city grime had made her relaxed suddenly; she had gained strength from the sight of nature, the realisation that the boys would return in time, that Cal would find them. At first she had worried that grief would trap them the way it had trapped her, would make death preferable to being alive, but they were young and resilient; Mairead's blood ran in their veins, her blood, the blood of her father and her mother. The death of a parent was different to the death of a lover; though the boys had suffered three hurts in all, starting with their father's accident, they were strong and they would survive.

She stretched and shifted slightly in her seat. 'I would love a glass of wine, if they have that.'

The shepherd looked out of the narrow leaded window at the sky and nodded to himself. The sunset was bloodied; he would be confident of the morning. He drained his mug, then nudged the dog awake.

Out on the moors his ewes were about to give birth; life was reassuring itself.

Haldane returned with a half pint of stout for himself and a glass of old tawny port for Tia.

'I didn't think pubs opened on a Sunday,' she said.

'This is an hotel. It's an old staging post.'

His inflection struck her, the silent h was something she had learned about in English lessons, but never heard until then.

They talked of small things, inconsequentialities. When Tia

331

had learned how to sell, she had learned to give away nothing of herself, but to listen to the other person, to draw out their thoughts and focus the attention on them. Haldane talked about the weather and his car, the garden in Rutherglen tangled with the winter, the trees that needed branches trimmed. He told her about the Ruglonian Society in a way that was almost mocking, as if he sensed the futility of history when the present collides with the past. At the end of the month they were giving a ball; he asked her to go with him and she agreed, surprised with herself.

When he left her outside her tenement in Hyndland she realised that she had enjoyed herself. Haldane Brodie's starchiness had lessened in the car; the arrogance of his stance at the store had gone completely. He smiled easily; Tia liked that. She had meant to make it clear to him that Marcus was so dear to her that she doubted she could ever have another relationship, but she could not find the words or the opportunity without sounding awfully presumptuous. She consoled herself that he probably felt the same way as well.

Her door opened just after she had closed it behind her. Cal walked in, followed by Tam and Willie, looking sheepish and cold.

'I . . .' She was flustered, taken aback by the suddenness of their return. Fiddling with matches, she lit the lamps and then went through to light the fire in the front room.

'I have a meal on,' she said, when she saw them standing so close to the range that the smell of drying clothes mingled with scorching. She fussed over them, took the wet coats, told them to go and take all their clothes off and have a bath. It was the only luxury she had permitted herself when she bought the flat; it had a bathroom with a big china tub, hot and cold water, even a shower stall which she never used. The water was constantly hot, kept that way by the boiler in the basement where the lobby dosser slept. It cose each resident £2/10/- a quarter, but the convenience was worth it.

She went and put the plug in the bath and turned the water on.

Tam and Willie went off meekly as Cal stood with his back to the range.

'Have a pleasant afternoon, did you?' he asked. There was a note of something in his voice, anger perhaps. 'Nice car your boyfriend has.'

'He is a colleague,' she said tersely. 'No more than that.'

He looked at her cynically. 'Well, I brought them back. I'd best get away,' he said.

'No!' She hesitated. 'Cal, please. Don't go like that. Have a meal with us at least.'

He thought for a long time before he took off his old war-time greatcoat and his cap.

She busied herself with the food, putting on more potatoes, heating up a loaf she had baked.

After a while Cal sat down. She handed him a steaming mug of tea. Beneath the coat, his clothes were rags. There were holes in the elbows of his jumper, his trousers were blackened with dirt. She did not dare to look too closely because she sensed that if she did he would be hurt.

The boys came back, even Willie squeaky clean for once. They ate quickly and ravenously and then went to their beds. Tia had not eaten anything.

'Sit down, God's sakes,' Cal said. 'You have to eat somehing yourself.'

His own food was almost untouched.

She tried very hard to smile. 'I will if you will.'

For the first time he laughed at himself; she saw a flash of the old humour again and was so happy that she could have cried.

Once they had eaten, she made more tea.

'You've made a friend of Brogan,' he said.

'Who?'

'The lobby dosser. Name's Brogan.'

'I didn't know that.'

Cal's face lightened into an impish grin. ' "*A goood woo-man, an' sure she is. A lady, is Mistress Cameron. She puts out food night and day, and never asks a penny piece. Never even swore that time I wass sodden drunk and she had to climb over me to get into her house. Never a word she said, jes' went and fetched a blanket and put it over me, a pillow aneath my poor auld aching head.*" '

His face straightened suddenly. 'We were at the corner when you went past in the Daimler with that bloke. Nose in the air like anything, you never even noticed us. Would've turned back if it wasn't Tam told me it wasn't a fancy man, you didn't have one. Would've taken them to the Green and kept them with us. Brogan made us tea. He said you gave him a kettle.'

She smiled. 'He used to make a brew with a billy mug on the boiler. He burned his fingers doing that.'

'You bandaged them for him.'

She looked away. 'Cal . . .'

He got up decisively. 'I really do have to go now.'

She turned back to him. 'Where are you going, Cal?'

'Home.'

The bitterness of his expression was as harsh as lead, as brittle as pig iron. She would have argued, but she knew there was no point. She would have told him that he had a home – two, if he wanted them. But he didn't want them, not yet.

She went to the big press in the hall and took out the military greatcoat that she had made for him to replace the one she had given to Willie. It was thick charcoal wool, lined and interlined, and with a canvas cape to keep off the rain. The canvas was waterproof, the cloth made by Birkmyres in New Lanark, famous before the war as makers of circus tents. The company had been started by Clydeside fishermen nearly two hundred years ago; Tia had begged the off-cuts and made the capes from the remnants of an order for tents for the troops.

She handed it to him.

Cal looked at the coat for a long time. 'Time was, I would've given my life for this.' The anger in his face looked as if he had been carved out of stone. He didn't bother to put on his old coat, he put on the new one instead.

Tia picked it up. 'I'll launder it, Cal.'

'No. I'll take it as it is. The men at home don't care to smell of soap.'

She winced.

'I'll come back tomorrow,' he said. 'The boys want to talk to you. I promised I'd be here when they did.'

'Where were they?' she asked, almost as an afterthought. She did not care; she cared only that they were safe again.

'Home,' he said, 'they went home.' And then, sensing the irony of his words, 'They went to the islands, I mean.'

Tia left them in bed; the soaking had given them each a cold and she made lemon toddies and told them to sleep it off, not to risk the weather, the rain that was pelting down relentlessly.

She got through the day at work, rushing along to the butcher's at Candleriggs in the afternoon where she managed to buy a joint of beef after she had dropped in to Weinstock's to repeat the order for serapes. Samuel greeted her like a long-lost daughter; she did not have time to stop and talk but promised that would visit them on Sunday. He told her to bring the boys, Miriam would love that.

She had forgotten all about Haldane Brodie until one of his assistants passed her a memo from him noting that the Colquihoun account was in order again. She dashed off a quick reply and then wrote a little note to his mother to thank her for her hospitality. Though she had learned painfully about the procedure that passed as manners, she would never get used to the rituals involved. It was Miriam Weinstock who had explained it all to her: if she was invited to someone's home she must write to thank her hostess afterwards. Though she had had occasional invitations from Weinstock's customers, she still did not understand the rule, more so when one of the machinists asked her over for Sunday dinner and burst into gales of laughter when Tia sent her a thank-you note afterwards.

'I dinna get fashed wi' all that,' Mrs Anderson had said. 'A lot of bluidy nonsense, so it is. If ye want ma advice, pet, dinna hae aucht tae dae wi' folks like that.'

She smiled to herself as she put the note into the little lilac envelope, smelling faintly of violets, which the assistant in the stationery department had assured her was the right thing for the job.

Just before she left that evening, Moira Wilson put her head round the foor of Tia's office, where she had been working on forward orders for the summer. Monday was a quiet day; the ladies' department could have been closed, customers were such a rarity. Tia had been thinking of asking if any of the women wanted to go on to part time, because a few had husbands who had returned from the war. She wanted to stagger the assistants so that fewer were on duty during the quiet days, and more were there in the afternoons and towards the end of the week. On Saturday she wanted the younger girls to work, because the day was a write-off as far as their married clientele were concerned. The departments were busy, but only inexpensive mantles and gowns did any business. The other sections were packed to the gunnels with gawpers.

'That was Mr Colquihoun on the phone, Mrs Cameron,' she said, 'he wants his wife to come in, and he wanted to know when it would be convenient.'

'You can take care of Mrs Colquihoun,' Tia smiled.

Moira blushed. 'He asked for you, Ma'am. "That elegant lady my wife chatted with the other day", he said. Mrs Colquihoun was most impressed with you, he said.'

'I see,' Tia said, carefully, not wanting to dent Moira's fragile confidence. 'I'm in the department every day this week and next. I don't have anything planned.'

'I told him that,' Moira said. 'He said he would bring her in next Tuesday, if that's all right.'

'Serving customers is what we're here for,' Tia said.


Tam and Willie were up, bathed and dressed when she got back, their beds neatly made, though they were hunched tightly against the range, sniffling.

She smiled to herself, but said nothing. When Willie heard her walk in, he jumped up to put the kettle on, while Tam took her coat and shook it, sending drops of water everywhere.

The beef roast had cost her five shillings, but the smell of it cooking was worth that.

Neither Tam nor Willie said much as she put on the vegetables and then checked the apple dumpling she had put on to steam slowly before she left for work. Not a crumb remained of the loaf she had left for them, not an egg out of the ten that had been in the bowl.

Cal came shortly afterwards; she was glad of the good meat that had cooked quickly and she served it proudly, but he said he would just take some vegetables, he would rather take his meat home with him. When the boys held their plates out for second helpings, she glowered at them and pretended not to notice the meat, heaping their plates with potatoes, parsnips and gravy instead.

After dinner they sat around the kitchen table, Cal smiling, Tia with her chin cupped in her hand.

'We had to go,' Willie said, after a long time. 'We didna

want to worry you, Auntie Tia, but we needed to know who we were.'

He shook his head. 'We met our folks, y'see. Our da's pa and ma, and your'n as well.' He had been crouched over the table; he sighed and leaned back. 'It's a guid place, so it is. The island. Good folks an' all. E'en yer pa, Auntie Tia, Ma's pa. He's no a bad man, ony more.'

She thought fleetingly of her father, the irony that her mother's illness had washed the rage out of him.

'But it's no for us, Auntie. Tam and me, we've no place there or here.'

'You always have a home with me,' she said softly.

'Aye, an' we're glad o' it, but we want to make a place fir oursels, Tam and me. We want tae wirk, we want a country that wants us. This country disna.'

She looked away.

'We want tae go tae America, Auntie. Once we get the fare, we're off, Tam and me.'

They sat in silence for a while, then she turned to Tam. 'What do you think of that?'

'Like Willie's says, we want a country that wants us. We want a life for oursels. Our ma, bless her, they never gied her a chance. An' she worked sae hard, a' the days o' her life. She wirked bluidy hard, Auntie Tia, she ne'er stopped wirking, a' day lang.'

Tia felt tears surge; she looked down to hide them. 'I loved your mother very much,' she said. She blinked and looked directly at them. 'I'll give you the money, if that's what you want.'

They began to protest, but she held her hand up to stop them. 'It's not my money, it's yours by right. It's money your mother made with her shop.'

Willie shook his head. 'She loved that wee place o' hers. Dinna close it, Auntie Tia. She widna'a wanted that.'

'I won't close it,' Tia said. 'It's still open, you know that. It always will be. But Mairead never took her dues, and her money is yours now.'

'We can wirk,' Willie said gruffly. 'We can get the fare oursels.'

She shook her head. 'If you want. It could take for ever. You know that. The money's there if you want it. If not, I'll put it into an account for you. Either way it's yours.'

Cal shook his head, as if to clear the mist. 'I told you,' he said, 'I told you she'd do that. She's a great one for keeping money for people. Even people who don't want it. Your aunt's a great woman for doing that.' He turned to her and smiled. 'My sister-in-law, I should've said.'

The boys looked at each other. Tam yawned; they were still riddled with the cold, still tired.

'We dinna want tae leave ye, Auntie Tia,' he said, 'but y'ken why, d'ye no?'

Once they went to bed, she busied herself clearing and washing the plates, making a fresh pot of tea to replace the one that had gone cold. She could see that Cal was getting ready to leave himself.

In Marcus's chest was a bottle of whisky she had bought for him at Christmas so many years ago, still undrunk for the most part. When she gave it to him he had told her he didn't want to shade a minute of the time he had with her with anything that would blunt his senses. Marcus drank sometimes, she supposed, all seamen did, but he hardly drank at all when he was with her.

She went to fetch it and handed it to Cal. It was Grant's malt, Glenfiddich; she knew nothing about whisky and had bought it because the grocer in Pollokshields told her it was the best.

He took it and stared at it. 'A toff's brew, that is. Trust you.'

She smiled. 'I got it for your brother. He never drank it. He'd want you to have it, I know. Keep the cold out.'

Cal got up and put his coat on, letting the bottle fall into the deep inner pocket where there was plenty of room for it.

At the door, he bent and kissed her gently on the cheek.

'You'll come back,' she said.

He nodded. She reached out for him but he pushed her away. She felt his anger again then.

'Why are you so angry with me, Cal?'

He looked at her for a long time. 'Because you're so bloody naive, Tia. You believed the lies.'

'I . . . I never . . .'

'You did. You still do. That job you do. that's a lie. Stewart and MacDonald paid the Excess Profits Tax, like Fraser's and

338

Daly's and all the rest of them. Two million dead and missing, and the fucking capitalists, all they fucking care about is what it cost. The bombs and bullets and the boats they sank. Not a penny for the men.'

'There's pensions being paid.'

'Pittances, you mean. The money went to the shipyard owners, the owners of the munitions works and the forges and the metals works and the mills that made the uniforms that were buried in the mud. That's the lie, Tia. And now they gripe about the Excess Profit Tax. If we're going to defend the country, we've got to defend it from people like that first.'

'Cal, as God's my judge, I did my best. I did what I could. We didn't know.'

He shook his head. 'You read the newspapers, you mean. You believed the lie.'

'I knew it wasn't the truth,' she said softly.

He punched the door frame with his fist, hard, bruising it. 'You believed the lie,' he repeated.

'*Only because you didn't tell me the truth, Cal!*'

He frowned fleetingly. 'What do you mean?'

She went to the drawer in her bedroom and took out his letters, the letters he had sent home and Bridie had copied for her. She read out a few lines until he put his head in his hands and told her to stop.

'Our mail was censored.'

'You could have told us when you got leave.'

'I didn't take my leave. Not till, not till after . . . I didn't take leave, I left. I was lucky I wasn't shot for deserting.' His voice tailed off into a whisper.

'You could have told us then,' she said, so softly, and then again when he looked as if he had not heard, 'You could have told Bridie and your mother when you came back from the Somme.'

'I have to go,' he said again.

'If you have told Eunice, Bridie, me, anyone, we would have helped,' she said.

'What could you have done?'

'Kept you hidden. Kept you safe.'

He shook his head. 'You see, Tia. I couldn't tell Ma or Bridie for fear they'd tell the others, with sons still there. We still had hope then, hope that we would make it through. There was six of us after the Somme. There had been twenty but the rest were killed.'

'You could've told me,' she said, 'come to see me. You had my address.'

He shook his head. 'You don't even know how your own husband died. You believed the lies back then. I didn't want to tell you the truth. I didn't want to hurt you.'

Her eyes narrowed.

'Cal.'

'G'bye, Tia.'

'*Cal!*' she screamed, following him down the stairs. 'What happened to him? What really happened? You have to tell me, Cal. *You have to tell me!*'

He stopped for the briefest moment. 'I don't know what happened, Tia. I only know what didn't happen.'

'What didn't happen?'

'The way they told it to you. The way that MacCallum told it to you. It didn't happen like that, Tia.'

'I have to find out,' she said. 'I have to know.'

His mood changed abruptly. He lifted her chin gently with one finger, wiped the tears from her eyes. 'It makes no difference, pet. Not to me and not to him.'

'It would to me,' she said.

He put his hands into his pockets and began to walk away, whistling as he did so.

She called after him and he turned back.

'How many's left?' she asked.

He did not have to think about what she meant; he told her that there was only him.

# Chapter Nineteen

*T*am and Willie were at the front door as she walked slowly up the stairs.

'Are ye a'richt, Auntie Tia?' Willie called down.

'I'm fine,' she said, as she turned the corner in the stairwell.

'We heard shouting.'

She shrugged.

'It wis ye shouting. Ye woke us up.'

She got indoors and went to the kitchen to make chocolate milk for them.

'It was nothing,' she said as she stirred the brew.

Behind her back she sensed them looking at each other. She turned to face them. 'It was an old story, a very old story.'

'Wis it the war?'

'No, Tam. It was before that.'

'Wis it aucht to do with our ma?'

'It was to do with Marcus. My husband. Cal's brother.'

'Cal's a hard man,' Tam said. 'It's like he's still fichtin'. Only God kens whit for.'

Willie shot him a look and he shut up.

Three days later she stood at the pier in the deep docks and waved to them on board the transatlantic liner. Though they had wanted to go steerage, she had insisted on buying them second-class tourist tickets and had made sure they had a cabin to themselves. She had heard too much about the way third-class passengers were treated to allow anyone she loved to travel like that. They had fifty pounds each, and Willie had two hundred American dollars she had ordered from the Linen Bank in Ingram Street. For a long time she had wondered if she should give them the deeds of Marcus's land in Montauk; just when she decided that she should, at least to be sure that they had a place to start, Willie told her arrogantly that they had arranged board for themselves. They would go to Jimmy Michie's place in the Lower East Side. Jimmy was from the

Gallowgate, and his aunt had given them his address and promised that he would give them a roof over their heads and help them find work.

Her heart was heavy as the horn sounded and the little tugs began to ease the liner out into the river; she did not want to let them go, but she sensed she had no right to keep them where they did not want to be, to try to take their mother's place when she knew too well that no one could. Their hurt was deep, the raw wound of their father's absence bleeding again.

She had given them the best start she could. There was no more she could do for them, except to hope. And pray, if there was anyone who would listen.

They had promised to write to her. She knew that Tam would.

The boat left early; she pulled her coat tightly around her shoulders and walked along the Broomielaw until she reached the railway line, where she turned towards Argyle Street, the streets thronged with shop workers and office workers, the lucky ones who still had a job to go to.

Mrs Colquihoun came that morning; she was flushed, clinging to her husband's arm. Though he wore a business suit, Tia saw from his stance that he was a man of the ocean, a man who understood its moods. He shook Tia's hand and told her that his wife must have whatever she wanted, it was time for her to have some new clothes again. His eyes were clear and honest; she warmed to him, feeling none of the resentment she sometimes did when she sold to the wives of the war profiteers.

Cal's anger still rang in her head, like a bell that tolled for so many of the dead.

Mrs Colquihoun asked him to leave; he said he would wait in the smoke room, but would not leave the store until she was decently clad.

Moira stood aside as Tia settled her in a little chair and began to show her some outfits that had just arrived from Paris. On a tidal wave of postwar exuberance, some of the designers had turned to Louis XV for inspiration; Lanvin had produced a blue serge suit trimmed with gold braid that was redolent of Napoleon. Mrs Colquihoun winced and Tia knew without being told that the style was too close to the military for her.

She began to wash her hands nervously. 'Mrs Cameron, I'm really not sure, I really don't think any of this is me. And the prices, they must be out of this world.'

Tia smiled and nodded to Moira, who showed her a tweed suit similar to but not the same as the design Tia had sold to Murielle's when she was working at Weinstock's.

'This is more my sort of thing,' Mrs Colquihoun said. 'It's comfortable to wear. I'll not go back to all that nonsense we had to put up with before the war.'

Tia left them alone until Mrs Colquihoun had finished choosing dresses and coats, when she showed her a cinnamon duvetyn coat with stitched silk detail at hips, wrists and neck which would show her lithe figure to perfection. Mrs Colquihoun was tall and thin, she could wear the narrow skirt and bloused top that was draped at the hips, and the high neck would not make her look dumpy. Tia had ordered only one of the style, convinced that there was probably only one woman in Glasgow who would wear a coat like that.

'Now that,' Mrs Colquihoun said, 'that is worth the money.'

The price was 30 guineas.

Tia ordered coffee when they were waiting for the alteration hand, who had to finish the seams of some of the suits.

'Tell me,' she said conversationally, 'do you ever see anything of Captain Jardine these days?'

'Why, no, my dear. Didn't you know? He died, let me see, it was so sad. He died in January of 1913. I remember now. It was just before the end of the month, and the Hunters, they said one of his ships wasn't sound. I remember my husband talking about it.

Tia felt faint. She sat down quickly.

'I'm sorry,' Mrs Colquihoun said, 'I didn't want to upset you. I thought everyone knew.'

'I wasn't sure,' Tia said slowly. 'I didn't know him, you see. But I knew someone who did, and he always spoke kindly of him.'

Mrs Colquihoun patted her hand. 'In the old days, they were all like that. Now, they don't think so much of whether a man is capable of keeping a ship, only how little they can get away with paying him. You'd think the yards would be busy with all the ships that were sunk in the war. Not a bit of it! Of all the compensation paid, I don't think a tenth of it has gone to build new ships. Most of the owners think themselves lucky to be out of it. I know we do.'

Tia found herself changing her mind about the woman; she had to be polite though, she had to chat until the alterations were chalked and the order signed and the customer escorted through to the restaurant where she met her husband for an early lunch. Thanking Moira and the alterations hand, Tia went into her office and closed the glass door before she sank into a chair and put her head into her hands and sobbed.

She had always wondered why Captain Jardine had not contacted her after Marcus died. For all of these years she had blamed the Jardines for denying her; now she realised that they couldn't've done, because Captain Jardine was dead before Marcus was killed.

For all of that time, she had blamed Jardine for her husband's death, her sorrows as well; the humiliation of the hospital and the agony of Mrs Gordon's, the terror of her lost memory, most of all the betrayal of Marcus's trust. The realisation that she was wrong cut almost as keenly as the original pain. Though she knew that it would fade she sensed also that it would never heal.

She had dried her tears and put a little powder on her nose, but the gloss of grief shone through like a beacon as she pretended to be working on invoices, tallying sales and costs. The soft knock at her door made her look up.

Moira hesitantly opened the door to her abrupt command. 'I'm so sorry, Mrs Cameron, but I wondered if there was anything I could do.'

'Do?' Tia spat sharply, before her voice quavered and she apologised.

'I saw the look on your face,' Moira said.

Tia was taken aback. 'I didn't think she noticed anything.'

'Mrs Colquihoun didn't. I did. Only because I'm a widow too.'

Tia pulled out the other chair. 'Sit down,' she said.

'I don't want to be forward,' Moira said, 'but I was lonely once, very lonely. In a way I was lucky, because so many were widowed during the war. We clung together and helped ourselves.' She smiled. 'We cried our hearts out and then we dusted ourselves down and decided to get on with it. That's why I applied for this job. My piano pupils, I loved teaching them, but I didn't make enough to keep a chicken fed. At least, this keeps the wolves from the door.' She shrugged. 'I live in Partick. There's a few of us. We go out together once a week. I wondered if . . . I wondered if you would like to come too . . .'

Tia sniffed.

'As I said, Mrs Cameron, I don't want to be forward. I know I've been rude . . .'

'You weren't rude,' Tia said quickly. She was crying again. 'My sister, my oldest sister, she died two weeks ago. I just put her sons on the boat to New York this morning. I didn't know if I did the right thing, but it was what they wanted.'

Moira touched her hand. 'Maybe you don't want to go out just yet.'

'But I do,' Tia sobbed. 'I'd like to.'

She was thinking of the empty days ahead of her and, worse than that, the empty nights, when she had nothing to think of but Cal and what he had said, and Marcus, and what had really happened to him on a cold winter's morning in New York six years before.

That night, as she left MacDonald's with Moira and the other sales assistants by the Mitchell Lane entrance, a man saw her and swung the door open; she hardly noticed him. A light rain had fallen and the alleyway was full of puddles. Tia sidestepped them carefully, turning round when the man, just behind her, swore loudly, having landed in one.

At the end of the lane, the women went off in opposite directions.

'Who was that man?' Tia asked Moira, just before they parted.

'That was Jimmy. Jimmy Stewart, Mr Stewart's son. The heir apparent.'

'Oh.'

'He was injured in the war. That's why he limps. He makes a joke of it, but he was down at Erskine for months.'

'I didn't notice his limp,' Tia said.

Tia didn't know what to do about the mystery of Marcus's death, about what Cal had said. At the end of the month she

345

went to the Ruglonian Ball with Haldane Brodie. She wore a dress she had made herself, a shirred silk sheath in dove grey, with grey bugle beads and a grey fringe sewn in a spiral that twisted around her torso, ending with the fluted hem just above her ankles. She was proud of the dress; the material had cost shillings and the work had taken up her evenings for most of the month.

'My goodness,' he said, when he collected her in the Daimler, 'you look stunning, Mrs Cameron.'

Obediently, she told him to call her Tia; they were off-duty, as it were.

When they arrived at the dance, in the Rutherglen Town Hall, gaudily decked out with paper streamers and hand-painted copies of the burgh's coat of arms, she looked around and knew with stomach-sinking certainty that her dress, so fashionable, so chic, was utterly wrong. None of the other women had anything like it; most wore designs from before the war; a few were in traditional white dancing attire with tartan sash draped over one shoulder.

'I am so sorry,' she said to Haldane.

'Sorry? Don't you mention it. This burgh could do with a breath of fresh air.'

He turned to talk to one of his fellow baillies, leaving her to make small talk with the wives. She sat at a table, nursing a glass of sherry, trying determinedly to pretend that she was enjoying herself.

Haldane Brodie did not dance, with the exception of an eightsome reel during which he stood on her toes so often that he nearly crippled her.

Mrs Brodie sat on a platform with the other dowagers, scanning the dance floor with eyes like periscopes as their necks twisted this way and that. Tia went to say 'hello'; Mrs Brodie ackowledged her but did not ask her to sit down.

The evening was an ordeal; she was glad the dance ended promptly at midnight in deference to the sensibilities of the Sabbatarians.

On the way back to Hyndland, crossing the Clyde Bridge, Haldane put his hand over hers. Unsure what to do, Tia did nothing, inwardly cursing herself for cowardice. Each time he moved to change gears she prayed he would keep his hand on the wheel or on the stick, but each time he placed it gently over hers. In a very small voice, she asked him if it was safe to drive with one hand. 'Of course it is,' he said, rolling down an almost empty Sauchiehall Street. When he coasted to a halt at the entrance to her close, he did not get out the door to open hers, but lifted her hand insistently to his lips and kissed it.

She shuddered reflexively.

'Mrs Cameron, Tia, I mean. It has been such a pleasant evening.'

'Haldane, Mr Brodie, thank you, but I am very tired.'

'We must do it again soon. A dinner, perhaps?'

'Perhaps.' She smiled, feeling as weak as water.

'My dear Louise left such a hole in my life.' His hands dropped hers and she snatched it back as he wiped his eyes dramatically. 'I never thought I would meet another lady who would interest me, but now I have. I have never . . . I never sought to marry again, but, Mrs Cameron, Tia, I mean, you, you are a lady who has made me think twice.'

Her courage surged. 'Oh, Mr Brodie, oh, dear me. I am flattered, very flattered, I truly am, but I do not want to get married again. I do not think I could replace Louise.'

With eyes as wide as the moorland sky she opened the door herself and nipped out and into her close before he could say another word.

The lobby dosser was at home, singing 'I Will Bring You Home Again, Cathleen,' in a voice so sad and rich that tears tingled her eyes.

'Ahoy,' he roared, hearing her footsteps. 'Is that 'ee, my lady love, my mistress of the bowls of soups and hot pies?'

She frowned. 'It is, Brogan.'

'Your friend wass here, the young soldier laddie. He wass asking for 'ee but I said you were away out, bedecked in finere-ee.'

She swore softly to herself. She did not want Cal to think she was out enjoying herself.

'Don't worry-ee, fine lady,' he sang, 'your secret is safe with me-ee.'

'What d'you mean, Brogan?'

'I says to him, I says, "Cal, my boy, Cal, my man, the lady iss out for the effening. She is with her young friend, the estimated

Mrs Wilson. They are off to the pickatures at Partick. *Oh!
Tralalala, tralalalee, the pair o' them's off to the cinema'ee.*" '

Brogan never worried if the lines of the song he made up off
the top of his head did not rhyme. He just added a long 'ee' to
everything.'

'I love you, Brogan,' Tia said.

'Fie, for fear, you do not, Missus Cameron. Only a fool would
love a man like me-hee. A truly atrocious marital prospect I
be-hee. Worse than Henry the Eighth, I am. *Oh, 'Ener, 'Enery,
'Enery the eighth I be I be . . .*'

When she got indoor she was laughing and crying all at once.
She slung her cape over a chair, then ripped off her sheath,
careless of the dozens of little self-covered buttons that fitted
into the handrolled eyelets. On impulse, she nearly tore it to
shreds but desisted and put it back on its hanger, wondering if
the fact that the buttons and eyelets had stayed intact was an
omen of better times to come, or just that she was good at
sewing. She would much rather have seen Cal than go to the
ball. She felt a wave of hatred for Haldane Brodie for keeping
her away from him. As she got ready for bed, she wondered how
long it would be if Cal came again, if he ever would.


At work, on Wednesday morning, she went into the office in the
storeroom behind the department, closed the door, picked up
the phone and in a shaky voice asked the operator to connect
her to Pacific Hunter.

The telephonist, a man, answered carelessly.

'H . . . hello,' she stammered, 'can I speak to Captain
MacCallum, please?'

'There's nobody of that name here,' the voice said.

'Captain MacCallum, who used to be with you just before
the war.'

'Retired, I think. Wait a minute, he died, didn't he? Who's
calling?'

'Mrs Cameron. My . . . my husband worked for you in
Jardine's day.'

'That's a while ago, Missus. The auld boys are gone, most o'
them.'

'Is . . . is Hector MacKenzie, First Officer MacKenzie, is he
with you still?'

'Jis' a minute.' Some papers ruffled, she heard a muffled question. 'He's no, no as far as I know.'

'He was going to emigrate,' Tia said, urgency creeping into her voice. 'He was going to emigrate, he said. D'you know if he did?'

'I do not, Missus. Some went to the Navy, some went to other lines. We lost a boat in the convoy, '15, it was, another two in '17, but there were survivors, those times.'

'Was he killed, d'you know? *D'you know if he's still alive?*'

'I do not, Missus. I only know he's not on the list now. I could check, maybe, but you'd huff to call back.'

'I will,' she said.

'But ye'd be better onto the Mariners' Guild. They'd know, better than us.'

'The Guild?'

'The Guild of Master Mariners, they'd know, right enough, if he was a member, and all of Jardine's men were.'

Shaking, she put the handset down in the receiver, jerking reflexively when it dropped with a clatter. For a long time, she sat with her head in her hands.

Moira's soft knock disturbed her. She put her head around the door. 'I'm just off for lunch, Mrs Cameron.'

The clock on the wall told her that it was half past eleven.

'Is the department quiet?'

'Dead as the grave,' Moira said, not seeing her wince, or perhaps ignoring that she had. 'I'll be back at noon. I'll do the modelling then.'

'That chemise with the long jacket,' Tia said. 'It looks like nothing on the rails, but it's beautifully cut.'

The door closed again. Decisively, she picked up the phone again and asked for the Mariners' Guild. There was a lady telephonist this time, who put her on to a man, and she asked the same thing.

'Just a moment,' he said, leaving the phone for a minute or two before he came back. 'This list isn't final,' he said, 'there's half a dozen MacKenzies on it, but not a Hector MacKenzie, ex-Jardine, ex-Pacific Hunter.'

'Are you sure?'

'I only know his death wasn't reported. See, his dues were paid to 1914. By then, he'd put in his twenty-five years and he took out life membership, so his dues weren't payable after that.'

'Do you know where he is?'

'I can ask around. Try to find out. What is it that you really want to know?'

A stab of pain shot up her arm, she was holding the handset so tight. 'My husband, Marcus Cameron, Captain Cameron . . .'

'That's a name I know,' he cut in.

'But he died, he died six years ago. In New York. An accident, they said. Hector . . . Hector came and told me. He took me home I . . I didn't take anything in then.'

The silence echoed. After a time, she said, 'hello' again, to make sure he was still there.

'Yes,' he said. 'Mrs Cameron, we have a report on your husband's death. We have a report on the death of every member who dies at sea or abroad.'

'Do you . . . could you . . .' she began, her voice breaking.

'Mrs Cameron, of course I could. If you just come round to the office, I can see you now.'

The office of the Mariners' Guild was in an alleyway off the Broomielaw, up a flight of stairs from a ship's chandler.

The man she had spoken to on the phone was waiting for her. 'I'm Jimmy Henderson,' he said; his face was open, bronzed by a lifetime on the ocean, and his blue eyes shone below eyelids draped like fire curtains. He did not shake her hand; he could not because his right sleeve was inverted, tucked into his jacket. She noticed his limp as he led her through to a tiny cubbyhole filled with a table, two chairs and a mountainous range of files piled in stacks that tumbled and slumped to the floor, the contents held together by rubber bands. He motioned her to one of the chairs and took the one opposite as a woman brought in two mugs of tea.

Marcus's file was on top of his desk. His name was written on it in heavy black letters. Jimmy Henderson opened it and handed her the first page, Pacific Hunter's accident report.

*My Lady Eilean* loading at berth No. 53. Captain Cameron checked hold and then proceeded quayside to check cargo. Cargo crane in operation. Captain Cameron gestured to proceed. Crane chain slipped, load fell, the load knocking Captain Cameron over. Crane secured. Once crane secured it was apparent Captain Cameron had fallen into river. Po NY A informed and search launched 0945 hours. Home office informed by telegram. First Officer Corbett assumed command. On hearing of accident, some ratings took to the sea. One rating dived repeatedly in vicinity of ship.

Po NY A instructed departure noon. Berth booked. Search continued, terminated 1600 hours. Po NY A assumed death.

Body recovered City of Jersey 3rd February 1913. Identified by uniform jacket.

The language was so bland that it made Marcus's death seem surreal.

Jimmy Henderson was watching her closely.

For a long time Tia stared out of the window, at the muddy sky just visible above the tenements of the alley.

He drank his tea, poured hers away and refilled the mug.

'Why . . . why did they secure the crane before . . .'

'Because it could've killed someone else. If a chain is swinging uncontrolled, it could hit anybody.'

'What . . .'

'The operator would've reeled it in. Takes seconds, Mrs Cameron.'

'Why didn't . . . didn't . . .'

'If the load dropped, if the Captain was beside it or behind it they wouldn't've seen at first that he was thrown into the river. It would've taken a minute, perhaps, they would've known then.'

'Why didn't . . .'

'The men began their own search, soon's they knew. They didn't see it. The ratings were in the hold securing the cargo. They didn't know until the loading stopped. In the hold, y'see, there's an echo, you can't hear what's going on outside. It was minutes later, up to ten, because cargo loading often stops, y'see, there's often a hold-up and they wouldn't think anything of it.'

She drank her tea for politeness' sake. He had added a tot of rum for which she was grateful.

'You don't believe it,' she said.

He took the paper. 'There's nothing here to doubt.'

'I suppose, you see, I don't know, and Hector, he didn't know. He was in the office when the telegram came and he came to me.'

'Mrs Cameron, we don't know either.'

'So . . .' She was shaking inside, clutching at straws; she had lived with Marcus's death as an accident for so long that the knowledge that it might have been something would be too much. '. . . It was an accident, then, there was nothing . . . nothing happened that shouldn't've . . . I mean, I saw Captain MacCallum and he told me that. He told me the truth. He told me the truth, didn't he?'

'Mrs Cameron, I'm sorry, we tried, and we couldn't find out much. It was too late, you see.'

'Too late?' She stared at him, realised that she was shouting, apologised quickly.

'I understand,' he said. 'You see, this note, the ratings, they launched their own search. *My Lady Eilean* sailed without them. There was half a dozen stranded New York side and the other owners, they wouldn't give them passage back never mind a post. By the time we got word of it it was the summer; we had the report then, but we didn't get any more until the war began. *My Lady Eilean* you see, she never docked here, she diverted to Liverpool and the crew weren't given shore leave because she was turned around straight away for Shanghai. She appeared at Manila in October 1913 but after that she was off the list.'

'What d'you mean?'

'Off Lloyd's list. No longer insured at Lloyd's.'

'Did she sink?'

'No, nothing like that. She was sold for scrap and then renamed. She's on the South China Seas somewhere now. That's where Pacific Hunter ply their trade, mostly.'

'Marcus said she was sound.'

'She was a good ship when Jardine's sold her.'

Tia gazed at him.

He reached into the file and handed her some other papers. She looked down, saw Marcus's handwriting, began to sob.

Jimmy Henderson became flustered. He fumbled for a

handkerchief and then, finding none, went and got one from the female clerk.

'Mrs Cameron, please,' he said, 'you don't have to read it. You don't have to upset yourself. I have tried to find out what really happened but I have failed.'

'No,' she said.

'I assure you, I have.'

'I won't fail,' she said. 'Not if I try, not if I really try, I won't.'

He sat down and meshed his fingers. 'You see,' he said, 'that's the Captain's log. There was a lad on board, your husband had taken him under his wing. The lad took his dinner one day and found the Captain keeping two logs. That is the second one. After the accident, he took it, but he was just a lad, you see. He was in the galley when Captain Cameron died, and the ship sailed without him knowing anything. He jumped ship in Manila and got back home a year later.'

'What's his name? Can I speak to him, can I see him?'

The seaman's eyes misted. 'That's just it. He joined up. Land side. The infantry. He was killed at Ypres. His mother brought this in. She found it with his things.'

'Can I see her, please?'

'Mrs Cameron, she knows nothing. She lost two sons, you see. She didn't even leave an address, just left the log in an envelope. I asked around. I checked the writing against your husband's membership form. It's the same. That's how I know it's his.'

She stood up. 'Thank you, Mr Henderson.'

'Jimmy.'

'Thank you, Jimmy.'

'Please come back,' he said. 'Please come back and let me know how you get on.'

The rest of the week passed; she went to work mechanically, clinging to her routine because anything else would have been too hard, going out on Friday evening with Moira and two of her friends from Partick to the new show at the Britannia. Just outside, a familiar face in the crowd struck her. She tried to smile, but, scared that she would cry instead, managed to say nothing beyond a distant greeting.

On Saturday, Haldane Brodie came to the department as

the store closed and asked her to a dinner the following weekend.

'I am afraid I can't,' she said.

His eyes darkened angrily. 'Tia, Mrs Cameron, I am afraid I must insist. You see, it is the Chamber, and the board have asked me to introduce our senior lady staff. Mrs Nish from Stewart's is coming as well.'

'Oh,' she said. She did not care too much about her job just now.

'I will collect you at 7.30,' he said.

She went home and ate food that she did not taste, then lit the fire in the front room and began to read the log.

Cal's fingers were blue with cold, though the weather had been warmer that month. She did not hand him the mug of tea; she put it down on the table. He was still wearing the greatcoat she had given him; the canvas cape was black with filth.

'I got your message,' he mumbled, his teeth chattering.

Wordlessly, she brought the log from her room and handed it to him. He stared at it for a long time before he got up and washed his hands, then began to read, turning the pages carefully as if they might crack.

*January 10th, 1913, 0600 hours*
*On deck for the change of watch.* My Lady *is sitting low. I took command as Wilson, the Pacific Hunter Captain, filled log. Being the old line's Captain, I act as his deputy on this last trip. He is right. She feels clumsy.*

*January 20th, 1913, 1200 hours.*
*The weather has changed. The wind has fallen;* My Lady *is slow. She is not the ship I remember. I will check her load in Kingston. The log records her tonnage as it was.*

*January 25th, 1913, 0500 hours.*
*Kingston, Jamaica. Customs come on deck; the Captain gives them a case of Haig. Unloading begins. As I was watching, Wilson called me below re telegram from head office. We take on molasses for NY, rum for Charleston.*

*February 1st, 1913 0100 hours.*

*We slip into harbour at the dead of night, unload before local customs appear. Rum from Kingston smuggled ashore. Later, Captain hands envelope to Port Authority master and to Captain of Customs. Bribe? Take on Cotton for NY and HP. Got chance to check hold; PH increased tonnage 20%. No wonder* My Lady *is a little sluggish.*

*February 6th, 1913 0400.*

*NYC, awaiting pilot, tugs. The purser and the Captain have each, apart from paid cargo, 100 cases of rum in fuel compartment and there's contraband in the ballast tanks. Will report to head office once ashore. Talked Wee Joe last night. Like me, he's trying to come up through the focsle, unlike me, he doesn't think he'll make it. Not with PH. He says Will Jamieson and Iain Cathcart, both good men, left in Wellington because Captain marked their books D.R. They went to the nearest cemetery and got new names, but he's not heard who they're with yet. Lachie Mor, my chief steward, he's gone to Cunard. Captain Wilson called him a belly robber! In any case, at New York, I'm going to call the Port Authority and report that the two main ballast tanks are full of contraband. I challenged Wilson, who said it was nothing to do with him. I said, everyone has their game, but this is going too far and it has to be stopped. He said that there was nothing to do to stop it. I have no alternative but to report the ship as unsafe; the crossing is not easy this time of year and she would be too unstable with the extra tonnage even if they empty the ballast tanks and use them properly on the way home.*

*I am going to stand on deck now, and watch for the pilot.*

Tia went to the stove and heated soup, poured him a bowl and put it down in front of him.

He swore under his breath.

'How did you know?' she asked him.

'I guessed,' he said bitterly. 'Marcus was too competent to allow himself to be killed in an accident.'

'What can I do?'

Cal's mouth twisted into a cynical grin. 'There's nothing you can do, Tia. There never was. Except now you know not to trust big companies and the men that run them.'

She had kept track of the Discharged Soldiers' Society in the paper. The Corporation had given a few work and some had lodgings now; the group on the Green that had been hundreds had now dwindled to a couple of dozen.

'I wrote home,' he said. She turned abruptly; she had been making up some sandwiches; if his pride made him ignore them she always put some out for Brogan anyway. As the seasons changed to summer, sometimes the old tramp liked to sleep out in Kelvingrove Park. He enjoyed watching the stars.

'Just to tell them I was alive.'

She sat down, pouring tea for herself. 'Cal, I . . .'

'I shouldn't've said what I did, Tia. I was angry.'

'I understand.'

The bitterness fell over his face again. 'Do you?'

'I try to,' she said softly.

'You don't know what it's like,' he said, standing up. 'Don't ever think that you do, because you don't. Nobody does.'

'You could tell me,' she said.

He shook his head again, not to refuse but as if he wanted to clear his mind. 'You don't know what it's like,' he said in a whisper. 'You don't know what it's like when you don't know if it's the future or the past, whether it's today or tomorrow or yesterday, when you don't know if you're alive or dead.

'D'you know what it smells like? Death?' He looked directly at her; his face shone, his eyes were glazed with tears. 'They tell you about the pain and the blood and the screams, but did they ever tell you about the smell? You smell it first in the distance, Tia, when you're in the countryside and it could be anywhere, it could be here, even, out in Ayrshire or Lanarkshire. You smell it first in the distance and then it comes closer and closer. It hangs over the trenches like a thundercloud but it never bursts, it doesn't break in the storm. It just smells stronger. Rain doesn't wash it away, Tia. There's no rain that can wash it away. Once you've smelled it it stays with you. It stays with you for ever, to the end of your days.'

He slumped down on the chair and held his hands as his shoulders racked with sobs. The air in the kitchen had turned sour; she looked towards the milk jug, to see if it had turned before she realised that the milk was fresh and it was something else. She watched him for a long time, then she got up and fetched the bottle of whisky she had bought, put it in front of him with a glass and then went to the window and opened it and let the fresh cool air evening blow in, the air that smelled of spring and hope and distantly of the city fug.

Dry-eyed, Cal looked at her.

She picked up Marcus's log, folding the papers gently before she replaced it in its envelope and then went through to her bedroom where she opened her bottom drawer and put it back with all her other memories of him.

'I will go,' she said quietly. 'I don't know when I will, but I will go to New York and find out what I can.'

'You'll find nothing, you mean.'

'I mean I will go to the Medical Examiner's office and ask to see the autopsy report. If the truth is anywhere, it will be there.'

His mouth twisted cynically. 'Didn't you hear, Tia? The truth, it died too. It died in France and it's buried there, along with all the men who fought and gave their lives for a lie.' He opened the bottle then and, ignoring the glass, drank steadily until he had drained it.

'Cal, for God's sake . . .'

'God's dead, too,' he mumbled thickly, as he stumbled towards the door. 'Ypres or the Somme or Passchendaele. I can't remember which, but God's dead too.'

'Cal,' she said, as he stumbled down the stairs. 'Cal?'

Brogan was there, watching from the shadows. He called to her as she made to follow Cal, in her thin blouse and stockings, because she hadn't had time to put her shoes back on again – she had never picked up the lowland habit of keeping them on indoors.

'Don't worry, Missus,' Brogan said, clasping her shoulder with a grip that was surprisingly strong. 'I'll go after the daft young bugger, make sure he doesn't kill himself under a tram.'

Next morning she made an appointment to see Mr William. She had not seen the director since she had refused to go to Paris, and was not sure of the reception she would get.

'I want to take some leave,' she began.

He looked at her sharply. 'I acknowledge that the sales figures have improved, Mrs Cameron, but why do you want time off?'

She explained that she had business in America, a property she had been left by her late husband.

'If you come back at the end of the week,' he said slowly, 'I will see what I can do.'

The days passed in yawning emptiness; she went to the store and did her work mechanically. On Thursday night she went to Glasgow Green with a bag of pies, but Cal was not there. She went on to the close off the Gallowgate and told the woman running Meg's Pegs that she was going away for a while. Marcus seemed closer to her these days; she wondered how she could have accepted Captain MacCallum's glib story. How naive she had been to sign the bit of paper without reading it and not to realise how convenient Marcus's death was to the new owners of Rankine's Line.

Mr Willian called her into his office on Friday afternoon. 'I've spoken to the board,' he said, 'and we've agreed to give you the month of July. The assistants can deal with the sale, and you are on top of your work. America is the home of retailing; it will do you some good to see how American stores operate.'

'That's very generous, Mr William.'

'Have a look around and pick up some ideas.'

She would have hugged him, but his off-hand demeanour prevented that.

# Chapter Twenty

$A$s the liner glided towards land the sun rose behind it, etching the buildings of New York, the quayside tangle and then the rise of the Woolworth Tower, making them like bronze caricatures against the blank canvas of the sky. Passing the mouth of the East River, the Brooklyn Bridge and the Manhattan Bridge beyond were like cobwebs draped over the branches of a giant tree uprooted by a storm.

The light changed as the tugs pulled the ship towards the pier on the Hudson River – on the quay ant-sized men waiting, a line snaking out and flopping into the water before being reeled in and thrown again, this time to be caught by a rating and made fast to the ship.

The sun shone like a searchlight between the lips of the land, New York this way, Jersey City that.

Tia stood on deck, alone, a little apart from the knot of tourists, the gaggle of wives of the Captain and officers, on board for a holiday whilst their husbands worked. Beside her were her case and a little leather valise in which she kept her toilet things, her purse and papers. As a second-class passenger she would have second call on the porters, and she did not want to lose a moment waiting for them. A steward who had befriended her had promised to meet her on the quayside and find her a cab. He was a Glasgow man, though his roots, like her own, were in the islands.

The gangplank edged out, hitting the sides before the chains caught and winched it up to the deck. The crew were already going ashore on their own gangway that had been secured first to enable them to assist the disembarking passengers. Tia walked down, slowly, fearful that she would slip on the damp wood and metal.

She stood for a moment, before the steward beckoned to her, helping her into a cab driven by a friend of his from the dockland bars.

The morning air was warm, a clamminess hung over the city though it was hardly past dawn, too early for the working day to begin. The driver checked the address with her, then set off through the streets, turning this way and that, until he reached Broadway and surged past the early newsvendors, the food stalls where wisps of steam rose lazily from urns of heating water.

The hotel was a solid building on 54th Street, in between Fifth and Sixth Avenues. She reached into her purse for a dollar, but he waved the money away, the steward had already paid him.

Tia murmured her thanks, got out and let a bellboy take her case as she signed the register.

Her case clanked suspiciously as the bellboy put it on the stand in her room; she had brought two bottles of whisky to use as bribes, if need be. He grinned and tipped his cap to her, pocketing the coin she gave him and leaving before she realised that it was a shilling and set off along the corridor after him, catching him by the elevator and swapping it for a dime.

'I wouldn't have you to think I swindled you,' she said.

He shrugged. 'I take everything, Ma'am. Save 'em and keep 'em till I can take 'em to the bank and change 'em.'

She smiled.

'Hey, Ma'am. You Scottish?'

'I am.'

'D'you know Carnegie?'

In the quiet of her room she took out the copy she had made of Marcus's log.

For a long time she stared at the words Marcus had written in the last minutes of his life. She wanted to see Tam and Willie, even to see the stores, but first of all she wanted to find out what had happened to Marcus.

She reached the street as the busy hour began, battled against a tide of office workers and hawkers until she reached the subway station, bought a ticket and asked directions to Jersey City, realising with dismay that she had bought the wrong ticket in the wrong station and would have to take something called the 'El' instead.

She ended up walking to Ninth Avenue and taking the

elevated railway to Hoboken, where she walked through a pathetic little patch of scrub called Canal Street Park and caught a ferry to the other side. The liner on which she had crossed the Atlantic was just a couple of berths down, the river so busy that freighters and liners jostled with tugs and ferries as a noise the like of which she had never heard echoed across the brief expanse of muddied waters, streaked with oil, the tide a swollen bulge that pummelled the timbers of the Jersey shore.

Tam had written to her twice, with his address, she had it now, folded into the pocket of her bag. She had written to him to arrange a meeting and he had sent a telegraph asking which boat she would arrive on so they could meet her, which she had ignored. She had things to do first.

Jimmy Henderson had written down the address of the Medical Examiner's office and had drawn her a little map of the streets with the route there marked in red ink. He said it was no more than a fifteen-minute walk from the pier; she did it in ten. Once there, though, she hesitated. The brownstone building with the Tudor arch above the door with little trefoil spandrels at the corners loomed large in her vision until the sunny day was obliterated and all that remained was a dark, funereal archive that held the truth about Marcus's death. She stood on the corner for a long time, until she summoned the courage to push open the heavy oak door and then, taking a deep breath, walk towards a clerk seated at a table. Her footsteps rang out along the marbled corridors rather like a bell that carries news of a death.

The clerk was young, female, disarmingly pretty.

'I . . . I'd like to enquire . . . I'd like to ask you about a death,' she began.

The clerk smiled sympathetically. 'Are you a relative, Ma'am?'

'Yes . . . I'm . . . it was my husband. I was his wife.'

The clerk motioned her to sit down. Tia slumped on to a wooden seat that felt unstable.

'Can I have the details?'

Tia opened her bag and handed her the form.

The clerk frowned and then rose. 'If you will excuse me, I will see if I can locate the file.'

She left and Tia listened to echoing footsteps, a door opening, indistinct voices beyond. The voices continued for a moment or two, then another door opened; she could not see where. She had never looked at Marcus's death certificate; when she handed it to the clerk it was still in the envelope that Captain MacCallum had given her. She had not needed to look at it because she knew he was dead; back then, she did not need to know more than that.

The clerk reappeared with a man, a small man with etched features and spidery grey hair that rebelled against the cream he had combed into it. His face was pale, his eyes bleached as if he lived indoors always, never saw the sun. 'Please come with me,' he said.

She followed him meekly, sat down at his command.

'I just want to know why he died,' she said. 'Jimmy said, Mr Henderson said, he said you would know. You would be able to tell me.'

'I'm sorry,' he said, 'but there was no autopsy performed. The ME said that it appeared as if your husband had drowned. There was no examination.'

The air swirled, dust motes drifted; she felt faint, loosened the collar of her blouse. Haldane Brodie had told her that New York was hot in the summer, suddenly she felt as if she was in an oven.

'What d'you mean?'

'The . . . the acting Captain, Wilson was his name, working for Pacific Hunter, he informed the Coroner's office there was fever aboard. So once the body surfaced, we took special precautions. We had to, you see. The docks . . we cannot take the risk of fever.'

'Marcus had no fever.'

'There was a report of shipboard fever, typhoid. They said they had lost a crew member.'

'That isn't true.'

'Mrs Cameron, that is what they said. We had no reason to doubt them.'

'The ship hadn't been to India.'

'They had been to Port au Prince. There was an outbreak of typhoid there. They warned us. We had to take precautions.'

She grasped the side of the desk. 'Where did you bury my husband?'

'Mrs Cameron, the fever, we did not bury him.'

'What did you do to him?'

'The body was burned. Cremated. Prayers were said.'

She bent her head, felt nausea rise.

'Mrs Cameron, there was no doubt, your husband was dead. There are often accidents at the docks. More often, there is fever aboard ship. We have to protect our citizens. We cannot take undue risks. The acting Captain signed his consent.'

'My husband wasn't found until three days after the ship sailed.'

'The acting Captain gave his consent before the ship left.'

She felt her head spin and then all went dark.

An hour later, she stood uncertainly outside the police station beside the courthouse, by the city hall that Boss Tweed had built with his plundered millions. Crowds milled around her; it was mid morning now, the courthouse busy with cases against bootleggers, hookers and tramps. They were not her kind of people; they sensed that and stayed away from her, making her like an island in the human river of chance and circumstance and bad luck that flowed around her.

Inside, the policeman at the desk stared at her for a long time before he told her to sit down, that he would get someone from the detectives to come to see her.

She had told him that she wanted to report a murder. He said, 'What, another one? Lady, ya husband's either downstairs, sleeping it off, or he's in the park, sleeping it off. Just because he's a drunk don't mean he's dead.'

When she told him this murder happened six years ago, he asked her if she was sure before he grudgingly agreed to get someone to see her.

She had to wait for two hours before anyone came.

Detective Connors was Scottish, like her, he said, when she paused in her monologue and he got up and brought her some coffee in a mug, the liquid as filthy and thick as the Hudson River.

'It is hot,' he said. 'And wet.'

Though the afternoon had turned the city into a furnace, the detectives' room was cold as ice. From the cells down the hallway, the cries of miscreants sounded like the howling of wolves. Every so often, a policeman in uniform would yell at them to shut up; otherwise nobody listened, or appeared to.

'That's it?' he said, when she had finished talking and had shown him the log.

'Isn't it enough?' she replied.

'Lady, this is a city, men are born and then they die without anyone knowing they was alive. Used to be, thousands camped in Central Park. Babies were born. The old died there, and the not so old. One time a man told me his life wasn't worth more than a penny piece. Men died for less in fights. They die now for a bottle of beer. The old days, used to be an asylum in Ward Island for the drunks and the lunatics. Still is, 'cept they should've added the Bowery an' Alphabet City. When they started Ellis Island, they said it'd keep the no-hopers out, but they just go to Canada and walk here. This city's the biggest draw for crazies since they closed the Colosseum.'

'My husband wasn't crazy,' she said shakily. 'He didn't die for a bottle of beer.'

'I ain't saying he was, lady. I'm saying, life is cheap here. It is now and it was six years ago. I don't know what happened that day. I don't know if he fell or was pushed or someone slipped one of the longshoreman a coupla' dollars to dump a load on him. I don't know. But I believe you, if it means anything. I believe your husband was one of the good guys, like our cowboys, and he fell in with a buncha Indians, the bad guys, and cos' he was one good guy in amongst a load of bad guys they killed him.'

He snapped his finger, the clicking sound rising above the scratchings and scrapings, the lowing of the herd of human misery from the cells along the way. She stared at him, too shocked to say anything, too shocked to do anything but listen.

'I got a motive. Motive's there. These Pacific Hunter people, they don't sound no good to me. So I got a suspect. But that ain't enough, see? To prove it, to convict, I need not only a suspect, but I need to know who did what, how, where, when. I don't even need to know why. If a suspect did something and I can prove he did, that's enough for me. And the judge. And the jury. Sometimes. Sometimes it don't matter iffen you don't know. Sometimes a guess is good enough. But iffen I've a motive, an' that's all I got, it ain't enough, lady.'

He paused and tapped some files on his desk, a pile of paper overflowing untidily against a debris of blank paper and pencil stubs, ashtray and cigarettes. 'I need evidence, witnesses, physical evidence, the weapon, the ME to say how a man died.' During the time she had been talking to him, he had taken notes. He tapped them then, with a stabbing motion, almost as if the paper on which he had written was in itself a culprit of a sort. 'All I got's a suspect, see, an' a motive. Nuttin' else. You can convict a man, lady, if you can prove he did what you think he did. But you can't convict a whole company.'

'But,' she said slowly, 'you could try . . .'

'Try what?' His tone was sharp; he seemed to think she had been wasting his time.

'You could find witnesses. At the docks. Men who worked there might remember. And the crew. They remember.'

'Lady, six years is a long time.'

Her eyes narrowed. 'Some people have good memories.'

He sighed. 'Okay. Say I try. Say I start with the crew. How many d'you think'll be with the same ship, the same line even? They're British, so some of them'll've died in the war. Some'll've retired, and the city won't pay for me to go find 'em.'

'You don't know,' she said, 'You don't know what you'll find. You don't have to find the crew. You could start at the docks, with the longshoremen and the shipping agent. You never conscripted, did you? The longshoremen, they'll still be there.'

He was drumming his fingers on the desk. 'Lady, lemme tell you one thing. I don't go on what I don't have. I go on what I know. I started with the department in '12. In '13 I was a patrolman. I was on the dock beat. That day, the day you say it happened, I remember that day. It was the first time I was sent to patrol the docks.'

She waited.

'Y'see, there was a strike, a lightning strike by the long-shoremen, because the Port Authority or the shippers, I'm not sure, it was very cold, they wouldn't pay the wages and they wouldn't give the men proper working gloves either. So the longshoremen went out and the shippers, they hired some scabs. It was scabs on the docks, that day. I bet your husband didn't know that. Hardly any of the crews did. Y'see, the men, the union men, the longshoremen, they were kept back, way behind the gates. They didn't even get into the docks that day. I know the scabs couldn't do the work. I know there were accidents that day. I also know, I *guess*, some things happened weren't accidents. I do know that the shore office of Pacific Hunter were the first to refuse the men's wage demands. Could've been chance, could've been design, I tell you one thing, lady, a man like your husband dies, he doesn't die by happenstance. Either there's an accident, clear as day, or he was killed.' He stopped talking, shook his head. 'Thing is, lady, don't ever quote me, but this here city's the best in the world if you want to commit a murder. Right now, anyway. City won't pay the money it'd cost to investigate every suspicious death. Lessen you're lucky enough to be killed in broad daylight in front of witnesses who'll talk, then chances are you'll be buried and forgotten about.'

She got up. 'To hell with you, Officer Connors.'

His eyes widened. 'Lady, it ain't me, it's the police department.'

'To hell with the police department,' she said, 'to hell with the lot of you. *To hell with New York!!!*'

It was late afternoon when she got out of the filthy air of the New York City police department into the street, where the day was so hot, the sun felt like a ball of flame that reached out of the sky and scorched the sidewalks, and made the telephone and telegraph wires above droop like the fibres of a tweed when the loom had split. She wandered aimlessly for a while, heading vaguely for Fulton Market, which she had heard about from the boys, who were working as barrowlads for a wholesale grocer. Tam was so proud of that, his job, his pay of 75 cents a day and whatever vegetables were left when the market closed. In his last letter, he had told her that he and Willie were saving hard to buy a stall for themselves and then a motor lorry to deliver groceries to customers.

Dreaming, she missed the Fulton turning, and carried on all the way to Wall Street where daylight was obliterated by the cables that hung from every window of every floor of every building, frayed like a widow's weeds.

The irony was that she understood the detective, knew there was truth in what he said, that if Marcus was murdered, that even though Marcus had been murdered, she would never know who, or how; only why. And she knew why already, without asking any more questions, hearing any more lies. Marcus's honesty had been his death sentence, along with his loyalty to old Allan Rankine. If he had kept quiet about the smuggling and overloading, he would be alive to this day.

She went back to her hotel, eased her clothes off and had a long, cool shower. Although she had not eaten, she was not hungry. For a long time she lay thinking, until sleep came in the small hours of the morning. She did not dream.

In the morning, she washed quickly and breakfasted on a pot of coffee that a waiter brought to her room. She had written to the lawyer whose name was on the deeds of the property in Montauk; she phoned and left a message with his secretary that she would see him later that day. The bellboy told her how to get to Brooklyn; there were many ways but she decided to use the boat, at least ferry travel was familiar to her.

The ferry was docked in the shadow of the Brooklyn Bridge, a tiny little spluttering boat that still stubbornly plied its trade though the real need for it had been gone for years. Tia bought her ticket and drifted out into the river, where she felt a breeze for the first time in days.

On the Brooklyn side she boarded a tram headed for Flatbush.

The station of the Long Island Rail Road was on Flatbush Avenue, next to the IRT station, which could have brought her from Manhattan in half the time. Tia felt drained, unable to think straight.

She bought a ticket, stumbling over the destination and did not catch the directions she got from the bored booking clerk, his pencil hovering over a paper listing runners in a dog race; it was too hot to run and she felt fleeting sympathy for the animals. The waiting room was oak-clad and stifling; she passed it and the tobacco stall, heading directly for the stairs to the tracks. There, she paused; the alternatives confused her. It was just before ten o'clock; she could take either the express or the local train; All Stops to Jamaica.

The irony struck her then; Marcus's last voyage had been to Kingston before it docked at Charleston, before it ended at New York. The string of sounds from the ticket collector made sense now: Jamaica Line; change at Hicksville for Babylon.

As the train pulled out from the station, filled with mothers and children, women with shopping bags, Jews and gentiles, a black woman with a bundle, a sad-eyed black man, a greasy-haired Italian who studied his quiff in the window before he tugged at it with a comb, the cacophony of humanity that is New York closed around her; she was no longer isolated, a visitor, but one of them, a fellow member of the lost tribe of humanity that had struck out in search of freedom and built a New World on the ashes of the old.

The train pulled into Hicksville, where black and white boarding passengers stood at opposite ends of the platform. For a moment she stared at them, wondering why, until she remembered that she had to change here for Babylon; she got up in a flurry, grazing her head on the luggage rack, opening the door and causing the linesman to sound his whistle just as the train was beginning to move. Mouthing an apology, she walked to the waiting room, went in and sat down, grateful for the fan that spun lazily from the ceiling where the electric light should have been. A timetable pinned to the wall told her that she would have to wait ten minutes for the next train. She sat back, closed her eyes and did not move when she sensed someone else come in and sit down, coughing weakly and then again.

She opened her eyes, looking into the face of a black woman with a bundle of dirty linen by her ankles. Tia smiled at her lazily, looked through the window. The memory was too raw; it hurt too much to remember, but it would hurt much more if she tried to forget before she had done all she could to find out the truth.

''Scuse'm, Ma'am, but you be in black room, yo be. White room issin along de platfoahm.'

'I . . .' Tia gazed at her. 'I'm waiting for the train to Babylon,' she said. 'Do I change there for Montauk?'

'Do'noah, Ma'am, I done go to Babylon m'sel. Reckon yo go to white room and dey tell you der, maybe.'

Tia did not understand. She shook her head.

'Ma'am,' the woman said again. 'Yo in room foah black folk. Yo go to white-folk room. Heah for black folks only.'

'I . . .' She rose, grabbed her bag. 'I'm so sorry.'

'Doan be sorry, Ma'am.'

'I didn't know.'

'That's why I tell yoah.'

The woman bent down and began to fix the string on her bundle of dirty linen as Tia walked out into the blinding light of the Long Island noon.

The train came; at Babylon it halted for five minutes, then carried along to the end of the line as she watched the farmland, the wheat that grew like candlyfloss, streaked by the motion of the train, the farmer's placard against the railroad that had burned his fields with sparks from its smokestack, the burned-out station where an anonymous countryman had taken his revenge at an encroachment of civilisation that had brought devastation to his crops. She cried tears of pain and loss and loneliness then pinched herself to remind herself where she was.

The lawyer was in Amangasset; once she reached Montauk and found nothing but the station building she had to take the same train back to Amangasset then walk along the single street until she found his sign hung over the drug store that offered cures for everything from apoplexy to unhappiness.

He was an old man, vaguely plump in his trousers and waistcoat, his shirt stretched over his stomach.

'I waited,' he said, 'else I'd've been in the saloon.'

She smiled.

'I rented Captain Cameron's place,' he said, when she handed him the papers, the deeds and Marcus's death certificate. 'He left four hundred dollars in the bank, but when I didn't hear from him when y'all were at the war, thought I better get a tenant in when I'd a chance. Place was empty, and there's a dozen acres where a crop could grow, and grazing land for a few cattle. So I got in a tenant and paid the taxes that way. Here. You see. Eight hundred dollars in his account now.'

The figures on the page of the ledger blurred into a wavy line.

369

Each year, the land tax had been paid to the county and the state, a fee of $10.00 deducted as well.

'That's me,' the lawyer said. 'Paid myself. Captain told me to, so I did.'

She nodded. 'The tenants?'

'Good folks, they are. Land's not as good as some hereabouts. Too close to the ocean. Too salt. But they made it as best they could, paid rent regular as the church clock chimes on Sunday morn.'

'Oh.'

'I have a vehicle outside, Ma'am. I told 'em you're coming, an' they'll have made a spread for you. The Cap'n's things are there, too. I piled 'em all into one room an' locked it when I figured he wasn't coming back, not till the end of the war, at least. I tried to do right, Ma'am. I hope you're not upset.'

'No,' she murmured. She had been in New York barely two days; the excitement and shock had worn her out.

The lawyer followed a track etched into the scrub that followed the sea around Napeague Bay, then stumbled until Montauk station was in sight, when the track veered left and he followed it to a little house set amidst fields full of potatoes and turnips.

'Montauk's going to be developed,' he told her. 'Get a good price for this, specially the Atlantic side.'

'The Atlantic side?'

'The Cap'n's land's either side of the railroad, right down to the ocean on the other side. He was going to build another house there, but he never got around to it. I reckon he loved this place.'

'Loved?'

'The ocean, Mrs Cameron, Ma'am. The Cap'n used to stand right there on a summer's morn and watch the sun come up over the Atlantic. He said he could see his way home from here. East north-east. Or something. I donno. A landlubber, that's me. You see.'

The car stopped, and a thin young woman came out and opened the door for her. Tia stepped out and saw the chickens in the yard, the children playing, a dog asleep under the shade of the porch.

The woman had made bread, apple pie, a chocolate cake.

The spread was arranged on the kitchen table with a pat of farmyard butter and a glistening ham, half sliced, with bowls of pickles.

The lawyer left, once he told her to get in touch if she needed anything.

'Will you be staying, Missus?' the woman asked, her accent Irish, traced with America and a harshness that Tia realised was Belfast.

She looked around at the wooden floor, whitened with many scrubbings, the rag rug, the twin chairs, the cushions carefully hand-stitched and stools for the children.

'Wil, that's my man, Wil, he had to go to bring the cows in. He'll be back soon. We didn't know when you'd be coming, see?'

Tia nodded.

The woman gestured that she should sit down.

Tia shook her head. 'I'll just go to my husband's room, if you don't mind.'

The woman showed her up a narrow stairway, a ladder made safe by the addition of rails, and left her once Tia had opened the door.

The attic room was dusty and dry; she coughed, and waited for her eyes to adjust to the low light before she found a chair and sat. From the kitchen the woman called upstairs to ask her if she needed a lamp.

'No,' Tia croaked, clearing her throat and repeating the word when she guessed that the other woman hadn't heard.

In the room was a set of old clothes, a homespun jacket and trousers, a pair of rubber boots. The desk held papers, but not personal ones, there were newspapers and union newsletters, a copy of the *New York Times* dated May 1912, a scribbled column of figures where Marcus had counted his money and worked out how much to leave in New York. There were no answers here.

She realised then that he had never lived there, had never even stayed there for more than a night, but had bought this place to be a home for them both and the children they would have . . . would have had. She blinked and found the final piece of paper, a scrawled note from the old owner, a Tom McKenzie, formerly of Seabost, wishing Marcus 'and your dear intended, all the good luck and the Grace of God in your new home'.

She broke down, cried for a while, then wiped her eyes and began to put the papers away.

During the journey she had listened with half an ear as the lawyer had gassed on about a wealthy man who was buying land, who was going to turn Montauk into a town just like the resorts further down the line, like Wainscott or the Hamptons.

There was a skylight set into the roof; standing on tiptoe she looked out over the dunes and the railroads, towards the distance where she sensed through the heat haze the blankness of the Atlantic.

She took off her suit jacket and loosened the neck of her blouse before she unpinned her hair and shook it free.

In the kitchen the woman was beginning to prepare the family's evening meal.

'Willie won't be a minute, so he won't,' she said, 'don't know what's holding him, sure I don't. Should've been here hours ago, he should. See? Isn't that men for you?'

Tia smiled. 'I'm leaving now.'

The woman put down the bowl of vegetables, reaching for a rag to wipe her hands. 'I'll hitch up the trap, have you at the station in no time. Sure and I don't know what he's playing at.'

'No', Tia said, too quickly, adding when she saw the woman's face fall that she had time to walk to the station, she wanted to.

Outside the house, she walked due west, across the railway track and over the dunes, until she reached the long stretch of sands where the breakers rolled.

She sat down at the water's edge, letting the waves brush her bare toes, then her feet, then her ankles. The events of the day thumped her memory, tumbling against her recollection of the past years, of Marcus's death, of her slow realisation that the accident was not an accident, but that Marcus's death was meant to be.

Anger tore her soul apart, ripped at the cords of her heart like myriad tiny knives that jabbed and stabbed and left her aching and sore, crying so hard that her eyes felt as if they would burst and pour out her soul to meld with the pounding waves. The tide ran in, soaking her skirt, then rising to her waist, dragging her skirt to and fro like seaweed straining at its roots.

That shocked her, momentarily, caused her to rise and walk up the sands until she found a dune cushioned softly with grass where she sank down flat on her back and stared at the burning ball of the sun overhead.

'Let me go,' Marcus said.

She did not listen at first.

'Let me go,' he said again, so loudly that she jerked up and looked all around to see where his voice was coming from, to search his mind, the soul that spoke to her still despite the years that had gone and the body that he had lost.

'No,' she said. '*NO!*' she yelled, catching a glance of the echo that rolled back from the distant bluff.

A wind rose and whipped her face, not harshly but hard enough to dry her tears, make her narrow her eyes against it.

'Let me go,' he said again.

She stared at the void of the ocean for a long time before she murmured that yes, she would, she would let him go if that is what he really wanted her to do.

The wind died as suddenly as it had come up, drawing the last of her agony out and away to the place beyond the horizon where she knew that the man she loved, and always would love, would be; waiting for her, watching over her, until with the grace of God they would meet again and laugh at the pain she had felt because she had not obeyed her promise not to mourn what was not death but simply a parting of ways for twin souls that had divided suddenly but not for ever, to join again in time.

Some time.

If she could only believe in God again, in heaven, in the promise of a faith that had caused her such pain.

# *Chapter Twenty-one*

*T*he sense of peace stayed with her during the journey back to Manhattan, along the length of the Long Island Railroad and then back to Manhattan by the IRT. It was late evening when she returned to the hotel and ordered supper in her room, where she took out the copy she had made of Marcus's log and addressed it to Andrew Furuseth, the President of the American Seaman's Guild at Washington, with a brief note explaining what it was and why she was sending it to him.

Jimmy Henderson in Glasgow had told her that if anyone could do something, Furuseth could, but since Pacific Hunter no longer worked the transatlantic routes she doubted if it would mean anything. The line had reported *My Lady* sold for scrap at Shanghai the voyage after Marcus's, but a crewman had told the Seaman's Union that an identical vessel was plying the South China routes under the colours of Pacific Hunter's affiliate Chinese line. That way, Jimmy Henderson told her, the Board of Trade would not be able to ask any questions, even if she managed somehow to excite their curiosity. *My Lady* had, in effect, vanished from the surface of the earth, the new vessel was manned by crew recruited from the Philippines and Shanghai who did not even know that a Seaman's Union existed, and would be too scared to join even if they did.

She signed the note and took it to the lobby to post in the mail box, knowing that she had done all she could.

The following morning she woke up feeling the same sense of peace, looking forward to seeing the boys again.

Tia was amazed at the change a few months had made to her nephews. Willie now stood his full six feet, the shoulder slump of old vanished like the stern cast of his face that had rarely smiled, almost always frowned. Tam was wearing a cap back to front, a jaunty grin beneath. They took her, reluctantly, to their room on the Bowery, not quite a slum but not a palace either, a clean, spartan place that they shared with two other Scotsmen, each paying $1.50 in rent to the landlady for the bed and clean sheets once a fortnight, a shower every night and a bath on Sundays, if they wanted one.

They ate their meals in a little cafe along the street from their lodging, that advertised on its window soup and bread for five cents, a plate of stew for ten cents. At first Tia had had ideas of taking them somewhere, maybe to midtown or Central Park, but they wanted to show her their New York and so they walked around, along the Bowery first, where they showed her the barbers' schools and then the Scotch Indian outside the Snuff Shop on Division Street, then along Hester Street where kosher restaurants jostled for custom with the chicken market and the Guaranteed Kosher Butcher, then down to the docks where they proudly showed her Fulton Market, where they worked from midnight till mid day and sometimes longer, bartering and carting fruit and veg which they sold on for a reasonable profit.

Very proudly, after they had walked back, Willie took her by the arm and led her into the Blossom Restaurant, where he grandly ordered sirloin steaks all round, and got change from two dollars even after he had ordered coffee and apple pie as well.

Fleetingly she felt regret that she had not been able to give them the purpose that this new city had, that there were in Glasgow few, if any, opportunities for young men whose only assests were their native wit and their strength.

The boys walked her along Broadway, all the way back to her hotel.

'I was going to take you to a show,' she said, as they passed the Grand Opera.

Willie, determined, put his hands in his pockets. 'There's time for that later, Auntie Tia. Right now, I've work to do, and so has Tam.'

'D'you come up this way much?'

Tam grinned. 'All the time. Willie even marked out the place he wants to live when he makes his first million.'

'Where's that, Fifth?'

Willie shook his head. 'Park. Fifth'll be taken over the stores soon. Wait and see.'

'And how will you make your million, Willie?' she asked, half joking.

His eyes narrowed. 'I'm not sure how yet. I just know I will.'

Her eyes turned misty for a moment as she thought of Mairead.

'Don't worry,' Tam said, 'he'll not go brewing hootch. He can't stand the smell, you see. However he makes his million, he'll make it legally.'

She laughed. 'I don't doubt he will, Tam.'

Willie's ambition broke for a moment into a smile almost as broad as the avenue. 'We had enough of being poor back home. If we weren't poor, Pa wouldny've got himself hurt, Ma wouldny've died. Maybe. Don't want to take a chance like that again.'

They would not come into the hotel for tea because it was already ten in the evening, and they had to go to work at midnight.

Tia had saved one day for herself, to have a last stroll down the Avenue, to Bendels on 57th Street and then way down to Union Square to have another look at Klein's, the woman's dress store just opposite Lafayette's statue.

She had been to Seventh Avenue, the sweatshops at the lower end and the manufacturers in the Middle District, watched rails of garments being pushed along the road like trams, and models as haughty as Liberty carelessly throwing off a $100,000 sable just for effect. An Astor or a Vanderbilt, she wasn't sure which, had paid that sum for a fur and now the furriers were vying with each other to see who could make the most extravagant coat of sable or chinchilla lined with silver brocade, with gold or platinum buttons sprinkled with diamonds that glinted like cats' eyes through the pile of the fur. She had touched sable so fine that one pelt could be pulled through a button hole, leather shaved so thin that it felt like silk, evening gowns embroidered with real pearls, rubies and sapphires.

The open display of wealth astounded her, especially the easy way that the Guggenheims flaunted the profits they had made in the war. There was an exuberance in the streets that felt strange to her, accustomed as she was to the grief that haunted Glasgow and all of Europe. In this city anything and everything was possible, the past was gone and the future was everything. She felt the promise that had drawn Tam and Willie and so many others to these shores.

Klein's intrigued Tia almost as Bendel's did, the way that store brazenly advertised its copies of Paris, flaunting them with such zeal that it was if they were thumbing their noses at the most expensive stores.

Of all the New York shops, it was Bendel's that had struck her as the most fashionable, the most in tune with the times. Henry Bendel, a Lousiana Cajun with just a crinkle in his hair, had met her and given her tea in a delightful little room decorated discreetly with just a touch of Louis Quinze in the gilded mirror and the legs of the chairs that were upholstered with Bendel's trademark cream and brown stripe.

From his eyrie on 57th Street, Henry Bendel promoted style in the true sense of the word and gently mocked the New York matrons who vied with each other to visibly display their wealth. That month, the hottest that anyone of consequence spent in the city before the exodus of August, his windows were dressed with plain white linen divided skirts and blouses, beautifully cut, sweaters almost like a man's slung carelessly over shoulders as his plaster models sailed, played tennis, toyed with golf sticks.

'I make clothes for women who live, you see,' he said, after she had flicked through his cuttings from the *New York Times*, studied the louche pyjama trousers that had scandalised the editors of American *Vogue*. 'Some of these ladies, these women,' – he paused and waved dismissively towards Millionaires' Row – 'they do not live, they exist to boast and flaunt their husbands' wealth.'

She showed him her own designs, those she had been working on for the autumn, the loose jackets and skirts with just two pleats, front and back, for ease of movement.

'I like these, but you may just be a little before your time,' he said.

She showed him the drawing of the Hebridean tweed jackets with velvet appliqué.

'That is *style*,' he said. 'Are you taking orders?'

She shook her head. 'I wanted your reaction, that's all.'

An assistant came to the door then to tell him that an important customer had arrived; he sighed theatrically and left, asking her to call in to see him when she was next in New York.

Tia stood, staring at his window displays for a long time before she turned reluctantly back to the hotel, where she checked her notes and then packed quickly before she went down to the lobby and ordered afternoon tea, sitting at a table alone, trying not to feel too lonely as other people chatted and laughed.

'Excuse me,' a voice said, a voice that was faintly American, but almost Scottish as well, 'but I think that all the other tables are taken. Would you mind very much if I joined you?'

She frowned reflexively, glancing around and seeing that what the man said was true, at least for the moment, though there were two tables nearby that looked as if they would be vacant soon.

There was something familiar about him, in his grey eyes and shock of brown hair, the easy way he stood there smiling at her as if nothing else mattered except the empty chair.

She began to rise, but he held up a hand to stop her. 'Please, I didn't mean to chase you away.'

'I was about to leave,' she said.

'Please don't. At least, not because of me. I can stand. I've been standing for a while anyway.'

'You can't have tea standing up!'

'Why not? I might as well. That way, one of the waitresses might notice me.'

She laughed.

'I'm Jimmy Cavanagh,' he said, shaking her hand briefly but firmly. 'Aren't you the woman I saw in Lord and Taylor's the other day?'

She thought for a moment. She had spent half a day in the store, studying the way goods were displayed on tables and rails, not in glass cases, how the less formal layout seemed to make people more likely to buy. 'I might have been,' she said carefully, wondering where she had seen him before. There was something about him, perhaps the openness of his face, that made her trust him, and she waved him to the empty chair. In

Glasgow, she would never take tea with a stranger; in New York she had the confidence to follow her instincts.

'I'm Tia Cameron, Mrs Cameron.'

'What brings you to New York, Mrs Cameron?'

Her face became serious. 'Some family business, also I work for a big store in Glasgow and I've been looking at the big stores here.'

'And what did you make of them?'

'Americans are brazen by our standards. At home, it's not quite the done thing to flaunt your wealth.'

He looked around for a waitress, but could not attract her attention.

'I hope you don't think I'm being forward, but would you like to join me for tea at the the Plaza instead?'

'I'd love to,' she said, then immediately wished she could bite back her words; she hardly knew him, yet felt instinctively that this man was destined to become a friend. It was the openness of New York that made her accept his invitation; the energy of the city that helped her to take a risk.

The Plaza was a gilded fairyland, a baroque fantasy that mixed the Sun King with a proto-Michelangelo and got away with it, the same audacity that allowed Sam Klein to put up a placard outside his store telling the outrageous lie that the World's Best Dressed Women Shop Here.

Tia stepped into the lounge beside Jimmy Cavanagh, her cheek swiped by a passing palm frond, her mouth gaping as she saw a diamond tiaraed woman taking tea at a table underneath which her pet cub leopard crouched. She had a plate of sandwiches and another of steak, and every so often would toss the beast a morsel that it devoured in one gulp. The waiters and the other customers were completely unconcerned.

Jimmy Cavanagh was known here; as soon as the head waiter saw him he strode forward and led them to a table, a prime spot for watching the clientele under the shadow of one of the vast plaster columns. Tia spent fully five minutes looking around before her eyes returned to him. There was a quaint little smile on his face, and he shrugged indulgently when she apologised for ignoring him.

'What d'you think?'

'It's kind of hard to believe.'

'D'you think it might work in Glasgow?'

She laughed. 'Everything but the leopard. He would end up being skinned.'

He looked wistful. 'I've been to Glasgow quite a few times.'

'Oh?'

'I have family there.'

Tia smiled. 'I might know them. I don't mean it like that. I mean MacDonald's is like, well, it's a bit like a mixture of Lord and Taylor and Saks, our customers come from far and wide but mostly they're pretty well off.'

He nodded to himself. 'How many of them are called Cavanagh?'

'How come they know you so well at the Plaza?'

He laughed, put on a broad Irish brogue and told her that some of the Irish had done quite well over here.

They talked right through the afternoon, until the tendrils of evening made lacy trails of the railings around Central Park.

Afternoon tea was over, the salon in the hiatus before the evening; Jimmy Cavanagh stretched and yawned. 'I don't suppose I could persuade you to have dinner with me?'

Tia was surprised that she wanted to. 'I should've told you,' she said, 'I'm a widow.'

His face flashed pain.

'It was a long time ago. But my husband, he came here. He was a ship's captain. He bought some land up in Montauk.'

'I would enjoy your company,' he said.

'Where . . . what shall I . . .'

'We'll start at Sherry's. Usually dinner there turns into something of a party, but you must wear whatever you want.'

He was waiting when she walked down the stairs of the Murray Hill Hotel, dressed in the Fortuny Delphos with the matching cape, the scarf tied around her brow, her hair arranged gently in a knot. As she dressed, she had been diffident, until she remembered M. Kassinsky and what Marcus had said when he talked to her on the beach. Jimmy Cavanagh was nice, kind, uncomplicated, not arrogant like Haldane Brodie; she sensed that she needed someone like him, at this time of her life, if only for an evening. She was sure she would never see him again.

His eyes met hers, followed her stately progress until when she stood before him he bowed deeply and then handed her a single orchid. 'Quite unnecessary,' he said, 'but I thought you would like the smell.'

A car was waiting outside the hotel, a long Duisberg driven by a chauffeur who wore his cap at a rakish angle and said, 'Sherry's now, Boss?' as he opened the door for Tia.

Jimmy Cavanagh eased himself into the seat beside her, wincing slightly, then smiling when he caught her look of concern.

The hatch between the back seat and the driver was open; the chauffeur kept up his chatter as the car travelled along Park, then turned into 44th Street, stopping at the corner of Fifth Avenue opposite Delmonico's.

Jimmy looked diffident. 'Maybe this is a bad idea.' he said.

'Ah, f'chrissakes, make up yah mind,' the chauffeur said. 'I gotta number running. I haffta be down the street to see if it comes up.'

Tia got out of the car, Jimmy wincing as he manoeuvred his leg on to the street. 'I always say, have a good relationship with your staff,' he said.

'I'll meet ya back here in a coupla hours,' the chauffeur said as he got back into the car, revving the engine roughly before he skidded around and headed downtown.

Tia gasped in surprise, as they walked into the reception area.

Sherry's was decorated in an American version of what Versailles would have been before the revolution curtailed the excesses of the French kings. Every inch of space was adorned by plasterwork, gilded and carved into nymphs and medallions, segmented by fluted pilasters framing flowering outgrowths that shed leaves and branches like a garden left to grow wild. The dining room was a fantasy of mirrors and chandeliers, topped by a mural so detailed that it defied description. The tables were set with porcelain, silver and crystal that shed light like diamonds, vases filled with a profusion of lilies and roses.

The hum of voices dropped as Tia walked in and took her place at a table in the centre of the room with Jimmy; women's faces turned to look at her as men's eyes followed her progress through the room. She let her cape fall over the back of the chair, where it was instantly whisked away by a waiter as another poured champagne from a black bottle with a gold label in the shape of a shield.

Jimmy smiled. 'I don't think they've seen a Fortuny before, else they're so jaded they've forgotten.' He leaned closer. 'These women are so fat a dress like that would make them look like a cherry fondant.'

Tia blushed.

'They're still doing a roaring trade in corsets here,' he hissed. 'Honestly, they have to truss themselves up like a Thanksgiving turkey to get into these awful dresses they wear.'

She took a sip of champagne, let the bubble blister and burst against the back of her throat.

'How come you know so much about fashion?'

'A lifelong fascination with the women who wear it,' he grinned. 'But don't go thinking I'm New York's answer to Don Juan. I trained as an architect, but then I got tied up with the family business.' He winced, and gave his attention to the menu for a moment. 'What would you like to eat?'

Tia looked at the menu, puzzled at the ornate frenchified phrases and ordered quail's eggs followed by chicken supreme as she wished for a moment she was back in the Blossom restaurant, where at least she undersood what each dish was.

Jimmy Cavanagh was smiling gently at her; he gave her order to the waiter, adding that he would have the same.

The chatter around them stilled again as Isadora Duncan strode in with her retinue and took a table not far from theirs. She was dressed in a white sheath over white pyjama trousers, adorned with gold chains that reached her waist. They eyes of her audience nearly popped out.

'I'd take you to see her,' Jimmy said, 'but you're leaving tomorrow, aren't you?'

She nodded. 'Your family business, what is it?'

He frowned. 'My father's a merchant. He's a partner in a business, a wholesale business really . . .'

'Oh?'

'There's not much more to tell, really. I'd rather design buildings, but I got dragged in. Duty, you know. My inheritance.' He laughed. 'The way things are going, I won't have one. They overbought during the war and now they've got a warehouse full of things they can't sell. When I hurt my leg, I couldn't get about on site easily, so I went in with Father. My mother nagged me like hell.' He winced again. 'You must think I'm weak.'

'I don't.'

'In any case, I'm going to have an operation on my leg soon. There's a surgeon who's going to try to graft a bit of bone on to my femur to fix it. If he manages it, I'll go back to architecture.'

'I see.'

'Until then, I'm the spoiled only son of parents who were wealthy once and think they still are.'

She laughed. 'I thought everyone here made a fortune from the war.'

He cocked his head to one side. 'A few did. A lot more tried and failed. My father's Scottish and my mother's Irish. The old country, you know. In his way my father did what he could to help.'

'Have you ever been to Scotland?'

'Och, aye. I used tae be able tae dae a guid Hielan' fling afore I jiggert ma leg.'

She laughed again. 'What happened?'

'A shooting accident.'

His face had turned grave.

As they ate they talked of little things, safe subjects like Henry Bendel's and the new vogue for sportswear, the dread rumour that prohibition was here to stay despite the open flaunting of the rules that went on at places like Sherry's and the Plaza.

The meal ended with peach melba and rich American coffee with lashings of sugar and cream.

'Do you like music?' he asked.

'Yes.'

'Well, if you like jazz there's a very good club quite close to here.'

'D'you mean the Cotton Club?'

He frowned. 'That's way up in Harlem. We can go if you like, but there's a better club quite close to here.'

The Duisberg was nowhere to be seen. 'Hell,' he said, 'we'll have to walk.'

The heat of the day had faded to a comforting warmth that held her like an embrace. 'Can you walk?' she asked.

'Oh, yes. It does me good to walk. Keeps the muscles exercised. The graft's got a better chance of working if the muscles are in good shape. I can't run though, or dance, or do anything like that.'

They walked up to Central Park, where a gentle breeze frilled the trees, through Scholar's Gate and along the path by the pond, where Jimmy paused and they sat down for a moment, listening to the birdsong that sounded above the racket of the city, and breathing the air leavened by moisture and the smell of grass. As they got up, Jimmy rubbed his thigh and winced; at the Artist's Gate they found a cab which whisked them alongside the park, screeched around Columbus Circle and came to a breath-stopping halt on a street of brownstone houses just off Broadway.

'This is a nightclub?' Tia said as Jimmy banged at a brass knocker on a heavy oak door.

'Wait till you see,' he said, as the door swung open. They were let in after a black man built like Goliath had stared them both up and down and then grinned broadly when Jimmy asked if Fats was there.

'Ya never know,' he said, 'don get e'rybody from Customs to FBI come heah.'

'I thought it was just the police,' Jimmy said.

'Don paid 'em off, we do. Police doan trouble us no moah.'

The music twisted up the stairs, a trail of notes so fast that when the door opened on the basement club the sound felt like a solid wall of noise that shocked her ears into quasi deafness for a moment before they adjusted and she heard the intricate rhythms and tunes that ran together and then separated, jostled and jived like the threads of some anarchic tapestry that held the tiny, smoke filled room entranced.

The piano sounded as if it was alive, the pianist's hands running up and down the keys, scampering like mice on scorching keys of ebony and ivory, as if the instrument was fighting the music. The tune wound on, like a bar brawl, growing louder and more strident with each moment, until suddenly the pianist, sweat pouring from his brow, pounded the same chord three times and then sat back and gave way to the briefest silence before the audience broke into resounding applause. To Tia, who had never been to a nightclub before, the place was a revelation, a playground for grown-ups where people danced and talked, drank and ate oblivious to the constraints of the city beyond. The musicians were black, the waitresses both black and white, arrogant and nonchalant, with pencils hitched into their hair and voices that rose above the cacophony, dumping orders on to customers' tables with all the finesse of coalmen. A man found space for her and Jimmy at a table in the corner, just beyond the tiny dance floor, abandoned them there as the first pianist bowed and left the piano and a younger, thinner one took over, singing a simple melody before he too broke into jazz.

They waited for a full quarter hour before a snarling waitress took Jimmy's order and came back with two bottles of beer, which she plumped unceremoniously in front of them.

'It's the only thing that's safe,' Jimmy hissed, pointing to the Canadian label. 'The spirits are hootch and the wine's dilute surgical spirit. I came here with a doctor friend and he swore that their claret is actually ACE.'

'What's ACE?

'Alcohol, chloroform and ether. The stuff they give you to put you to sleep. He said it was flavoured with raspberry cordial. He put a match to it, and it went up in smoke. It did. Honestly! Phewfft! We would've been thrown out 'cept he said he was trying to light a cigarette and lit his drink by mistake.'

He twisted the cap off with his teeth and handed the bottle to her.

The first pianist noticed him and came to sit down, and Tia caught that look again, the look that passed from Jimmy to everyone who knew him.

'Man,' the pianist said, as Jimmy handed him his beer and looked around for a waitress to bring him another. He turned to Tia. 'This's only white boy I know can play the piano.'

'Don't talk horse shit,' Jimmy said.

'Have it yoah way, man,' the piano player said amiably.

'This is Tia, Mrs Tia Cameron,' Jimmy said. 'This is J.P. Johnson, Jimmy Johnson, the best stride piano player in the whole of New York.'

'The whole of US of A, you mean.'

'Ya going on later?' J.P. Johnson asked Jimmy, who shook his head and said he didn't dare.

They stopped talking for a moment to listen to the man playing; he was singing a song of sadness, gentle, toning notes, as rich as velvet, within a moment changing the atmosphere from exhuberance to introversion.

'Blind Lemon,' J.P. said softly. 'Blind Lemon Jefferson.'

'Really?'

'Boy can't see his own nose, n'mind any moah. Boy was working as a wrestler in Dallas when we heard him and brought him up heah, but he a Southern boy, he goan back to New Orleans acos he cain't stand the city winter. Freeze a man's soul, he said.'

As the song finished, the audience clapped and threw dollar bills on to the tiny stage, which one of the waitresses collected and gave to Blind Lemon as he smiled his thanks and began to play again.

'Theah is a spot foah you,' J.P. said. 'After Blind Lemon and Fats and the Duke.'

Jimmy gave up waiting for the waitress and stole a beer from the next table, tossing a dollar down in its place.

'You could have mine,' Tia said.

'I could not!'

'You see,' she blushed, 'I'm not drinking it. I don't really like it.'

J.P. frowned. 'What sort of chicken shit is this, Jimmy? You bring a lady heah and you buy her a beer?'

'I didn't want to poison her.'

'Shit, man.' He got up and went through a door behind the stage, coming back with a bottle wrapped in a napkin; disguised as cola, it was claret, the real thing. He even had a glass, a heavy tumbler that he wiped with the napkin before he plonked it down in front of her. 'I'm sorry, Mam, don't you go thinkin' we don't know how to treat a lady at the Double Deuces.'

She laughed.

'My hands are stiff,' Jimmy said.

'They *will* be, man, iffen you doan play.'

'I'll get laughed off.'

'This ain't no Savoy, man. We is kind to the white man heah. We is tolerant of our pale brethren.'

Jimmy turned to Tia. 'Should I play, or shouldn't I?'

She shrugged. 'Why not?'

Tia's heart was pounding as Jimmy took the stage after Blind Lemon's blues, played a shimmering chord that he stretched out like elastic before he pounded the keys and launched into a rhythm that had the dance floor jumping.

'Mam, I hardly dare ask,' J.P. Johnson said, 'but would you dance with me?'

'Of course I will,' Tia said, 'if I can.'

The dancers were moving strangely, jerkily in time with the rhythm, spinning on one heel and then the other, she had never seen anything like it before. 'I come from Scotland,' she said, 'I've never danced like this before.'

He took her by the hand and made a little space on the floor, then began to pull her towards him and then push her away, spinning her one way and then the other, until she caught the idea and began to dance herself. She caught Jimmy out of the corner of her eye, waved at him and he waved back, playing with one hand until he started a new tune with the other.

They danced for ages; sweat pouring from her brow but she didn't care, the Fortuny was so light she felt she was dancing on air. Halfway through, a saxophonist and a trumpet player came on and played along with Jimmy; and a photographer with a huge cumbersome New Graphic camera took pictures, the flash exploding and giving off sour fumes of phosphorus that caught in her throat.

'That's the Duke,' J.P. yelled. 'He's making a recording. They taking picture for the record cover.'

'What's a record?'

'A victrola. Mam, doan yo know *nuthing*?'

The music stopped suddenly; winded, she slumped down in her seat, as J.P. wiped his brow and Jimmy fanned her with his handkerchief.

J.P. said he hoped Jimmy didn't mind him dancing with his woman.

Tia blushed scarlet, so red that she excused herself and ran for the ladies' room.

In the mirror, a look of happiness stared back at her. The time had passed in a flash; half a day since she had met Jimmy Cavanagh; fleetingly, she frowned at the thought that time had not sped by like that since she had been with Marcus. Her hair was damp, matted to her brow; she struggled with a comb for a while, thinking of Jimmy, wondering if she would ever see him again in Glasgow. The attraction was so strong, it was as if a magnet was pulling her towards him.

When the club closed at five o'clock in the morning Jimmy took her by the arm and they walked slowly back to Park Avenue, as the morning chorus of birds heralded a new day.

He draped his jacket around her shoulders because the air was sharp and cool.

'I had a wonderful time,' she said.

He looked down at the ground; she could tell that his leg was sore.

'Can I get them to call you a cab, Jimmy?'

He grinned. 'I can manage, Mrs Cameron.'

'I wish you would call me Tia.'

He nodded shyly. 'Maybe, if . . .'

'If what?'

'If this surgeon cures my leg, maybe we could go dancing together next time.'

'I would like that, Jimmy.'

'I'm sure we will meet again, Tia Cameron,' he said, as he gave her a cheery wave and then turned and walked off jerkily along Park Avenue. She stood watching him, feeling a strange sense of regret.

Alone in her room, she took off the precious Foruny and eased it into its sheath, then put it in the top of her case, along with the orchid, which she wrapped in tissue paper and then put in the glove box she had bought from the wholesaler on 7th Avenue. MacDonald's had glove boxes of their own, but she thought that the American one was more stylish, more suitable for customers who could pay up to five guineas for a pair of the finest silk-lined kid gloves.

She gazed at it for ages before she finally closed the case and secured the buckles of the leather straps around it.

She felt light-headed, strangely energetic, though she should have been tired.

She smiled when she thought of Jimmy Cavanagh, of how easily the hours had passed in his company. With a twinge she remembered Marcus, then Cal, then immediately the pain on

Jimmy's face when he had turned to walk away. She did not have his address and he did not have hers; she panicked for a moment before she thought that she had no right to.

When the bellboy knocked softly at her door at 6.30, she was still in her underclothes. She wrapped her gown around her and he brought in her breakfast and then left with her case.

She dressed quickly, putting her night things into the valise she carried, then walked downstairs and paid the bill before she got into the waiting taxi and headed for the docks. The desk clerk had handed her a letter, the address typed, which she put in her bag without opening it, assuming it was some mundanity connected with the store.

The passengers boarded quickly and the big liner began to part from the dock, roped to its tugs like a dead stag being dragged by a pack of terriers. She stood on deck as New York faded, this time thinking not of Marcus but of Jimmy Cavanagh, and the magical sense of fun she felt when she was with him.

It was almost as if she was young again, a virgin rather than a widow. Deep in her bones, she felt the same sense of longing, the same need to look around to see if he was there, although she knew that he would not be.

'*I'm sure we will meet again, Tia Cameron.*'

She shook her head in an effort to move off the meandering trail her mind was following.

Jimmy Cavanagh was a nice man, an immigrant New Yorker who still felt something for his old country, as all New Yorkers did. A pleasant escort for an evening, a kind and gentle man who made her feel comfortable and happy to be herself.

He had become a friend within the few hours she had known him.

Circumstances decreed he would never be more than that.

Just a friend, that is all, she told herself.

In her cabin she checked that the steward had unpacked her bag and then sat down on her bed and opened the letter.

*

*American Federation of Labour Building
Washington, D.C.*

*25 July 1919*

Dear Mrs Cameron,

*I was very sorry to recieve your letter, and to hear of the very sad way in
which your husband died. Captain Cameron was respected and loved
not only by his own crews, but by everyone who worked with him at the
Port of New York. As you were informed by the docks Police, there was
a longshoreman's strike on the day your husband died and for that
reason our brother members were locked out of the port. The Pacific
Hunter's line is one which we have long advised our members to refuse
to sail on and indeed we have no member with the line and have not had
for years, because it is the line's practice to hire foreign crews who are
not protected by either the laws of the United States of America or
membership of our Union.*

*I am ashamed that you were treated in such a careless manner by the
Port Authority police. I shall, of course, lodge a complaint because they
have no right to treat the widow of a member of our affiliate union like
that. I will do what I can to try to discover more about your husband's
death and I will write again once I have talked with our branch
members to let you know what I find out and also to let you know of the
response of the Port Authority police. In the meantime I hope you will
accept both my most sincere condolences and also the wish that you will
not judge all Americans by the reception you recieved from the Port of
New York police.*

*Yours Sincerely
Andrew Furuseth*

Clutching the letter in her hands, she broke down and sobbed.
She was still crying when the liner left its tugs beyond the
Verrazano Narrows, and steamed towards the emptiness of the
ocean and her own country, three thousand miles away.

Haldane Brodie met her at the quayside, as he had promised.
He was still courting her in his way; her protestations that she
did not want to marry again had no effect on him.

'I trust you had a pleasant trip, Tia.'

She nodded and waited as the porter put her bags into the
boot of his car.

'You look a little pale, if I might say so.'

'The sea was a bit rough.'

The journey to her home passed in silence.

'I will see you on Monday,' Haldane said.

She remembered herself. 'I have a written report,' she said, 'but I'd like to get it typed for the board to read before I talk to you all.'

'That is an excellent idea, Mrs Cameron. We are giving a luncheon for the Memorial Fund in the Central Hotel in a fortnight. I trust you will be there.'

'Of course,' she said. 'I'll give you a list of my customers who might buy tickets.'

'Please, Mrs Cameron, if they are customers, they must be our guests. The directors are giving the luncheon to announce their donation to the fund. It is very generous, if I say so myself.'

She smiled and excused herself just as soon as the chauffeur had carried her bags up the stairs and left them at her door.

# Chapter Twenty-two

$S$amuel Weinstock peered at her over the little half-moon glasses he had taken to wearing on the end of his nose ever since he had misread a bill from his button supplier and sent the company a cheque for £118/10/- and not the £11/18/- they had asked for.

It was only Tia and his wife Miriam who understood his terror of debt, the horror that his experience with the US German Guitar Zither Company had branded him as a thief for ever, despite the fact that he had long since paid back all the people who had bought the zithers.

'There is something different about you, Tia,' he said.

She smiled. During the afternoon she had spent on the beach at Montauk her face had tanned golden and when she looked at herself in the mirror it was as if a different woman looked back

In the island summer, her skin had always been like that, golden brown against her honey hair, which bleached almost silver in the sun, but in her years in the city her skin had stayed the same pale tone all year round.

'I have a sun tan,' she said.

He reached over the desk that was piled with bills and sketches, swatches of cloth and scribbles, all the debris of his working life, and put his hand over hers. 'It's more than that, darlink Tia. It is your grief. Your mourning for your husband is finally over. You have healed at last, no?'

She winced and looked away for a moment before she told him that she had. That morning, she had received a letter from Andrew Furuseth which told her of a rumour at the docks that Pacific Hunter had hired a thug to kill Marcus, that the rumour could not be substantiated because the man involved had been killed in a brawl a year later.

Samuel nodded to himself, lifted his glasses and wiped his eyes. 'To business,' he said, jumping up from his seat and leading her over to a rail of coats. 'I could let you have the lot for fifty pounds, Tia. Wool serge, tailored. A cancelled order from the Polytechnic. That's just one pound per garment. The order was five dozen, but the girls have taken some themselves.'

He pulled a coat from the rack and held it before her. Tia stepped back and looked at it, then took the hanger from him and examined the seams, the lining, the fold of the collar.

'It's a nice-looking coat, Sammy.'

'Tia, I charge Andrew thirty shillings a piece, and even then I make *bubkes*. One pound a garment is costing me money.'

She looked around the workroom. All the machinists were busy; two tailors worked on the cutting table so fast that the movement of their scissors was a blur that caught the reflection of the sunlight and scattered it around like a cascade of splintered diamonds.

She touched the cloth, rubbing a fold between her fingers. It was wool serge, that was true, but it was not good quality, it was the mediocre fabric churned out by the mile by the Lancashire mills. The coat would wear, but it would not wear well. After a few pressings, the cloth would become shiny and dull, the tailoring would sag. She could sell it as a special in the inexpensive mantles sale, but it would never pass muster in the fashion deparment proper.

She held it away from her and looked it up and down one final time. 'All right, Sammy, I'll take the lot, but you have to change the buttons.'

He frowned, his face turning hard and hurt all of a sudden. 'The buttons are good, Tia. What do you expect for a pound a piece? Solid gold? With pavé diamond inset, perhaps?'

She laughed. 'What I want, Sammy, is the navy brass-rimmed ones I saw on my way in.'

'One pound and sixpence.'

She shook her head.

'One pound and fourpence.'

She said nothing.

'Tia, these buttons are a penny each. It costs time to change, and the girls are busy. I have to pay overtime.'

'You're a hard man, Sammy.'

'You're a hard woman, Tia. You and I, we should go into business together. We get shops in the suburbs, we make a fortune . . .'

She laughed.

'I tell you, Tia, in a year we put MacDonald's out of business.'

She laughed again.

'You think of it, Tia, like Meg's Pegs, but more expensive . . .'

'I will, Samuel,' she said, casting the notion out of her mind as utterly ridiculous.

They shook hands, and she left.

The summer sun was warm; she walked quickly along Argyle Street and into Buchanan Street, feeling the usual thrill when the doorman opened the doors of MacDonald's and welcomed her in with a flourish. She walked through the ground floor, nodding to the sales girls before she took the stairs to her own departments and saw that every assistant had a customer, even though it was only just before noon.

Her departments were doing well, despite the grim warnings of recession, strikes and industrial unrest. The chairman of the board, Sir Ian Stewart, had written her a letter to congratulate her on the sales figures from ladies' fashions for the six-month period ending in July, which had broken all records. Mercantile Glasgow, the heirs of the tobacco merchants and the sugar importers, the wives and daughters of the ship-builders and armaments manufacturers, the new rich who had made a fortune supplying the country's hunger for the artefacts of war, was spending money with a vengeance.

Just the other day she had heard one woman remark to another that her husband's works in Clydebank was laying off workers, that they could have done with the war lasting another year or two until their sons were through Fettes College. The women had spent the best part of a hundred pounds each on outfits for dinners and a ball to raise money for the Erskine Hospital.

Tia took satisfaction from her 'great success', but she did not feel a sense of triumph.

She enjoyed much more the Sunday morning shift she did in Meg's Pegs on the Gallowgate.

The rest of the summer passed without Tia knowing anything more of the season beyond the store's takings during the sales.

She tried to find Cal but, wherever he was, he did not want to be found, and she felt heartache for him as if he was her own brother. When she went to Glasgow Green to leave food, the older man she left it with told her that Cal would heal in time, but meanwhile there was nothing she could do to help him. The helplessness hurt her most of all; when she got back to Hyndland Brogan often had to coax her to eat. The only thing that cheered her was when a photo arrived from America, showing her dancing with J.P. and Jimmy Cavanagh playing the piano in the background. With it was a note from Jimmy saying he hoped the picture was a happy memory. She took it to Annan's and got it mounted and framed, then put in on her desk at work.

When autumn came, it took her by surprise; the first chill wind of winter came to the city on a day in October when the sun shone briskly as if it was June. Tia left the store in the light-weight linen suit she had copied from one of Bendel's. That night, she took out her sable-collared coat and steam pressed it for the following day, and also began to cut the Island-tweed suit she wanted to wear during the winter.

In November, Haldane Brodie appeared in her office un-expectedly; she had asked the girls to alert her to his little visits but that day they were short staffed because of the latest flu epidemic that was sweeping the country, killing men and women in their thousands, some because they could not afford to pay the doctor or they were so weak with malnutrition that they did not have the strength to fight off a disease that caused just a few days in bed in the wealthier part of town. Brodie's manner was pleasant for once, he had come just to make sure that the department was surviving with so few staff.

That night, he was waiting at the staff entrance when she left.

'Good evening,' he said. 'I mean, it's hardly a good evening, is it? If you don't object, I would be honoured to drive you home.'

The hailstones biting at her calves made her mumble nonsense and climb willingly into the passenger seat. She had not seen Brodie outside work since that evening when he mentioned marriage and she had fled. Since then, she had been to Montauk and said a proper goodbye to Marcus, now Jimmy

Cavanagh still danced in her memory, although she told herself often that she would never see him again. Haldane Brodie's manners were impeccable, but so formal that she spent most of her time with him on edge, for fear that she might make some tiny infraction of the rules. He had given her the job at MacDonald's; she did not doubt that he could take it away again, and she needed the money to make sure that she had enough for Cal's needs, if he ever came to her. She still blamed Brodie for that evening when she missed Cal; she would never forgive him for that. In a way, she was living a split life: during the day at MacDonald's she was the epitome of style; during the evenings and on Sundays she wore a shawl like everyone else. Brodie was part of her life at the store; she wanted him to have nothing to do with her life outside it.

The hailstones battered at the roof, made little round bumps on the surface of the windscreen. Talk was impossible; Tia was grateful for that. When they reached her close, she had thawed a little, and smiled warmly as she thanked him.

'I'm sorry that I can't ask you in,' she said, 'but I live alone.'

'I would love to, Mrs Cameron,' he said, 'but we mustn't throw fuel on the gossips' fire, must we?'

Tia got out of the car as fast as she could without breaking an ankle, a leg, or both.

It became Haldane Brodie's custom to drive her home from work. Once or twice, on particularly bitter mornings, he even collected her and Tia became accustomed to the attention he paid to her, the aura of power that surrounded him. His attentions took her mind off Cal, who she had not seen since before she went to America. She found herself looking forward to the ball of the Ruglonian Society that was held on the first Friday of December.

She made her own dress, a sheath of dark grey charcoal satin, its collar embroidered with jet and cushioned flowers. When the collar stood up, it framed her face; down, it was like a fur wrap, except infinitely more gracious. When she walked into the hall on Haldane's arm, every woman in the place noticed her and some gawped openly.

As she whirled around the room, she did not believe she was the same woman who went most nights to Glasgow Green to give food to the discharged soldiers in the hope she might see

Cal. In fact, as the colours before her eyes changed and twirled like a magic lantern, she knew she was not the woman she usually was, but an actress playing a part. She enjoyed the role, even relished it. When Haldane Brodie asked her to MacDonald's Christmas Dance, she agreed willingly.

At the Christmas dance the directors sat at a table on a rostrum, and did not participate beyond a quick foray on the floor for the opening waltz. Tia felt a fleeting anger at the condescension of their attitude, but she said nothing; it was more than her job was worth because she had been in enough trouble when she had backed the sales staff in a demand for increased wages. She wore a dress she had copied from the best sales line in French gowns, itself a copy of a Vionnet. She did not notice the young man who briefly visited the head table. During the evening, almost everyone came up, rather like schoolchildren on prize day, either to be grudgingly praised or just to thank the directors for arranging the dance. At the end of the evening Haldane Brodie drove her home in his habitual silence. When he drew to a halt outside her close, he did not immediately get out to open the door for her but instead sat listening to the crackling of the car engine once the ignition had been turned off.

'I've been thinking,' he said. 'Don't you feel that we should think about making our liaison permanent?'

Tia had to think for a moment before she coughed and mumbled that she didn't know what he meant.

'I mean, we should perhaps think this is the time for us to wed. I mean, I am a widower and you are a widow . . .'

She winced, and sneezed to hide the expression on her face. 'I'm sorry,' she said after a moment, 'it's not what I expected.'

He turned to her as the streetlights caught the sallow glare of his features. 'I suppose you need time, my dear, but I am sure marriage is the right thing for both of us.'

When she got upstairs she could hardly breathe for a moment; she opened all the windows and sat gasping for a while until the sensation of being choked faded. The distant carols she heard were her only reminder that it was now Christmas Day.

\*

The knocking disturbed her in her sleep. It was low but insistent, regular, not anarchic as if made by the wind. She got up groggily and threw her dressing gown over her nightie, wondering who could have avoided Brogan and slipped up the stairs.

Cal stood there grim faced. 'I want to come in from the cold, Tia.'

She opened the door to let him in, catching a glimpse of Brogan fleeing down the stairs.

Cal's features were grey, lifeless like a statue's. He followed her into the kitchen, and stood until she told him to sit down. Though he had been living rough, he did not have the stale smell that went with it. Tia wondered if he would be insulted if she offered him a bath; once he had drunk his second cup of tea he asked for one.

She gave him some trousers she had made for Willie, a sweater of Tam's.

When he had finished, the church clock chimed three times.

'I failed,' he said, 'we failed. The Discharged Soldiers' Society failed. We wanted to make it right, Tia, we wanted to gain the promises they'd made us, but all we did was make tramps of ourselves. The reason is we're too greedy. One man gets a job, he takes it and no nonsense about not take a job each until there were jobs for us all. Or we love too much. There's not a man out there who would refuse to work if his children were hungry.'

'Cal . . .'

'Tia, I was one of the lucky ones. I had no family . . .'

'You have a family, you have me.'

'It's not the same, Tia.'

'It's exactly the same, Cal. We love you, all of us.'

'There's nothing to love in me. I'm just a tramp, another street beggar, that's all.'

She gave him the bottle of whisky she had bought when he drank the old one, and watched him drink doggedly until he fell asleep.

When the day came, she slipped down the stairs and asked Brogan what had happened.

'Nothing,' he said. 'He just found out the difference between lies and promises, dreams and the world of Man. We all do, some time or another. We all do. Nothing else to say for it, pet. 'Cept be around when he comes to, and let him know that you dream too.'

'I haven't dreamed for years, Brogan.'

'Why not start then, pet?'


She went back upstairs and into the kitchen as quietly as she could, to begin cooking the brisket she had bought for her and Brogan's Christmas dinner. There was enough for a dozen; she had planned a treat for the Discharged Soldiers as well.

Cal woke up at mid day just as the meat was ready.

He sucked in the air, as if eating it, then suddenly stood up.

'Who was that rich bastard who brought you home last night?'

Tia winced.

'You think you were watching me, I was watching you as well.'

'He is the accountant for the company I work for.'

'He's a rich bastard who made money from the war, from killing men like me.'

'I don't think he did that exactly.'

'Oh, no? What did he do then?'

'He worked for the company. He didn't go to the war because of something to do with his health, or maybe he was older. I don't know.'

'And the company made nothing from the war? And then they kick up a storm about the Excess Profit Tax?'

Tia sat down. 'I know what you mean, Cal.'

'Well, what the bloody hell are you doing with him? Didn't Marcus mean anything to you?'

'Cal, I . . .'

'Cal, I . . .' he mimicked her cruelly.

'Cal, CAL!' she shouted. 'How dare you say that? Marcus meant everything to me.'

'I note you use the past tense.'

'Cal, you don't know.' She went to the dresser and got the letter from Andrew Furuseth.

Cal took it from her and read it once, and then again aloud.

*My dear Mrs Cameron,*
*I am afraid all I can do is say that I share your belief that your husband*
*was murdered. A number of our members heard that he was killed by a*
*thug Pacific Hunter hired for $10 a day. The man I refer to was killed a*
*year later in a street brawl. I am sorry, but someone who is dead cannot*
*be charged with murder; all we have is rumor, there is no one who*
*actually saw the money being handed over or the deed being done.*
*With very deep regret and the hope that you will contact me again if I*
*can be of help.*

*Andrew Furuseth*

'One of the reasons I work for MacDonald's is that they let me go to America.'

'Tia, I would've taken you to America.'

'I seem to remember you were with the Discharged Soldiers at the time. You didn't have any time for me. You ran away from me, Cal. Correct me if I am wrong.'

'You have an answer for everything, don't you?'

'Cal, I . . .' She had the beef on a plate, was slicing it. 'Cal, you have to understand . . .'

He got up and strode towards the door. 'I could never understand you.'

'CAL!'

She ran down the stairs after him, but Brogan was already after him as he ran into the bitter cold of that Christmas Day.

He came back at seven o'clock, and ate a meal silently with Tia and Brogan. Afterwards he stood up. 'I am sorry,' he said, and then he went to bed.

'God love the pair of you,' Brogan said as he rose to leave. 'There is aught as selfish as a man in pain. Or a woman, come to that.'

Cal slept on through that day, as Tia laid out cloth on the kitchen table and cut and sewed him a new coat with a cape of canvas. He no longer had the one she had given him; she guessed he had given it away to somebody else.

She went to work as usual, the next day; Brogan had the keys to her door and promised to go in and heat up soup for Cal.

It was the day after Ne'erday that he came to life again, coming almost shamefully to the kitchen to watch her baking black bun for Brogan, who had always been her first foot in all the years he had lived in the close.

'Cal,' she said, 'there is something I would like to say to you.'

'Tia, I was wrong, I am the one who should be saying something.'

'Cal, I only want to say this. In my job, I keep a small factory going and I send money to my nephews in America . . .'

'What about that place in the Gallowgate?'

'That is something I did with my sister before she died. I don't like that man who drove me home. I did once enjoy myself when he took me out, but that isn't a sin, is it?'

His look reminded her so much of Marcus, that she could not say any more. He stood up and hugged her briefly. 'Give me time, pet. In time, you won't need people like that.'

Tia shivered and then pushed him away. His expression was bitter until she told him that he reminded her of Marcus.

'Pet, I want to go home. Will you come with me?'

She called Mr William and negotiated a week off work without pay on compassionate grounds; she told him that her brother-in-law was a victim of the war.

The islands were wreathed in mist when the ferry drew into Benbecula. Cal took Tia's hands as they crossed the causeway to South Uist, taking their direction from the stones left to mark the way. The landscape was a blank page, but the sounds were there, of the wind and of the birds, the soft thrum of the sea as the tide turned just as they reached the southern shore. Bridie was there to welcome them. She hugged Tia in silence for a long time.

'I've been thinking,' Cal said, as they walked over the machair to the cottage, 'I might go back to the Church.'

Tia looked at him sharply.

'God just came back to me,' he said, 'you see.'

Eunice came running to meet them. She threw her arms about Cal and then around Tia. 'It's been too long, precious. Far too long.'

In the morning, when the mist had cleared, Tia went home. The sands stretched out, long and lonely, and she remembered the time she had crossed the causeway with Marcus, on the eve of her wedding. She thought of the time that had passed, of her mourning and her healing. She wanted to see her mother again, but had not written to say that she was coming.

When Tia reached the inn at Carinish the sun was high in the sky. She stopped to put her shoes back on and then walked slowly up the incline towards her parents' cottage.

Her mother was outside, feeding the hens. Tia was right next to her before Janet realized. She threw her arms round her daughter and hugged until Tia was afraid she would not let her go.

'I never thought I would see you again,' Janet said.

Tia could not speak for fear that she would break down and cry.

'The minister, Reverend MacQuarrie, he's gone,' Janet said. 'And your father, Sorley MacIain, he's a changed man.'

Tia reached down and picked up some eggs.

'Come,' Janet said. 'Come and let me make you a cup of tea, and I will tell you everything.'

Tia followed her indoors. Janet told her how the minister had fallen out with Sorley because he wanted to exclude women from the main Sunday service, saying they were a distraction for the men. Her mother handed her a mug of tea with milk, which she drank slowly. The cottage had hardly changed at all; Janet just seemed a few years older.

'Your father's a changed man,' Janet said again. 'Since my fever broke, when you came. He wants to make his peace with you.'

Tia shuddered. She had no feelings for her father, nothing but a vague sense of dislike. Suddenly the cottage door opened and his shadow fell over her. Janet busied herself mixing a bannock.

'Tia,' he said.

'Father.'

He sat down on the chair opposite her. 'I wanted to talk to you when you came to Janet.'

She said nothing.

'A long time has passed, you see, and many things have happened. I wanted to tell you that I was wrong when I refused to allow your marriage, and even more wrong when I threw you out when you came back.'

Tia felt her eyes prickle with tears.

'I am sorry,' Sorley said.

She looked away, thinking of the pain of the years, how if she had not been thrown out Marcus's baby would be a child going to school now. Time had lessened her pain, but there was still enough to feel anger.

'It's too late, Father. You see, I was carrying a child, and I lost it, probably because you hit me.'

Sorley put his head in his hands. 'I know that.'

There was something pathetic in the way he sat there, his gnarled hands red and raw against his white hair; he was no longer a preacher, just a simple man, faced with his mistakes. Tia felt her anger begin to wash away, replaced by a sort of pity.

'You see, Father, it was Mairead as well, two of us.'

Janet finished mixing the bannock and balanced it on the grid above the fire to cook.

'It's too late for Mairead.' Tia thought of the slum, the smell of hops, the woman with a large dog to keep the police away.

Sorley looked up. His face was shiny with tears. Tia saw his pain, and hated him no longer. Impulsively, she threw her arms around him. Sorley cried openly then, and so did she.

In the morning Janet walked with her to the beginning of the causeway; they both cried when she took Tia in her arms.

'You will come again,' Janet said.

'I will, if I can.'

'You will write,' Janet said.

'I will always write, Mama.'

Cal was waiting for her at Lionacleit; he took her hand as they walked in silence back to Eunice's. 'You know,' he said, 'I don't have to be a priest.'

# Chapter Twenty-three

Cal said, 'You have one day before you leave. Give it to me.'

Briefly, she resisted him. 'The boat sails at midnight.'

'There is the afternoon.'

The weather was a hypocrite; the air cold but sun dominant in a cloudless sky. Tia had only the clothes she stood up in; her spare undies were drying on the rock outside Eunice's.

The day was silver green, the tired green of winter machair, the hills naked in the wind. Wordlessly, Cal led her to the shore, then carried his tiny rowboat to the edge of the tide. He helped her in first, then pushed it out and got in himself. He rowed out a few hundred yards and then hefted the oars in the locks and let the boat drift. Because the tide was coming in, there was no danger. Tia watched him, the sun against his face that washed the grey of the city away, the way his eyes looked just like Marcus's. She knew somehow that this was not her normal life, that Cal would never be part of her normal life, that the love she felt for him was not the love that would lead to marriage. The knowledge that she loved him came to her suddenly, though as soon as she accepted it she knew it had been there all along. Cal had broken free from the torment of the war; he wanted to work for a better world – she loved him for that too, and wanted to show him that she did.

The dolphins came then, dancing around the boat, flirting and then flapping their tails naughtily. Cal leaned out to touch one that was just out of reach; he missed and fell overboard, laughing as the dolphins jumped over him. Tia reached for him, but he waved her away and caught the ring at the prow of the boat and began to drag it towards the shore, with the dolphins nudging the sides. For a moment Tia worried, then she suddenly had the sensation that there was nothing to worry about, that Cal could bring the boat in effortlessly. He was whooping and shouting; a boy again, no longer a troubled man.

When he reached the shallow water she climbed out and they stood together waving at the school of dolphins who danced on for a while before they turned back to the deep.

The setting sun blistered the sea, casting ruddy wounds on the surface as the whole sky glowed like a lantern. Tia slipped, reached out for Cal, and caught the strength in his body as he steadied her with just one hand. They reached the dunes and he set the boat down, then turned to her.

'God forgive me, Tia.'

'God will not blame you,' she said, as she began to undo the buttons of his shirt.

He fell on top of her; there was no struggle until they were both unclothed and she reached for him again and suddenly they were making love like animals, soundlessly beyond little grunts that spoke of their need. For Tia, it was like being cleansed and made new again. She had never thought that she could make love with another man after Marcus. Cal's body was different, younger, leaner, harder in a way; he had been toughened by the war years. His touch was less certain, as if he was unsure of himself until he understood the language of the sounds she made, and then he learned how to make her cry with joy. They were like that for hours, like puppies learning how to play, until the sun was long gone over the western horizon and the bleak northern wind brought them back to themselves.

'Tia, I . . .'

She put a finger to her lips. 'Don't say anything, Cal . . .'

'I love you, Tia . . .'

'Least of all that.'

'I could marry you, Tia.'

'Cal, I can't.'

'Why not?'

'Because . . .'

In the night, she could not see the expression in his eyes; she saw only the hard cast of his features, like stone set against the sky. For a moment she fell against him but when he did not respond she stood away.

'I am sorry,' he said.

'Cal, you've no need to be,' she said as she picked up her clothes and began to shake the sand off them. As she dressed stray particles of sand etched her skin. When she looked again

Cal was already clothed and it was as if nothing had happened between them. He stared at her so intensely that she felt as if she was a specimen at the museum, squashed between glass slides under a microscope.

'You marry for the future,' she said. 'If we wed, we would be marrying the past.'

He said nothing.

She looked upwards and saw the moon, and then she turned away and headed for the ferry, with tears streaming down her face. She cried so hard that it seemed as if her body was water; as if she herself had dissolved when she had made love to Cal.

When she got home Brogan took one look at her and led her down to his place beside the boilers, and fed her hot sweet tea until she cried again.

When the January sales were in full flood, one of the assistants knocked at her door and shyly offered her congratulations.

'Why?' she asked distractedly; she was working on some adverts for the new spring lines.

'Your engagement, Madam, Mrs Cameron.'

'My what?'

The sales assistant showed her the notice in the *Herald*.

'My God,' Tia moaned. Haldane Brodie had given her no idea; in fact, she had hardly noticed him for weeks, she was so used to him driving her home. She was struck dumb for a minute or two, then she eased the assistant out of her office and sat thinking.

She called up Haldane Brodie on the house phone and protested vigorously.

'I really am sorry if you have been surprised, my dear. I did give you the time you asked for.'

'But you never . . . I never said I would.'

'You said you needed time, my dear. I have given you time. I thought that your assent was implicit in your request for time. I believed that once you became used to the idea you would agree. Only a foolish woman would not.'

'I'm a fool then, Haldane, I mean, Mr Brodie. I did not consent or assent, whatever that is. I won't either. In fact, I never will.'

The timbre of his voice changed then. 'I can hardly take it

back now, can I? As far as the public and officers of this store are concerned we must stay engaged. If not, one of us must leave.'

Tia's blood ran cold. 'If that's what it means, I'll resign.'

'Think of all the money you spend with that Jew. Think of your nephews in the winter of New York. I read the other day that the temperature there stays below freezing until the middle of March.'

Tia gripped the receiver. 'I hope you don't mean that, Mr Brodie.'

'I wouldn't try me too hard, Mrs Cameron.'

She put the phone down, cursing aloud, as if swearing would make any difference to the dull fear that caught her stomach. What Haldane Brodie said was true. She needed the security of her MacDonald's salary; and if she quit then Samuel Weinstock would lose his orders too.

For a while she sat staring at space, her chin cupped in her hands.

After work she did not go out the staff exit but the revolving doors at the front of the store, where she hailed a cab for Candleriggs.

Samuel Weinstock was not there, the place silent and empty apart from Miriam in the office going over the accounts. When Tia told her what had happened, Miriam held her in her arms and said that Brodie was blackmailing her, that it was illegal. Samuel came in at that point and told her that it was not blackmail, that it couldn't be because Brodie had nothing to blackmail her with, just a simple threat to get her fired if she did not marry him.

He shook his head. 'I doubt the other directors would stop him, Tia. My impression is that they are all the same.'

'I'm the best buyer they have ever had, they all said that,' she murmured.

Miriam shook her head along with Samuel. 'You are expendable, dear heart. As a designer, you are unique; it doesn't take your skill to run a department, especially when the manufacturers are hurting so hard with the slump that they would almost lose money just to sell.'

Tia thought for a moment. Her face muscles relaxed and

then tensed again. 'The hell with Haldane Brodie,' she said. 'I'm going to keep my job in spite of him.'

Way out of the city, in the annex of the Erskine Hospital, Jimmy Cavanagh Stewart lay with the right leg in plaster from ankle to thigh. He had already read the news in the paper. It was by accident that he saw the notice of the forthcoming marriage of Mrs Cameron to Mr Brodie. At first he did not believe it, but then he read it again and threw the paper away angrily, cursing so badly that the nurse, who was used to caring for fighting men, came over and briskly told him to mind his tongue.

Tia made an appointment to see Mr William. His manner was friendly now; the first thing he did was to congratulate her on her engagement. Tia waited until he had sat down before she told him that was what she had come to see him about.

'It's a misunderstanding, you see. I will not be marrying Mr Brodie.'

Mr William's eyes narrowed. 'I'm afraid I don't understand.'

Tia struggled to keep her composure, to keep anger out of her voice. 'Nor do I, precisely, Mr William. Mr Brodie brought the subject up and I said I needed time. A month later, he put the notice in the paper without asking me again.'

The director fidgeted with some papers on his desk before he found the winter sales figures. The slump was beginning to show; on average, the figures matched those of a year before, there was no longer the dramatic increases that Tia had achieved when she started work at the store.

'I expected you to hand in your resignation. As a married woman, you would no longer be able to work for us.'

'What I am trying to explain is that I will not be getting married, not in the foreseeable future at least.'

Mr William fiddled with the half-moon glasses he wore to read. 'It is true that you take care of your departments very well, Mrs Cameron.'

'What I want is to be able to continue to do so, Mr William.'

He sighed deeply. 'The board will not tolerate any whiff of scandal, Mrs Cameron. Mr Brodie is a powerful man. He has been your friend until now. I would warn you that it would not do to make him your enemy.'

'I only want to keep my job, Mr William.'

'I have no intention of asking for your resignation.'

In the pit of her stomach, she felt anger mixed with fear. For a moment she considered reminding Mr William of her successes, but she sensed that he was not of a mind to listen. Thanking him for his time, she returned to her department.

Tia was working in her glass booth when one of the assistants came to tell her that two ladies she had never seen before were trying to charge three hundred pounds' worth of clothes to a company that the assistant had never heard of. Tia asked Sheena to phone Accounts for verification, and then went on working on the sales staffs commission payments. When she saw Sheena nodding, she put her pen down and went out herself. The women were talking to each other and ignoring the sale assistants, who were struggling to wrap everything for the waiting chauffeur.

'Wait a minute,' one of the women said, just after he had been handed two huge bags. 'One of those has to come to me.'

Tia got a pen and began to write out a label. 'Mrs?'

'Hunter,' the woman smirked. 'That is Hunter, as in Pacific Hunter. I am afraid we have been away too long. We spent the war years in Hong Kong, and we've become used to oriental standards of service. I'm afraid you don't match up, my dear. Servility is in the Chinese blood.'

Tia's own blood began to run cold. 'That is, Pacific Hunter, the shipping line?'

'I don't know of anything else there is,' the woman snapped.

Reflexively, Tia's hand hit the ink pot, spreading midnight blue over the ochre and scarlet ball gown.

'You silly brat,' the woman shouted. 'Now you'll have to give me another one.'

'I will not,' Tia said, as she took the other parcel from the chauffeur. 'I am afraid that I will give you nothing at all.'

'How dare you? We've paid already.'

'You have merely signed an order. I am the buyer; I can give you credit or refuse to give you credit and I have just decided to refuse you credit.'

'How dare you? You can't, you stupid little bitch. I am Mrs Bryce Hunter, and this is Miss Hunter, my husband's sister.'

'I don't give a tinker's curse who you are. You are not buying on credit from this store.'

'We'll go to Daly's.'

'Be my guest. It's straight up this street and then turn left at Sauchiehall Street.'

'This is not the last you've heard about his.'

Tia stalked back to her office, as Sheena and the assistants stared after her.

Five minutes later Haldane Brodie strode into her office without bothering to knock. 'What do you think you're playing at?' he ranted. 'Bryce Hunter is one of the richest men in the country, and you have his wife and sister virtually thrown out of the store?'

Tia stood up. 'I have my reasons . . .'

'Which are? If it wasn't for our relationship and my standing in this firm I would sack you here and now.'

She had a vision of Cal's body, its strength and its power, the way she was drawn to him not only because of who he was but because of what he did, then Marcus's face. 'You won't do that,' she said quietly, suddenly sick at herself because she had spent so much time kowtowing to a man for whom she had nothing but contempt.

'Why not?'

'Because I am leaving. You can keep your standing. I mean, a man like you, you don't need a mere woman, do you?'

His face darkened. 'You can't do that.'

'Watch me.' She began to tidy the papers through habit, then stopped and went to take her coat from the stand. Haldane Brodie stood fizzing like a firework; for a moment, she thought he would hit her, then he picked up the framed picture of her and J.P. dancing at the Double Deuce. He stared at it for a moment then tossed it down. 'I should have known you're a slut at heart. My mother told me. All teuchters are the same. You have no class.'

Tia's hand whipped back then lashed him across the cheek, leaving a vivid welt.

'I'll have the police on you for that.'

'Oh, yes? So then the world will know that you have not only

410

been jilted, but also that a woman slapped your face. Wonderful for your reputation, I should imagine.'

She picked up the picture, put it into her bag, and left the store with its entire work force staring at her. The first thing she did was to go to the *Herald* offices and put an announcement in the forthcoming weddings column: Mrs Tia Cameron was not marrying and never would marry Haldane Brodie, Chief Accountant to Stewart and MacDonald. The next was to go into a tiny tearoom in Queen Street, where she had a long cry.

It was then that she felt the aching loneliness that had been typical of her life first when Marcus died, then Mairead, when the boys had emigrated, and most of all since the night when she had left Cal on a Hebridean beach. Since Mrs Anderson had died, her only real friends in the city were the Weinstocks. She walked the city for a long time before she crossed the river to the Gorbals where Samuel and Miriam lived with their two children. Miriam, there alone for once, welcomed her with open arms.

'It had to happen, dear heart,' she said. 'The man is not good. He is evil.'

The coffee was thick and sweet, perfumed with cinnamon and cloves.

Tia told Miriam about Cal.

'Dear heart, you could marry him. In the old country, it is not uncommon for a widow to marry her husband's brother. It will happen here too, I am sure.'

'I've never heard of it.'

'Who cares whether you have heard of it? Is it what is right for you?'

'Don't you see, Miriam, if I married Cal, I would be marrying the past? I loved him because he is Marcus's brother, not as himself. I should never have done it.'

'Tia, when you reach my age, you learn that life is too short for regrets. You are a young woman still, what age do you have, twenty-four isn't it? I promise you, you will find a love again, one who is the man for you, and not just a shadow of your past.'

'Don't call Cal a shadow of my past, Miriam. I loved him, I still do. I am not in love with him, that's all.'

'You are a wise woman if you can make that distinction,' Miriam said. 'Most cannot, even till the day they die.'

Tia took part-time work designing for Samuel; she filled up the days by sending for some bolts of *clo mor* and making them into gently tailored walking suits which she sold to Murielle's. By the end of March she realised that she was earning almost exactly the same as she had at MacDonald's.

The knock came unexpectedly one afternoon. She opened the door to Bridie and Eunice; if she had not been so strong she would've fainted with the surprise.

'We are not staying,' Eunice said, once she had them sitting around the oven in the kitchen drinking tea. 'The boat leaves this evening and we will be on it.'

'Why did you come then?' Tia murmured, as she opened a tin of ham for their tea.

Eunice got up and took both her hands. 'Because of my sons. You cared for them both, and you gave Cal back to me. You did not come to say goodbye, you did not give me the chance to thank you.'

'I did nothing,' Tia said softly, thinking of the long journey they had taken.

'You did everything for him, for Cal. He told me that if not for you he would still be on the streets or dead of the cold. You gave him back his belief in life, his faith in God.'

'But . . .' Tia whispered.

'No buts,' Eunice said, hugging her tight. 'I had to come. I had to thank you.'

Tia looked into her eyes and knew then that Eunice knew everything.

'He's gone back to the Church, pet. The Bishop talked to him and they have taken him to Valladolid. It was your grace that put him there.'

'I was selfish.'

'God has strange ways sometimes. I just came to thank you and to tell you that however long you live, you will be my daughter, in law and in fact. You have not one mother, but two.'

Tia turned away, sobbing softly.

'I don't deserve you.'

'Yes you do,' Bridie said. Then she smiled. 'It doesn't matter if you want us or not. You have us.'

They all laughed as Tia went to the sink to wash the potatoes and Bridie put on the kettle for another cup of tea.

'I must give you both a walking suit,' she said, 'I make them and sell them to a shop in Sauchiehall Street.'

'You must not, Tia,' Eunice said firmly.

'They're the latest fashion . . .'

'That's the second reason we don't want one,' Bridie said. 'We would be the laughing stock of the island. Walking suit indeed.'

It was the beginning of April 1920 when Samuel sent her to Paris again, to buy trims and buttons and have a look at the designer collections. She stayed at the same hotel; she had only two days there, and once she had done the buying she had just an afternoon to walk down the Champs Elysées and breathe in the hope and the heady air. Paris had recovered from the war quicker than Glasgow; strangely, because France had been the major battlefield and had lost so many soldiers. The people seemed to throw off the grief and take it in their stride somehow, perhaps because they were used to having revolutions and maybe even a little more used to death. Tia crossed the bridge to the Left Bank and took a table outside the café Haldane Brodie had taken her to. She remembered how much she had wanted just to sit there, to watch and absorb the style of the women and the nonchalant arrogance of the men.

Her table was teetering on the pavement edge, the cloth frilling in the breeze; she ordered just a coffee and croissant, because she had only a little money.

She was midway through the croissant when a voice spoke close behind her.

'*Excusez moi, Madam, mais je pense que vous etes la femme la plus belle dans tout Paris.*'

Tia only had the vaguest notion what the words meant; the only thing she was sure about was that the man was not a native of Paris. She spun around, almost knocking her cup over, amazed at the feeling of familiarity, almost *déjà vu*.

Jimmy Cavanagh stood there sheepishly. 'If you remember, I did say that I would meet you again.'

Tia felt a sudden urge to stand up and hug him, instead she

gestured for him to take a seat. 'I thought you were joking. I thought you lived in America.'

'I told you, I have Scots blood. My mother is Irish and my father is Scottish.'

'Oh . . .'

'Tia, before we go any further, I have a confession to make. My name isn't just Jimmy Cavanagh. It's Jimmy Cavanagh Stewart.'

'So?'

'You must promise me not to get up and walk away . . .'

'Why?'

'Just promise me and I will tell you . . .'

'I won't promise you that.'

'Oh, well, hell,' he said. 'I may as well tell you anyway. If you get up and run away I shall have to run after you.'

'You can't run, at least you couldn't in America.'

'Yes, but, I just spent several months in Erskine Hospital. A surgeon called Sir William Macewen fixed my leg. I can run now.'

Tia looked down at the pencil-slim skirt she wore under a long flared jacket that almost reached her knees. 'Jimmy, I . . . I . . .'

'Jimmy,' he teased her. 'Jimmy I what?'

'Jimmy, this skirt I'm wearing, it's very tight. I can walk, but I can't run.'

He put back his head and roared with laughter. 'You can't run because you're in fashion. Why on earth don't you take up golfing, dearest, and then you could run away and I would have to find a way of stopping you – because although I can run now, it'll be a year or two before my muscles get their strength back. I can run, but I can't run very fast.'

'So tell me,' she said, 'this confession of yours. What is it?'

His face changed. 'I am Jimmy Stewart, eldest son of James Stewart, that is, the man who owns Stewart and MacDonald.'

Tia stood up in a flash. 'How dare you . . .'

His face hardened. 'Quite easily. I didn't want you to think that you had to be nice to me because of who my father is. I guessed you wouldn't, but I didn't want you to feel on edge, or anything.'

Tia suddenly felt heavy. She sat down again. She was still hurt that Mr William had taken Brodie's side.

'The only thing I want from life,' he said, 'the only thing I want that I don't have already is for people to treat me as I am, and not as my father's son.'

'You work for them, don't you?'

'I do at the moment. I didn't used to. I have to, in a way, because my operation cost a lot of money.'

'It must be wonderful to have the money to pay for it. Thousands don't.'

'Macewen operates on everyone. He doesn't expect them to pay if they can't. I could hardly turn around and tell him that because of my pride I couldn't pay, could I?'

'What are you doing for them now?'

'Right now I'm having a look at the Paris stores to get some ideas for them. The only thing is that fashion isn't my strong point.'

'You'll go far, then.'

'I am an architect. According to my father, architecture and fashion are exactly the same thing.'

'I know the difference,' she said slowly.

'I'm like a bastard, in a way,' he said. 'I've spent most of my adult years trying not to be my father's son. Before the war I was a junior partner in a practice in Glasgow. Then I went to fight.'

'Were you called up?'

'No. I believed the propaganda. I volunteered at the end of 1914. I was a private. I was lucky to survive the first day of the Somme. I was shot in the thigh during the second.'

'Do you believe it now?'

'The propaganda? Of course not.'

The air was soft, slightly scented with flowers from the stall just down the street. The breeze was warm, it spoke of summer, drifting gently like the waves of a receding tide. They sat at the table until a waiter came to ask them if they wanted dinner, and then they moved inside and sat under the twin Chinamen, utterly careless of where they were, both ordering coq au vin because it was the first thing the waiter suggested.

At eleven o'clock Jimmy stretched. 'I must tell you something, Tia.'

'What is that?'

'You are the only one who could make me oblivious of Paris.'

She laughed.

'I mean, it's nearly midnight, and I was going to have canard presse'.

'It's nearly what?'

'Midnight is an hour away. I was going to a restaurant over the other side of the river that is famous for its pressed duck.'

Tia stood up. 'I have to go. My train leaves at midnight.'

His face fell. 'Can't you get one in the morning?'

'No. I have some trims, and the garments they go on have to be delivered by the end of the week.'

He stood up, holding her chair for her. Outside the café, he hailed a taxi and took her to the station. 'We must meet again,' he said.

'Why?' she teased him.

'Because I am in love with you.'

She said nothing; the sensation was too fragile to disturb with words. Her legs turned to cotton wool, her vision blurred; when he took her arm it was as if a jolt of electricity ran through her. When the whistle gave the train permission to leave, he brushed her lips with the quickest of kisses and she felt herself melt towards him through the open window. She took a seat and sat through the journey in a daze, eyes closed, as his words repeated themselves again and again.

Jimmy's face stayed in her mind, and the realisation that she loved him came slowly, as the train pulled into Calais docks. She had thought that love would never come again, but it had, unbidden. Crossing the Channel, she stared at the night sky, felt deeply alone and wondered when she would see him again.

Back in Glasgow, Samuel and Miriam noted the change in her but did not ask any questions. At the end of the month she began to ache for Jimmy Stewart, to count the days before he was due back in the middle of May. Sam called her into his office one day, and handed her a piece of paper.

'What is it?' she asked, handing it back.

'It's the lease of a shop in Pollokshields, my dear. You and I are going into business together.'

'But I have no capital.'

'You don't need it,' he said. 'I have paid the first three months' rent.'

'That's not fair,' she said.

'It is perfectly fair. Your investment is your expertise and your ideas.'

Tia had the walls painted gloss white, which she decorated with line drawings of the summer styles. There was a coat stand in old oak, and an aspidistra. Cameron's opened on the first of June: each customer was offered a glass of champagne and given a single red rose; the shop was too busy advertising its wares that day to sell anything, but the next day women came back and began to buy.

The strange thing about Tia's meeting with Jimmy Stewart was that he had not fixed a day and time to see her again; she wondered about this and then knew that he would find her, because he knew she worked for Weinstock's. At the end of two weeks, she counted the sales and realised that she had made a profit, if sales held up through the rest of the month.

On Monday of the third week she had just opened the shop when a man dressed in uniform turned up and asked her loudly if she was Mrs Tia Cameron. When she said that she was he handed her some papers and picked up the keys from her little desk at the back of the shop.

'What . . .' she fumbled.

'I'm a bailiff, Mrs Cameron. I've come to serve a court order. Macdonald's have taken out an interdict to ban you from trading.'

'But what, what can they . . .'

'They allege that you have stolen ideas from them. They have drawings of clothes that you have on sale here. You made those drawings when you worked there, and they allege the designs belong to them.'

'They can't do this. It's not even my shop, its Mr Weinstock's.'

'Oh, yes they can. In your contract you signed a pledge not to take part in retail trade for a year if you left the store.'

'Contract, what contract?'

'The contract you signed when you joined the staff, Mrs Cameron.'

She slumped down; suddenly his manner softened.

'Mrs Cameron, I only serve the order, I don't know the rights and wrongs of it. What I do know is that this isn't the end. You can fight them in the courts.'

'I know nothing about courts,' she said dully.

'Well, you don't need to. You hire a lawyer who does.'

'But don't you see,' she said, 'don't you see that I haven't any money for a lawyer? And nor does Samuel Weinstock.'

'Maybe you can find one anyway, one who will take on the case for a reduced fee.'

'How can I find one? I didn't steal the designs. They were mine. How can I steal my own designs? This shop isn't a store, it won't make any difference to MacDonald's . . . it's just a little shop.'

'Nevertheless, I have to close it now. Or have your assurance that you will close it immediately and not continue with the trade until the case is resolved. If you read the summons, you will see that MacDonald's are sueing you for ten thousand pounds . . .'

Tia sat there, not listening, just hearing the words. It was only when the bailiff had left and the window shutters were closed that she felt anger rise; she got up and put her coat on and then walked into the spring weather, hoping that the walk across the river would bring an idea that made sense.

When she got to Weinstock's, she discovered that Samual had been served with a writ too.

# Chapter Twenty-four

*T*he lawyer spent fifteen minutes reading the summonses and then ten more reading Tia's copy of her contract with MacDonald's. He was a young man, just finished his apprenticeship; he was Jewish also and so he had offered Tia and Samuel Weinstock his advice for free.

When he put the papers down, he looked into space for a moment before he spoke.

'The contract does forbid you from engaging in similar work, Mrs Cameron, but it says nothing about designing. You were employed as a buyer, the designs you did for nothing, as it were.'

'So what does that mean?'

'It means that a sympathetic sheriff might overturn the part of the interdict that prevents you from working as a designer, but not the part that prevents you from working in the retail trade.'

'Can you represent me?'

He took his heavy reading glasses off; in an instant he looked young and vulnerable. 'No, but the firm I work for can.'

'Ach.' Samuel put his hands in his pockets, pushing against the cloth so that the pleats at the top opened and his trousers were the shape of a kite. 'Miriam will run the shop and Tia will stay here and design. It is stupid anyway, jealousy, that is all.'

'Miriam can run the shop, but the name must change and Tia can't do any work until we get the sheriff to vary the terms of the interdict.'

Sam spent fifty pounds instructing the young lawyer's firm and hiring an advocate, but at the end of the day the sheriff went with the arguments of the famous King's Counsel the store had instructed.

'Is it not true,' he asked Tia, 'that part of your work as buyer was to roughly design garments made up by the firm called Weinstock's Haute Couture of Candleriggs?'

'It is true, but it was not something that the store asked me to do, it was something I offered to do.'

'And so you did a range every season that you were with the store?'

'I did, but . . .'

'But nothing, Mrs Cameron. What you did in law was to amend your contract verbally to the effect that you were also the store's house designer in effect.'

He turned to the sheriff. 'I believe it is reasonable therefore to request that Mrs Cameron does not design for a period of one year to give my client the oppprtunity to make good its loss incurred by her untimely and, if I may say so, undignified departure.'

The sheriff nodded. The interdict remained as issued; a full hearing was set for August. Tia bit her lip and drew blood, rather than scream out at the injustice of it all. She could not be seen to have anything to do with Meg's Pegs because that was in breach of the court order and if MacDonald's found out they would have closed the tiny shop too.

Tia ended up working as a machinist for Sam; she was so angry that when she started she worked for twenty-four hours without a break. Her mind was like porridge: half rage against MacDonald's, the other half telling her that despite her dealings with his father's company, she had fallen in love with Jimmy Cavanagh Stewart.

He came to see her three days later, with a sheaf of drawings under his arm and a bright smile on his face.

'How could you?' she asked him.

He did not know what she meant.

'I mean MacDonald's. How can you do this to me?'

When she told him what it was, he told her the wholesale side of the business had lost eighty thousand pounds, that the wholesale firm Campbell's had bought a share in it otherwise the entire business would go bankrupt. She told him about Haldane Brodie; he said only that he would find out exactly who had started it all. Through pride, she refused to go out with him; she agreed only that he could meet her after work in two weeks' time.

He asked her to marry him; she refused resolutely.

Afterwards, she spent two hours crying on Miriam Weinstock's shoulder.

The court hearing was set for August; Sam was glad because it gave him time to learn the law; they could not afford more legal fees so he decided that he would defend himself and Tia. He thought that the issues were too important to be delegated to anyone else; the young lawyer who had advised them for free did not have the experience to fight the case.

Tia paid the rates on her flat and then took the last of her savings and went home, to stay with Eunice and Bridie, or her mother, she did not care which. The one thought running through her mind was that she would go mad if she stayed in the city. In the end she went to Janet's through habit; she even smiled when her father stood up to welcome her home.

'What's wrong, pet?' Janet asked as she carded a fleece to make it ready for the wheel.

Tia told her; Janet barely understood a word of it but she understood the need Tia had for peace.

On the second day she walked over the north causeway to Benbecula, where Ceit showed her how to work her grandmother's loom. It took her three days to thread it properly; another week to make her tweed; it was lumpy, not smooth-surfaced as it should have been, but she was calmer, gaining strength to fight again. The wild irises had opened, the edges of the island looked like they were trimmed with gold.

One day, as she was crossing the causeway back to North Uist, in the distance a stranger waved at her; when he got closer she realised that it was Jimmy Stewart. He was waving a paper in his hand, she stopped and would've turned back if the tide had not been coming in.

'It's rubbish,' he said, 'the engagement announcement. I'm not engaged at all.'

She sighed, 'You don't know, but I've already had that experience, thank you.'

His face clouded. 'I do know. I read it in bed in the Erskine Hospital.'

She suddenly had the feeling that if she did love him, then he would die, like Marcus had, that she would lose him again as she lost her first husband.

'It was my mother,' he said. 'She wanted me to marry Catherine Campbell, the Campbell that's bailing out Stewart and MacDonald, that is. She wanted the firm in the family, that's all.'

She thought of Sam struggling to learn the law, Miriam running a shop when she would rather have been at home caring for her family, herself in North Uist only because she was wary of MacDonald's power.'

'Jimmy, I . . . I don't think it would be right if we were to marry.'

His face fell. 'How do you know?'

'You see, Samuel and I, Miriam too, we have had to work for our money, work for our lives. You have never had to work for anything.'

His face sharpened. 'I didn't work in the war, did I? I didn't work when I was an apprenticed architect? I'm not working just now, when I am trying to stop the whole business collapsing and all our staff ending up on the street? I mean, for God's sake, Tia, you have to understand, I didn't choose my parents.'

'MacDonald's should close,' she said spitefully. 'They closed me.'

'Tia, you have to believe me. It wasn't MacDonald's board who issued that writ. It was Haldane Brodie, acting beyond his powers. The writs will be withdrawn after the board meeting next week. I promise you.'

'Haldane Brodie is still the accountant. The lawyer who explained the writs to us said Brodie had a legal obligation to collect money if he thinks it's due.'

'After the board meeting next week Brodie won't have a look-in. He's the one who didn't watch the wholesale side, and let the losses build up. He'll be sacked, if my father has his way.'

'And what was your father doing, playing golf?'

Jimmy winced. 'If you had ever seen him, you wouldn't say that.'

'Why not?'

'Because he has rheumatics. He's been a cripple for the last twenty years.'

Tia felt a shard of sympathy until she remembered

Mairead's husband; what she had to do to pay for his hospital bed.

'When you're rich,' she said, 'it is easy to be a cripple.'

'For God's sake, Tia, is there nothing you care for apart from money?'

'I care for people, Jimmy . . .'

'I know one thing, now. You don't care about me. Not enough.'

He was over the eastern horizon, making for Lochmaddy, when she curled up into a ball and fell on the sands, crying like a baby.

She was picking herself up when Janet found her took her in her arms and coaxed her back home. Sorley was not there, he had an elders' meeting that day to consider yet another applicant for the parish charge. Janet settled Tia in front of the fire, and made tea.

'What the matter, pet?' she asked, when she had finished the cup.

'I don't know. After Marcus, I thought I would never love anyone again. I went to America, you know, I went to the house he had brought for us, and then I felt different somehow, as if the loss had changed from being a weight to being a memory. I still thought I would never love again but then I loved Cal and now, this Jimmy Stewart, I love him too.'

'Did Cal leave you, pet?'

'No, Mama, I left him.'

'You were not in love with him, then. This Jimmy Stewart, he's the young man who asked the Post where he could find you?'

'Yes.'

'Does he love you?'

'He says he does, but the store, I should never have gone there. It was a stupid argument I had with Samuel . . . I'm not like them, you see. I'm not like the women who are married and who come in just to spend their husband's money. I make money to keep myself . . .'

Her voice tailed off into silence.

'I think,' Janet said, 'I think you are confusing this Jimmy with MacDonald's the store. I don't know about these things, pet, but there's a good few who have made good in the city and I suppose then they become greedy. I don't know. But the son is not the father and the father is not the whole of that great big company.'

'He works for the store, Mama.'

'Yes, but it seems that he thinks he is obliged to.'

'He's an adult. He could refuse.'

'Tia, there's good and bad in everything. I remember you saying that Mr William, the man who gave you time off to see me when I was so ill, I remember you saying that he was a good man.'

'He is. He wanted to give the assistants a pay rise. It was Haldane Brodie who refused . . .'

'This Haldane Brodie, I think, I know – you see, pet, men set traps for women, just like some women set traps for men. This Haldane Brodie, he wanted you for his wife and when you would not agree he turned vicious. He's like the Reverend was, the man you turned down all those years ago. Christian minister though he was supposed to be, he behaved like a pagan after you were gone. And your father, he respects the cloth, it took him a long time, it took him years to see through the cloth to what the Reverend was, which was a bad-tempered, nasty, greedy man. Think of it this way, when Marcus asked you to marry him, if you would have said no he would not have hurt you. You only said no to Haldane Brodie; he had no right to do this to you. But don't blame the whole store for the action of one man.'

Tia stretched and got up. 'The thing was, what I loved in Cal was the strength of his belief. And the strength to get up and start again. He fought for his ideals, you know. With the Discharged Soldiers' Society he fought for the things they had been promised in the trenches. Jobs, decent wages. Decent homes to live in. And he had the strength to give that up when he knew he wouldn't win. But he didn't give up his belief, he went back to the Church and he is going to try again, I know, like these priests in Ireland. I know he will.'

Sorley came in then. 'What is this about you sending a fine young man packing?'

Tia looked at Janet; they laughed so hard that Sorley left again, muttering that he would never understand either of them. In that moment, Tia forgave him for everything; it was as if another weight had been lifted from her soul.

Taking Janet's shawl, she walked out into the gossamer night, the air so soft that the touch of the breeze felt like eiderdown. The edge of winter still touched the islands, Eaval was wealed with rifts gouged by the early storms, rivulets that died almost as soon as they had sprung in the heavy rains.

Tia had her drawing pad with her. She sat on the rock facing the shore and began to draw simple, slim, tailored clothes, not adorned like Coco Chanel's, but almost mannish in their sobriety, the difference being in the eight-gored skirts that would flare like a tulip when a woman walked, the lapel of the jacket that was not split but continuous so that the jacket could be buttoned like a railwayman's smock. She drew for hours, making clothes that matched the landscape, until rain fell as gently as talcum powder and she wrapped her pad in her shawl and ran home.

The evening meal was as always preceded by prayers; she tried to concentrate but could not, and ate quickly once her father had said Amen.

He sat at the fire afterwards, reading his Bible as she and Janet cleared away the dishes.

'This young man, this Jimmy Stewart. You do love him. I can see it in your eyes.'

'Its madness, though. I've only met him three times.'

'How many times did you meet Marcus?'

Tia winced. 'Mama, I had known him all of my life.'

'Yes, but it was only two times you saw him as a loved one. The first when you were fifteen, the second when you were sixteen. That was all.'

'What are you saying, Mama?'

'What I am saying is that you love him. And because you love him, you should give him a chance.'

'And Cal, what about Cal?'

'Cal you loved and you do love; Jimmy you are in love with . . .'

'But if I am in love with him, it should be magical, like it was with Marcus . . .'

'You are mature now, the difference is that you are a grown

woman. Being in love isn't easy, pet. Sometimes being in love can be like being in hell.'

'If I do go with Jimmy, what about Samuel?'

'Have you asked him, pet? He'll not stand in your way. All these obligations you have, you are like an old woman, and you're only twenty-four. Your youth isn't done. Samuel knows that. He will survive. The workroom will find other customers. You said yourself that Meg's Peg's alone keeps them busy enough.'

'But the slump, they keep on talking about the slump. There's no work for thousands now that the war's over.'

'Rather the war had never started, pet. Rather no work than men killed in the trenches.'

Tia suddenly felt the pain in her mother, the empty space left by the death of her brothers. 'I have no right,' she said suddenly, 'I have no right to your love.'

Janet reared as if she had been hit. 'What on earth do you mean by that, pet?'

'I've always had so much of you, Mama. The others don't get the same.'

'Oh, but, precious, of you all there's three dead, for God to care for, and three living for me. I care for your sisters, pet, as much as I care for you, but they don't need me, you see. You do. You're the only one not wed and settled. Of course I care for you, all this time I have since you all left home. If I was sure he wouldn't take me seriously, I might go to your father and confess to idleness . . .'

'Idleness nothing,' Sorley cut in, 'away with your daft talk, Janet, and you, too, Tia. The pair of you, I have never heard such nonsense in the whole of my life.' Tia would have been hurt, but as he spoke there was a wry little smile on his face. The next time he spoke, it was to ask for a cup of tea.

Back in the city, Tia thought for a long time before she wrote to Jimmy, asking him to join her for afternoon tea in the Willow Tearoom; her pride would not let her do more.

He had been as good as his word; both interdicts had been lifted by the time she returned and the story of Haldane Brodie's resignation was in the business pages of the Glasgow *Herald*. When Jimmy did not come for tea Tia just supposed he had changed his mind; she did not realise that the invitation had reached his father, also called James, who would have written to thank her and refuse if there had been a return address on her note.

The workroom was busy when she walked in. Samuel looked pleased to see her, but there was a reticence in his manner.

'Dear heart,' he said, in the office over a cup of coffee, 'I have reached a decision. I am not going to chase fashion any longer. I have the contract you got for uniforms. I am going to try to get more. I will make for Meg's Peg's and customers like that, but I am not going to get involved with a store like MacDonald's again. It's not worth the risk.'

Tia slumped. 'But what do I do, Samuel?'

'Either you come back as a non-equity partner . . .'

'What the bloody hell is that?'

He smiled. 'I read so many law books these days, I am a lawyer without a wig and gown. A non-equity partner is someone who has no capital in the business, but who gets a share in the profit. I guarantee you a wage of two pounds a week; your commission on order and your share of the profits should make it up to four. Think about it my dear. You are an excellent saleswoman.'

She thought for only a moment. 'But I am a designer, Samuel.'

'Well then, you still have Cameron's. You design for yourself. I will make up the garments, the only difference is that you cannot return them. I will open a credit account for you.'

'But Sam . . .'

'You take the risk, Tia. If you want to be a designer, you take the risk . . .'

'But it won't be like Paris, or even the lines you were doing for MacDonald's . . .' She opened her case and showed him the suit she had made up from the design she did in North Uist.

He looked at it with his professional eye. 'Tia, this costs a lot to make up. The tailoring and then the sewing. I could make four other suits in the time it would take to do this one.'

She flinched. 'I want it in Island tweed.

'It'll cost the best part of a guinea just to make it up.'

'Oh, Samuel, I know, but it looks wonderful on.'

'Any woman with any sense of style will want one, but the

difficulty is there are not so many women with style these days. There are the wives of the war profiteers; they want to look rich. The old rich, the aristocrats, all this talk of socialism frightens them. They no longer want to look rich. Plus fashion is not something they deign to follow. They expect to lead it by right. The war, this stupidest act of mankind in a history of stupidity, it has turned everything topsy turvy. You have to know that. If you go into Cameron's Fashions again, then you have to cater to the nouveaux riches. They want to look the part. They have no confidence, only greed.'

Tia turned away. 'All right, Samuel. I won't design –'

'Don't say that, you will design; just now you have to wait a little, maybe, or design for the market.'

'I hate the war profiteers, Sam. I'd rather take the Devil's money.'

'All money is tainted. It is so in my faith and also in yours. It is not so much where it comes from, Tia. It is that you must be fair when you have it. Don't you remember that row we had, when you would not stay with me? I realised something later. You were right. I have an obligation to the people who work here as I have an obligation to my family. But in a way, I was right also. If you have an obligation to others, so too do you have an obligation to yourself.'

Cameron's had a tired air about it; Miriam had stocked the shop with the simple, workaday clothes she wore herself and there was little call for them in Pollokshields except from the housekeepers and maids. The atmosphere in Albert Drive was gloom, tinged with desperation; one of the butchers had gone out of business, there was so much less beef being bought.

The summer made the air heavy with the exhausts of the cars and smoke from the shipyards just along the river in Govan. The whole street was paved, with not a growing thing in sight. Once or twice, Tia walked along to the houses, almost as far as Baillie Cuthbert's had been; he was dead now and so was his wife; dimly she supposed his son would be living there. Jimmy Stewart lived in Kelvinside; that comforted Tia because she felt there was no risk of a chance meeting. She hurt inside, but she would never have showed it. She did the best she could with Cameron's, holding a sale to get rid of the dead stock and carefully buying Paris copies, the differences being the price and the fact the ornate trims would fray and fall off.

She spent much of her time wondering why Jimmy had not come to tea; if he had capitulated to his mother and was now happy to marry the Campbell girl instead.

# Chapter Twenty-five

$J$ane Cavanagh Stewart was an unhappy woman. Her marriage had ended twenty years ago, or so she thought; she dated it from the day her husband took rheumatic fever because after that he was a man no longer, just a shell of a person who could talk but not do. She was Scots Irish, bred of the salty tough settlers who have been granted land by King James three-hundred-odd years before. Her father still farmed a thousand acres of Antrim; her brothers had done well in trade in America. When she married James Stewart, she thought the match was good. She would never admit that she missed making love, that the lack of physical union left an emptiness inside her. Her own mother said she was not the daughter she knew; most other people avoided her, except for the Women's Guild at the kirk.

One day, she was having afternoon tea with James Senior when he read out a sales advertisement for Cameron's of Pollokshields. 'I always wonder about Mrs Cameron,' he said, 'I wonder if I should ask her to return to the firm.'

'It's true that the takings aren't so good as they were,' Jane said carefully.

'She is a very nice woman, I hear. She certainly bears no grudge against us. She was kind enough to send me an invitation to tea.'

Jane's mind began to turn then. She and Jimmy hardly spoke, but she had a mother's sense that he was in love; she just did not know with whom. She did not believe that Mrs Cameron had sent her *husband* an invitation to tea.

That evening at dinner, she asked Jimmy if he had ever met Mrs Cameron. His expression told her exactly what she wanted to know.

The difficulty with Catherine Campbell was that she was a flighty young thing; she did not want to marry James, as his mother always called him, either. It had taken the combined wits of Elizabeth Campbell and Jane Cavanagh Stewart to engineer the engagement announcement, but as soon as Jimmy issued a fervent denial, Catherine up and ran off with a golfer, one she met on the golf course at Newton Mearns. The worst of it was that Catherine stayed openly with the man in a hotel, so from Jane's point of view the marriage possibility was beyond salvation. She was beginning to think of trying to do something with a Campbell niece, a sweet little thing called Mary Louise.

'I've been thinking,' James Senior said over his after-dinner port. He sat in his bath chair with the bell for the nurse handy; Jane felt a wave of rage at him for succumbing to an illness that older, less fit men had fought off. She did not realise that the disease affects different people in different ways; she did not even try to understand James's pain, so she did not care about it. 'I should perhaps write to that Mrs Cameron and ask her for tea here. The store did treat her very harshly.'

Jane was doing her needle lace, the ephemeral, ornate work done without cogs but just thread and one needle. She did needle lace every evening, making perfect collars and cuffs for her blouses and dresses. She was proud that, in the discomfort of her marriage, she could still produce something of value.

'I think the store was perfectly fair to her, in fact more than fair. She got a very good salary and was paid to go gallivanting all over the place. I'm afraid that although the war's changed some things, it has not changed the fact that it is not done to fraternise with staff, no matter how deserving they be – and she is not. She walked out on us, remember.'

'I remember the day I took on Haldane Brodie as an accounts clerk. I didn't expect him to go much higher than that, but he did when I wasn't looking. You know the rest of the board apart from Will just rubber stamp things and Will, God bless him, couldn't read a balance sheet if you paid him, which nobody would.'

'The Brodie affair has nothing to do with it.' Jane had a sneaking regard for the accountant, not because of his work but because of the perfectly deferential manner he assumed when he was in her company. 'The man's paid off, and there's nothing more to be done about it. Except having to end our lives in penury, having to watch every penny.'

'We're hardly in penury, my dear. We still own forty-nine

percent of MacDonald's, and Campbell, Stewart and MacDonald's, as it is now. Apart from that, I have shares and capital of about fifty thousand, which brings in enough in interest to pay all the bills.'

'Forty-nine percent isn't anything. The control's gone. We would as well have sold up.'

James Senior's mouth twisted into a painful grin. 'But that's where you're wrong, my dear. My aunt has five percent and her daughter has two and a half. We vote these shares – me or Jimmy, if he ever comes around to it. That means we still have control. Campbell's have only forty-three and a half; the fact is they couldn't afford any more. They paid a hundred and fifty thousand remember? That left us with sixty-five thousand once the loss had been made good.'

Jane came back with another question but James Senior never listened for long when his wife talked like that. He put the port down as gently as he could manage, then turned slightly in his chair and went off to sleep.

Nevertheless Jane had the last word: 'I really am not prepared to entertain hired hands, James. You must content yourself with that.'

The lease on Cameron's was paid six-monthly. Tia was shocked that once the lease and rates had been paid there was no profit left beyond the pound a week she paid herself. Samuel was making nothing at all from his investment.

She began to think; she remembered Albert Drive in the old days, when a haberdashery had done good business besides the two butchers and the grocer. In the *Scottish Field* that month there were two articles on how to make do without spending a fortune on an autumn wardrobe.

The idea formed slowly; to stop selling dresses, suits and coats, to stock only blouses, hats, bags and shoes and the costume jewellery that sold so well in the stores in Argyle Street.

'You see,' she said to Sam, 'we're not asking them to spend anything *like* as much money . . .'

'It's worth a try,' he said slowly. 'But hats I can't do. For hats you have to go to Greenbaum.'

'I thought,' she said, 'I would get simple little berets and add feathers and the like myself.'

The first line she put on sale, of little brown berets trimmed with brown and green pheasant feathers, sold out at five shillings each within the week. The tussore blouses Sam made, perfectly plain except for a scarf tie at the neck, sold steadily at seventeen and six.

'Don't look so glum,' he said, when she dropped in after closing to order some more. 'You are learning how to be a business woman.'

That night Brogan, the lobby dosser, banged on her door at midnight. He had won a bet on the horses and had twenty pounds in fresh new notes. He told her that he was emigrating to America, to his sister who had a land grant in Idaho. He asked her to come with him. She did not believe him, but in the morning he was gone, leaving only a note in which he promised to write. She felt empty then, lonely. Brogan, when he was around, had made her feel as if she was not quite alone, he had taken the edge off her solitary state. For just a moment she closed her eyes and prayed for him, then she strode out of the close to take the tram to Cameron's.

Tia made little bouquets of velvet violets for buttonholes, fake carnations from silk stiffened with starch. She worked at these little things all the time she wasn't in her shop, and realised that the activity soaked up the ache of the loss of Jimmy Stewart, just as she had staunched the hurt she felt about Cal with endless work. The little shop began to pay its way, even to pay her enough to send some money to Tam. When she saw women in the street wearing brooches made of mink tails and velvet, she got some fur and made some too, even though the finished article made her wince. Samuel and Miriam encouraged her, telling her that if she learned the trade thoroughly, in the end she would be a better designer.

The letter from Henry Bendel arrived months after she had sent him one of the suits she had designed and made from island tweed. The postmark was weeks old, the mail had been held up by a dock strike in America. In it he said he loved the suit and if she ever wanted to come to America, he would give her a job.

She folded the letter carefully and put it in her drawer, next to the box where she kept her mementos of Marcus.

433

'You know,' Miriam said one day, 'sometimes I think you're a little bit crazy.'

Tia looked at her.

'I mean, the money your husband left –'

'It's all gone, Miriam, I spent it on Cal and the boys, remember?'

'I mean the money in America.'

'There is no money in America, just the rent I'm paid. It's very little.'

'But Sam's cousin in New York, he says the land is valuable now, that all the land in Long Island has become very valuable with the developers. They're making summer homes, you see.'

'Marcus's house is not a summer home. It's a farmhouse with some land, and people live there.'

'But you could serve notice on them. They could find somewhere else.'

'That is the one thing I would never do, Miriam.'

'I don't understand why, Tia.'

'Because that's what the rich did to my people on the island. The landlords served notice on them and moved them away to nothing. The people in Marcus's house are a family; I know they're not rich. If they were, they'd buy land for themselves.'

'Like the Zionists, yes, hungry for land . . .'

'Not like the Zionists. They don't want a whole country, just a few acres to call their own.'

'I don't understand you, Tia, sometimes. You start Meg's Pegs, you have a good business there and you give it away; you have land, you let it out for a pittance.'

'I have ideals,' Tia said. 'I got them from Cal.' She did not tell Miriam about the emptiness she felt at the core of her life.

The woman came in one Tuesday in August; the shop was quiet, most sensible people were out of doors or away to the coast. She brought carefully, a couple of light silk cloches and a matching bag, a little posy of roses that Tia had spent a whole evening making, not caring that it had to go on sale at the same price as the others, 4/11d.

'What a charming shop this is,' she said. 'My family is in trade, but the wholesale side. I must bring some friends. We live in the West End, so there's never much reason to come over the river, but I just had to visit the WVS here, to arrange the Calton children's day outing. We do it jointly, you know, we help them and then they help us.'

Tia nodded discretely. She could tell that the suit the woman wore was a Paris original, albeit eighteen months old. She packaged the things she had brought and handed them to her at the door, thinking fleetingly that she would never see her again. When she tallied the takings at the end of the month, including the lines she had cut for the sale, she was gratified that the business had shown a profit of thirty pounds over her wages, costs and the lease.

Jimmy Stewart was drawn two ways in life; he wanted to work for himself in his own way but he loved his father and so tried to work for the family business. With the Campbells' share, the warehouse side had changed; only MacDonald's remained the way it had been, competing with Daly's for the title of best store in the city. He had gone over the store with his architect's eye and drawn up plans for its remodelling. His heart ached when he found the sketches Tia had made for Mr Williams; he refined them and put them in along with his own for the other departments. He knew that he would have to find a way to see her again, to somehow make up the row. He could not spend his life working for the family store; he would find a way to persuade Tia to share it with him.

'I've been thinking,' Jane said, one day at dinner. 'I've decided to go into business for myself. There's a little shop over the river that Agnes Brown and I have our eye on. We're going to buy it and stock it from the warehouse. We can't lose.'

James Senior's eyebrow lifted; his jaw ached too much to say anything.

James Junior paid little attention to what his mother was saying; he was concentrating on eating his steak pudding.

'It's a little hat shop. I bought the hat I wore to church on Sunday there. I went back with Agnes yesterday . . . the woman eventually agreed to sell the lease for two hundred and fifty pounds. She's going to New York, I believe.'

Jane rose to go through to her living room, to work on her needle lace.

James Senior winced and then began to speak. 'I must say,

the only thing I regret was that we did not lure Mrs Cameron back. She was a very pleasant woman, I think, and she did have a dreadful time with that Brodie character. She wrote me a note, you know, a little letter apologising for the row and asking me to tea.'

'She did what?'

'She wrote me a letter, asking me to tea at Miss Cranston's . . .'

'Father, what did you do with the letter?'

'It's there in the bureau, with all the others. It came the end of springtime, beginning of May, some time like that.'

Jimmy went to the bureau, took out all the letters and began rifling through them, ignoring his father's expression of surprise and then annoyance, at the mess Jimmy was making of his personal mail.

When Jimmy found it, he read it twice and then ran for the door.

'Wait a minute,' James Senior said.

'I can't, I haven't a minute.'

'But . . .'

'Don't you see, Father, the letter she wrote, it wasn't meant for you, it was meant for me?'

# *Epilogue*

*Life goes forward, not backwards.*

In the cabin of the great ocean liner, Tia sat on her bunk and felt the pull of the tugs, the change in the engine note when the big ship was midstream and beginning to move under its own power. She had paid for a second-class ticket, but at the last minute the other passenger had cancelled and so she had the cabin to herself. In her wallet she had a hundred pounds, the money left after she had split the proceeds of the sale of Cameron's with Sam Weinstock and paid her ticket. She also had the address of his cousin's wife's lodging house off Hester Street and Miriam's brother's address on Seventh Avenue.

Once the liner reached open sea, instead of veering west it headed north. She was so surprised she went on deck to ask why; one of the ratings said they were avoiding a bad storm over the north of Ireland.

She stood on deck, seeing the familiar islands, feeling the change of direction as the ship turned to go west of Barra. Alone, she watched her own island fade in the soft, low mist that hung around Eaval like a cloak.

She turned to face west. At the cusp of the horizon, night stained the sky, above the ochre thrust of the sunset. For a moment she watched the two mingle, and then she turned back to watch North Uist until it became a narrow strip and then a memory.

*Janet was wrong; she would return.*

She had no regrets on leaving, only the ache of leaving Jimmy. She still could not understand why he had spurned her invitation to tea long ago.

A school of dolphins tumbled by the ship; she thought of Cal, of loving him for his bravery and his resolve, of not being able to love him any more because he was Marcus's brother – or maybe because he was Cal. A man like that didn't need women, she thought, because all the need in him was drawn up in the urge to change, the search for justice.

She had had enough of false promises and of the people who made them. The whole of the war had been fought through false promises, made by those who risked nothing, probably even in defeat. There was talk now of the wreckage of the German economy, yet no talk of the wreckage of lives. She had no will to go on, in a country like that, not even with the vote *because she sensed that so many would vote contrary to her. She wanted the newness that only America could give, the chance to start her life again as if the future was a blank page.*

She gripped the rail and prayed briefly, then let her body relax as she swayed with the breeze.

The sense of somebody behind her made her turn.

Jimmy Stewart stood there; she yelped reflexively as if he was a ghost.

He put out a hand to steady her. 'You have to listen to me now.'

The vestiges of her spurned pride frayed and Tia smiled her agreement.

'You see, my darling, your invitation to tea went to my father. He would've replied except you did not give your address. I only found out about it last night. My mother was the one who bought you out.'

'The privilege of money, yet again.' Deep inside, her hurt was still raw.

'No longer for me, my darling. I had a talk with my father. I left this morning without a penny, apart from the clothes I stood up in.'

'How did you know where I was?'

'I guessed, dearest.' He had more sense that to ask her to marry him now; and also another reason.

'You must have had some money.'

'No. I have none.'

'Well, how did you get your ticket?' She was flirting with him now, no longer bothering to hide her feeling.

'I didn't.'

'Well, how did you get here?'

'I stowed away. In that lifeboat. I pretended to be somebody's valet. I carried my own case and then I just hid. I came out because there's no way they'd turn back now, it would be too expensive. I thought of confessing and then offering to play the piano in the first-class saloon.'

'Jimmy, I . . .'

'Jimmy nothing. I love you. I'll take care of your needs.'

At the side of the ship a dolphin jumped and twisted, showering salt water towards them.

'I mean, I shall confess, and offer the money I have in my pocket, which is just short of a pound. I shall offer to wash dishes or scrub the deck or something . . .'

'Jimmy, I have a cabin all to myself. I can go to the purser now and pay your fare.'

'On, no you won't. I have some drawings with me; I know some architects in New York. They will take me on as an assistant . . .'

'I have a job with Henry Bendel.'

438

'Oh, no, you haven't, precious. At least, you don't unless that's what you want. I was thinking of playing rag time piano for a couple of months, and then heading out west, finding a little town that needs someone to make them something to wear and someone to design decent houses. You do what you want, precious. The only thing is, you do it with me.'

Night had fallen now, as they hugged each other their shadow was defined by the light of the moon, and chorused by the dancing of dolphins.

The loneliness that had haunted Tia for so long left her forever; she was secure at last, at peace in his arms.